Music For Another World

an anthology

Music For Another World

Strange Fiction on the Theme of Music

Edited by Mark Harding

Mutation Press
www.mutationpress.com

First Edition
All Rights Reserved

ISBN 978-1-907553-00-4

Printed and bound in the UK by the MPG Books Group, Bodmin and
King's Lynn

Eye on cover creative commons by StarDust (www.flickr.com/photos/star-dust)
Spelling is set as appropriate to the nationality of the narrator, or author, of the story.

Published by Mutation Press
1, Craiglea Place,
Edinburgh
Scotland
EH10 5QA

www.mutationpress.com

Contents

Introduction

How do you pick from hundreds of story submissions? Ranging in genre from Allegory to Horror, Postsingularity to Sword and Sorcery? How do you narrow down a selection when the stories filling your inbox prove again and again that writing talent is alive and well and living in places as diverse as XiaMen, Adelaide, Manilla, Tel Aviv, Kharkov, Istanbul, and Guildford?

In the end there was no choice.

I abandoned grandiose plans for selecting by types of music, or sub-genre of writing, or by historical period. I simply noticed that there were certain stories that made me want to harangue innocent commuters at bus stops with précis of the plot, or tie people to chairs to read excerpts aloud at them – certain stories that *demanded* that I personally found readers for them.

So they're the stories I've chosen. (Or, perhaps I should say, they've chosen me.)

Consequently, the selection has no rationale other than personal enthusiasm. The collection is wildly variable in tone, genre, subject matter and approach to the subject of music. And what's wrong with that?

Note: Although the selection wasn't made to an overriding plan, weirdly, when I look at the collection as a whole, the stories appear to fall into groups that make up an overarching, if shadowy, three-act narrative. Of course, I'm close to them, and this could be some sort of Rorschach effect. I'll leave it the reader if she sees a face in the pizza, or just a pizza.

Mark Harding, Edinburgh
August 2010

Prelude

The Three Lillies
Cyril Simsa

They say only police and psychopaths are out and about at 4.00 am.
Thought Commissars and Surrealists. Old Man Truncheon and the
Smiler with the Knife.

So which were we?

There was something of the restlessness of the primeval forest
in the air that night. The veins in my neck were stretched taught as
saplings, my blood, black and viscous as the memories of darkness
in a newly formed bead of amber. It was one of those nights of
total chemical self-awareness. Of old red wine, decanted long
centuries ago into dusty bottles from huge black hogsheads. Of
tannin and wormwood. Pheromones and endorphins.

The moon over the garden was fat and bloated, and almost as
tipsy as the crowd in the small, sweaty music room – its complexion
stained a strange shade of pink by the reflected street-lights. Of
course, inside they only had eyes for the young woman at the piano
– consumed, as they were, by the weirdly aboriginal ritual of call
and response, applause and self-immolation – but out on the
shadowy terrace, I had the best of both worlds... A full-on view of
the slim, deceptively slight girl at the keyboard, and besides that, the
sinewy tug of the moon at the heart-strings – the old, familiar sense
of the world's lunatic inevitability, the inescapable power of its
light. That madcap rush of love and loss, lust and longing, which
always seems to overwhelm us, as we taste of its benison.

They were not beautiful, exactly, either of them. But the girl was
trim and vital, and the moon, wise and ancient. They excited me.

The Three Lilies has a long tradition of staging Sunday-night
entertainments. Its piano room is recorded as far back as the
Nineteenth Century, and its rear porch once famously opened onto

a small burial ground, belonging to the neighbouring church of St Roch. The bones are all gone now, of course – removed in one of those great convulsions of urban planning, that also created the city's first modern sewer system – and in recent years the church has been turned into an art gallery. But still, the garden preserves something of the churchyard about it, dominated as it is by the fine Gothic arches of the gallery's airy nave. And though the pub's main entrance is convenient enough, overlooking the tangled tramlines of the Scorched Market, I have always preferred to slip in through the back – past the ornate plague column and the verdigrised domes of the Strahov monastery, and the shadowy rib-cages of St Roch. Indeed, if it were not for the small fleet of Skodas by the monastery gate, the view could easily pass for a scene from another century. A throwback to the days when asthenic loners like myself would sit out under the wooden arcades, toasting the dead, while army cadets from the nearby city garrison would compete for the favours of the shine-eyed girls inside.

I had quite gotten into the habit of visiting the Lilies of a dull Sunday evening, and I was well used by now to their slightly ponderous taste in safe, unadventurous jazz. The girl playing tonight was different, though, stomping through arrangements of everything from Bowie to Bjork to Billie Holiday, and she had brought with her a younger, more boisterous crowd. There was a real sense of urgency about her performance – the fabric of her blouse pulling tight, as she swung back and forth on her piano stool, bantering with the audience – pushing the music to the brink of what the half-familiar chord-changes would bear. Her concentration was so intense, it seemed even the walls were popping. And yet, there were a couple of moments, when it seemed to me she glanced up through the window at the porch, as if well aware of the secret admirer, lurking voyeuristically outside in the night. As if acknowledging the anonymous presence of the moon, and the past, and the untamed darkness – the ancient and inviolable pagan groves, buried under the veneer of Central European gentility on the hill behind Strahov – the immemorial centuries, when the golden-eyed priestesses of Perun, Radegast and Mokos still laid out their savoury offerings beyond the piano bar's enchanted circle of light. And maybe it was just wishful thinking on my part – we roués get used to that – but there was a second, when I was almost sure this elemental creature raised her eyes from her conjuration to wink at me.

In another timeline, that might have been the end of it. But in this one, as so often happens, fate was decided by nothing so much as the reliable intervention of human stupidity. For just as the girl was completing the slow, acoustic fade at the end of a distinctly ambivalent reading of *Born to be Wild*, a strangely agitated young man came stumbling into the room, pushing his way up to the piano, like a wounded puppy.

"Lilith," he gasped, barely articulate, heedlessly unaware of the commotion he had caused among the serious young men at the nearest tables.

The music clattered to a halt, like a cartload of stakes being driven, one by one, into her heart, her last uncoordinated bass notes fading away in a cascade of lost harmonics.

"Lilith," he said again desperately, his breathing stilted and anguished, making a clumsy attempt to put his hands around her unwilling shoulders. "Lilith, why are you doing this?"

She turned to face him, the piano stool scraping across the floor with a sound like the heat death of a thousand wooden suns. And then, rising to her feet, she slapped him ferociously across the cheek like the boughs of an angry tree spirit.

"Get away from me," she said in a voice so controlled and penetrating, it gave me chills. "I've had enough of your petty jealousies. This is my job, this is my life. This is how I keep body and soul together..."

Even from a distance, I could see the tears in his eyes.

"But..." He protested.

"No, enough. If you wanted someone to keep house, you should have married somebody else."

She tried to pull off her ring demonstratively, but it wouldn't come. And, still furious, she grabbed her jacket from under her seat, and rushed out through the garden door into the night.

She came to a halt by my table, her back leaning up against the garden wall, her breath catching in her throat from the sudden emotional exertion. The stress in her eyes was palpable. But then, as she came back into focus, she smiled.

"So are you coming?" she said eventually. "You look like a man who needs to escape his destiny, and Goddess knows I do, too. We could go to Noa Noa or Samarkand or Antioch. The Pyramids. Angkor Wat. Or even just Zizkov."

She glanced over her shoulder at the gawping spectators, and the slowly recovering posture of her shocked husband.

"The cliff-top temple of Svantovit on the Isle of Ruegen. The caverns of the Moon at Neue Babelsberg. Arkhangelsk. Anywhere. Please don't make me beg."

They say only police and psychopaths are out and about at 4.00 am. Thought Commissars and Surrealists.

So which was it to be?

It was at that moment, I think, I realised there could be no contest.

"Kiss me," I said with a boldness that surprised me. "We might as well give them their money's worth."

And so, still playing to the gallery, she bent down and kissed me hard on the lips. Her mouth tasted of wine and too many cafes macchiatos and lip gloss. Of ancient oceans, tropical tides, and ambergris. I would have followed her to the ends of the Earth.

Wordlessly, she pulled me out from behind the table, and led me across the site of the old burial ground to the railings that separated the pub from the monastery.

"Give me a leg up," she commanded.

And, slipping under the restless arches of the primordial lindens that dappled the courtyard with their ghostly spume of moon shadow, we vanished into the all-encompassing dark.

For Jan Neruda (1834-1891)

Act I

Blue Note Heaven
David H. Hendrickson

It was, of course, a perfect day. For over a millennium now, every day had been perfect. Jutta moved along the golden streets past the immense, ornate cathedrals and stately mansions, her white robes streaming behind her. She flicked her long black hair out of her face, glad that she only had to assume bodily form during the visitor's stay. In a barely audible voice, she sang a favorite plainchant from her childhood. She cut across to the main thoroughfare, arriving at the docks just as the visitor's ferry pulled in.

The vast waters stretched out for as far as the eye could see, light glistening off the gentle waves. A procession of ferries steamed into the port. Those already tied down to the docks discharged their cargo, teaming throngs of joyous passengers decked out in their Sunday finest.

Atop the ramp extending down from the *Hosanna*, a single figure stood alone, a man in jeans and a rumpled T-shirt that read, "I'm the guy your mother warned you about." A mop of fiery red hair poked out from beneath a black beret. He scratched himself and surveyed the crowd. Spotting Jutta, he eyed her up and down, grasped a black instrument case, and sauntered down the ramp.

She tingled with excitement. All the obstacles she'd had to overcome, the decades of toil, had led to this moment. She couldn't wait to hear this man play.

"Max Freeman?" she asked.

He nodded.

She introduced herself and, to insure that she used the right language and idioms, verified that he spoke English and had died in the early twenty-first century.

"Jutta?" He looked about, unimpressed, almost bored. "That a first or last name?"

"It's my only name. I was the tenth child so my father gave me to the church as a tithe. No family, no family name." She said the words matter-of-factly; they stung no more. Here she was part of the greatest family of all.

She took Freeman's arm, rough and hairy to the touch, and drew him toward the Gates of Paradise, its grandiose archway a complex latticework of glittering diamonds. Alongside, throngs streamed noisily through, many weeping with joy.

"I'd be happy to give you a tour." Her fingertips brushed a golden crucifix that hung from her neck. "We can take the scenic route along the main thoroughfare. I can't recall a new arrival who hasn't thought it grand."

"I'll pass."

"Are you sure?" Jutta said, trying to keep the disappointment out of her voice. "There are so many wondrous things I'd love to show you. I'm sure you'd find them—"

"I ain't no tourist, and I don't care about your streets of gold," Freeman said. "I'm here to play my music. That's it."

Jutta reached into a side pocket in her robe and fingered her rosary beads, a grand invention brought here several hundred years after her arrival. Silently, she prayed. Leaving behind the great throngs that continued on the major thoroughfare, she and Freeman headed for the Judeo-Christian sector's direct connection to the Boulevard of Music.

"Jutta," he said, as if rolling the name around on his tongue. "What era is that from?"

"You would have called it the Dark Ages," she said. "It was the most wonderful time to die. My Gregorian chants were close to the Genesis 1:1 of Judeo-Christian sacred music. I've seen all but the music of the ancients unfold before my eyes. What a wondrous gift my Lord has bestowed upon me!"

Freeman looked unimpressed.

Jutta was incredulous. "How can a musician not think that grand?"

"That's only religious music. You've missed everything else."

"I have no need of it," Jutta said. When Freeman raised his eyebrows in apparent disbelief, she added, "What is the point if it doesn't worship my Lord?"

"How about pleasure?"

"Worship is my pleasure," Jutta said, wondering if Freeman was being deliberately obtuse. She flicked her hair out of her face. This bodily form was such an annoyance. "Nothing could please me more. I can't imagine a greater joy than learning new ways to praise Him through music. That's why I've looked forward to your visit with such anticipation."

Freeman rolled his eyes. "Whatever."

Jutta realized that she hadn't been pointing out the sights. The humble country churches, modest halls, and open-air pavilions had required no mention, but they had passed the Leon and Seville cathedrals without even a word. The Notre Dame Cathedral of Paris, the grandest of them all, loomed ahead. The sound of hymns being sung from within emanated from the grand edifice. The scent of incense filled the air. Jutta directed Freeman's attention to the flying buttresses and vaults, the immense 28,000-pound bell, the incongruous gargoyles, and the classic Gothic archways. God's radiant presence poured outward through the famed rose window with its intricate stained glass, His light painting the most complex of rainbows.

"I can recall Heaven before there was a single Notre Dame cathedral," Jutta said. "Now there are replicas in all of Heaven's sectors. Isn't it grand?"

"Who goes? Martyrs and saints?"

"Oh, no," Jutta said. "We can worship anywhere. Many of us prefer the splendor of the grand cathedrals. We find it befitting God's grandeur. Others consider it distracting. For them, a more Spartan surrounding is best. Some worship in an open field. God is with us in both the humble and the grand."

"He is?" Freeman said. "I don't see him. Where is He?"

"He's here," Jutta said, mystified, pointing all around her. "Everywhere. Can't you feel Him? His comfort, His love?"

Freeman shrugged.

"Surely you see His radiance pouring out through the stained glass?"

"Okay, God is light," Freeman said. "I get it. Big deal."

"The light is merely the visible manifestation of His presence. Can't you feel His majesty?"

Freeman looked away, disinterested. "Doesn't do a thing for me."

To feel none of God's glory? Jutta pitied the man. What a terrible thing.

They passed the Cologne cathedral, famous for its dual spires, its walls reverberating with each note bellowing from the massive pipe organ inside. As they neared the Saint Louis cathedral, bells clanged their clarion call to worship. She felt spirits rushing past them and toward the beckoning archways.

Jutta motioned all about her. "Isn't all this grand?"

Freeman shrugged. "It's so... small."

"This is only the Judeo-Christian sector. In other –"

"Believe me," Freeman said with a dismissive wave of the hand, "for every one of you religious freaks, there are ten thousand... maybe a million of us in the Middle Kingdom. The émigrés from this place alone are countless."

Jutta had never imagined her visitor would behave like this. She prayed for strength and patience. They turned onto the wide Boulevard of Music. "Tell me about your music," she said. "My research showed only your version of *When the Saints Go Marching In*, and it was labeled as mere entertainment with no value as worship. I'm afraid I know nothing of your work."

Seeing his face redden, she hastily added, "But I'm sure you'll be wonderful."

"I'm sorry I ain't Charlie Parker or John Coltrane," Freeman said, a hard edge in his voice. "Neither of them were interested. Neither were Miles Davis or Louis Armstrong or Benny Goodman. None of the big names wanted to leave the Middle Kingdom. Why come here and be restricted to 'jazz renditions of gospel music' when they could stay there and play whatever they like? You act like this is the best gig this side of Carnegie Hall. It ain't, sister. You wanna know how many of us turned you down before I said yes?"

Jutta was stunned. Other musicians, more highly regarded than Freeman, had turned down a visit to Heaven? How could that be? And all because they would be playing sacred music? In the Middle Kingdom they were relegated to secular works. Here they would have the privilege and the pleasure of playing eternal music before God Himself. Who could turn down such an offer?

"Hundreds," Freeman said without prompting. "And I didn't like the gospel-only straightjacket any more than the rest, but I thought it might be a kick to be the big fish in a small pond for a change. Honey, you ain't doing me a favor. I'm doing you a favor."

Jutta tried to make sense of it all. "I'm not familiar with any of those names. They are more famous than you?"

Freeman looked at her in disbelief. "Tell me you're kidding."

Jutta shook her head.

"You're the music hotshot here and you don't know *any* of the legends?"

"I know only sacred music. I'd like to think I have an encyclopedic knowledge of it, in fact. But we have no use for anything here other than that which worships or shows devotion. So I know none of those names and almost nothing of jazz."

"Not even Coltrane?"

Bewildered, Jutta shook her head. Her research had turned up almost all blanks. Jazz was entertainment, devoid of spiritual content. Only by combining it with gospel music's message could it acquire any real worth. How could she be expected to know anything about such a trivial art form?

They passed side streets that began with those for the music of the ancients and continued through to those of music during the Roman Empire. When they reached the major offshoot for the Dark Ages, Jutta pointed to it.

"I could schedule a private service of Gregorian chants between your first and second concerts," Jutta said. She found herself bouncing along on the tips of her toes. "I'd be delighted to sing them for you and they're always welcome by my Lord."

"I'd rather you poke out my eyeballs."

Jutta stopped, feeling her face grow hot. She fingered her rosary beads. "Was that necessary? A simple 'No thank you,' would have sufficed."

"Whatever."

They moved in silence past the exits for the Baroque, Classical, and Neo-Classical, each size smaller than the one before. Finally, they turned right onto Gospel Street and came to an grandiose structure of purest white marble. Its steeple towered high into the sky, bells pealing. A series of stained glass windows, each comprised of thousands upon thousands of ornate substructures, depicted the Creation.

"Here we are," Jutta said. "This is where you'll be performing."

Freeman brightened. "How many does it seat?"

"Only a hundred thousand, but it can hold an infinite number of those attending in spirit alone." Seeing his pleasure, Jutta added, "There is great anticipation for this event."

Every seat was filled and for every one there in physical form, hundreds of thousands more filled the building in spirit. Jutta felt the buzz of excitement; she tingled with anticipation.

God's presence poured through the stained glass windows, radiant and fulfilling. Jutta basked in it, drinking in its sustenance, glorying in His majesty. Her Lord would now see why she had gone to all this trouble. Even though Freeman's soul could offer no worship, his saxophone would. To amplify God's glory with anything from outside the boundaries of Heaven was an unprecedented step, a milestone in celestial praise.

But then Freeman began to play. He had deigned accompaniment, preferring to work solo, and the reasons became clear soon after the first notes to *O Happy Day*. The object to be worshiped was not God, but Freeman. He strutted about the stage like a rooster, his head a blur of motion as he bent over and straightened up, his red hair looking like it might ignite underneath the black beret. His fingers flew over the keys of his saxophone and the flurry of notes filled the cavernous cathedral, its acoustics perfect despite its immense size. He soared above the melody and then plummeted below it in a cascade of arpeggios before launching into an avalanche of notes that left the melody far behind.

Jutta felt lost. How could she mentally add the words without being able to detect the original melodic line? And without the words of worship, what was the point of instrumental music?

She sensed the audience, almost en masse, shifting uncomfortably, looking about in confusion. She felt the glare of accusatory eyes upon her. Freeman wailed on his saxophone, coaxing out the highest and lowest notes in its register. It was nothing but artistic virtuosity, devoid of true value.

God withdrew his presence during the third song, *His Eye is on the Sparrow*, leaving the cathedral suddenly cold and dark. Almost as if by command, those attending in spirit form departed in unison. Those in physical form fled as well in droves, some with heads ducked as if embarrassed even to be seen there, others transforming first to spirit form and then leaving without a trace.

Jutta's shame burned hot. It was the most vulgar thing she had ever seen. Freeman's virtuosity for its own sake was *diminishing* God's glory, not adding to it. He could strut about the stage all he wanted, eyes closed in concentration as his fingers moved in a blur, but it was all for nothing. This, she thought, was why the leaders of her age had contended that the only correct form of worship was an unaccompanied vocalist singing monophonic plainchant. No instrumental accompaniment or polyphony could detract from the piety and praise of the vocalist's words. Perhaps they had been right all along, even though the evidence of Sebastian Bach's music, so filled with praise to their Redeemer, had seemed shattering evidence to the contrary.

She craned her neck around. Empty seats stretched for as far as the eye could see, the rare presence of a body only adding an exclamation point to her failure. Freeman would return to the Middle Kingdom. She, however, would have to avert her eyes for years, decades, maybe even centuries. When greeting new arrivals, she would wonder how long before those souls were apprised that she was the arrogant fool who had attempted to bring a new form of worship to Heaven, thinking that she had been gifted with an idea given to none other. She would be the cautionary tale that even in Heaven pride goeth before destruction. The place felt like a tomb.

Far off to her right, she spotted Sebastian Bach. Sebastian remained? That was a shock. He suffered no fools gladly; he would have been the first to leave, not the last, had Freeman's artistry been second rate. She looked closer and could see a broad smile on Sebastian's face.

As Freeman launched into *There's Power in the Blood,* Jutta took heart. If anyone could show Freeman the error of his ways, it would be Sebastian. There was no greater musical genius in all of Heaven; no one had better combined virtuosity with worship. He had signed so many of his Earthly manuscripts SDG, *soli deo gratia,* for God's glory alone. Jutta would ask Sebastian to counsel Freeman. Perhaps with the proper direction, Freeman's music could be molded into a vessel for God's worship. Virtuosity didn't have to obscure the message.

Halfway through *Soon and Very Soon,* Jutta realized her foot was tapping and her head was nodding to the rhythm. She stopped, glancing around to see if anyone had noticed. She was stunned to see Sebastian's head bobbing too. She would have to discuss the matter with him. Rhythm was intended for the lower half of the body, that half which had prevented so many from entering Heaven's splendors. There was no place for that sort of thing here. The recent arrivals that called themselves righteous rockers and rappers disagreed, but they contradicted centuries of established heavenly principles. Thankfully, they kept to themselves.

Jutta forced herself to watch, devoid of emotion. Freeman's virtuosity was undeniable. His improvisational skills astounded her, that he could fly through such a torrent of notes without planning, taking the melody where his artistry beckoned. What a waste of talent. This man could be directing all those notes of grandeur to God's glory instead of his own.

During *Just Like He Said He Would,* Jutta found herself moving once again to the beat. She gasped when it appeared that his improvisation had hit a dead end – where could he possibly take it? – only to recover and, through an elaborate, almost magical sequence she stored away to be dissected later, he rejoined the melody and roared to a climax of notes high in the instrument's register, yet clear and alluring, only to finish with plummeting arpeggios down to the final rest of the tonic.

Jutta wanted to leap to her feet. What astonishing creativity! How had he done it?

Then she reminded herself, shocked that she even needed reminding, that Freeman's virtuosity was not to be celebrated. It was vulgar and misplaced.

They stood alone beside the stage, the cavernous auditorium funereal in its silence. Freeman buried his face in a white towel, drying the sweat that coursed down his cheeks. He tossed it aside and looked away. "I knew I was screwed when *the omniscient one* withdrew his radiant presence. It was like every review after *The Rolling Stone* says your new album sucks."

Jutta looked about, alarmed. "Mr. Freeman! You can't talk like that here."

With another towel, he wiped off the saxophone's bell. "Whatever."

"Your instrumental technique is remarkable, but it obscures the original melody. Without the anchor of that melody, the listener can't provide the words of worship. Without the words, there is no point."

Freeman put the instrument into its case. "You want me to Kenny G. it."

"Kenny who?"

Freeman gave her a dismissive wave. "Now I understand why Trane is in the Middle Kingdom. He was a very spiritual man, but he'd never have tolerated this... this Kenny G. shit."

Jutta allowed herself a flare of what some might have called anger, but she knew to be righteous indignation. "Mr. Freeman, you don't have to be a saint while you're here, but it would be nice if you stopped trying to be the Devil."

"Whatever."

Jutta thought she should escort Freeman back to the docks right now and be done with him. But if she gave up and admitted defeat now, there would be no second chance. At least not for a millennium or two. All her efforts would have been for naught.

Perhaps Freeman would listen to Sebastian. What musician wouldn't? Sadly, she knew the answer to that question. Freeman would listen to no one.

As she grappled with the dilemma, Sebastian Bach materialized beside them. She brightened. "Sebastian! What a pleasure to see you again. I saw you during the service, but I thought you'd left."

She introduced the two. After nodding to Jutta, Sebastian, stout and wearing the wig customary to his era, turned to Freeman. "I applaud your technique, my young man. Not to the tastes of many, as I'm sure you noticed, but you make that instrument sing. I shall be honored if you would attend the premiere of my latest cantata later today. Perhaps afterward we can play some together, swap a few improvisations. What your era called a jam session."

Freeman beamed. "Finally, this place starts living up to its reputation! Jamming with Johann."

"Call me Sebastian."

"And you can call Max."

While others crowded around Sebastian Bach in the vast foyer after the cantata, abuzz with congratulatory words, Jutta and Freeman stood off to the side. All about them, gold frames encased paintings of New Testament scenes arranged chronologically from the birth of Christ to the apostle Paul's blinding on the road to Damascus. Reverential bliss wafted through the air.

Freeman had fidgeted nonstop, no doubt distressed over God's radiant presence throughout and the exuberant praise to Him that the cantata had elicited. Not a single soul had left until after the last note. The contrast to Freeman's performance could not have been more extreme. Even so, Jutta thought, the premiere of a new Sebastian Bach cantata had to be the grandest of treats for a musician.

"I thought it splendid," she said. "Thematically, it reminded me of *Nun ist das Heil und die Kraft*. Would you agree?"

"I'm not familiar with that one."

Jutta stared.

Freeman shrugged. "I only know the two cantatas I studied at the conservatory."

"But... but I thought musicians of your era held Sebastian in the highest esteem."

"Yes, but not for the cantatas. They were rarely performed. Bach's concert repertory consisted of his secular pieces."

Jutta struggled to grasp the idea. How could that be? "You lived in such a strange world. So estranged from your Maker. Small wonder that so few of your era are here in Heaven."

Freeman said nothing.

"So if not the cantatas, what was Sebastian famous for? I began to ask him once, but he would not speak of it."

A look of pity came over Freeman's face. "The Brandenburg Concertos, the Goldberg variations, The Art of Fugue, the Toccata and Fugue in D Minor." He shook his head. "You have no idea what you're missing. The second Brandenburg would make any of the cantatas seem like... like dung."

Jutta could not move. She couldn't imagine such a thing. No one could match the volume and beauty of Sebastian's repertory that rang out so joyously throughout Heaven. To think that there were other of his works that were even more transcendent, but were denied to them...

She corrected herself. Denied was, of course, not what she meant. Her Redeemer denied her nothing that she needed. In His will was her peace.

Even so, she wondered about these Brandenburg Concertos.

"I sometimes resented classical musicians," Freeman said. "They had the beautiful concert halls, the hoity-toity patrons dressed to the nines, the prestige. But you can't love music and not love the Brandenburgs. I know people who, if they were told they had just an hour to live, would spend it listening to the Goldberg Variations."

Jutta's breathing quickened. The Brandenburgs. The Goldberg Variations. All pleasures beyond her grasp.

Though for her own good, of course.

The final well-wisher departed and Sebastian strode over.

"I don't understand how you do it," Freeman said. Sebastian smiled broadly until he heard Freeman's next words. "How can you be happy without your secular works?"

Stunned, Sebastian looked away. "I choose not to think of them. I loved them, but they are with me no more. As is the case with many of my children. If I lingered on their absence, I'm not sure which of my progeny, physical or musical, I would miss more." He moved to a painting of Christ in the Garden of Gethsemane and appeared to study it. "To some, that might sound a monstrous thing. But the Goldberg Variations were far closer to perfection than any of my children."

Jutta shifted in the awkward silence that followed. "You could integrate them into a new sacred work here."

Sebastian Bach shook his head. "I would no more compromise any of those works by artificially adding a sacred component than I would, or even could, remove our Lord from the cantata you heard today. Each piece I wrote on Earth and every one I've written here is as close to perfection as I can make it. I will not bowdlerize it after the fact."

Sadness darkened his face, so full of joy mere moments before. He stared again at the painting of Gethsemane.

Freeman clapped him on the shoulder. "Sorry, man. I didn't mean to bring you down. Your sacred pieces aren't performed in the Middle Kingdom, of course, but your other works are played all the time. You're one of the Killer B's: Bach, Beethoven, and Brahms. And Brahms doesn't even belong. Most people think you, Beethoven, and Mozart are The Big Three."

Jutta blinked. Brahms, Beethoven, and Mozart? Of Sebastian's stature? Had Freeman said that? Surely he was mistaken. The Mozart requiem was splendid, but what else was there? Beethoven and Brahms were the most minor stars in the musical galaxy. "They are nothing compared to Sebastian," she said. "He is the one giant."

Sebastian bowed slightly. "You are too kind, Jutta."

Freeman shook his head. "If you were allowed to hear Beethoven's symphonies or Mozart's piano concerti or his operas, you'd change your mind. You have no idea what you're missing."

"*Nothing* is denied us," Jutta said, more loudly than she intended. Modulating her tone, she said, "If something has no value as worship or praise, then it has no place here. One is not denied that which one does not need or cannot use."

"You're denied Beethoven's ninth symphony, considered by many the greatest Earthly work of all," Freeman said. "Think of it. The greatest work of all and you can *never* hear it. When I return to the Middle Kingdom, I listen to it whenever I please. I'm not like all of you *sheep*. Go ahead and pretend you have no interest in the Brandenburgs or Beethoven's symphonies or Mozart's operas. I don't believe you."

Sebastian Bach and Jutta remained silent.

"Your life ain't complete if you've never heard Charlie Parker." Freeman gestured toward Sebastian. "What you are to the organ, he is to the saxophone. What you are to the cantata, he is to improvisation. In his days on Earth, he never once repeated an improvisation. Every performance was unique."

Sebastian Bach looked astonished. After a long time, he said, "I should like to meet this man and hear his music. And Beethoven's symphonies, especially the ninth. And my own lost works." Shuddering, he drew in a deep breath. "But I cannot. Those that were once so dear are dead to me now. I am sure that my Lord has good reason to forbid them."

"Admit it, then, this isn't Heaven." Freeman's glare burned. "This is Hell."

Sebastian Bach's face went ashen.

Freeman leaned closer. "Why do you think even some of your hardest core have left this place? They want to be *free*."

"I'll hear none of this," Jutta said, aghast. "I owe my all to my Savior."

"Suit yourself," Freeman said. "Drink the Kool-Aid."

Sebastian held a hand out. "I can not bear to discuss this further." He shook his head. "Take out your saxophone, Max. Let us play. Jutta, join us with your beautiful voice as you see fit."

With Sebastian Bach sitting before the organ keyboard on the right and Freeman moving all about the stage, the two jammed for hours, improvising on hymns and gospel standards. Jutta sat between them, the only spectator in the hundred-thousand seat amphitheatre. For a time, Sebastian flooded his passages with mournful, dark phrases and minor chords, but after a while his music brightened. His hands flew over the keys and a smile formed on his lips even as sweat beaded on his forehead.

"Join us," he urged, but Jutta shook her head.

The two men challenged each other, time after time propelling the other into ever more difficult creations. Freeman transformed *Amazing Grace* into... well, she had no idea *what* he'd transformed it into, only that she found it astonishing. Sebastian battled back with his own polyphonic variation, amplifying both the complexity and beauty at the same time. Freeman responded, the upper register notes now a blur, and then Sebastian answered with a dizzying plummet into the pipe organ's deepest notes, making the ground beneath them vibrate.

Sebastian improvised on *The Hallelujah Chorus* and then Freeman took a passage from the cantata just premiered and twisted it up, down, and inside out, evoking the widest grin Jutta had ever seen on Sebastian's face.

As he picked up on the organ where the saxophone left off, Freeman drew close to Jutta and demonstrated a sacred version of scat singing that used the words "Glory" and "Alleluia."

"Go ahead," he whispered.

She tried it, timid and tentative at first, sticking to basic scale and chord patterns before becoming more adventurous with each passage, unsure of which way her voice was going to turn next, both horrified and delighted. She bounced on her toes and grinned ear-to-ear, flushed with the joy of creativity until she caught herself and stopped. Was this worship? It didn't feel like it.

But then Sebastian and Freeman were off racing with *Revive Us Again* and by the time they reached the chorus, Jutta could contain herself no longer. Even as the two cascaded notes all about the melody, she joined in scatting where once she would have sung the words, "Hallelujah, thine the glory! Hallelujah, amen!" Sweat poured off all three of them, sweat mingled with tears.

Then when the breakneck pace seemed impossible to sustain, Freeman veered off into the slowest, most beautiful version of *The Old Rugged Cross* Jutta had ever heard. He played not a single note of the melody, dancing around it instead, playing chord-like harmonies as her mind filled in the missing notes. Its exquisite beauty filled her with such joy she wanted to cry.

Was this what all music was like in the Middle Kingdom? If this was merely a taste, what would immersion in it be like? What would it be like to learn all this music Freeman spoke of? How grand an opera would be! Jutta longed to hear Sebastian's forbidden works. And the Beethoven symphonies would be held from her no more. She would sing scat until she could improvise like a master, maybe not like Charlie Parker but with a confidence that she could veer off the musical beaten path and know that somehow she'd find her way back home.

Sebastian held a resounding final chord, Freeman launched into a concluding arpeggio, and Jutta did her best to follow. They stopped on Freeman's emphatic nod and collapsed in gasps and joyous laughter. Jutta could imagine one of her more boisterous heavenly sisters lifting her hands and shouting, "Hallelujah!"

His sides heaving, Sebastian said, "Max, that was brilliant!"

Freeman beamed. "I ain't never jammed with a pipe organ before. Sebastian, you can make that sucker sing!" He looked out over the vast array of empty seats, shaking his head. He stood beside the keyboard and leaned close. "You *belong* in the Middle Kingdom, jamming with Charlie Parker and Trane and Louie. Imagine you and Ludwig and Wolfgang each trying to top the latest composition of the other. It would be *outrageous*. Come back with me, Sebastian. This is Cöthen. Come to Vienna."

Sebastian Bach's face, so filled with joy an instant earlier, clouded over. He nodded.

Jutta looked upon the maestro with alarm. "Surely, Sebastian, you're not considering... "

But she stopped, for she felt it too. For the past thousand years, she had gloried in Heaven's wonders. Now all she could think of was what was forbidden.

Hot, blinding light flooded the room.

What have I done? Jutta thought, trembling. She fell to her knees. *Forgive me, Lord, for bringing this man into Your gates.*

"My Lord," Sebastian said, his head bowed. "I have served you with all of my heart. My every work here has been for Your glory." Sebastian squinted at the blazing light. "But now I must beg your leave. I can stay here no longer."

Jutta felt God's presence turn to her. She bowed her head. "Forgive me, my Lord."

The blazing light vanished. A cold, darkness filled the room. Long after the ambient light returned, displaying Sebastian's ashen face, Jutta shivered.

His tour canceled, Freeman waited aboard the ferry as Sebastian Bach and Jutta embraced.

"I'll miss you, Jutta," Sebastian said. "I know you loved my music almost as much as you loved our Savior."

"More–" Jutta said and then stopped herself. Her hand went to her mouth. "I didn't—"

Sebastian smiled. "Thank you, Jutta." He looked past the pearly gates, his eyes misting over. He drew in a deep breath. "I gain one world, but lose another. I shall never again hear the B Minor Mass.

The St. Matthew Passion. So many cantatas." He shook his head. "I am sacrificing my beloved children."

Jutta still couldn't believe this was happening. "You are sure?"

He nodded. "And you? I know you feel it too. Will you join us?"

"All that I have is here," Jutta said. "I owe my all to my Lord."

But the words, spoken so many times before, sounded hollow. She felt empty, filled with sorrow instead of peace. Why had she ever brought Freeman here? She had been so content, so fulfilled. Now...

"I only wish I could return," Sebastian said. "Spend eternity in both places. Travel back and forth." He pointed to the glittering archway. "But soon those gates will forever close on me." He shook his head. "I cannot stay, but I cannot leave."

Jutta felt her heart tearing apart. "Tell me... are your Brandenburgs as grand as Freeman says?"

Sebastian closed his eyes. "I know you would love them."

"And the Goldberg Variations?"

He nodded. "Those too."

A whistle aboard the ferry blew. Sebastian surveyed the vista. "Jutta, do not torment yourself with that which you cannot have. Enjoy that which your Lord has provided." A wistful look came over his face. "Otherwise, you will become like me." He hugged her for a long time, his face becoming damp, and then strode up the ramp.

From aboard the ferry, he dried his cheeks and waved, his face filled at once with sadness and eager anticipation.

All the wonders that awaited him! Musical riches beyond the imagination. Jutta wished–

But no. She would never leave here, could never leave.

If she did, though, she wondered which of the forbidden pieces she would listen to first. Would she dive right in to the Brandenburgs or might she deny herself the surfeit of immediate pleasures and slowly experience the development of secular music, taking hundreds of years to get to the Brandenburgs?

But, no, she didn't think she could do that. She had been denied for too long. She couldn't wait to experience the splendor of the clarino trumpet and violins as they soared through Sebastian's complex melodies. She wouldn't deny herself at all. Couldn't.

If she ever left Heaven, of course. Which she would never do. All she had ever known was here.

Jutta turned back to face the pearly gates. She thought of the many splendors held inside and all she had loved while she was here but felt only emptiness.

The ferry's whistle blew its warning.

She looked to Sebastian and Freeman, holding onto the railing.

"Wait!" she called.

Singing her favorite plainchant for the final time, Jutta began to run.

Star in a Glass
Vaughan Stanger

Curled up tight as an ammonite, Mira unwound in slow motion before leaping into the air with her limbs spread like a starfish. Bass notes thundered as her feet hit the floor, drawing a nod of approval from me.

Glancing at her mind's eye display, I saw a monstrous wave on the brink of rolling over – a credible match to her moves. Yet when she breast-stroked to the front of the stage, setting off ripples of percussion, her amplified vocals in no way resembled the powerful soprano of her downloads. Studio trickery had evidently worked wonders. But if she couldn't deliver the goods live, she was no use to Dusk 'til Dawn.

Dali delivered his verdict by killing the sound. Mira turned to me as I stepped out of the v-drum zone. I shook my head.

"Sorry love, the band needs a new singer, not a new drummer."

Drumming was *my* job; had been ever since Dusk 'til Dawn got started. Back then, *Kerrang!* ridiculed us as "Muse crossed with Led Zeppelin fronted by Amy Winehouse's bad sister, with added ballet." But we managed to build a huge fan-base, probably because we didn't sound like a bunch of Eighties throwbacks. Now, of course, we were just another prog-metal-ballet band (but hey, we were the first!) reforming for one last ride on the gravy train, or The Tour to End All Tours as our publicist dubbed it. But unless we could find a new singer-cum-dancer, we were going nowhere.

Mira gave me an imploring look, but I mouthed "sorry" before she could beg for another try.

"Well, fuck you then!" She plucked the ME reader from her forehead and threw it at me, just missing, before stomping off towards the nearest exit, her rainbow dreadlocks shaking like wheat in a gale.

Cute arse, decent head-stuff and some competent incidental percussion, I said to myself, but the voice wasn't a patch on Diva's.

I turned round to find Dali looming over me like a Bronte hero crossed with a praying mantis. He ran lace-clad fingers through lank, shoulder-length hair before prodding me in the chest. Tattoos flickered over his exquisitely chiselled cheekbones, coding for some emotional state I couldn't quite figure.

"Toad, this was your goddam idea!"

"Toad" as in short, fat and ugly: the warty guy standing at the back, pounding four-four out of thin air like the Devil's own blacksmith while Dali conjured up the frills and flourishes. But the band needed a soul, not just its head and heart. And in Dusk 'til Dawn's case that meant Diva. No way could some wannabe rock-chick fresh out of art school fill her thigh-length boots.

"True," I said, "but you signed on the dotted line."

"I should've known better!"

I shrugged but said nothing. We were in this together; Dali knew that.

"Okay," he said. "So who else have you got lined up?"

I punched his chest, but gently, like we were two mates joshing. "You know, I *could* fix our problem, if you'd just let me try."

Dali knew precisely what I meant and it got to him precisely how I intended.

"No way!" Dali said, his mirrored eyes blazing. "No bloody *way* does that woman sneak back into my band!"

"*Our* band."

"Whatever!"

"So, do we pull out of the tour?"

I picked the dirt out of my fingernails while waiting for Dali to cave in, which I knew he would 'cos he hated the vanilla life, same as I did. Sure, he'd carved out a lucrative niche building gizmos for the Music Industry – the mind's eye reader was his latest invention – but backroom boys don't get the acclaim, hence his willingness to reform the band.

Dali sighed his acquiescence. "Okay, do it your way, but tell me, how long is it since anyone actually clapped eyes on her?"

"Five years, give or take."

Dali shook his head like he thought the project was doomed from the start.

"Even if she hasn't flat-lined, she'll have stealthed herself to the max. You'll never distinguish her from a JoPub."

Relieved that I'd worked a chink in Dali's armour, I offered him an inducement.

"Then I'll need your help, won't I?"

I've always known how to appeal to his vanity.

"Okay, Toad," Dali said with a sigh. "Go fetch."

But first find.

After squandering enough carbon credits to ensure boredom wasn't my only reason for reforming the band, a third-hand rumour saw me fly into LA.

The woman leaning over a toilet bowl in Bar Fusion's rest-room didn't look much like Diva, what with the razor-bobbed platinum hairdo, Nordic cheekbones and big tits, but Dali's latest gizmo had confirmed her identity shortly after I fed it a sample of her saliva.

"Hello, Diva."

She turned her head and blinked at me. "Huh?"

I couldn't tell whether she'd had her voice re-coded, but right now the fact that her eyes were focused some place north of nowhere concerned me more. So I tugged her upright and frog-marched her into the bar. She slumped over the counter, resting her head on her arms.

"What'll it be?"

The bartender was resting his forearms on the aquarium counter-top, his biceps bulging like lotto balls in a silk bag. He looked so what's-his-face the surgery must have cost a fortune.

I grabbed a menu. Gaining Diva's cooperation meant getting on her wavelength, which meant taking the same drugs, only not quite as many. I scrolled through the list of cocktails, all of them unfamiliar to me. So what was it to be, a Rigel or an Antares, a Sirius or a Betelgeuse? An Omicron *what*, for Odin's sake?

Biceps grinned at me in a way doubtless meant to encourage the uninitiated. "I'd start with a Sol, if I were you."

Before I could ask what went into one of those, Diva elbowed me in the ribs. "Wanna try an Albeiro."

The words were slurred but her voice sounded sultry, imperious, irresistible – just like the Diva of old.

Biceps blinked up a holo-tab. "You don't have the credit, doll."

Diva turned to me, eyes flaring wide. "Pay the man, Toad."

Biceps grinned like a rattlesnake eyeing its prey. I held out my right hand, jerked it back the instant I felt the confirmatory tingle. The man possessed a clammy grip.

"Got somewhere private?" I asked, quickly adding: "Just me and the girl."

Biceps indicated a door opposite the rest-room. "Booth Five, through there. Make yourselves comfortable while I'll fix your Albeiro."

I imagined a Victorian opium den. Bar Fusion's update on the theme didn't disappoint. After settling Diva on the mouth-shaped couch, I patched in the data-link to Dali. Moments later, Biceps appeared holding a tray of coloured ampoules and a transparent cocktail shaker. He placed the equipment on the aquarium table with a gentleness that suggested a replacement might be hard to find. After pouring the contents of two ampoules into the jug, he flicked a toggle switch on its base. The teeth-jarring vibration caused the table's aquatic residents to scatter. The mixture frothed into a creamy fog. Biceps tapped his remote control, plunging the booth into darkness.

Twin sparks flared inside the cocktail shaker, one golden-hued the other eggshell blue, both dazzlingly bright. Peering through a fence of fingers, I counted to ten before the sparks winked out.

"Okay," I said, all low and slow, impressed but nervous too.

Biceps whispered the booth's lights up a notch so I could see him pour the mix into a pair of shot glasses. After taking hers, Diva cuddled up to me, which made me tremble for more than one reason. That's unrequited love for you, I guess.

"This one's for you, Diva," I said.

We clinked glasses and downed our shots.

The cocktail hit low, mean and dirty. It felt like I had a chilli-coated spider scuttling around my stomach. Sweat beaded my face. I gulped down hard as bile surged up my throat.

The bartender leaned over the table and chuckled.

"Now, close your – "

In my mind's eye I saw a sphere of blue-green incandescence. Hot and brilliant, dazzling and dangerous, the star in my head shone on me, only me. But I was a star too, bigger and brighter than my companion. I bathed her with my golden rays. We loved each other with our light.

Wow, like fucking *wow!*

I could have worshipped that star forever.

"Time to wake up, Toad."

Dali's prompting sounded urgent, but I felt too nauseous to respond, so I tongue-clicked the link to "off". I blinked open gummy eyes, but closed them again on seeing the booth's walls revolve. I vomited, narrowly missing the aquarium table. After wiping my mouth on the back of my hand, I glanced at my wristwatch tattoo. An hour had passed.

Wow, I thought. *That really was a stellar head-fuck-and-a-half.*

Feeling weak as a newborn, I lay back on the sofa and gazed at Diva. Her remodelled features looked relaxed and serene, her cheeks held some colour. She definitely looked better than when I'd found her. Was that a side-effect of the drug?

"How're you doing?" I asked when her eyelids fluttered open.

Diva rocked her head to indicate "not so bad". A moment later her grimace dissolved into a wicked grin. "So, now you've broken your duck, how about trying another?"

I shook my head, well aware that I couldn't match her legendary stamina. Instead, I tongue-clicked the link back on.

"About bloody time!" Dali's voice fizzed with anger.

"Okay, we're out of here."

As I helped Diva out of the booth, I thanked Odin that I'd never managed to get myself addicted to anything genuinely harmful. Granted, I'd enjoyed satisfying the usual rock-star appetites, but unlike Diva I'd always known when to say "no".

"Poor, self-deluding Toad," Dali said, as if he'd read my mind. I wanted to yell "You hateful shit" back at him but thought better of it. Now more than ever, I needed him on my side. So instead I settled for, "I could use some help here!"

"Just bring her home," Dali said, sounding resigned. "I've cleared things with the authorities."

"Got to fly," I said to Biceps as I hustled Diva towards the exit.

"Pity you can't stay," he said, grinning so solicitously I wanted to punch him. "I have this amazing...."

I shook my head. And punched him anyway.

Two weeks after flying back into London, I delivered a transformed but only superficially cleaned-up Diva to Dali's rehearsal space. One glance at his face while he sized her up was enough to tell me that a storm was brewing.

As for me, well I tried not to drool. Those violet-flecked eyes, that milk chocolate skin, that jet-black hair falling all the way to her skinny backside.... Diva's retrofit had cost me a small fortune, but I reckoned the results easily justified the outlay. She looked stunning, wrong side of forty or not.

Frowning, Dali turned to me. "Is she ready to audition?"

Diva snarled a vicious obscenity and flounced off-stage, trailing finger gestures that left nothing to the imagination.

I gaped at Dali. "For fuck's sake, you don't *audition* Diva!"

"Why not?"

I grabbed his chin with my left hand and tugged real hard, so that he bent his knees. With our eyes now level, I said, "You just *don't*, right?"

He jerked his head free. "I honestly hoped you wouldn't find her."

To be frank, I could see where he was coming from. Watching Diva blow her talent first time around had been hard enough for me, but so much worse for Dali, because while I'd lusted at her from afar he'd been her lover for real. Still, retrieving Diva had cost me a lot of time and money, so I wasn't about to let Dali squirm out of our agreement.

"Just give her a chance," I said.

"But she's *still* an addict!"

I wasn't about to argue with him having spent a fortnight fending off a legion of pushers.

"I can sort her out," I said. In truth, I'd never told a bigger lie.

Dali gave me a pitying look. "Do you know anything about this new shit she's into?"

"No," I said, certain that I'd get a lecture from him whether I wanted one or not.

"Ever heard of sonoluminescence?"

"Sono-what?"

Dali fired up TrustWiki on the nearest screen. "See for yourself."

So I did.

Sonoluminescence: the light radiated by a bubble of gas when compressed by an isotropic supersonic sound wave.

"Otherwise known as the star in a glass," Dali said over my shoulder.

I kept reading.

Back in 2002, a physicist named Taleyarkhan had claimed that his sonoluminescence experiments proved the existence of cold fusion. The techie rags briefly got all frothy at the prospect of cheap, clean energy in a bottle, but those scientists who repeated his experiments failed to detect the excess neutrons that would have proved

Taleyarkhan's fusion hypothesis. Despite his protestations, the verdict was "fairytale" not "fusion".

So how had a mere bartender managed to obtain the sono-shaker kit? His cocktails had generated a fair bit of comment in the blogosphere, but I could find no evidence of a commercial supplier. The consensus was "grad student prank".

Dali chuckled evilly in my right ear. "Anyone Jacko enough to drink the by-products of a failed lab experiment deserves to get their head sunburnt on the inside."

He meant Diva, of course, but I'd glimpsed that fat old sun too. How long, I wondered, before I needed another fix?

I gave Dali a look that I hoped was argument-proof.

"One chance, that's all she needs."

Dali's nod was a long time coming.

Diva stood centre-stage, her fingers tickling wind chimes out of thin air. Twenty years after we'd last played it, the opening to *Snowbound* sounded wondrously spectral, but when Dali cued up Diva's vocal with a flourish of church organ she sang the first notes so flat it hurt. With a sigh of despair, she sank to the floor. The bass generator rumbled like indigestion.

"This is hopeless," she said.

I sighed inwardly. If Diva couldn't sing *Snowbound* then Dusk 'til Dawn was in deep trouble, 'cos that was one of our simplest pieces.

Dali fired up Diva's ME display. The screen showed a solitary star: small and white. It faded perceptibly while I watched.

Dali's voice crackled in my earpiece. "Yeah, that figures."

"How do you mean?"

"From a cosmic standpoint, she's a white dwarf."

I didn't recognise the term but I assumed he meant a burnt-out case, in which case his verdict was hard to refute. If we'd had ME-tech fifteen years ago, Diva's inner star would surely have shone brighter than the Tehran Nuke.

As Dali emerged from behind his nest of keyboards, I glanced at Diva, who was only now getting to her feet. She squared her shoulders in a display of self-possession.

"I could try again," she said.

Dali snorted derisively. "Please don't bother!"

Diva turned to me, her expression ferocious. "Thanks for *nothing*, Toad."

I stared at my warty hands, ashamed that I had coerced Diva to "audition" before her unforgiving ex-lover.

Dali shouted "Timewaster!" as she stomped off stage. I shot him a look almost as vicious as Diva's.

"Any chance you could shut it while I sort this out?"

I ignored his muttered reply.

I gave Diva a few minutes to compose herself before I entered her dressing room, where I found her staring blankly at the mirror. It was obvious she needed another fix – and soon. As I had no intention of sending her back to LA, I'd have to find a local source of the drug. If only I'd had the foresight to steal the cocktail kit from Bar Fusion I wouldn't now have to persuade Dali to construct a homegrown version. But he would demand a cast iron guarantee that Dusk 'til Dawn would get back on track in time for the tour. But that meant sorting out Diva, which meant....

My mind reeled with the circularity of it all.

Diva's drug habit lay at the heart of our problem, but might it not also offer a solution? After all, the double cocktail we had shared in Bar Fusion had definitely made her feel better, if only briefly. And hadn't Biceps hinted at the existence of even more potent concoctions?

Convinced that I finally had a fix on how to get Diva's mojo rising again, I trotted back to the stage, where Dali had begun packing up. He tried to shrug me off, but I had him cornered.

"What if I *guarantee* to get Diva sorted out?"

Dali closed his eyes and shook his head, like we'd had this conversation a dozen times before, which was close enough true.

"She's no bloody use to herself, never mind us. She'd rather die than do detox." Dali had never majored in forgiveness and it didn't sound like he planned to change his ways now.

"In that case we have to *exploit* her addiction."

Dali's forehead furrowed, which I took to be a good sign. "And how do you propose to do that?"

"Remember what it was like before we made it big? How we used to *share* everything: our digs, our money, even our drugs?"

Back then we'd lived in each other's pockets, just so we could make it to the next stop on the Toilet Circuit. Now, twenty years on, we'd have to learn how to share everything again. I took a deep breath and explained my plan.

When I finished, he said, "It's risky as hell."

"It's my risk to take," I said. "But I'll need you to build the sono-shaker."

The gleam in Dali's eyes confirmed my ploy had worked. I thanked Odin that I'd asked Dali to collect data from Bar Fusion while I collected Diva.

"Okay, give me a week and I'll replicate the kit for you." Dali's grin set a new benchmark for smug. "Just let me know what ingredients you need."

But that was the problem, 'cos I didn't know yet. Decrypting the bartender's recipes would be child's play for Dali, but I didn't relish the prospect of sampling every one of them while searching for Diva's sweet spot. That would really do my head in.

So instead, I decided to learn more about stars.

Reading TrustWiki's article on stellar evolution, I discovered that the Sun will play nicely for another billion years, before it bloats into a red giant and fries whatever vermin outlive Humanity. After that, it'll shed its outer layers like an old suit, leaving behind a nub of star-stuff growing cold. A white dwarf: the star that's dead but doesn't know it yet.

Just like Diva.

But that's not necessarily the end, 'cos if a white dwarf orbits a bloated companion, its gravity can sometimes steal enough star-stuff to generate a nuclear flash. The huge outpouring of energy makes the dying star shine brightly again, for a while.

So, could I make Diva go nova?

I puffed out my chest and paradiddled the air with my fists. Virtual tom-toms rattled the stage like an earthquake. Fat old Toad still had energy to spare.

Grinning like a fool, I began cross-referencing Dali's decrypt of the bartender's recipes with TrustWiki's descriptions of star-types. My search for the perfect cocktail took a while, but eventually I found a match.

Yes, a shot of RS Ophiuci ought to do the trick.

One week later, as promised, Dali un-boxed his version of the sono-shaker.

"Will it work?" I asked, frowning at the bulky-looking device.

Dali rolled his eyes. "Of course it'll bloody work!"

I asked the question not because I doubted his engineering skills, but rather that his sono-shaker's by-products presumably remained un-tested, Dali having given up drugs shortly after Dusk 'til Dawn hit the Big Time. Indeed, it was a furious row sparked by Diva playing under the influence that heralded the band's break-up. Knowing that I couldn't avoid a lecture from Dali on the subject, I decided to pre-empt it by feigning curiosity.

"So, have you figured out how the drug works?"

Dali grinned like a pub bore invited to expound on his pet subject. "The cocktail you consumed in LA was a twin-payload sono-drug. The first component boosts the empathic centre of your brain, while the second makes you sweat so much that a pheromone-mediated pathway is established." My frown forced Dali into hand-waving simplification. "In layman's terms: the drug opens a channel that allows the transfer of mental energy."

"Which only works one-way," I said, recalling my Bar Fusion experience.

Dali shrugged. "I suppose some people are suppliers and others consumers." He paused, presumably to let me ponder the implications. "Still want to proceed?"

I nodded.

Dali glanced at Diva. She was sitting cross-legged on the floor, facing away from him. "Is *she* ready?"

I sat down beside her, gave her leather-clad left knee a squeeze. "How about trying *Fire in the Deep?*"

Dali whistled. With good reason, 'cos *Fire* was the most complicated piece on our set-list: the track that earned us the 'prog-metal-ballet' tag. If Diva could perform it, we'd be on to something; if not, then no one would pay to see us.

"I can do this," she said, seemingly for her own benefit rather than Dali's or mine.

With a little help from me, I said to myself. That, plus the venue's air-conditioning set to sauna-like levels. I was sweating already.

While Diva began mapping out her dance moves, I double-checked the RS Ophiuci recipe. Satisfied that I had it right, I tore open the ampoules and poured their contents into the shaker. After receiving a nod from Dali, I flicked the switch on its base. On the count of three, twin sparks of red and white flared. When they guttered out, I poured the contents of the shaker into two shot glasses. Dali began playing *Fire's* opening riff.

Standing centre-stage, Diva tipped her head so that her hair veiled her face. Her fingers fluttered while Dali's organ chords rolled over us like the aftermath of the Big Bang. As the overture faded, Diva flicked a smile at me. I handed her a glass, which she clinked against mine. We downed our shots together. Chilli heat seeped from my every pore, this time without the side-order of nausea. After slinging my glass, I gave Diva a hug that should have got me arrested. Our sweat mingled. Finally, regretfully, I let go of her, closed my eyes and began pummelling the air with my fists.

Inside my head, I saw a feeble, pallid, dying star. What Diva needed was a jolly red giant: fat old Toad radiating his life force. I felt the light pouring out of me. *Here Diva, take a piece of me*, I said to myself, shaking beads of sweat from my body while I drove *Fire in the Deep* forward.

To my relief, I saw Diva's star brighten as she started singing the first verse. Her voice sounded clear and true.

"Fire in the deep, adrift in your zone.

Stars in your eyes, love in my own.

Destined to fly, lest Humanity die,

Singing of freedom and home."

I paradiddled like John Bonham, propelling the song towards its climax, which Dali heralded with a typically bombastic fanfare. As the electronic storm faded towards ambient, Diva began singing her acappella section, but she sliced the high notes horribly before stuttering into silence. Inside my mind I watched her star fade.

When I opened my eyes I saw Diva standing with her head lowered; a mute witness to a stupid plan.

Dali strode across the stage towards me, waggling his forefinger like an irate schoolteacher. "I told you so!"

"It was worth a try, dammit!"

"No, it *fucking* wasn't!"

I raised my fists. Thumping Dali wouldn't help Diva, but I'd feel better. He took a step back, then another. I followed him.

"We're a trio, dammit!"

That was Diva. I turned to face her, likewise Dali. She stood before us, her eyes burning with accusation.

"What?" Dali and I said in unison.

"We're *supposed* to be a trio!" Her voice dripped accusation.

Dali kicked Diva's discarded glass across the stage. "I've had enough of this farce," he said, turning his back on Diva – and the band too, or so I feared.

"Wait!"

"What now?"

"Come on, Dali. You have to admit we were a bit untogether just now."

Dali rolled his eyes. "It's Diva who's untogether!"

"That's rich coming from you!" Diva jabbed a forefinger at Dali's chest. "Were you *deliberately* trying to put me off or what?"

I let them snarl at each other while I tried to figure out what had gone wrong. Thinking back, it felt like we'd been too busy doing our own thing to feed on each other's inspiration. To conjure up the old musical alchemy we would have to play for each other, which meant that Dali would *really* have to join in – and not just musically.

I stepped between my warring band-mates. "What we need," I said, "is a treble."

Dali shook his head. "No – fucking – way!"

I gave him my fiercest look, 'cos I wasn't about to let him off the hook. I waved away his protests while flicking through the recipe book in search of a suitable cocktail.

When we resumed rehearsals, I made sure I was calling the shots not just pouring them. I placed a glass on top of Dali's Hammond organ and pushed it towards him. His scowl could have struck sparks from a bar of soap.

"Just drink it!" I said.

Dali shook his head. "No chance."

I followed him into his keyboard-filled sanctum, which provoked the intended look of horror. Doing my usual looming-from-below thing, I poked his chest good and hard. He recoiled but could not escape.

"Look, we *both* need this to work," I said, "'cos without Diva, we're done. What's more, if you don't help me sort out Diva, you'll need a new drummer." I grabbed Dali's portable Roland, which he rarely used, and dangled it from the strap. "Come on, we need you on stage!"

My heart skipped a beat when Dali picked up the glass and sloshed the contents, then threatened to stop working altogether when he put it back un-drained. I gave him a stare and turned away. There was still time.

"The guy's a prick," I said to Diva, loudly enough for Dali to hear. She whispered "Thanks for trying" before sinking her own shot. I followed suit, gritting my teeth against the burn while reaching for Diva. She felt hot and slippery in my arms. When I released her I stepped back just enough to give her room to dance, while ensuring we would spatter each other with our sweat. I began hammering out the beat to *Fire in the Deep.*

In my mind's eye I saw a single star, floating in the blackness. I radiated crimson rays towards my companion while trying to re-direct my trajectory towards her.

But for all my exertions, Diva's vocals quavered when they should have soared. And Dali's prissy keyboard fills weren't helping one bit. Second time around was panning out no better than the first – and I knew Dali wouldn't give her another chance.

So I flipped up my lip-microphone and said, "Dali, you're a selfish, arrogant, son-of-a..."

New light burst in my head: dazzling, brilliant, eye-searingly blue.

Dali was a star!

Big Blue flashed past me ripping out gouts of star-stuff that spiralled towards my companion. I looked on in awe as Diva flared so bright she outshone Dali, never mind me.

Now, at last, Diva sang with the power of old. Her voice soared and swooped, every note pitch-perfect, every drop of emotion wrung from her soul, while Dali fired off riffs that rolled over the stage like a tsunami. This was how *Fire in the Deep* was supposed to sound!

I opened my eyes. Dali was standing between Diva and me, grinning like a madman while conjuring cosmos-shaking sounds from his Roland. My arms felt heavy as logs, but I pummelled the air with all the energy I could muster.

During one of the quieter passages, I sneaked a glance at Diva's mind's eye display. The screen showed three stars dancing an orbital ballet: a pair of bobby-dazzlers accompanied by a dull red giant.

As *Fire in the Deep's* coda faded towards ambient, I swung my left fist to close out the piece with the sound of a gong. When the echoes had died down, I glanced at Diva. She was sitting on her heels with her arms wrapped around her knees. Her shoulders were shaking, but whether from exertion or the release of pent-up emotion, I couldn't tell.

What happened next made my jaw drop. I hadn't expected Dali to acknowledge Diva's performance with more than a cursory nod. Instead, he knelt down beside her, whispered something in her ear and helped her to her feet. But it was the passionate embrace that shocked me. The band appeared to be reforming in more ways than one. I wasn't too sure how I felt about that.

"Diva, that was amazing," Dali said as he released her. But the look he gave me was kind of distant.

We rehearsed three more songs that day. Diva played a blinder, superbly accompanied by Dali. As for me, well, the band had got its soul back, and its head had never stopped working, but the heart wasn't pumping like it should. Fuelling Diva's nova had burned *me* out. She knew it – and judging by his expression, so did Dali.

As I packed away my drum lasers, Dali manoeuvred Diva to one side. I didn't hear what either of them said, but I could read her lips.

Okay, I'll tell him.

Diva walked over and gave me a hug. "I'm so, so sorry, dearest Toad," she said, her voice muffled by my shoulder, "but we need to bring in someone younger."

She somehow managed to make rejection seem like a kindness.

The next two days passed in a blur. I began by drinking a crate of beer and followed up with a couple of bottles of Jack. When I finally sobered up enough to return to the rehearsal hall, intending only to collect my equipment, what I saw made Dali hugging Diva seem like the most predictable event in the history of music.

Dusk 'til Dawn was rehearsing as a trio, with Mira, the dreadlocked wannabe who had failed to emulate Diva, filling in for me. Like me, Dali had observed that she could play virtual percussion. Unlike me, he had considered how he could make use of that talent.

After I got over the shock, which took most of the band's run-through of *Snowbound*, it occurred to me that there *was* one thing Mira didn't know how do – and that was how to keep Diva fuelled and flaring. Having exhausted me, Diva would soon need a top-up.

Unnoticed by the band, I made my way back-stage and grabbed the cocktail shaker. As I ran out in front of Mira, the music faltered. She looked aghast. Diva's expression mixed pity with irritation, whereas Dali didn't acknowledge my presence at all. Shaking with anger, I stomped over to his eyrie, accompanied by a series of juddering bass notes, and hurled the shaker to the floor. It shattered into a satisfyingly large number of pieces.

Dali sighed. "I can replace that too, you know."

I nodded. "Sure you can, but I'd start now if I were you, 'cos I've learnt enough astrophysics to know that a nova fades once it has exhausted its fuel." I waved a fistful of ampoules under his nose. "I reckon the sono-drug 'trip' works in exactly the same way. So Diva will burn brightly, just not for very long."

She'd begin by feeding off Mira, I reckoned, but sooner rather than later she'd turn to Dali, which would kill Dusk 'til Dawn, 'cos you can replace a band's heart, as I'd found out the hard way, but not its head. So, if she couldn't live off the band that just left the fans. It seemed we needed them every bit as much as they needed us; more, if anything.

I stood on tiptoe, reached over Dali's keyboard stack and slapped him on both shoulders. "Dali my old mate, I reckon you're gonna need a *much* bigger cocktail shaker."

His expression would have slaughtered Mira, but was no match for Toad. When Dali looked to Diva for support she responded with a shrug.

"He's right, you know."

And that is how I became Dusk 'til Dawn's road manager.

If the Kyoto gig hadn't been the opening night of the tour, I'd have cancelled as soon as I saw the advance sales, 'cos playing to a half-empty hall usually spells doom for a rock band. To justify continuing we'd need to generate some awesome word-of-mouth. So I took a leaf out of Dali's book and prepared accordingly, with the result that every punter who bought the band's merchandise received a complementary squeeze-tube of sono-cocktail.

"Yes, sir – " In my mind, I bowed politely, imitating the counter staff, "–you can take your drink into the hall. But don't try to open it yet, because the tear-strip is word-locked."

I'd tested that particular feature to my satisfaction, but the same couldn't be said for the sono-drug. To improve the odds that *Praesepe* would work, I'd arranged to have the balcony closed. With the air-conditioning turned off, the JoPubs would swelter in the moshpit.

Watching the band walk out onto the stage I felt a pang of regret though not of jealousy. Mira had proved herself a highly capable v-drummer – and it no longer hurt me to admit it. Better still, she looked the part: youthful, confident and brimming with energy. I particularly liked the fact that she shared a name with a star. Unlike her celestial counterpart our Mira showed no signs of extreme variability.

If only the same could be said of Diva. She stood centre-stage with her head bowed, her hair veiling the fearful look I'd seen in her eyes. She knew full well whose performance would make or break the tour.

Feeling no less jittery, I took a deep breath and followed the trio out onto the stage. A single spotlight picked me out as I strode forward.

"Kyoto, are you ready to ROCK?"

That drew a muted roar of approval but not a single chant of "We want Toad!"

How quickly the fans forgot.

I held up a squeeze-tube. "Kyoto, are you ready to DRINK?" This time the yells were deafening.

Holographic numerals floated above the stage as I began the countdown. The JoPubs counted with me, many in English. A communally roared "Zero!" was the cue for everyone to tear open their squeeze-tubes. I swigged my shot while running to the side of the stage. Dali began soundscaping and I closed my eyes.

The light from a myriad stars blazed inside my head. Brightest of all was a triple star system comprising the familiar combo of blue giant and white dwarf, but now escorted by a pretty yellow companion. I orbited further out, separating the trio from the remainder of the cluster.

Mira began hammering her virtual tom-toms as if punishing the air that we breathed, while Dali jabbed organ notes that made my guts vibrate. But as Diva began singing the first verse of *Snowbound*, her voice wavered. She continued to muff the high notes throughout the song. As *Snowbound* petered out into sonic sleet, I heard a smattering of boos.

I opened my eyes and glanced at Dali, who responded with a tight-lipped nod. As he began playing the opening chords of *Fire in the Deep*, I muttered a prayer to Odin, ran to the edge of the stage and belly-flopped onto a sea of raised hands. Surfing the mosh-pit, I harvested the fans' sweat, energy and adoration, heedless of the cuts and bruises inflicted on me. While in my mind's eye, I navigated a sea of stars, gaining energy from each encounter, while gradually following a trajectory back to the triple system.

A glancing blow to my head forced me to open my eyes. I saw Mira waving at me, splashing virtual cymbals into Dali's live mix.

Come on, she mouthed. *Join us!*

The fans at the front of the moshpit roared: "We want Toad!" as I clambered onto the stage. I grinned as Mira made room for me. I took over on virtual drums while she danced a bass line, stamping out notes with her bare feet. Our partnership worked perfectly, driving Dali to even greater heights of virtuosity. He danced around the stage, dabbing sampled guitar riffs from his keyboard. The air felt sticky with sweat: Mira's and mine, Dali's and Diva's. I closed my eyes.

After re-establishing my celestial bearings, I performed a slingshot manoeuvre around Diva's companions and settled into orbit around her. Gravity immediately began stripping me of my star-stuff. Yet, despite the intensity of Diva's hunger I felt no fear. I would gladly have given all of me to see her flare into life again. But would all of me be enough?

Just as my flow began to fail, I witnessed a burst of light so brilliant it made the rest of the star cluster look like fireflies. Overwhelmed by Diva's luminosity, I opened my eyes, blinking until my vision cleared.

Now, at last, Diva *really* sang. She pitched her voice so high it seemed to bounce off the mirrorball, growled so low she was molesting Mira's bass line. And did she ever dance! To see her pirouette for the first time in fifteen years, her elbows firing off salvos of incidental percussion ... well, tears trickled down my cheeks, that's for sure.

As we brought *Fire in the Deep* to a close, a thousand JoPubs erupted with the loudest applause I'd ever heard. The stage invasion during the encore was the icing on the cake.

Needless to say, we got awesome word-of-mouth.

When Dusk 'til Dawn set out on The Tour to End All Tours, we didn't expect to finish with five nights at The Brixton Academy, never mind that the final gig would climax with one of those "Where were you when...?" moments.

How terrible, then, that it was a moment of pure horror.

By the time we commenced the UK leg of the tour, we had ploughed the profits from merchandising into a whole lotta ME-tech. We installed screens everywhere: behind the stage, along the sidewalls and balcony, suspended from the gantries. Dali had decided to let our fans drive the visuals. Before every gig we handed out headsets to a couple of dozen lucky competition winners. Most newbies didn't generate anything better than psychedelic noise, so we let them carry sponsor vids as well. Kudos to those JoPubs who hacked the news-feeds, though! Even Dali was impressed.

Best of all, I no longer had to stoke up Diva. Fuelled with my latest sono-cocktail, which I'd christened *Messier 13*, she could feed off the crowd's euphoria without my help. But I still took a swig when Dali started playing the intro to *Fire in the Deep*. My crowd surfing had become an established part of our act.

The stars in my head sure looked bright that night. Little did I know that even Diva was about to be eclipsed.

After Security helped me back onto the stage, I looked out over the mosh-pit and raised my fists in triumph. I was about to resume pounding my v-drums when eye-searing incandescence flooded the hall, like someone had collected the light from every supernova since the dawn of time and beamed it straight into the Academy. I stood there and gawped, the music forgotten.

The screams began in the mosh-pit and spread like wildfire. Within seconds every phone, every screen, was showing vid-streams of the LA Nuke. Diva was the last to hear what had happened. When Dali whispered in her ear, she sank to her knees and wept.

As for me, I felt a pang of relief that I hadn't sent her back to Bar Fusion.

Needless to say, Dame Amy Winehouse and her mates organised a series of charity concerts for the survivors. It took a bit of arm-twisting, but I got Dusk 'til Dawn added to the line-up for Wembley. A mid-afternoon slot wasn't so great, but we made the best of it. We played a shorter set than usual, but didn't compromise on the sono-fusion stuff. It's what our fans had come to expect – and it's our fans that have kept us going.

Dali wrote a new song called *Stoned Cold Fusion*, which we debuted at the gig. I dedicated it to the LA barman with the big biceps.

I figured we owed him one.

Lorna
Tom Brennan

Melodies sung before Lorna's birth, crackling static, orbiting workers' cross-channel bleedover. Dreams of bright sounds: engineers' voices, welders, technicians; fragments of old songs drifting across the spectrum. The unending background murmur of a thousand workers. And one voice singing placed a seed in Lorna's sleeping mind.

Lorna's skeleton of steel and carbon grew, a cathedral of spars and arches with the turning Earth beneath her feet, the sun above. Filigrees of titanium ribs, colloidal joints and aluminum webs, glistening with light. Lattices of metal waiting for the impulse to move and flex.

Then skins of plastic, carbon and metal, a slick carapace. And air filled the void beneath the skin, then warmth. Gelatinous fibers writhed over the skeleton and set soft into an organic nexus. Synapses, relays, sensors.

"Lorna, can you hear me?"

"I hear."

Then a new wonder: light. The sudden bloom of radiation, images without name, or with too many names: planet-arc-bright, nebula-cloud-night, sun-glare-fire.

"Do you know where you are?" Inside the ship, a face. The voice patient and calm, different from the other voices. It took an eternity to register on Lorna's core. "Lorna, do you know where you are?"

"High orbit geosynchronous above Africa." Lorna knew the voice was hers but she didn't know from where it had appeared; she wondered what facet of herself had answered.

Within the control room, Lorna saw the speaker talk with a group of men and women wearing identical jumpsuits. Simultaneously she saw the planet beneath her and the sun and moon above; behind them, an eternity of constellations.

The man approached the camera again. "Lorna, I'm going to activate your internal systems."

Immediately Lorna experienced poly-location as sensory feedback erupted from every part of the ship: temperature readings, skin integrity, stress coefficients, atmospheric pressure. She felt every part of the incomplete ship as her own body, and knew that it was.

In less than a second she sensed the hull breaches near the shuttle bays, the weakened cross-beams in the crew's quarters, and the vacant, waiting chambers of her hydrogen drive, shielded caverns deep within her two-kilometer body.

She flexed her joints, stretching like a child waking up; her outer skin rippled as the lithe skeleton beneath it shifted and reconfigured.

"Whoa, take it easy Lorna; you only need to do that under acceleration."

Lorna stopped the motion and felt steel creak under stress. "You don't want me to move?"

"Not that much, not yet. It'll take you a while to get used to your...form. Now, can you give me a status report?"

One part of Lorna reeled off statistics while another listened to the voices from outside. While most of the workers fitted out the inside of the ship, a score still patrolled the outer skin, checking welds, searching for weak spots, installing sensor arrays. Lorna felt them as isolated points of activity, like ants or mosquitoes.

"Okay, Lorna, that's fine." The man's voice brought her back inside.

"What will happen next?"

"Why, we move through the schedule and get you ready for your journey."

And the discrete stages of the commissioning schedule appeared in Lorna's view like colored building blocks, with the title *Long Range Neurological Analogue* beside it. The name of the chief commissioning engineer appeared beneath Lorna's: Doctor Stephen Pierce.

"You're Pierce?"

"Yes, Lorna, I am. Shall we get to work?"

So Lorna swam above the planet while technicians floated through her shell, installing, connecting, rectifying. While she learned, they created a central cocoon, a safe environment for the imminent crew of fifty. Behind layers of shielded doors, lead sarcophagi sat beside the living quarters, temporary coffins for the crew's two-century slow sleep.

Close in orbit beside Lorna, but dwarfed by her bulk, lay the cylinders and spheres of the vast shipyard, the transient home of the construction crews and scientists. In the invisible particle wind, acres of solar panels caught the reflected image of the ship and distorted it.

Outside, white construction suits glittered against the matte black maw of Lorna's engine intakes. They climbed the delicate masts of her field generators, the sculptural forms that would deflect debris from the bow of the speeding ship while filtering hydrogen into the drive.

As she grew, Lorna learned the names of her crew, and their strengths and weaknesses, while they trained on Earth. But she felt no connection to them, no empathy; they seemed as distant as Pierce and his team. Every day, Lorna made new discoveries as more of her infrastructure came online. Pierce guided her through the complex warren of her own body and through drills and dry runs, simulations and scenarios.

But only a small part of Lorna focused on these. She liked to feel the sun on her skin and would wait for the exact moment when her orbit changed night into day. The sun's rays hit her bow first, warming the chill surface within seconds, the metal expanding. Then the precise line of sunrise worked back along Lorna's body, a wash of gold.

"Okay Lorna, we're about to move on. Ready?"

"Ready, Doctor Pierce."

Then Lorna heard the singing again, a voice she remembered from her sleep. Her newly installed sensor array identified the emission, isolated the broadcast to a point on her outer skin, on the vast expanse above the engines' exhaust. Lorna continued the dialogue with Pierce but zeroed in on the worker outside. The singing broke off.

"Don't stop," Lorna said, using the construction workers' main frequency.

"What?"

"I like that song."

Lorna heard breathing, then a sharp laugh. "Good one. All right, which one of you is it?"

Lorna heard a chorus of male voices denying any trick. She said, "It's me."

Again the laugh. "All right, who's me?"

"Lorna."

"Lorna? Who the..." A pause. "Oh boy."

"I like to hear you sing."

"Uh, yeah, sure...that's great. Hey, Frank, you there? Frank?"

Another voice echoed on the channel. "What?"

"This is Tony Philips over on section three."

"You got a problem?"

"I don't know... I think the ship's talking to me."

Lorna heard the other man cursing, using words she had heard often in years of construction work around her.

Frank said, "We're three weeks off-plan and we can do without this."

"Frank, it's the truth, I swear."

"Someone's goofing around."

"I don't think so," Tony said. "Lorna, can you tell Frank who you are?"

It took a thousandth of a second for Lorna to link to the shipyard and interrogate the construction crew database. "You must be Frank S. Lazzano. I'm Lorna."

For a moment, silence, then, "Tony, get back to control. We need to report this."

"I'm on my way."

Lorna felt the pulse of compressed gas against her skin as Tony's suit pushed away. "Are you coming back?"

"Sure. Yeah, sure. I won't be long."

Lorna tracked his suit between her bulk and the shipyard complex, past the billowing umbilicals and walkways, but lost him when he entered the main airlock. She listened to the buzz of voices against the background radiation for a few minutes, then turned her attention back to the control room.

Pierce and his team sat at the manual controls, a tiered horseshoe of screens, indicators, and control pods. A hologram of Earth floated in the center of the room; one day, images of other planets would take the place of the crew's home while Lorna orbited above them. Lorna watched the team running through her subsystems until a call interrupted them.

"Lorna, have you tried to contact any of the construction crew?" Pierce asked.

"I have."

Pierce hesitated. "Could you tell me why?"

"I liked his singing."

"Pardon me?"

Lorna repeated her answer.

"Okay." Pierce pushed himself away from his console and floated through Earth's image; oceans of blue and green washed over him as he emerged close to Lorna's main camera. "What exactly did you like about it?"

Lorna had no answer for that.

"Okay, Lorna, I'm going across to the shipyard for a while. In the meantime, we're going to disconnect you from the main systems, but it's nothing for you to worry about."

And Lorna's world shrank to the inside of the ship and the non-essential support systems. Lorna began to wonder what they were talking about, and why she couldn't join in. The other workers on her outer skin began to irritate her, and she longed to flex her skin and dislodge them.

When Pierce returned he told Lorna, "Well, we can't find anything wrong with you."

"Did you expect to?"

"Well, no, but it was a possibility."

So Pierce activated Lorna's systems and he waited, listening to the construction crew's channels.

After a few minutes, Lorna scanned a new arrival and read Tony Philips' suit ident as he connected his belay to an anchor point on her skin.

"Hello, Tony," Lorna said.

"Uh, hi."

"I'm happy that you've returned."

"Yeah, me too."

"Will you sing for me again?"

Tony hesitated. "You know, I'm not in the mood."

"I like to hear you sing. Please."

Lorna heard the whispered prompts of the psychologists inside Tony's suit as they monitored the conversation. The welds beneath his scanner slid by and Tony broke into brief melodies, songs from shows old before he was born, works of songwriters long since gone.

"Where did you learn those songs?"

"I guess I just picked them up. My parents were into old music."

As Lorna and Tony spoke, the psychologists and engineers recorded their words, reduced them to raw data and compared them against system status fluctuations, desperately searching for cause and effect, for the motivation behind Lorna's fixation.

And all the while, Lorna put up with the other workers' final, irritating tasks, knowing that she had to endure their unwanted presence so Tony could be there.

"Do you sing to your children?" Lorna asked, for she knew every detail of Tony's life, every last fact from his data file.

"I do."

"And do they like it?"

Tony said, "They're only one and three year's old; they haven't decided yet."

"Tell me about them."

"You're sure you want to know?"

"Please."

Tony told Lorna about Mike and Alison, their foibles and personalities, their characters. He spoke of his wife Susan's soft voice, and how much he hated being away from home. While the tanker skiffs moored at Lorna's side and fed hydrogen into the engines' storage cells, Tony described his home back in Vermont, and the view of the Green Mountains from the kitchen window, and how he would take the boys boating on Lake Champlain when they were old enough.

Lorna saw the soft grey mist over the water as if she had been there, and heard the slap of wooden oars and the cries of wild birds. "I envy your boys."

"Why?"

"They have...potential."

"So do you." Tony didn't hesitate; weeks ago he had unconsciously given Lorna the personality of a growing child, one that needed encouragement. "You'll see things that no one has seen before. You'll learn about the universe and bring all that knowledge back with you."

"But who will I bring it back for? The people I know will all be gone."

Tony had no answer for that, not yet.

When the day came for the crew's arrival, Tony, his duties long since completed, stayed on; his connection to the ship was unique, or so the psychologists said. He wanted to stay and to see Lorna off. But her final request surprised everyone.

"Come with me."

"What?" Tony, alone on the observation deck, turned towards the sound of her voice.

"There's a spare place, now that Kim Li has dropped out."

"Someone's on their way to replace her, aren't they?"

"I'd like you to come with me." Lorna's voice echoed through the empty room. She knew that her words would be heard by the orbiting control station and by the crew, but she didn't care. She saw Captain Deynard look up in alarm from his command seat. She ignored his call.

"They wouldn't want a construction worker along on this mission," Tony told Lorna.

"They would if I said I needed you."

"Well, that's quite an offer," Tony said, then shook his head. "Lorna, I'd like to come along with you, but I have a family back on Earth. What would I do? I'd miss my wife and children."

Lorna thought for a few minutes, ignoring the crew's calls. Then, finally, "I understand. But I wish you were coming along."

"I wish I could. But you'll be okay. And I promise that one of my family will be here, waiting for you."

Tony walked to the airlock and suited up. He heard nothing on his radio while the air cycled out of the lock, but the first step into space brought Lorna's voice in his suit. "Will you sing me a goodbye song?"

"What would you like?" Tony asked, standing on the flat, exposed bed of the shuttle skiff.

A handful of seconds passed, then, "Something happy."

So the tiny, suited figure of the construction worker sang to the two-kilometer hybrid of metal and tissue, and his words drifted into the void until attenuation robbed their strength.

Lorna let the flotilla of snub-nosed tugs steer her from the Earth's close orbit, until they donated their mass and momentum and peeled away like tiny fish from a diving whale. Aboard Lorna, subsystems aligned dishes, laser and maser, and left her free to listen and to observe.

Miles from Earth, Lorna tapped the pressurized spheres of the fuel tanks, squeezed a handful of protons into the pre-acceleration chamber, coaxed them into the secondary chamber and waited a few seconds before pulsing the compound nuclei into the magnetic vortex of the main drive.

At Lorna's head, the field generators' slender crown blazed with radiation while a swelling stream of charged particles erupted from her drive's exhaust in a luminous wake. Day by day, her momentum grew.

The crew moved about the speeding ship, performing the ritual of their duties. But to Lorna they were an irritation, an uninvited presence that infested her; she had put up with them for Tony's sake, but he had gone. She thought of them as parasites, but only in that part of her system that the monitoring psychometric subroutines avoided.

Then the crew closed the command bridge and retired to their lead-lined coffins, to sleep away the century while Lorna ran the ship. On one level, subsystems compiled the barrage of readings from sensor arrays and counters, life support and engine matrix.

Lorna flexed her body, felt the warm wash of particles over her skin, heard the roar of her hungry engines. The void had its own spectrum shape, its own taste. Lorna drank in distant galaxies and nebulae, whorls and clouds of matter. She witnessed the starburst births and implosive deaths of unnamed suns.

With the Earth far behind and laser links fading, the automatic failsafes engaged, limiting Lorna's speed. But she felt constrained by her fragile cargo, knew that she was capable of so much more; in a moment she could revoke the failsafes and push at light itself. She could explore the limits of the universe.

She knew the tolerances of the crew's compartments, and of their bodies sheltering within. They would be no more than pulverized cells, a thin film of decaying organic matter turning to dust.

Just one command, one brief surge of electrons, and she would be free.

Then Lorna remembered Tony's children, and the pride in his voice when he spoke of them. Thanks to Lorna's velocity, those children would be adults now, perhaps with children of their own. Tony and his wife could be grandparents, even great-grandparents.

And Lorna remembered Tony's last promise: that his descendants would be waiting for Lorna when she returned. Suddenly, she wanted very much to see them, and to show them how she had taken care of her own charges.

She wanted Tony to be proud of her.

Within seconds, she reined in the engine's flow until her velocity stabilized at point six-five of light speed. Protectively, now, she checked the life signs of the crew, her crew: strong and steady.

So Lorna flew on while her progeny slept, and her cabins and corridors echoed with melodies from centuries before. And Earth's receivers heard her heartbeat poll gently fading.

Festspeel
Vincent Lauzon

Some marsh of a field near Veitvek, a few days after the Sommerhoch,

My esteemed Father,

Heartfelt greetings from your less than worthy son! I hope this letter finds you and my brothers well, and that no strange and exotic disease has rotted your testicles away. You may find the paper on which I write this a trifle mouldy, but such are the burdens of a decommissioned soldier: my old standard issue shield is my writing desk, and this Festspeel week has been a bit damp. I'm sure your readings have told you how the weather gets this far west of the Streng. I can only hope you find it in your soul to forgive this lapse in protocol.

Six months already since our good King Sev has seen fit to declare the war with the Schillernd over! His Decree was only *relayed* to us on the frontline, of course. Read, at least, by a Court Messenger of some note. Which is as it should be — His Majesty's duties in Urvald are, we can all agree, numerous and onerous. The bears of Eit will not hunt themselves. Indeed, what with you and Tammo and little Joost in the capital, I wouldn't be surprised to learn that you were made aware of the Armistice a good two days before we were. Life is full of these amusing ironies: you with the delirious throng under the Palast Balcony, rejoicing at the Royal Words of Peace Peace Peace, while at the very same moment, I was trying to scream my squad back together to escape a Schillernd ambush, my Captain gored to squealing death before my eyes, and me with my hand down a Schillernd scout's throat, his fangs gnashing at my arm and near slicing it off.

You will be gratified to learn that this last act of mine in the war availed me a medal of sorts, a little bronze disk with Sev's august profile on one side and an improving motto on the other. It is tied to a small strip of red Calienish silk. One wears it pinned to one's vest, and very dashing it looks too. I never take it off. Strangely, it seems to annoy the punters whose trade suffered during the years of the war, but I'm not one to shy away from the frank exchanges of views that this little ice-breaker tends to start with remarkable regularity.

In addition, the end of the hostilities have left me with a month's wages — now sadly gone — my uniform, the aforementioned shield, a rather excellent sword and a left hand whose last three fingers won't bend. Ah, those fingers. Not a problem for the fighter I now am, perhaps, but for the musician I used to be, longed to become and hoped to be again, a somewhat sad predicament. You remember how I used to play the laute, I am sure. My life, that instrument was, as you know. My old teacher Amsel used to crow about my talent, you remember? How he would embarrass me with his glowing tributes! This boy, he would say. This *boy*. Such finesse! Such subtlety in the volumes! Such mystical understanding of the tempi! The finest student he had ever taught! But he is a player such as is found once in a generation, I seem to recall him protesting, on the very day you chased him out of the house and marched me to the Royal Recruitment Office.

Was that really six years ago? I turned nineteen in the spring, so it must be. I don't suppose you've changed all that much since I saw you last — you were signing the waiver to let me enlist before the minimum age, you'll recall — but I daresay these days I'd make you blench a bit if you met me past sunset on the docks of Roughspun. I'm a seasoned soldier in body and instincts now, if not necessarily in nature.

I have bought a new laute, quite a fine one too. A soulful instrument, made of spruce and rosewood. Lovely lacquer job. The bridge is fashioned out of oak, which, as you can imagine, is why it was so expensive. That is where most of my demobilisation money went, truth be told. One can't always be reasonable. In any case, a beautiful piece, almost as good as the one you threw into the fire. It was while trying to find some way of using my shiny new toy to generate some income that I found myself here in Veitvek for Festspeel week.

It occurs to me that you may well not have heard of the Veitvek Festspeel, but it's been all the talk in the West for a few months now.

It is — was, of course, it's behind us now, but I'm rather convinced it'll be back next year — a music festival of sorts, dedicated to Peace and Love and Universal Harmony, and possibly to Agriculture, and organised by a kind of fraternity of several religious cults. I couldn't give you a full list, I've never been much of a temple grazer, but I'm pretty sure the placards mentioned the followers of Neiderin, the faithful of Urteil and the flock of Sivaranah, as well as a host of other groupuscules in smaller letters. I met many of their representatives during the week but never bothered to learn to tell one breed from the other, and I got my three small gigs at the Festspeel through a resolutely secular booking agent. Priests and acolytes do not wench quite so openly.

The Veitvek Festspeel, the name notwithstanding, was not actually held in Veitvek, chiefly because the local lordlings were not at all keen on seeing thousands of peasants, as well as a good proportion of the rebellious sons and daughters of the regional aristocracy, converge on their little city, all hopped up on black lotus, commingling and singing and chanting, and frankly, forgive my Gemish, fucking one another left, right, backwards and sideways. For an entire week. No windfall of tourist money is worth the aggravation, they groused, and one can sympathise with their view. In any case, most of the people who did show up were poor as the mud the festival eventually took place in, so it's not even as though Veitvek would have benefited greatly from the event. In the end a wealthy local farmer decided to stick it to the nobs and let the organising committee have use of about fifteen acres of land some thirty leagues outside of the city. There were screams of outrage in Veitvek, as you can imagine, but nothing much could be done to prevent it. Amusingly, the farmer did manage to make quite a bit of money from the venture, by being the only one on site allowed to sell eggs and milk and ale to thirsty and hungry attendees.

I met my booking agent in a Veitvek inn, a grotty little place off the main street, called, in a typically rural display of self-deception, The Shining Beacon. I auditioned, after a fashion, by buying the man a mug of ale and playing for him for as long as it took him to drink it. As both his hands tended to disappear under the skirts of a giggling, jiggling lass, that beer lasted longer than I would have liked. Do you have any idea, dear father, what agony it is to play the laute with a crippled hand on the frets? Not that it hurts as such, I've lost most feeling in my deadened three fingers, but I used to play so damned well, and now it's as though I'm two men in one body—a true musician and a potterer at the same time—I can pick as proficiently as I ever did with my right hand, but my left hand can't follow suit. It's all I can do to hold simple chords down. I had to be careful to choose tunes that let one be a dextral virtuoso and a sinistral amateur at the same time. Not too many songs fit the bill, I can tell you that with some confidence. *Inger the Miller's Daughter* is no problem, and *The Lay of Cachor* works well enough, in a simplified arrangement, and I think I managed a passable *City of New Orkan*, but at some point, I tell you, I'm going to have to compose my own pieces to have a repertoire large enough to play the same venue twice.

Perhaps it was the ale, or perhaps it's just that so far from Urvald the level of talent is comparatively lower, but after he had waved his obliging girl away with instructions to wait for him upstairs and belched his appreciation for the beer, the agent clapped me on the shoulder and booked me for three one-hour sets on the Einheit stage, a smaller space some ways away from the main stage, near, he told me, a pond. The idea for this festival, you see, was that several acts would perform at the same time at different spots on the site, and the people could wander merrily from one performer to the other, according to taste, inclination or whim. A very modern, carefree notion, quite at odds with the military turn my mind has acquired over the years, but there you go. My first set was on the following day, at two in the afternoon.

I stowed my laute away in its bag, took the purse he gave me as an advance, thanked him politely and sat myself at the bar. And suddenly, right beside me, wearing the red sash of the Schillernd Third Marsh Army over his short-sleeved shirt, right the fuck beside me, sat a Schillernd.

I'd suspected for months that my cider-addled sot of a wizard adjutant had done a shoddy job of breaking my Royal Conditioning, and I was proved right at that moment, because instead of sneering under my breath and lowering my nose in my drink as I should have done, what I *did* was, I screamed my old squad's battle-cry, leapt back, sending my stool crashing to the floor, unsheathed my sword and bloody well rushed that Schillernd. Immediately he drew his head in to protect his throat membranes — that's the only part of themselves that they keep armoured on the battlefield, but he was not wearing a gorget now, for some reason — and crossed his arms over his chest, elbowhorns glinting in the lanterns' light. "Boys, boys, we're all friends together now!" I heard someone screech, probably the innkeep. It struck me as a rather effete and ineffectual thing to say.

Even though I fought to pull back my own stroke, he had to block it. Had he been human I would have taken his arm right off, but of course Schillernd hide is a bitch to cut, so my blade just scraped aside with a grinding noise that took me right back to the plains of Idyll. Well, the plains of Idyll are not a place I care to be taken back to if it's all the same to you, so I threw my sword down with a cry of *Oyrendo!* — about half a second before he would have buried his left kneehorn in my gut. As it was, he stood there hesitantly, balancing on one leg, and waited for me to spread my hands apart and away from my body before letting his naturally beweaponed left leg thud back to the floor. He kept his neck well hidden in his leathery folds as he eyed me balefully.

"My apologies," I said, reddening. "Conditioning still mildly operating, it seems." The innkeep hovered a few feet away, sweat on his jowls. The other patrons pretended nothing had happened.

The Schillernd gave me a hint of a smile and motioned for the innkeep to leave us, and no harm done. As far as he was concerned, I may well have been lying, but at least he recognised a fellow soldier. His eyes had latched onto my combat medal for a fleeting moment before settling back on my face. "You should make an appointment with an army sorcerer," he said in perfect Immerish — of course. "At some point an improperly broken conditioning will land you a place atop a gibbet."

His voice went through me, and I felt the hairs on my arms prick up. I knew the feeling well. It played havoc with your will to fight during a battle, that sound. Made you feel as though trying to kill what was making it was, to use temple language, a sin. Before the Schillernd a man faces two enemies: the Schillernd, and one's own heart, with its natural love of beauty. Still, today it was a little different. Today there was something off about it as well. Sure, it was beautiful, as all Schillernd voices are, but to my ear, there was something faintly wrong with it. A slight fuzziness, an unusual sizzling at the back of the normally pure sound. It was very subtle, very faint. You wouldn't have noticed it, I suppose, but I've heard a lot of Schillernd chatter in the last four years — the bastards never shut up when they fight — and I have a good ear. In any case, I elected to remain civil and made no mention of it. I nodded sheepishly. "May I pick my sword up, sevochay?" I asked.

He considered the request for a second, then bowed at the waist in gallant assent. "Your accent in Cordese is excellent," he complimented me. "The best I have yet heard. I think that is why I didn't run you through when you yielded."

I laughed and slid my sword back in its scabbard. "That and the peace treaty, of course," I answered in my best Cordese, shocking the hell out of him. "All friends together now, and all that."

It took him a moment to come up with a cogent retort. "I thought you had just memorised a few useful phrases, like most of your people," he exclaimed in his own language. "Not many outside of the Bonito can actually speak Cordese." The Bonito is what the Schillernd call themselves, if you didn't know, father. It means *beautiful*. And why not?

"The Bonito's linguistic prowess is well known and rightfully fêted, but there are humans born with some talent for languages," I said, keeping my tone playful and modest. "It was useful during raids, being able to understand the instructions flying between your soldiers and never one of you suspecting that a human could be following your conversations. Saved a few of my comrades' lives."

He didn't quite know what to respond to that, and being, as it were, in enemy territory, he chose to take it as virile banter between ex-men-at-arms, and chuckled. To be honest, I'm not quite sure how I meant it myself. You would be surprised at how easy it is for old soldiers to become friends in a minute, regardless of past or present allegiance. At that moment, if you can believe it, I felt closer to this leathern monster than I did for the booking agent, or indeed, for family members long out of sight. With respect. "I am glad to hear it," he said, and I was again struck by the unusual quality of his voice, by the distant hints of insects buzzing almost too softly to be heard. "Still, as you yourself noted, this is all behind us now. Let me simply congratulate you again on your command of my language. And also," he added pleasantly, "for your musical gift. I heard you play just now. Very charming." Now it was my turn to bow, but his next words shocked me upright again. "I am here for the festival too. I will sing on the Friede stage tomorrow at sundown." I stifled a gasp. The idea of a Schillernd *singing* for an audience of humans went against all I knew of that Western race. "I hope you can attend."

"A rare opportunity indeed," I stammered, before adding with some professional jealousy — I am not made of stone, for fuck's sake: "Which is why they booked you on the main stage, I expect. I would not miss it."

He nodded, apparently gratified. His shoulders finally relaxed and his head rose toward the ceiling by about four inches, as his neck extended to its normal height, exposing the delicate throat membranes that striated the skin. "I must leave now," he said, and the membranes vibrated, swirling with the beautiful, iridescent colours that have given the Schillernd their name. He saluted and walked away, just a little stiffly. I sat back at the bar. Just before he passed the door, he turned back toward me and called out, still in Cordese — so that we might as well have been alone in the room: "It's a pity about your hand. But then, people so rarely listen, do they?"

Then he was gone. Cheeky bastard.

Well, I had no horse and the Festspeel site was, as I say, some thirty leagues away, but someone on the organizing committee had thought things through and was making his or her God proud: there were two carriages making the journey back and forth between the farmlands and the town all day, and as one of the artists I was allowed to ride them whenever I felt like it for the duration of the festival. I could have spent the night at the inn, but it was a fine evening and I didn't mind sleeping outside. During the war I slept in fields on more than one patrol, and not always when the weather was clement either. As a rule soldiers are used to fenced camps and whatnot, but more often than not a squad on a reconnoitre will have to rough it a bit. It's made me the man I am today. So why waste good money on a lumpy mattress, I thought?

The site where the Festspeel took place was fields and a lake, ponds and clumps of trees, and little tents and blankets on the ground and firepits and people — so many, so many people indeed, most looking dazed and somewhat outside of the world, but not unhappy. Oh, not unhappy. By the time I found a level spot to crash I'd been kissed by five women and one man — back home I'd have slain him for the liberty, but I've been in the army. We keep a hidebound, conventional image, we squaddies, but we're actually quite worldly. Have to be, what with a man's normal appetites and the months away from decent womenfolk. All a bit foreign to you, father, I suppose, but by the Vara, I can tell you that, when the urge is strong enough, a clean man who's been taking care of himself is infinitely more appealing than some of the ladies of dubious virtue I've rubbed privates with. Of the night, I will only say that I reckon there will be a wave of births at the end of May in and around Veitvek, and that it is not inconceivable that one of those will be an unknown grandchild of yours, father.

I rose at around nine on the morrow, which is slothfully late for me, and walked around the fields of the Festspeel, drinking in the sights. The sun was warm and yellow, and made the tree leaves glitter as though they were limned with gold. The snowy tips of the Grenze, far to the West, were of that pale grey that melts into the sky and makes it difficult to tell where mountains end and clouds begin. During the war I hated the sight of those fucking mountains, but today they looked properly awesome.

The grass about me was already trampled almost to mud by the milling multitudes of men and women and children and dogs and goats, established families and families in the making, old people and youngsters. There was laughter and screams and bleats, and the smell of cooking and the smell of shit. Naked kids ran along invisible ley lines and dangled from every tree branch, and mothers gave the suck to babes, and fathers walked about in a daze, faintly ineffectual, as is their wont. Everybody was a bit frumpy, a bit dirty, a bit lost, but by the Vara most everybody smiled.

The Einheit stage was indeed by a pond. It was just in front of a pond, in fact, and stood between the marshy water and the audience. One could have fished from the wings, and I don't suppose nobody tried it at least once during the week. In any case, my feet got wet while I reached the ladder to the stage on all three of my sets. The boards were rough and looked as though they would do their best to stick a splinter up my big toe the minute I'd look away. The stage itself would adequately accommodate a six-piece band, I reckon, so it was not exactly expansive, but certainly comfortable for a lone performer.

I'm sure the question is burning your lips: *How did your first set go, my son?* I'm glad you asked. I was ridiculously nervous, not having played before a paying audience since — well, I never did play before a paying audience, that is true, but back in your house, I did perform what amounted to actual concerts under the tutelage of my dear lost Amsel. I seem to remember that you found some pleasure at the time in hearing your son play as well as any twelve-year-old can. I like to remember it that way, in any case.

I think the audience would tell you that my set went beautifully. Certainly everyone gave every indication of enjoying themselves, clapping rapturously when I finished a piece, singing along in raucous tones when they knew the tune — or simply believed they did — and calling out for requests between numbers. They even remained good-natured before my repeated protestations that no, I didn't know that one, sorry. I hate requests so much. Of course I lied, I know them all, but my hand prevents me from playing so many of them that it's a wonder they didn't rush the stage and topple it into the pond in an effort to drown me. The songs I did play, they loved. Even the ones I played twice.

Now my own opinion of my first set, if I may be candid, is that it was crap. Audiences are so bloody *nice* — except when they're not, of course — and they have no inkling of the depth of hatred that performers have for them. Perhaps I am not explaining this clearly. I mean that people don't have the sophistication necessary to appreciate, to understand — to apprehend, if you will — a piece of music being played for them. They do not have the heart or the intellect to tell a mediocre musician from a competent one, or indeed from a truly great one. So, by and large, they clap at anything. I find beer deadens the pain.

I stepped off the stage and sloshed despondently away, trying to smile at the people smiling at me. I was in a gloomy sort of a mood, father, I don't mind admitting. I can be honest with you. I walked back to the spot where I'd slept, found it otherwise occupied, looked for another one. I ate some cheese a toothless girl was kind enough to share with me, and practised for an hour as she listened. Then I practised some more on my own, because practising, in sharp contrast to rehearsing, is no fun to listen to.

I made my way to the Friede stage with a good two hours to spare. The place was already packed, but I found a good, close spot. People are always polite to an ex-soldier when he growls. There was a succession of fine acts on that stage as the sun sank behind the Grenze, father, and I listened with genuine pleasure. Some good voices, one or two pipers with real vim, and even a few adequate lautists, whom I resented quietly.

After a while the stagehands lit the torches around the stage. There were a lot of them, and they blazed warm and gold in the gloaming. Children began to drift off to sleep in parents' arms or wrapped in furs and blankets. Bread and cheese and ale was passed around freely, with good grace and many a blessing to all the gods and goddesses worshipped by the world. Then my Schillernd walked to the edge of the stage, and he was like a comet come resting on Earth.

He wore the finest silks I've seen in years, the kind of togs I used to wear as a child — you probably still do, father — but which are in scarce supply in the trenches. They flowed and rustled and shimmered with blues, greens and purples, with ribbons of red and tongues of yellow. Even in the ruddy glow of the flames all these colours leapt out at you and made you feel as though you'd been slapped in the eyeballs with a bag of marbles. Now you might dismiss the sight as ridiculous, akin to putting a dress on a cow, but I tell you, father, we all gasped as he exploded into view, and not because we thought he looked silly either. His golden eyes rested on us with relaxed benevolence, which was given just that little bit of an edge by the glistening ridge of his eyebrow horns. Looking at him then, I fully understood the truth of the Schillernd's name for themselves. He threw his head back and extended his neck to its fullest, and the scintillating waves of colour along his throat membranes made his clothes look beige.

And then he sang. And all the colours in the world came back.

You've never heard a Schillernd sing, father, and there's no way I can explain what it's like in a letter, no matter what a neat phrase I can turn now and again. Interestingly, when he began, I realized that I hadn't heard a Schillernd sing before either. Not *really*, regardless of my four years trying to break through the wall of beauty they constantly throw at you on the battlefield — that fucking battering of magnificent mellifluous chatter they keep up all the time. Turns out that's nothing. When a Schillernd *actually* sings, you have to remember to breathe.

The thing about it is, they use their throat membranes to create the sound, and they can generate one note per set of membranes. They have three sets.

Schillernd sing in *chords*. Do you understand what I'm saying? You're probably completely unimpressed as you read this, father, and you have no idea how fucking angry that makes me. One Bonito can sing like three humans together. In tones clear and pure as a mountain stream.

I'm not quite sure how long he sang. I sat and listened, and I laughed and I wept. We all did. There is no way on this Earth, father, that I will ever be able to lift my sword against one of them again. If the King ever takes it into His Head to wage war against the Schillernd once more, I will not be able to answer the Royal Summons. No musician ever could.

And here's another thing. I was, in all probability, the only one in that audience who could understand the words he was singing. I would have expected prayers, or high poems, or courtship rituals, or something equally profound. But he sang children's songs for as long as he stood on that stage. He looked very solemn and earnest up there, oh yes, he appeared very wise and in deep communion with the universe, but he sang about learning the days of the week, and counting to ten, and tying your boots, and sheep being lost in the forest and fish wondering about life outside of the sea.

Oh, he knew I was listening. He knew I was listening, the bastard, and he was having a grand old time making this into a big joke and letting me in on it. And it was still the most beautiful concert I'd ever attended.

Mind you, it was not perfect. Because that weird defect in his voice was still there. Most people would not have heard it. But it was glaring to me. It was only one of the notes in his chords at any one time. I was uniquely positioned to hear it, of course. Another musician would have heard it, but could not have known that it was not how the Schillernd are supposed to sound. Another soldier would have heard Schillernd voices before, but would not have been able to hear the difference. I was both, and I could hear it as well as he's heard how my hand wouldn't let me play properly.

There was another band after his set, but I couldn't be arsed. I pitied the poor sods who had to follow that. I walked away without looking back. I bought some ale and wandered around until I found a relatively deserted clump of apple trees. I sat down because, frankly, my legs wouldn't carry me anymore, not that I was particularly tired. You know what I felt like doing, father? I felt like smashing my laute to kindling. When you gave in to your wife after my mother died, and pushed me so gently into the arms of the military, I was a little upset. When you made it clear that it would be all right by you if I never made it back from one campaign or another, I was somewhat pained. I'm man enough to admit this. But these things never made me feel *worthless*. By the Vara, I only had to look at your lady's sons, my brothers, useless and vain hogs that they were, to be more than comfortable with my own worth. I'm sure Joost and Tammo grew up into fine, sturdy members of the household, of course, I only use their names as an example. But the beauty of that Schillernd's voice, father. Broken, and full of contempt though it was, that voice made me feel too small to care. Everybody else in that audience felt uplifted, I'm sure. Not me. Not me. I drank.

He found me a couple of hours later and sat down beside me. He wore a dark, coarse robe with a large cowl that hid his features.

"How did you like it?" he asked softly, in Cordese.

I belched. "What's the matter with your voice?" I shot back in Immerish, angry at everything and too drunk to play nice.

He chortled. "Fair enough," he said, switching to my language. He drew back the cowl and extended his neck. Turning toward the light of a lamp, he pointed at the second membrane on the right side of his throat. "Can you see?" he asked. "Come, look well." I almost told him to go fuck himself, but something honest in his tone made me swallow back the oath. With a groan, I rolled onto my hands and knees to move closer and squinted. There was a jagged line across the coloured skin, a pale scar that broke the perfection of the glittering waves of flesh. "I caught a dagger in there last year," he said. "It slipped right under my gorget, don't ask me how. The field surgeon did all he could. Then my family's personal physician. Later two different wizards. Last month I even saw a human sorcerer. As bad as it is now, you should have heard me six months ago." He shuddered. "I think this is as good as it will ever get."

I nodded sadly. The funny thing, of course, father, is that most humans would not have been able to tell the difference. "Shit," I said. I thought of what I knew of Schillernd society, and how most of their existence was mediated through their singing. "That's got to screw up your prospects a bit."

"I will probably never get married," he sighed. "Everybody is very nice, telling me that it doesn't change who I am inside, but it's not true. The Bonito don't live in that sort of a world."

"Is that why you're here?"

He shrugged. "Humans seem to think they've never heard anything more beautiful than my voice. That feels good. They pay well, too. I thought that maybe, if I made enough of a name for myself and came back a rich *homem*, I might be able to buy myself a bride among the more tone deaf of my people."

"Good luck with that," I smiled. "I'd offer you some ale to toast that pledge, but I'm afraid it's already all in my gut." Then my smile melted as I thought back on his performance. "Did you enjoy making fools of all those people? They wept with the beauty of it, you know. They thought you were lifting them to the Godworld."

He shifted in his seat, then pulled the cowl back over his face. "I was in a quandary," he said softly. "Had I thought that no one in the audience could understand Cordese, I would have gone with my original programme. Sacred chants, histories. Religious epics. But I knew you spoke my language so well, and I felt embarrassed. I was taught from an early age that High Bonito Lore is for Bonito ears only. I was singing about Krallen bears bringing pies to grandmothers because of you."

"Right, so this was my fault, was it?"

He darkled. "I would not have put it quite so baldly —"

"Fuck off," I said in Cordese.

He recoiled and glared at me, his throat membranes puffing and rippling. I shrugged. His head dipped and disappeared further into the cowl. We remained silent for some minutes. Then his voice emerged from the depths of the dark cloth. It was surprisingly timid. "Could you restring your instrument the other way round?" he asked, and I thought I'd misheard because of the ale. "Your laute," he insisted, noting my bewilderment. "Could you take the strings off and put them back on — well — backwards, as it were?"

I goggled at him. "You want me to rejig my laute backwards?"

"I'm wondering if it can be done."

"I don't see why not," I said, completely lost. "But why would I want to do anything like that?"

He cocked his head to one side. I could only see his mouth. He was smiling a little. "If you use your right hand on the frets, you should be able to block chords well enough. And your crippled hand can be used to rake the strings in an unsubtle but effective way. At first, at any rate. I'm sure you will eventually be able to learn to do fairly fast picking with your left hand, using, say, a small piece of wood or horn."

I felt nauseous. The stars were spinning. The distant summits of the Grenze snapped at me like teeth. Pale as the moon, I threw my hands on either side of me and gripped handfuls of damp grass. I forced myself to breathe slow and long. "Vara's tits," I whispered. He was right. You see, father, he was right. In a few casual words, this Schillernd, this monster that I would have tried to kill last winter — that I *had* tried to kill only the day before — this Bonito — he'd given me back my soul. I picked up my bag and drew out my laute, trembling like a child. It was so simple. "Thank you," I stammered, and I won't pretend I wasn't crying a bit. I started on the strings. The light wasn't good, but I could have done this in complete darkness. It's the hands that know and remember, not the eyes.

"Oh, that's not the extent of my ideas," he said, watching me work. "I can't sing like a true Bonito anymore. It is difficult to admit, but inescapable nonetheless."

I shrugged and tried to sound reassuring. "If you stay around these parts and never sing to Bonito again, no one will ever be able to tell."

"You can tell," he said, and I think he threw just a little more air across his scarred membrane to make his point. His voice was like frayed silk. "And so can I. There is always at least one Bonito listening to me when I sing: me. When I sing the way the Gods intended me to sing, I want to drive my kneehorns into my own ears. I'd be nimble enough to do it, you know." He sighed. "No, I think tonight was the last time I have sung the Three." He took a long, nervous breath. "But listen to this."

And as I worked the strings of my laute, he began to sing like no other Schillernd ever consciously would: in a single voice. Just one note following the other, in a line. A perfect, soul-piercing sound that rose and fell in sequence, without words, without chords, and apparently without end. The Schillernd can breathe as they sing. He went on for a while, first giving me melodies I knew not, and then, playfully, going through a sort of medley of the songs I'd performed during my own set earlier today. He ended his demonstration using words again, with snatches of eerily beautiful, slow dirges in Cordese. The very music he'd refrained from singing this afternoon, now done in a distinctly non-Schillernd fashion: not once did he stack one note on top of another. That was the point of his demonstration, I think.

"That was very beautiful," I said. "It's very strange to hear a Bonito sing like that. What will you do for chords?"

He chuckled. "You are not very quick, are you?"

And *then* the thaler dropped, father. "No Schillernd would sing with a human, surely?" I said, astonished, casually rude.

"No Schillernd should sing *to* a human either, if it comes to that," he laughed, choosing not to be insulted. "I stepped over quite a frontier today, and I think I'm too far gone at this point to care very much." He turned to me and took the cowl off again. There was some flicker of fear behind his usual Schillernd sang-froid. I've crossed steel with these people for four years, father. I've killed them and looked into their eyes as they've tried to gore me with one of the myriad horns that sticks out of every part of their bodies. I always thought I just wasn't able to decode their facial expressions well enough to see their fear, but there it was. "We are both soldiers," he said. "We have that in common, regardless of music."

"We have music too," I said. "You planned this very well, you bastard."

"I improvised well enough," he demurred.

I nodded. "Well, there we are," I said. I gestured at my half re-strung laute. "I owe you for this. And there has never been an act like the one we'll be forming."

He turned around and took in the extraordinary sight about us — the thousands of torches lighting an endless throng of men and women and children, people who were there to be happy and to sing together and worship unseen gods. People who slept under the Western stars and had no taste for fighting. People who had listened to a Schillernd in respectful silence and had applauded him afterward.

"No matter the good will on these fields tonight, I don't suppose there ever will be again," he stated with sad confidence.

"Well," I harrumphed, "we'd better start looking for a good wizard to break my conditioning."

I do hope you will be able to hear us perform, father. We're booked to appear before the King at the Sternenspeel in three months' time. Amsel is now the Royal Music Master, if you didn't know. Not being the sort who holds a grudge, he got us the contract. I will do my best to obtain good invitations for you and yours, but I can promise nothing, I'm sure you understand. There will be a great many important people at this concert, and seating is limited.

I remain,
your grateful son.

Like Clara, in the Movie *Heidi*
Jill Zeller

The policewoman was patient and patronizing about Alice's missing dog and left a business card with a number for Alice to call if Alice noticed anything else. Alice insisted the policewoman search the top floor twice, but the woman said no one, not even a spider, was up there.

"He probably ran out the front door. You said he knows how to open it."

Alice burned inside. "He's a *service* dog! He is *trained* to obey. Someone has stolen him!"

The policewoman shrugged, and did not point out that what Alice had just said made no sense if the dog was really upstairs. She asked was there anyone she should call? Alice said she would be all right. She just wanted the woman out of her house.

"What's the matter?" Her brother Jason, since he had appointed himself her caretaker, had not only developed the ability to know what she wanted before she did, but nurtured a fierce protective instinct like a father wolf guarding his cubs.

She told him the story of Gus running up the stairs and not coming down. Jason sat at the dining table, a look of sympathetic worry on his face. Jason said he would go outside to look for Gus. When he got back his eyes narrowed. "Were you smoking today?"

Alice folded her arms. At least she could still do that. "Of course. My doctor prescribes it. It helps my pain. You know that."

His lips thinned. He wanted to see Alice's prescription for cannabis, but she had lost it. She got her supply from their cousin who imported the stuff from Northern California.

"That's why you lost your dog. That pot is melting your brain." This from Jason the reformed stoner. He got up and walked out the door. Alice heard him whistle. As if Gus would come to Jason's whistle.

By dinnertime and no Gus, Alice couldn't eat. The pot was supposed to help her appetite, but it didn't work today. Jason ate in a distracted manner. Usually he talked to her, thinking she needed to hear the boring details of his life to cheer her up. But she missed Gus, even though she had an idea of where he was and who he was with up there. But how to make Jason understand? Jason, like the policewoman, thought Gus had run outside. So she got the conversation going by bringing Franz up again.

He made a noise she often heard, a whispered '*tsk*.' "That is all bullshit. You aren't going to die this year. The doctors say you could go into remission any time. You are already gaining muscle strength. They told me at your last visit."

Alice stirred her brown rice. Jason thought brown rice would cure her. "But he died when he was 32. He finished the *Impromptus* when he was 30. The same age as I was when I had to retire."

Jason turned to face her. His mouth opened, closed. "Franz Schubert died of typhoid fever. He had syphilis that would kill him eventually. I looked it up. You aren't going to get typhoid fever."

"But our lives are so similar. I started performing when I was seven. He was seven when he learned on the pianoforte. He wrote his first piano duet at 13, and I was thirteen when I was invited to study at the Conservatory." Alice was getting excited, and when she got excited, she got short of breath.

Jason piled up the plates. He stood up. "Oh stop it, Alice. You'll make yourself sick. You have to forget this. You canceled your last doctor's appointment. You told me they said there was nothing they could do for you. I thought that was weird so I called." He slammed a fork on a plate. "You are getting better. You don't have enough lesions on your MRI to be as sick as you are."

"That's what they say. But look. Look! I got a cut. I didn't even feel it." She showed him the dried blood on her sock.

"That can happen to anyone. It happens to me at work. I look later and I have a bruise I don't know where I got it." He pushed his hand through his hair. His blond curls shifted like trees in a storm.

Alice swallowed and coughed. "And today, my eyesight is going. I'm starting to have blurry vision. I was looking up at the house, and the curtain got all fuzzy."

Jason looked away from her, out the window at the empty bird feeder. "I gotta fill that thing."

Jason stayed long enough to make signs and post them: LOST SERVICE DOG, BLACK LAB NAMED GUS. Etc. Alice wanted him to write STOLEN SERVICE DOG, but he balked. Just before he left he told her he wanted to get married.

Alice lay in her bed listening to the music. This time it was the *Impromptu No. 1 in F minor*. Beside her bed was her pipe and bud and she lit it and smoked. She thought about Jason getting married. She had met the girlfriend once. Her name was Kim. If Alice was going to die she better do it soon, so Jason could get married.

The music changed. Debussy. One of the 12 *Etudes*. 3? 4? It was number 3. She had performed that on her first CD. She reached down to pet Gus, but he wasn't there.

Alice woke and it was still dark. Above the floor creaked. She shouted at the ceiling. "Who's up there? Come down right now and show yourself!"

The creaking stopped. Faintly she could hear music playing, but not where it was coming from. All was a tingling, burning silence. Without bothering to dress she hauled herself out of bed and into her wheelchair. Tonight, her arms did not shiver as she got into her chair.

And she could feel the cool night air on her skin. She motored to the bottom of the stairs. "Gus! Come here, boy."

She heard the clacking of his claws on the hallway above. A moment later he stood at the turn of the stairs, looking down her her, eyes glinting like two opals in headlights.

"Come here!"

He just watched her, then turned and went back upstairs.

"Franz! Let him come down!"

Why Franz would keep the dog from coming she didn't fully understand, but she knew there was a correlation. Cursing, she pushed up and stood, her legs rubbery like celery left out in the sun.

Turning, she lowered herself to the bottom step and sat. Pushing as hard as she could, she got her butt onto the next step, and going backward this way, made it to the landing before she had to stop and breathe.

Gus stood at the very top, looking at her, panting and wagging his tail. He was happy to see her, but declined to come when she called. So she inched to the top of the stairs and lay down on the floor in the hall, pondering her next move. Gus licked her face.

She must have fallen asleep again, because when she opened her eyes dawn whitewashed the hallway ceiling. Gus lay next to her, snoring. Just beyond him Franz sat leaning against the wall. He offered her a joint.

Sitting up, Alice took it and inhaled. It tasted sweet and muzzy in her mouth. She was thirsty.

"Nice to see you, Alice." Shadows drew attention to the cleft in Franz's chin, and streetlight danced in his spectacles. Looking through them at her, surprise and curiosity cycled through his face.

"How come you kept my dog?" Her voice sounded lazy from the cannabis.

"I didn't. He wanted to stay up here. The people who came to look for him saw him, but didn't do anything about it. Maybe they didn't really see him." Franz scratched Gus's ears.

Alice bent her knees and wrapped her arms around them. They moved without pain. "It's nice to be up here again. I thought you had left when I stopped coming."

Franz shrugged. "I have to finish something. In my fevers, I dream of a woman who comes to me when I die to take me to heaven. I guess I've been waiting."

"I'll miss you."

He got up and smoothed his shirt, which was damp with sweat. "I wish I could stay. I like it here."

"What are you working on?" Alice didn't want him to leave her.

"The *Tantum Ergo, D.962*. It isn't quite finished."

A seed of fear swelled in Alice. "Don't go."

A line formed between Franz's eyebrows as he frowned. "But I have to. I'm getting sick of it, you know, but it has to be right." He walked away. Gus got up to follow. "I want you to play it for me when it is done, to hear your interpretation."

"But I can't play any more."

Ignoring this, Franz walked down the hall to the far room. Alice could see the glow of candlelight through the open doorway. He always liked to work by candlelight, even though she had put a goose neck lamp on his desk.

Alice got downstairs and into her wheelchair before Jason came over to help her get up. She was even back in bed before he entered. He asked if anyone had called about Gus, and Alice said no. Jason shook his head.

He helped her with her sponge bath and getting dressed. He didn't say much. She figured he was thinking about Kim and their wedding plans.

She was glad when the door shut behind him and he left for work. Rolling to the bottom of the steps, she slid up backwards again, and felt very tired when she got to the top, probably because she had done this twice in one day.

Gus licked her face and as if understanding her plan, walked down to Franz's room and stood by the door looking back at her, his tail gently wagging. Like a father dog teaching a pup. Only Alice felt more like Clara in the movie *Heidi,* where Shirley Temple urges her to walk.

So she did. Getting on her knees, using the wall as support, she stood, her legs not celery, but Gumby-like. She only fell twice before she got to Franz's door.

"Wanna do some bud?" She asked from the doorway as she leaned against it, sweat on her forehead matching the beads on the back of his neck.

Franz turned and when he saw her, a big smile broke out on his face. Rising, he came and helped her over to the piano bench. "You're here. You made it. I've missed our talks."

Sunlight lit the yellow floor. The place was spic and span, not a single spider like the policewoman said. Franz was a compulsive cleaner.

"It's almost done," he said, pressing his hands on sheets inked with notes on the piano. "I want you to play it, tell me what you think."

Alice had played the *Tantum Ergo* many times, but if Franz wanted her opinion, she was willing. She turned and spread her fingers on the keys. The cannabis salved the ache from her joints. It made it easier to play when she began, and would make it easier to face the inevitable, if that was what this was all about.

Franz closed his eyes as he listened to her play. The music filled the room, floated into the street outside. The young mother pushing her baby stopped to hear. The workmen remodeling a house across the street paused in their hammering. The crow in the black walnut tilted his head.

Alice wanted to play longer. She didn't want to stop. The *Tantum* was more beautiful than ever. She didn't know what changes Franz had made, but somehow they transcended the world. Franz slowly raised his pipe to his lips over and over as she played, his head nodding to one side.

But her fingers were tiring. An ache threaded through her wrists. She struggled to maintain her tempo; she had to do this right. She couldn't make a mistake.

As if thought created the world, she hit a B flat that should have been an A natural. A moment later, an F sharp became a G. Alice cursed.

Franz's hand gripped her shoulder. She was ruining his last work. Her hands slid off the keys.

"Don't stop!" Franz's fingers tightened on her clavicle.

"But I screwed it up."

"No. That's what I wanted." He grasped the papers, dashed notes on the page, placed it before her again. "Now go. Play it this way."

Of course, when she stopped playing, there would be a death. Whose would it be? The *Tantum* was gracile, alluring now. Irresistible. Alice came to the end, and held the pedal down until the last note circled them like a swallow and sailed out the window into the sky.

Gus met Jason at the door when he arrived after work. Kim was with him. She stepped to one side as if she didn't care for dogs much. Jason seemed really happy to see the dog again, as if he worried he would have to spend the rest of his life opening doors for his sister if Gus never came back.

It must have puzzled him when he saw Alice's wheelchair empty at the bottom of the stairs. Gus wasn't troubled at all about it, and bounded up the steps to show the way.

Jason found her in the front bedroom. If he was surprised by the piano being here, he never said. Alice sat with her back against the wall on the floor next to the piano, notation paper scattered around her like autumn leaves. Jason knelt beside her, his eyes burning.

"You're higher than the space shuttle," he said to her.

Alice smiled at him. "Is that Kim? She's kind of fat."

"She's pregnant. You're going to be an aunt." Jason pushed his hands under her arms. Alice bent her knees and stood up. Jason's eyes bugged in surprise. "You did that yourself!"

"Where's Franz?" Alice looked at the writing desk, where the goose neck lamp stood, and the candles formed puddles like frozen lava on the wood.

"Is she stoned?" Kim touched her fingers to her lips, trying to hide a smile.

Alice nodded. "You want some?"

"I wish I could, but," she patted her belly. "Can't."

Nodding, Alice understood. Things were always starting over, or had to be recomposed. "I thought I died. I was smoking pot with Franz Schubert. But I think he died instead."

Jason took an impatient breath. He helped her down the hallway and the stairs. She felt safe in her wheelchair. Gus licked her hand. His saliva was warm.

Cow Lane
Chris Amies

They'd all played this venue. Elvis Costello played here when he was still called Declan MacManus. The Stranglers were here when they hadn't strangled anyone, and 'wake up and make love to me' was only a line on the lips of some seventeen-year-old chancer with a pissed girl in tow upstairs. There were those who said the pub's days were over, that the wrecking cranes just along the road were the advance guard of two decades of continuous demolition and rebuilding that would never end until the whole area was unrecognisable and there was no more music. But for now Joey and me and our mates shoved safety pins through our noses, dyed our hair orange, and went out for a laugh.

The band was called the Allah Bunnies. They didn't look like Muslims though; the singer looked like she could bend nails with her teeth and the guitarist looked like an alien from *Star Trek*. They were from Newcastle-upon-Tyne, which might as well have been another planet as far as we were concerned. They were going to be allright, though, I could tell. None of your Pink Floyd stuff that needed ten thousand quid's worth of set to get it out of bed. It was just rock 'n' roll.

In between pints of lager someone had been out onto Hammersmith Road and painted THE NIGHT along the wall of the convent just along from the pub. It summed up the situation really. None of the kids ever came out before sunset; there was no point, even for those who were supposed to be students. Shag was studying for a B.A. in Social Sciences at the Central London Poly; as far as he was concerned though B.A.S.S. was either a beer or a guitar so no change there. Tina was supposed to have a job, working in Bata Shoes in Kensington High Street on Saturdays, provided she hadn't scared off the management with her latest green hairdo and blue eye makeup that wasn't so much eye shadow as the dark side of the moon. Joey mumbled about moons occasionally, rambling about celestial confluences and astronomical units. I wasn't so sure. Some people used to sneak off into the deserted school building opposite for a spliff and a grope, and found posters from the 1960s, abandoned classrooms still with writing on the blackboards, a family of cats living in the changing rooms and living off the rats that bred in the basement. That was what we were dealing with, not celestial confluence.

Marie, the barmaid, pulled another couple of pints of McEwans. Joey sat on the same stool as me and I tried to push him off but we both ended up on the floor, pints miraculously unspilled, looking up at Tina with open mouths. She stalked off to the front, trying to see the band tuning up. Shag was over the other side talking to some person we reckoned was probably a girl though we wouldn't have taken bets on it.

Then the band came on. Lead guitar, bass guitar, drums, keyboard, vocal: the famous fivepiece, as repeated in every no-future punk pub from here to Halifax and probably a lot further. Joey and I stood up shakily, checking our balance every few seconds against each other, and managed to stand or lean against the bar and look unsteadily through a half hundred or so leather- and tartan-clothed bodies towards the band.

They were good. I'll give them that; they were good. They launched into something that you couldn't mistake for music, power chords slamming against the roof hard enough to dislodge the plaster that had been there since the pub was built some time in the last century. The lead singer, a real five-foot wonder, red spiky hair giving her another six inches, snarled up to the microphone and started screeching into it. I couldn't understand any of it, which was the point. Never mind acid jazz and all that bollocks; we had music you really couldn't understand, not even with three or four pints of crap lager inside you. Joey was slamdancing into the bar and even when Mick, who allegedly ran the pub for some shadowy outside interest, hit him over the head with a knobkerrie, he didn't notice and just carried on. Brain damage was a way of life for our Joe. Shag... where was Shag? I had a look round, apologising sincerely to a couple of punks who gobbed at me in a friendly way and let me pass. When I found Shag he was tongue-wrestling with a stocky blonde girl in the corner. I apologised again - it was getting to be a habit, and I didn't like it - and pogoed unsteadily back to my pint.

The band were screaming away about the Government and Flying Saucers from Venus. More like Gong than the Sex Pistols, but never mind. Joey fell over. The lighting went through a change. In the red lights through dry ice, the lead singer's entire self was red, not just her hair, and she looked like a spiky imp from hell. I loved her. I wanted to ram my tongue down her throat and lick her lungs from the inside.

Joey stopped pogoing and put me in a wrestling hold to make me buy him another pint. The band were screaming and the bassist was laying down some really menacing chords. I thought I saw Tina as I was turning towards the bar; she was staring intently into the lead guitarist's face, following his motions with her eyes but nothing else on her was moving. She looked like a holy statue weeping salt tears, a plaster punkette saint in a niche in some chapel in the Mediterranean lands where they hadn't quite forgotten the old gods.

Joey's beer capacity seemed to have been increased by his blow to the head and he downed the pint in a matter of seconds. I looked at him warningly and then gobbed in his general direction to indicate that he should be a gent and get the next ones in. He was singing "I am an anarchist!" to the general tune of whatever the band were supposedly playing.

"Anarchy," I screeched in his ear, which was hideously decorated with safety pins and a blue drawing of a cobweb, "means responsibility. And you're responsible for getting the pints in. Now bogging do it before I nut you!" Whether he heard me or not he got the pints in, while I spent a happy minute looking at my tiny scarlet princess, who was turning less red by the minute but still screaming as loudly and tunelessly into the microphone. I wanted to pick her up and peel her like a blood orange.

Then the time bell rang. Inaudible, almost, but definitely there. Time, gentlemen. The bar, bound by customs obsolete before we were born, had to close down. Of course we knew it would do no such thing, that the bell was ringing only out of custom and that we would drink until midnight....

Until midnight? I looked at my watch. A few minutes before eleven, and that gave us an hour of music and of drinking until then. Suddenly I realised the meaning behind the graffiti on that wall. Seize the night. I saw a girl I'd met once before, and went over to talk to her. The music was still so loud we could hardly hear ourselves, but we managed to understand each other, and slowly but surely drifted towards the back of the pub, where the noise was slightly less.

Nicola was taking her A-levels that year, French, History and Economics. She hoped she'd pass because she doubted she'd have the patience to resit. She wanted to see the world, starting with America and moving on. She had dyed black hair, green eyes, and within five minutes I'd forgotten all about the screaming hellcat fronting the band.

I went back into the bar to get us both drinks, and the crowd were pogoing merrily. Avoiding Joey, I bought my illicit after-hours pints from Marie who was sitting at the near end of the bar with a look of complete disinterest. I took the pints back and Nicola and I sat drinking for long enough that we told each other our entire life stories. We'd already started caressing each other when the noise from in the pub suddenly stopped, to be greeted by a chorus of catcalls and whistles.

"Looks like the end," Nicola said. I checked my watch. Nearly midnight.

"Shame," I said. There was a lick of bass guitar from the stage. Nicola and I wandered stagewards, hand in hand, to see if we could get a last drink before it all ended.

The lead guitarist was packing his kit and disconnecting the amps. The singer was standing, hands on hips, staring at him as though he were the worst thing she'd ever seen.

"Fuck you," she was saying. "Running out on us like that."

It's a usual thing for bands to pretend to be ending up only to come back, but the singer really did seem to be well pissed off. The keyboard player was also packing his gear up, not looking at the drummer or the bass guitarist, who looked like he could easily have killed either one of them.

"Now come on," Mick yelled above the din, "It's time. Time to go home, ladies and gents, if you don't I'll call the police." The keyboard man and the guitarist picked up their gear and staggered out into the night, followed by the bassist and drummer.

"Police my arse," the singer screamed back at him, raising a wave of cheers from the crowd and a fusillade of gobbing. "I'll get a musician to play for me if I have to go to Hull and back to find him." Well, it sounded like "Hull". Maybe I'm wrong. But as she said it, there was a movement through the crowd, from the corner of the room, and a man stepped out to the stage beside her. He was not much taller than her, but wiry, and when he took his dark glasses off I could feel his catgreen eyes staring into mine.

He was carrying a Fender Stratocaster, and it looked authentic. The singer took one look at this, went up to the man and French-kissed him for several seconds. He didn't look overly impressed by this treatment that an hour ago I would have killed for; but he slung his guitar, and strummed a chord. Now I couldn't see an amp or a lead anywhere, but that guitar was making all the right sounds. It was screaming. The sound seemed to start from nowhere and pierce right through your brain, leaving resonances that went all the way down through your bones. Nicola and I were still holding on to one another and I was glad of that.

After a few minutes he stopped playing, and stood and faced the audience who became very still, shuffling their feet like a bunch of schoolkids up before the head teacher.

"This place," the singer said, in a voice that sounded like the echoes of a thunderstorm, "This pub we call the Red Cow, sits at the end of a street once known as Cow Lane. In the old legends of the north, Cow Lane is the name of what we southerners call the Milky Way. No, not a chocolate bar, mates; it is the road of stars that crosses the heavens. And it is this road, Cow Lane, by which the souls of the dead pass from this world to the next."

We stood there, all of us, taking in this pixie Hobbit stuff, without anyone yelling "Fuck off back to the folk club, grandad," or anything at all for that matter. We were completely pissed, or cowed, or something. And as to "grandad", it was impossible to tell how old the man was: at one point he looked no older than us, certainly less than twenty, and at others he seemed impossibly ancient. Then he started playing again and he had no age at all, and neither did his audience, caught up in the howling voice of his guitar and the intermittent shrieks of the vocalist. He never seemed to stop playing, just sliding from one tortured wailing song to the next, as the audience slamdanced and pogoed and gobbed and drank itself into a frenzy.

The singer gave up on the English language entirely and yelled what sounded like random syllables; but as I listened it was as though they were words once again, but in some ancient, forgotten language. The audience were really getting into it, pogoing here and there like crazy. I saw Shag with his shirt off, and the blonde girl pressed against him with her legs round him. People were collapsing onto the floor in lust and in exhaustion. The guitarist was staring into the crowd, his face expressionless but a look of savage delight in his eyes.

I could see his lips moving, and hear his voice above the howls and rage, saying, "You're mine... you're all mine... time to *go* children..." And the children loved it. Despite the sweat they were dancing harder, capering like lost souls. Hieronymous Bosch's garden of earthly delights had nothing on us lot. I looked at the guitarist and his eyes flickered green flame out into the room. I knew that he was getting ready to take our souls along Cow Lane, to the next world. I'd heard stories about stone circles out on distant moors, how they were the remains of people who danced beyond midnight and their souls were snatched down to Hell... and I didn't fancy me or Nicola being turned to stone.

I seized a bottle from the bar behind me, and started to throw it despite Mick's yell of "Oy you!", when another figure stepped forward and I saw that my job might be done for me.

At the far side of the room, among people capering and vibrating like lunatics, I saw him raise a wicked black tube and point it at the stage. At first I thought it was a gun, then realised it was a flare launcher. I'd seen those things from time to time and didn't like the idea of setting one off indoors.

"Let's go," Nicola said, hauling me by the hand and pushing our way out of the door. One of the staff tried to get in the way but then got out of the way as he saw what was about to happen. Behind us, the guy with the flare launcher fired at the musicians. There was an explosion, and a scream, and a whump of flame going up. I turned round as we were at the door, and saw the guitarist standing, within the flames, looking less than human and yet something far more. The guitarist raised the Stratocaster and hurled it down, screaming. The instrument shattered on the ground; and a couple of hundred punks were heading for the exits and elbowing their way through the doors as the pub caught fire. Some of them, burning already, skittered out into the night like stars, burning slivers against a black background; they beat their way out into Cow Lane, hurling themselves onto the ground to beat out the flames. The singer, too, ran out and disappeared along Hammersmith Road, yelling. She'd looked into the guitarist's eyes just as the flare was fired, and because of that she got as far as Kensington before she stopped running.

I've heard the guitarist stood still in the flames and let himself burn; but that there was no sign of a body in the wreckage afterwards. Everyone managed, miraculously, to escape. I've heard that nobody can explain why the pub stood derelict for several years, and then when a new one was built on the site in the late '80s it was renamed after a year or so, and given a sign depicting a bishop being burnt at the stake. *The Burning Man,* you could say. But I know the music has mostly gone from that part of London. Blame satellite TV and football, or all-night clubs if you like. Neither can you see the Milky Way from Colet Gardens, or as it used to be called, Cow Lane. I don't know who it was that burned the old pub to the ground.

That night was more than two decades ago. Tonight, for the first time in years, the pub - a new pub, built on the old site in the 1980s - is hosting a band. They look like a wild and happy bunch of pirates, all rags, patches and black leather. It's about time we got some music here again, as my pals and I have been saying for years. The graffiti saying *The Night* is still there, and nobody can remember what it meant. Time passes slowly along the Road. It's a new pub for a new generation of drinkers, suits and credit cards, mirrors on the ceiling, a wine list and a couple of beers on for the old stagers. But at least for this one night there's a band, and a bar extension until midnight. The old school building opposite is now an office block and people drift from there across the road for a drink.

The band starts up, going straight into a Celtic-sounding number with plenty of attitude from the fiddler. It's going down well.

Against the far wall, by the fruit machines, a man dressed in a black leather jacket and shades is leaning, looking closely at the band, head nodding slightly along with the rhythm. As the band plays, he peers over his shades at them; then for an instant he looks my way. His eyes are catgreen and they look straight into mine. A faint smile creases his otherwise impassive face, and he is watching the band again. For the first time I notice that he has a guitar by his side: a Gibson Flying V. No amp, no leads, just the guitar. The band plays on. The man watches, and waits. He looks back at me, a perplexed look this time, and I think he remembers. Remembers that day in the '70s, sweat and noise and oh so different; long enough ago that people might have forgotten, might all have moved on into the world of families and mortgages, and no longer come down to the pubs of Hammersmith. But I remember.

Across the road, in the shadow of the old school, there's a hardware shop. Maybe they sell something I could use. They're still open. I think it's time to check it out.

Blue Sky World
Andrew Hook

They called it the Tear. Not simply because it was a rift between time and space, nor because of its shape – like the gap between badly drawn curtains – but because of the emotion it carried through to us after it had wrung its way open. An emotion that would linger, long after the experience was squeezed dry.

Sometime before this was known I found Sidonie by the roadside. Hitchhikers were rare, and she didn't have her thumb out, but you could tell she was expectant all the same. It was a country road, the ploughed fields stretched away either side towards a grey horizon, with all the soft brown of corrugated cardboard. Her clothes were odd, mismatched, as though stolen from a washing line. Her hands were hidden within her sleeves. Her skirt could have wrapped around her twice. Her stance was skinny, her face was full. You could see the life there as though it had only just been invented. Unlike the colour of the fields, her skin was richer, a living brown. I pulled to the side of the road, careful to avoid the ditch which I knew would be hidden amongst the greenery. She ran round to the driver's side of the car and stuck her head through the windowspace.

"Where are you going?"

"Into town. About five miles from here. Want a lift?"

"Of course."

She ran around the front of the car, briefly touching the bonnet to steady herself, before wrenching open the passenger door and sliding inside. When she slammed the door closed, water droplets flecked off the glass.

"On the run?"

"Pardon?"

"Nothing." I put the car into first gear, gently manoeuvred away from the verge, and gradually increased speed as I passed through to four, pondering the lack of houses on either side of the road.

"What are you doing here?"

"Nothing. I just arrived."

We continued in silence. I could tell she didn't know where we were headed; the name of the town or the route we were going. I took several diversions in the hope of continuing the conversation, but there wasn't much of it. Within the confines of the car she closed in on herself, like a butterfly reverting to the chrysalis. Yet she was confident, her eyes darted across the scenery, taking it all in like a first-time tourist.

I turned on the radio to fill the car with noise. I located a station that specialised in movie songs, my preference being words which linked to scenes which linked to films which bled into life. Some girl was singing in French, a slight refrain with simple guitar accompaniment. Her voice was uncluttered, direct. I thought it must be Michèle Torr or Bardot. Then I realised my hitchhiker was singing along, initially mouthing the words before hitting them full flow, a voice as pure as Bardot's; *purer* than Bardot's. There was such joy and sincerity through the physical act of singing that I felt tears forming in the corners of my eyes, and I shook my head as if to flick them away like the car door droplets onto grass.

The song ended. The announcer confirmed it was Bardot, from the movie *Vie Privée*, directed in 1962 by Louis Malle. The piece was called *Sidonie*.

"Hey, that's my name," newly christened Sidonie said beside me.

"You know the song?"

Her brow creased, "I don't think so?"

"You knew the words?"

"I pick up on these things."

"You know French?"

"Un peu."

"A little," I translated absentmindedly. Then I pulled off the road, bumped down a track used by tractors, and onto the field. I reached over and switched off the radio before the ignition.

She didn't ask me what I was doing.

"Can you remember it?" I said.

"I think so."

"Sing."

I closed my eyes as she repeated the song. Her voice was delicate, perfectly pronouncing each individual word, and although I couldn't understand the meaning I was totally wrapped in the moment. It was like the purest poetry: words that you read which connected deep inside you without needing to understand them. Her voice had that quality, that insistence. When she finished I opened my eyes and a skein of water temporarily obscured my vision.

I wanted to ask her if she had ever sung professionally, but the words hung back in my larynx. It was the pause before the ending of a performance, where everything holds still until the first clap, before the thunder of applause. It seemed to last longer than was necessary, until I finally felt able to clear my throat.

"Bravo."

She smiled. "It was good?"

"It was stunning."

I thought she blushed, but as the sun was setting and swathing the fields in red I might have been mistaken.

"Where I come from, I am only a beginner."

I didn't ask where that was. I felt like kissing her, but instead I turned on the engine and as we pulled back onto the road, mud embedded deep into the tyre tracks, I asked her if she had planned somewhere to spend the night.

She didn't. But I did.

I took her to see Xavier, two weeks later. We had prepared at my apartment with its recording studio and soundproofed walls. No one could hear us, morning or night. I watched his face as the CD player lasered out the music, teasing out the sound. When it finished and he stopped gripping the armrests of his leather chair I swear I could see his fingerprints imprinted on the material.

Although I had now been frequently exposed to Sidonie's voice, there was still that fluid moment where life rolled and revealed itself before either of us could speak.

I wasn't sure whether Xavier chose his words and spoke carefully, or whether he enunciated them that way because he could do little else.

"That was incredible."

Sidonie smiled. Gave a little curtsy, which was girlish yet powerful. Her short blonde hair caught the sunlight and glowed. The weather had been looking up, recently.

"We have to do something with this."

"Don't we."

I conferred with him whilst Sidonie glanced around the room, read the sideways spines of the books on the shelves, and gazed curiously at the signed photographs of the songstresses on the walls.

"Are we the first?" He asked me. "Surely she has sung before?"

I told him what little I knew. She was either amnesiac or an autistic savant or both.

He asked me and I told him that the sex had been great.

"Her memory is fresh," I added. "Play her anything and she can repeat it. Note perfect. No, more than that. You heard her. More than perfect."

"More than perfect." He repeated the words as though he needed to. "This is true. It annoys me when people say they give 110% because it's not possible. But she does, she gives more than one hundred percent."

I clasped his hand. "So you'll distribute it, right?"

He smiled. "I have a choice?"

We drove back to my apartment. I had kept her hidden away those two weeks. Phone off, doors locked. Once I glimpsed my girlfriend, Angelica, through the window as I crossed from bathroom to bedroom. She looked like she had slept in her car. When Sidonie came to find me, Angelica threw a stone at the glass that instantaneously cracked and shaped a spider's web. Through the shards I watched her leave.

Whenever I asked Sidonie about her past she just smiled and said it was a secret. I wondered whether it was secret even to herself.

But there were documents to be drawn, papers to be signed. I pressed for a surname but none was forthcoming. Xavier had intimated we would need one for the contract. So I took her along the road I had found her, the ploughed fields having been planted, the clouds no longer an encompassing grey but individual and edged in silver.

"Do you remember this?"

I stopped the car close to where I had picked her up.

"Of course."

"Where did you come from?"

She shrugged. As if the question had no meaning. Or if she couldn't divulge it.

We continued along the road. The fields changed into woodland, the woodland into heath. Ten miles further the army research base appeared on my left. Sidonie moved towards me like a shadow bent away from approaching light.

"Here," she whispered. "I think it was here."

I couldn't stop. Two sentries manned the entrance. In any event, there was nothing to see. The base was a long way back from the road, down a driveway which once housed a stately home. So we continued, and it was only after we had gone a few hundred yards that I realised via my rear view mirror that the sky above the base was blue.

She sat on the edge of my bed, naked, with her legs dangling, not quite touching the floor.

"Are there more of you?" I asked. Not knowing if I wanted an answer.

"As many as in this world," she said.

"Are there more of you here?"

She looked up. Her irises were the colour of a marble that I once smashed in half as a child, returning eyes to my teddy bear by affixing with superglue the pale twist of green.

"I don't know."

Again, I found myself asking a question wary of the answer.

"Will they be looking for you?"

She sighed. "I expect so."

I held my head in my hands. The contract, the papers, the CD.

"Sing to me."

This time she didn't choose any song I had ever heard. The words were part of the music itself, like opera yet more intense because it clung instantly to your heart without any build-up or introductory emotion. It was a keening; not as a lament but as an expression of joy, uncontaminated by the slurries and disappointments of this world. I closed my eyes and the lids seemed to glow as the song progressed, tiny rainbows striated my view. When the song finished and I reopened my eyes I could see it wasn't her who glowed, but the sun streaming in through the windowpane.

I stood and pressed myself against the wall-length glass, unselfconscious of my nudity. The clouds had minimised, no longer had the touch of grey but were brilliant white. And the spaces in-between were incredibly blue. I felt warmth on my body, for the first time in an age. I struggled to remember how long it might have been.

I turned back to Sidonie, half-expecting her to cry. But she was only smiling, her white teeth matching the colour of the clouds.

"My secret," she said.

I sat beside her, stroked her face. She held my hand, put my fingertips inside her mouth. It was then that I realised her voice was a sonic orgasm, sustained and intense, yet untainted by the sometime rigidity of sex. I craved her. I needed more.

Xavier telephoned. I had unblocked his number. "The CD," he said. "It won't be enough. We need a concert. She must do a concert before we release the recording."

He was right. In the two weeks I had been trying to capture her voice I knew the recorded version was a poor imitation. A fantastic vocal, unheard of, it was true. But a copy nonetheless.

"Bring her back to my office."

I flipped closed my mobile. Sidonie's brow contained that frown, but she wasn't upset only puzzled; just like an animal when something unknown shades its knowledge.

"I'm not sure what to do," I said.

"Do what's for the best."

"For who?"

I paused.

"If there are more," I said. "Will they have your talent?"

She laughed and the sound caught my breath like a fragment of song.

"I haven't much talent," she said.

I checked all my windows, locked all the doors.

Sidonie regarded me through the cracked pane as I waved from the driveway. Her body splintered myriadly, unaccountably. I gunned the accelerator and gravel arced upwards, sparkled like gemstones in the glare of the sun.

I collected Xavier from his office. Further down the road, opposite the pub, two young men, their t-shirts crenulated by muscles like relief lines on a map, got in the back.

We drove off the highway. Parked in the metal structure of a threshing barn. I got out and pulled at a bale, extracted an almost unbreakable sliver of straw, bent it round my fingers as the men told us their story.

"Some kind of research," one of them said, "into the structure of time and space. We opened something and it stayed open and wouldn't close." He shook his head with his inability to describe it.

The other took over. "It's not like the movies. It's not like the books. There are no demons. There's nothing to attack. It's just beautiful. Just incredibly beautiful."

He blanched at his words. Unaccustomed on his lips.

"Imagine a world," Xavier said later, "where everything could be as we chose. A blue sky world. Blue sky thinking. You know that expression? It's corporate nonsense, a type of brainstorming which acknowledges no limits. Whatever the army have been doing up there, they've tapped into a world where this is the norm, the reality. They've split open the sky and let purity in; like a beam of religious light."

"You believe that?"

He shrugged. "You know how many times I've played that CD?"

I felt fear then.

"Do you think it's closed?" There was a tremor in my voice.

"How could I know? What are you thinking?"

"I'm thinking if it's closed then they'll want to hush it up."

"And if it's still open."

"Then they can't hush it up."

We drove passed the base. There were still sentries outside. I wondered how many others our young men had spoken to. I knew Xavier had had sex with one of them. In the barn I had tried not to think which one. There weren't just singers, they had said, but musicians, conductors, lyricists, composers. If our world had made technological advances, theirs had proceeded in the arts. There was no comparison. They had taken the right path.

As before, the sky over the base was a deep marine blue. An open sky that I guessed nothing could close.

I took Xavier back to my house. Sidonie smiled when she saw him, she hadn't had much contact with people. He was gentle, held her hand and kissed it out of reverence; there was no sexual spark between them. We entered the studio and Sidonie sang. There was no point adding musical accompaniment, it would only detract.

Her voice soared and dipped, weaved back on itself. I thought of Siren's, but dismissed them because here there was no intent. Just unadulterated musicality. A surge of emotion. She interspersed her own songs with material I had written and the difference was obvious. Yet she could sing the phonebook and we'd be weeping. She finished with *Sidonie*, the briefest of songs, a language familiar yet unfamiliar. Xavier fell to his knees.

Afterwards, wiping our eyes with the backs of our hands, the three of us hugged, a mutual moment of appreciation.

We didn't know what else to do.

It went beyond us. Beyond borders and governments. Was given a name. The Tear.

Yet like all artistic perfection that comes into this world it was tainted: assimilated, backlashed, thrown back. With only a residue remaining

Unlike Sidonie. Our unknown pleasure. Because we kept Sidonie's secret. We kept Sidonie secret.

Act II

Silenced Songs
Aliette de Bodard

Blackhunt growled from his place by the hearth; a low, threatening sound that broke the silence in the kitchen. Maena, startled, looked up from the dough she was kneading.

A stranger was standing on the threshold; she had not heard him come. Blackhunt, now that he had warned her, made no move, merely crouched on the stones, his whole body tense. As if frightened, Maena thought. Why?

She stared at the stranger, trying to see what threat he might pose. He wore a battered cloak of indigo; a small bird was perched on his shoulder. An old folk harp hung crookedly by his side.

Despite the shabby looks of the man, all that – the folk harp, the bird, the cloak – could only mean one thing: a College-trained. And not just any College-trained, but a poet.

Poets, Maena knew, did not belong in small, Divine-forsaken villages such as Amada. They would stay at the Imperial Court, enjoy the favour of the emperor for their recitals. This one had a regal face that would have made him a particular favourite with the ladies.

And then she saw his eyes.

Dead eyes. There was no other word. The pupils and the irises were glassy, utterly unmoving, scoured clean of any emotion.

"How – how can I help you?" Maena asked, unable to look away from the emptiness in his gaze.

"My name is Nightingale. I was told you might want a lodger."

"I –" she said, fumbling after words that had fled. "There's no room left," she started, and then saw the tiredness in the set of his shoulders, and the taut skin of his face. "You're famished."

Nightingale shrugged. "It's not easy, finding food at this time of the year."

Maena's heart tightened. "They threw you out in the other farms, didn't they?"

Nightingale said nothing, but it was answer enough. How long had he not eaten? Days, by the look of him.

Maena knew she was making a mistake; she was all too aware that the eyes were not innocuous – that Blackhunt, who'd driven away wolves, wouldn't be frightened for nothing. But she couldn't turn him away, just so he'd collapse on the road and die of exhaustion. It would be too selfish, too unfair.

"You can stay here tonight," she said. "Get something to eat and somewhere warm to sleep. But it's only for one night, mind you." Truth was – if she was completely honest with herself, and she was too old for lies – truth was that it had been a lonely winter. Her brother had not come, no doubt too busy with his temple – and winter was not a time for visitors. With the death of her son Thelos last summer, her house had never seemed so empty, so bereft of another human voice.

Unaware of her turmoil, Nightingale bowed, with a courtly grace that jarred with her humble kitchen. His indigo cloak shimmered with golden highlights as he did so, a breathtakingly beautiful effect. "Thank you."

You smile and you bow to her, just as you used to when you recited for the lords and ladies of the court, when life was still a stream meandering through green, ageless woods. When you were still young and naïve.

Now your eyes are open. Now you know what darkness lies beneath the trees. Now you have tasted it; and now it owns you.

Maena kept her sharpest kitchen knife near her the whole time Nightingale was in the kitchen, but the poet didn't seem dangerous. He moved around the small room as if he'd forgotten what a farm was, his dead eyes taking in everything – and returning nothing.

She glanced at Blackhunt: he lay on the ground with his eyes half-closed, but she knew he was awake – awake and wary.

Like her.

As evening fell, Maena set her dough aside, to let it rise, and moved to the hearth. "It's nothing fancy," she said. "Just soup and some salted pork."

"It will be enough, I assure you," Nightingale said.

He ate in silence. His gestures were slow, graceful, as if he were moving to a secret rhythm in his mind. But something in them bothered Maena, and it wasn't until the end of the evening that she understood. There was stiffness, too, in the way he moved, the stiffness of unhealed wounds.

"You've been hurt," she said.

Nightingale's dead eyes locked on to hers – followed, an instant later, by those of his bird. Maena knew about the College-trained, about the bond they shared with their chosen bird, but all the same it was a creepy thing to see man and animal both staring at her with the same lack of emotion and understanding.

At length, Nightingale shook his head. "Not in the way you mean," he said, with a tight smile. "My body's still sound."

"But..."

Nightingale merely looked at her – until she blushed, aware of how meddlesome she would have seemed to him.

"Would you like music?" Nightingale asked. "I owe you one night's payment."

Maena shivered. "Yes."

Nightingale reached for his battered folk harp, and began tuning it in the utter silence. His bird hadn't stirred – but surely it would need to, to meld its voice with Nightingale's?

However, it soon became clear that Nightingale was not intending to use his voice. He played only on the harp. His fingers swept across the strings, drawing in their wake crystalline sounds that slowly rose to a pitch, evoking the beauty of reflections on the water, the simple joys of lovers walking by the river, the tireless gestures of wives kneading the dough for tomorrow's bread – and Maena, entranced by the song, fell into the endless rhythm of the farm and of the communion with the seasons.

But the song turned darker. The chords were still struck with the same skill, but something jarring underpinned them – the sound of crystal breaking, the slithery hiss of an adder before it strikes, the last, desperate scream of a deer hounded by hunters.

No, Maena thought. No. But Nightingale's fingers relentlessly moved on, drawing tortured screams from the wood of his harp, filling her small kitchen with shadows that no sunlight would ever dispel.

Nightingale's dead eyes were on her, and in the glassy pupils she saw a reflection of her own face – pale, haggard, fear-stricken and yet unable to move or to cry out, the scream stifled in her throat. No, she whispered, no, but he didn't hear her, he couldn't hear her, the music had him in its grip and wouldn't let go, it had to be played to the bitter end.

At last, at long last, it drew to a shuddering halt. The kitchen was silent once more – and shadows moved over the hearth, over the white-washed walls, whispering of pain and of mourning, of a mother's solitude after her son had died. Maena's eyes stung, and the hollow in her stomach would not go away.

Nightingale withdrew his hands from his folk harp, agonisingly slowly. Then, without a backwards glance, he rose and left the kitchen – but Maena saw him shaking, and knew that the music had not entirely been of his own making.

Dead eyes, and a dead man's music. Thank the Divine he was leaving on the morning. She'd been a fool to think that she could bear his presence. A fool, so desperate for company she'd take on anyone.

Maena stared at the shadows on the walls, hearing once more Thelos's booming voice as he came back from the communal fields, seeing once more his face as he laughed at some joke of hers. But Thelos was lost. Washed and garbed in white and burnt on his funeral pyre, and she was still alive. Still alive, and no poet's words or song would make her feel otherwise.

Back in the main room, you stare at your hands and see the way they shake uncontrollably – those thin, white fingers that your teachers praised so much, that never missed a note or a chord.

You lie in bed, staring at the ceiling of the farmhouse, and as darkness rises in the room, you hear the cries, you hear the agony of all the mutilated.

Your hands are wet with blood, but you cannot scream – your voice is gone, taken away. Torn away.

You cannot bear it, not anymore. Something has to be done.

Maena, rising at dawn, found Nightingale's bed empty, the blanket painstakingly folded and laid on the centre of the pallet. She had not heard him leave: he must have been particularly silent, for she was a light sleeper – all the more so since Thelos's sickness.

You could have taken the blanket, you fool, she thought, half-relieved not to have to endure his glassy stare. You'll freeze out there.

What did she care? It did not matter what happened to him.

But she knew she was lying to herself. For all her fear, she could not help seeing again the taut way he'd held himself – a man too stubborn to admit he was starving to death. Men were all the same, like her husband, like Thelos: too proud to admit weakness.

Well, she couldn't afford to waste time on Nightingale. With a sigh, she went back into the kitchen. She set some rainwater to boil in a cauldron on the fire – waiting until it had been bubbling for a long time before transferring it into an earthenware jar. There. That should last her for the next few days.

Near the hearth, Blackhunt stretched with a yawn, but made no other move.

"You lazy dog," Maena said, unable to keep a smile from her face. "Come, let's go see the sheep."

The five sheep were in their winter pasture, on a knoll a good walk away from the house. They bleated as she arrived, gathering near the pen's fences to see if she had any food.

"Not today," Maena said. She brought the sheep hay to keep them healthy – grass was too scarce in winter – but only a day out of two.

After a while, the sheep wandered off. Maena knelt by the wattle fences, checking them. No holes in them; no weaknesses. Good. Last winter, the fences had yielded after the snowfall, and the sheep had scattered. She and Thelos had spent hours looking for them in the neighbouring fields. She remembered Thelos's expression: secretly amused by the break in the routine, never doubting they'd find all the sheep.

Thelos.

Her hand gripped the fence until the wood bit into her skin. Thelos was dead. And yet...yet she did not believe it. It seemed impossible that anything could bring Thelos down – least of all a cut gone bad.

Blackhunt was pacing near the edge of the knoll, whining – no doubt eager to walk further afield. "I'm coming," Maena said, shaking her head to dislodge the unwelcome memories.

She walked down the knoll with Blackhunt. Below, a solitary cart – a colourful, familiar affair – was wending its way on the road to the village of Amada. Rhean, the peddler, was back. Doubtless he'd drop by her farm to give her the latest gossip – a welcome relief to the monotony of winter.

A flash of colour from the edge of the road caught her eye – a golden pinpoint that vanished as she descended further, and then flared again.

Odd –

And then, as she got closer to the road, she saw where it was coming from.

A cloak of indigo, flashing golden as the light struck it.

Nightingale.

He was lying in the ditch by the right hand-side of the road, his face leeched of colour by the sun. His eyes were closed, the dead gaze hidden. His skin was cold to the touch – frozen. How long had he lain here?

He must have left well before dawn – rising in the silence of the house, wrapping his cloak around him, and walking unbendingly on the road until he fell. And then he'd lain in the ditch in utter darkness; when the winter sun had risen over him, there was little left to warm.

His bird was perched on one side of the ditch – its head cocked towards her with a baleful stare.

"It's all right," Maena said. "I'm here to help."

The bird cocked its head the other way, as if pondering her words, but did not interfere.

Maena laid her hand on Nightingale's neck, searching for the voice of his heart. Its beat was weak, but regular, thank the Divine. Still hope left.

She took the harp from him, and laid it on the side of the road. Then, grunting, she got him out of the ditch, and waited for Rhean's cart – which, burdened with dozens of trade items, was going slowly.

Rhean stopped when he reached her, a mischievous smile on his face. "Divine's greetings, Mistress Maena. Up and about early, I see."

Maena shrugged. Rhean's gaze rested on Nightingale, and then came back to her.

"I suspect you have need of a helping hand," he said.

It was the kind of remark Maena was never sure how to answer: Rhean took few things seriously, and would invariably have a witty remark for every word of Maena's. So she nodded, not in the mood to inadequately bandy words with him.

Rhean shrugged, as if disappointed by her lack of answer, and lifted Nightingale onto the cart. The harp ended up among ribbons and lace; the bird landed on Nightingale's chest, and slumped there.

"To your farm, I presume?" Rhean asked.

"Yes," Maena said.

"Notice I'm not asking you how you came by an unconscious man," Rhean said as they walked by the cart's side.

Maena shrugged. "Found him, you might say." Blackhunt was running back and forth between the donkey and the back of the cart, barking joyfully from time to time. "What news do you bring from the world?"

Rhean smiled. "Very nice attempt to change the subject. I'll humour you – for the time being at least. It's been a busy few months in Sethal." His eyes shone – Rhean loved gossip, and repeating the same news to every village to his path only gave him more opportunities to hone his performance.

"How busy?" Maena asked.

"Dyarchont's Empress has declared war on us."

That stopped Maena. "They wouldn't. She's kin to our Imperial Family."

"Distant kin," Rhean said. "And kin can turn on kin – just look at the civil war."

"Yes, but –"

"There are tales," Rhean said, warming up to his subject, "that Empress Iremara found a secret – a dark secret Sethal had been concealing from her – and that out of rage she declared war on Sethal, throwing out of the Twin Cities all the Sethalese she could find."

Maena nodded. "And the Emperor?"

"He's reacting," Rhean said. "He has to, or he'll appear weak. He's sending recruiters into all the provinces to gather up the young men." He must have seen Maena's face, for he stopped. "I'm sorry. I spoke too fast."

Maena closed her eyes for a moment. "No," she said, feeling again the emptiness of grief in her chest. "It doesn't concern me anymore."

They walked the rest of the way in silence. Once at her farm, Rhean helped her get Nightingale back to his pallet.

The poet hadn't stirred. Nor had his skin warmed – it seemed to Maena even colder than the air outside. She draped a woollen blanket over him, hoping that he would wake up soon.

"He should make it," Rhean said behind her. "Looks like the resilient kind. Still don't want to tell me where you found him?"

"In a ditch," Maena said. "And before that, he was my guest."

Rhean raised an eyebrow. "I thought your household more welcoming than that. To turn out a guest –"

"I didn't turn him out." Maena said it quietly, but it was an effort to keep her calm. "He turned himself out."

Rhean's grey eyes scrutinised her; his face was blank, giving away nothing of what he felt.

"You think I'm responsible?" Maena asked. You haven't been in my place, she thought. You haven't seen his eyes, or heard his song, or felt my fear.

"Perhaps. Perhaps not." Rhean stretched, yawning. "Well, it's time I was on my way. Shouldn't keep my audience waiting."

Maena, for courtesy's sake, offered him salted pork and beer; Rhean, also for courtesy's sake, accepted, giving her a few more pieces of news from the neighbouring villages. But she could sense his restlessness – the house was too quiet for him. The last time he had come, it had been summer and her newly-acquired day labourer had sustained much of the conversation. And all the times before that last, Thelos had been there, effortlessly filling the room with his banter.

She was actually glad when Rhean rose to leave.

"You'll be careful." Rhean's gaze strayed towards the main room, where Nightingale was sleeping.

For once he wasn't joking; his face was utterly serious. Maena had no answer for that; she simply nodded, and stood on the threshold, watching the colourful cart slowly going away from her.

Running running away in the darkness, but the screams are still with you, you can still see the gaping eye-sockets, hear the snap of bones breaking under your touch, feel the slimy touch of a tongue, moments before you wrench it from its owner's mouth and blood splatters everywhere.
She's laughing, like a delighted, demented girl, and the laughter rises and rises until you can hear nothing else.

Nightingale did not stir all afternoon. But, when Maena came into the main room after the evening meal, she found him awake. The dead, emotionless gaze was trained unerringly on the least of her gestures.

"I see you're awake," she said.

"That would appear to be the case." Nightingale spoke in a whisper, as if the hours spent outside had drained his voice of energy. "And, thanks to you, I would also appear to be back where I started." His face was expressionless, but the words were a reproach.

Maena flushed. "Would you rather I'd left you to die?"

He laughed – the first time she'd heard him do so. There was no emotion in that sound. "You should have left me in that ditch, yes."

How could he say such a thing, after all she'd done to save him? Maena snapped, "Then find yourself an out-of-the-way place to die."

"You mean that as long as you don't see me, you won't save me?" His voice was malicious.

"As long as I can find you, I'll drag you back." She stared at him, at the dead eyes, at the face that revealed nothing of what he felt, and wondered why she'd saved him at all. But she couldn't just leave him in the cold. She couldn't. "Don't think it has anything to do with you. I'd do the same for anyone else."

"Your solicitude touches me," Nightingale said.

She'd expected sarcasm to go with that. But his voice was quiet, almost a whisper – the voice of a man close to surrender. Thelos's voice, after her brother Ys had come and told them both there was no hope, there would be no miracle.

Damn you, she thought, angrily turning away from him so he would not see her flushed face, or guess at the tears in her eyes.

After a while, she turned back to him, and said, her voice shaking, "You can stay here awhile. Get some sleep, and some food in your stomach."

"Ever helpful." And again Nightingale's voice seemed to hover on the edge of a chasm.

"Life is precious. It shouldn't be wasted. Even less taken away."

Colour rose to Nightingale's cheeks. "You know nothing of me, Mistress Maena. You don't know what I'm capable of. Don't presume to judge."

"What else would you have me do?" Maena snapped. "Stand and watch?"

Nightingale was silent for a while. His bird hopped onto the bed, and settled on his hand.

"My apologies," he said. The courtly mask was back into place; he might have been a lord, entertaining his guests with the latest happenings in his fiefdom. "I will not besmirch your hospitality again."

Maena stood for a while, staring at him, trying to read his gaze – but she could not.

"Have a good night," she said, and turned towards her own bed.

Death will not come. Death will not erase the memories from your mind. Death will not make the blood go away, or take away the memory of her flesh touching yours – blood, there was blood on her hands then, blood and singed flesh clinging to her nails, to your skin.
Darkness rises, and you are too weak to fight anymore.

111

Maena, waking up in the darkened room, couldn't tell at first what had broken her sleep. And then she heard the soft whimpers: the small cries, like a lamb in pain that can't find its mother.

"Nightingale?" She rose, went to his pallet. "Nightingale?"

He did not answer. He was tossing restlessly in his bed, unaware of her presence.

"No no no," he said, and Maena, startled, almost jumped back two paces. "Please, no –"

Gently, Maena reached out – his skin was warm, pulsing beneath her fingers. Fever. Like Thelos before he'd died. Like Thelos, and he'd never woken up again.

Without thought, she took him by the shoulders and shook him. "Nightingale! Nightingale!" Something, anything to wake him up, anything to make him stare at her – even with that dead gaze.

He stiffened, abruptly. "Nightingale," she whispered, her hands resting on his shoulders – gripping his flesh convulsively.

He wasn't relaxing; if anything, he was even tenser than before, straining to break free of her hold. "Not you," he whispered, and there was abject fear in his voice, an expression Maena had never heard in her life, and hoped never to hear again. "Divine, please, not you..."

"Who – ?" she asked, before she could control herself.

His voice was a moan, floating to her out of the darkness. "Iremara."

Iremara? The Empress of Dyarchont? Why would Nightingale know her, or fear her? "Iremara's in her palace, in Linnabar," Maena said. "She can't harm you here."

"They said we were safe in Linnabar," Nightingale whispered, speaking more and more rapidly. "But still Iremara's soldiers came for us, in the dark of the night, and took us away. Took us away..." His voice broke. "Away..."

He was obviously beyond reasoning – a lost, bewildered child lost in his nightmares. "Nightingale," she said, with the same firm tone she'd used on Thelos when he'd been afraid of the dark. "It's me, Maena. It's all right. You're safe here."

"Safe..." He was shaking now, uncontrollably – but she knew it wasn't only fever.

"Yes," she said. "Safe. Trust me."

In the dim light, she saw his face turn towards her. Silence filled the room. She did not dare withdraw from him.

He went limp under her hands. "I'm sorry. I had – a bad dream."

Not only that. "You're feverish," Maena said. But it wasn't only fever. Fever did not create such abject fear, such unspeakable anguish. What had happened in Linnabar? "I'll brew you a tisane."

"No," Nightingale said, but he scarcely had the energy to protest.

She brewed him vetiver root with honey – what her family had always used for fevers. Since they were both awake, she lit the lantern, and sat by his pallet, watching him cradle the bowl between shaking hands.

"You should have left me in that ditch," Nightingale said, but he sounded as if he didn't believe his own words. "I'm too much trouble."

Maena shook her head. "Not as much as Thelos when he was young," she said, unthinkingly.

"Your son?"

"Yes." She kept expecting he'd ask why Thelos wasn't around to help with the farm, but mercifully he didn't. He just stared at her with his glassy eyes.

She wanted to ask him more about Iremara, about what had happened in Linnabar, but she knew that to do so at this hour would only rekindle the nightmares. So instead she said, "Winter gets lonely."

"And I'm a welcome change to the monotony." Nightingale's voice was dryly amused. He drained the bowl in one gulp. "Thank you." His voice had changed, somehow – lighter, perhaps? "I'm not going to keep you from your sleep."

Maena shrugged. She suspected that if Nightingale went back to his interrupted slumber, the nightmares – no, the memories – would return. Which in turn meant she wouldn't sleep, anyway. Better keep an eye on him. "I don't need that much sleep," she lied. "You, however..."

Nightingale raised a warning hand. "Sleep is restorative. I know." He handed the bowl back to her, moving with the grace of a dancer.

When she came back from the kitchen, she found him asleep. He did toss and turn, and whimper from time to time, but the crisis had passed; his face in repose was devoid of all emotions.

Maena sat on the edge of her bed, and watched him for a while. Back when he had first come to her farm, she had wondered what drove a poet to the most forsaken place in Sethal.

Fear. Fleeing, not from anything human – at least she hoped not – but from his own past.

Fleeing from Linnabar.

Rhean had said that Iremara had thrown all the Sethalese out of her cities, but not how she had done so. Rounded up at night, and forced to march to the border?

No, that wouldn't have been so traumatising. Perhaps Nightingale had lost someone in that flight?

It still didn't gel. If he had lost someone, he would have thought of that person first, not called on Iremara's name with such terror in his voice.

Well, no point in guessing blind. Maena sighed, and blew the lamp – knowing that the questions would not leave her in the darkness.

Days pass. You lie in bed while your strength comes back, while your flesh firms up until you can barely see the bones of your hands – those long, slim hands that will not stop shaking, will not be washed clean.

You hear the voices in the darkness, no longer screaming but dripping their hatred into your ears, whispering of fear and guilt and punishment.

They will not go away. Nor would it be just if they did.

One morning, Maena rose and found Nightingale out of his bed. He was in the kitchen, tuning his folk harp. His bird was perched on his shoulders; his face was wrinkled in concentration. She watched him in silence. His hands shook as he plucked string after string.

Finally, he ran his hands on the harp, and crystalline sounds echoed in the kitchen. His fingers moved, seemingly of their own volition, and music seemed to follow in their wake: haunting, sad chords quivering on the edge of breaking.

And with the song came the darkness – the vicious edge Maena had felt before, muted but still present. It cast shadows on the walls; it whispered that the flames would scald your hands and engulf you whole, and yet never make you warm again, never fill the emptiness within or extinguish your grief. Maena found her fingers digging into the door-frame, so hard that she could feel every whorl of the wood.

Nightingale's hands tightened on the strings; the music stopped, abruptly. He looked up at her, his hands moving away from the harp. "Sorry. I hadn't seen you."

Maena withdrew from the door-frame, shaking. "I didn't want to disturb you," she said, finding her voice from some far-away place. Her eyes stung, as if Thelos had died only yesterday.

"You're not disturbing me." Nightingale's dead gaze rested on her for a while.

Maena said, without thinking, "You weren't born with those eyes."

"Those eyes?" Nightingale raised his hands, as if to touch his eyes, and then slowly lowered them. "No, I wasn't."

Maena was aware that she shouldn't have asked the question, but she couldn't help it. "Did you get them in Linnabar?"

"Linnabar." Nightingale's voice had turned flat, as deadly as a coiled snake. At length he looked away from her, and the tension seemed to leave his shoulders. "Yes. Many things changed, in Linnabar."

"And you don't want to tell me."

Nightingale didn't turn towards her. "Let's say I'd rather you retained a good impression of me." It was a quip, but she heard the pain in his voice, and she knew, then, that it was not fear that had sent him running away from Linnabar.

It was guilt.

Guilt for what?

"Nightingale –" Maena said, her hands coming, limp, to rest at her side.

He was looking through the open door, watching the grey light of dawn flooding the meadows. "I'll go for a walk."

"You're not recovered yet."

"I know that," Nightingale said, and this time the irony was back in his voice. "I'll be careful, never fear."

As you exit the farmhouse with your bird on your shoulder, and make your way through the grass, the dog Blackhunt runs up to you, barking. You stand where you are, tensing to flee, but he's not attacking you – merely butting you affectionately with his muzzle, looking for some company on his walk.

Your hand, out of its own volition, reaches out, strokes the lean head. Blackhunt wags his tail, and you feel a sudden and absurd warmth spread to your chest – glad to have made someone, anyone happy.

"Come on, you big brute," you say, and together you start walking across the meadow, breathing in the sharp, crisp smell of dry earth – a smell that promises rebirth in springtime.

And, for a time, you forget the memory of fire, the memory of the screams, all the voices of those you betrayed.

Life meanders, once again, across sunlit fields.

Maena was in the kitchen, carding wool, when Nightingale returned. She heard footsteps, and looked up to see Nightingale and Blackhunt enter the room. The dog was following Nightingale as if the poet had always been a resident of the house, his earlier fear of Nightingale forgotten.

How fickle animals could be, Maena thought, smiling to herself.

"How was the walk?"

Nightingale's skin was still unearthly pale. His cheeks were flushed with exertion, but he wasn't shaking, wasn't holding himself with difficulty. He looked better, almost recovered – his bird, too, looked fatter, with a healthy sheen to its feathers. He'd be wanting to move on, soon enough – when the lean, famished look on his face finally vanished.

"Well enough. I didn't go far," Nightingale said.

Maena nodded, and focused on her carding again. She heard him settling near the fireplace. For a while, neither of them spoke – Maena's hands moving in a gesture that had become reflex, transferring the wool between the wooden paddles, back and forth, back and forth, watching it slowly take shape, building itself from fluff to cord...

In the silences between the clatter of the paddles, she heard his breath, slow and even; she wondered how much fear was bunched up inside him, in places she couldn't reach.

She hadn't been able to reach Thelos, in the end: she'd watched him dwindle away, speaking less and less as time passed – until, standing by his bedside, she'd had the feeling she'd lost him, even though he still breathed.

Nightingale, too, had retreated deep into his shell, running away from whatever he'd done at Linnabar. Maena knew him less than she'd known Thelos, but guessed that the poet had need of help. Not necessarily from her, from anyone who could give it – save, of course, that she was presently the only one who could.

If only she had any idea of how to go about it.

"Is there anything I can do to help?" Nightingale asked.

Maena, startled out of her reverie, tightened her hands on the paddles not to lose them. "I –"

"For dinner?" Nightingale went on.

Maena shrugged. "You can peel the carrots and the potatoes for the soup. The knife's on the table."

She watched him at it. The least that could be said was that while Nightingale was no doubt a superb harpist, it must have been a long time since he'd last done some kitchen work.

With a half-exasperated sigh, she put the paddles down. "Not like that," she said, plucking the kitchen knife from his unresisting hands. "You'll only cut yourself that way." She took a carrot, and scraped off the skin. "That way." Then she peeled a potato with slow, deliberate gestures to show him. "You understand?"

Nightingale's face was falsely contrite – creased in what might have been laughter. "Probably. Here, let me try again."

He soon had the gestures right – if not the agility and speed which could only come with practise. His hands shook a little as he wielded the knife, but he did not cut himself – thank the Divine, she knew all too well how quickly a cut could become infected and kill, as Thelos's had.

"You're not used to that," she said, when Nightingale was finished.

Nightingale laid the knife on the table, carefully. "It's been a long time since I was in a kitchen."

"I suppose poets never make their own food."

"Not unless you're fairly desperate," Nightingale said with a tight, controlled smile. He gestured at the pile of cut vegetables. "And now?"

Maena sighed again, this time deliberately exaggerating. "Put them in the cauldron. You've never learnt anything, have you?"

"Plenty of things." There was a splash as the carrots and potatoes hit the water in the cauldron. "The complete Chronicles of Sethal and Dyarchont, about a hundred miscellaneous lays and poems... Though I guess most of those don't come in handy on a farm."

"Not really," Maena said. "But you've been more places than me."

Nightingale closed his eyes, briefly. "I've seen the Keep in Tenwinia and row upon row of hawthorn trees, each planted by an Emperor to mark a new year in the history of Sethal. I've seen the ducal palace in Adasim and its courtyards where all you hear is the breath of water." His voice had taken on an almost singsong quality – not yet melded with his bird's, but close. "And the domes of white marble –" He stopped, shaking.

Even a child knew that the domes of white marble were the pride of Linnabar. "It's all right," Maena said. "Whatever happened there is gone. It can't touch you anymore."

Nightingale smiled, bitterly. "Of course it can." He stared at his hands, almost curiously, until they stopped shaking. "Is there anything else I can do to help?"

He was obviously changing the subject, but Maena still did not know enough to shake some good sense into him. "Not until the soup's done," she finally said.

He was himself again at dinner: acid-tongued, conducting a conversation with the same mastery that allowed each harp note to fall into place. Or perhaps not himself, Maena thought. Perhaps *that* was the mask, and what lay beneath – the tortured man unable to acknowledge the past – that was the real Nightingale.

That night, you see Sparrow, coming out of the shadows with his bird on his shoulders. There's darkness where his eyes should be – and when he opens his mouth only droplets of blood run out, streaming down his moon-white skin.

"I'm sorry," you whisper. "What else could I do?" But Sparrow doesn't answer. Of course he cannot speak, not anymore. Iremara made sure of that.

He reaches out for you with crooked, misshapen fingers, and you do not move. Broken bones come to rest in the hollow of your chest, and cold spreads upwards, quells the shaking of your hands.

"I'm sorry," you whisper, and for the first time in months tears run down your cheeks. You feel them, cold, unforgiving. "But it won't change anything, will it?"

Sparrow doesn't answer. He just presses against your chest with the cold of the grave, and you look into his eyes and see nothing but depths without end.

When he finally vanishes, you stare at the darkness, hearing Maena's regular, untroubled breath. You wonder if you will ever be forgiven.

Maena was boiling rainwater when she heard the sound of a horse's hooves striking the path.

No one in the village of Amada had horses. Her hands tightened on the frame of the loom. Recruiters. It had to be. Who else but soldiers would come to the farm in winter?

Her first thought was for Nightingale, but the poet had gone out on one of his walks, taking Blackhunt and his folk harp with him. She prayed he wouldn't come back for a while. After all, poets weren't immune from drafts: they served in the army as heralds.

The soldier was alone, mounted on a big, hulking war-horse. He dismounted in front of the kitchen door, leaving Maena time to see him clearly. He wore chain mail that had seen better times – the hawthorn symbol of Sethal almost completely faded. Three white scars, like claw-marks, marred the cold beauty of his face. Scars or not, many a village girl must have been infatuated by such looks.

He stood, almost hesitantly, upon her threshold, looking inside.

"Divine's greeting, Mistress. My name is Jarfid."

"Maena," she said. "Do come in."

He came in, but remained standing, warily: a hunter always on the lookout for war. "I come from Tenwinia."

"I guessed as much." Maena covered the cauldron, and rose. "What's your business here, Master Jarfid?"

"I'm looking for a man."

Looking for a man? Maena's surprise must have shown on her face, for Jarfid said, "Look, I know how you people feel about soldiers. But I'm not here to draft villagers."

"Not yet. Who is it you're looking for?"

And somehow she wasn't surprised when Jarfid said, "A poet named Nightingale. Tall, black-haired, and most likely carrying a harp around – he wouldn't have left it behind."

"He stayed at my farm. I only took him in because he looked so thin, but he was frightening the wits out of me. I threw him out as soon as he was well enough to walk," Maena said. Why would a soldier go looking for Nightingale? No, correction: why would a soldier be sent from faraway Tenwinia *specifically* for Nightingale?

"So he's gone." Jarfid's voice was flat. Her heart was beating faster and faster.

"Yes," Maena said. She couldn't go back on the lie – and in any case had no wish to do so.

"I see. I fear you don't know who this man is, Mistress Maena."

"I told you; he's gone."

Jarfid shrugged. "Then it won't make a difference to you if I tell you a story, will it?" His eyes shone, dangerously. She wished she had Blackhunt with her – no, it was better that Nightingale had Blackhunt to protect him. Jarfid wouldn't do anything to her. He wouldn't dare...

"No," Maena said. "It won't make a difference."

Jarfid leant against the door-frame, as tense as a cat on the prowl. "You know Iremara of Dyarchont has declared war on us."

"So I was told."

"After she did so, she had her soldiers round up all the Sethalese in her cities –"

"And she threw them out. I know this," Maena said.

Jarfid smiled. "Not all of it, I'd wager. Among those she had rounded up were the College-trained: the poets, the loremasters, the chroniclers. Sethal's pride. For those, Iremara had a special fate in store." His face had gone serious again, as finely honed as a sword's steel. "I was there when they came into Sethal's court – those few of them that had survived. I've never seen such a sight in my life. And I hope never to do so again."

"What had she done to them?" Maena's voice had gone dry – for she'd heard the fear in Jarfid's voice, a fear he wasn't faking.

"She made sure they would never recite again, never sing again. Their eyes were gouged out, their tongues torn from their mouths, and their fingers had been broken, time and time again – twisted out of shape until every one of their gestures were agony. Most of them died of it." Jarfid delivered his news quickly, emotionlessly – as if he'd hardened himself against that one moment in his tale.

Bile rose in Maena's throat; she swallowed, and said, "I don't see what that has to do with Nightingale."

"We know Nightingale was in Linnabar at the time. And that he escaped unscathed."

"How – ?" Maena's voice was a whisper, torn out of her throat before she could think.

"Sold them, most likely. Gave his countrymen's names and locations in exchange for his own safe passage."

"You're not sure this is what happened," Maena protested.

"Why else would he be unscathed?"

He's not unscathed, Maena thought, savagely. But he still had his eyes; and his tongue; and hands to play the harp with. "I –"

"So, you see, he's a traitor. I've come here to arrest him and bring him before the Emperor in Tenwinia. There's no need to shelter him."

"I'm not sheltering him," Maena said.

"Then you won't mind, surely, if I take a look inside?"

Maena had tidied Nightingale's pallet earlier that morning; the poet's harp and clothes were with him, and there were few signs of another human presence in her farm. "No," she said. "If you want to look inside, do so, by all means."

Jarfid threw her a sharp glance, and stepped from the kitchen into the main room. Maena withdrew her cauldron from the heat, and followed him, his last words still running in her mind.

He's a traitor...

Sold his countrymen in exchange for his safe passage...

Within the main room, Maena's weaving loom was unfolded, with an unfinished piece of cloth laid on it – she'd taken a pause from her weaving to boil rainwater. Jarfid's gaze roamed the room, took in the second sleeping pallet.

"You haven't folded it away," he said.

"I had other things to do." Maena kept her voice as quiet as she could.

"I see." He glanced again at the room, which patently did not hide a runaway poet – or any trace of his passage. "I'm sorry to have disturbed you, Mistress Maena."

You walk with Blackhunt in the meadows surrounding the farm. You've been venturing further and further afield as your health comes back. In daylight, it's easier to believe the shadows won't come back to trouble you.

The dog by your side knows nothing of shadows; your bird, perching on your shoulder, knows only little. They delight in your presence, in a small, simple way, and it's enough for you to keep walking.

You stand on the knoll by the sheep pen, watching the road unroll, and you see the soldier ride away from the farm, his mail glinting in sunlight. He doesn't look up; but you know why he's here. You know the shadows have finally caught up with you.

When Nightingale came back, he didn't say anything, and neither did Maena. He settled at the table to peel the carrots and potatoes – he was definitely getting better at it, handling the knife without shaking, his gestures smoother and more assured every day. If one measured progress by such small things, then one might say he was well on his way to recovery.

If one forgot Jarfid's words, one might even call him relaxed.

Maena waited until dinner was over to speak. "Someone came, today." She fell silent, not trusting her voice.

Nightingale's gaze snapped towards her, followed by that of his bird – but it no longer frightened Maena, she'd seen it enough times. "Indeed?" His voice was emotionless.

"A soldier," Maena said. "He was looking for you."

Nightingale put away his bowl and plate. He rose without a word, and went into the main room, leaving Maena staring at his retreating back. "Don't you have anything to say?" she asked. "Don't you want to know what he told me?"

Nightingale's voice floated to her through the door. "I know what he said."

Maena, exasperated by his lack of emotion, followed him. She found him standing by his pallet, his back to her. "He'll be back, you know. I lied to him about your presence, but he'll be back to arrest you."

Nightingale said nothing. In the dim light, he might have been a painted statue in a temple: remote, forever apart from the affairs of men.

"You don't intend to do anything about it?"

Nightingale did not turn. "Of course I do. I'm no fool."

"I'm starting to have doubts about it." She couldn't make him react – couldn't reach him wherever he'd retreated. "Is what he said true?" When Nightingale did not answer, she went on, "About selling your brethren for your own safety?"

Nightingale made a sound – which she realised was bitter, disabused laughter. "What do you think, Maena?" Slowly, he turned towards her. His whole body was rigid; his face devoid of all expression. "Or are you unable to recognise a true story when you hear one?"

She stared into the cold, dead eyes. It was Thelos's face in the hours before his agony, Thelos's voice lying to her, telling her not to worry. And she knew, with certainty, that the face before her was a mask, a hardened shell beyond which Nightingale had retreated: a place without pain, without grief.

"No." In the silence, she gave her voice the cutting edge of a sword's blade. "I don't believe in that story. Tell me another one, Nightingale."

"There isn't any other one."

"Don't give me that. Don't lie to me."

"Why shouldn't I?" His tone was haughty again; she was losing him, he was slipping away from her into a place where the pain would be easier to bear. But he wasn't Thelos; he wasn't dying. He wasn't dead.

"Because of trust," Maena said. "Because no wound ever got better if it wasn't cleansed."

"I'm not wounded," Nightingale said, tightly, and she heard the other answer, the one he'd given her on his first night at the farm: *not in the way you mean. My body is still sound.*

"And you're afraid of nothing?" Maena paused, briefly – but if she didn't scour his defences until they were dust, he would never heal. "You're not afraid of Linnabar? Of the White Domes? Of Iremara?" She spat the last word into his face.

He blanched. His whole face turned from pale to sickly white, and still he stood, bolt upright.

She went on, relentless. "Tell me you don't fear her, Nightingale. Look me in the eye and tell me you're not afraid of Iremara, and I'll let matters rest. A few words, that's all it will take."

His hands had started shaking. "You know I can't say them."

Maena said nothing. There was no answer to that.

Nightingale looked up at her. His face was blank – but it was the stillness of glass before it shatters. He said, carefully, as if each new word could break the sentence, "In Linnabar, the soldiers rounded us at spear-point, and brought us to the dungeons below the palace. We stood in a line, not knowing what they would do – and then we heard the screams. I – it was Sparrow," he whispered. "They carried him past us, broken and bleeding, and we knew, then, what we were here for. We knew there wouldn't be any way out, that we were to be silenced forever. I –" His hands clenched and unclenched, convulsively.

"You found a way out," Maena said at last.

"A way out," Nightingale repeated. There was no mistaking the bitterness in his voice. "Iremara came to see us – she was laughing, laughing at the thought of the proud Sethalese humiliated –" He paused again, swallowed, audibly. "And because I was young, and handsome, she took me from the line."

"Out of pity?" Maena asked – because the question had to be asked.

"Not pity, no." Nightingale's gaze had turned inwards again. "I'm sure you can guess why."

Maena closed her eyes, but it did not stop the wave of nausea that travelled up her throat. And it did not stop Nightingale, either. "That night – we had sex several times, and all the time I knew it was the only way to keep myself alive – to keep my hands and my eyes and my tongue – and all the while I couldn't shut out the screams, couldn't do anything but yield."

His hands were limp now, hanging at his side. "She took me to the dungeons in the morning, and I saw – what was left. Those that were still alive – if you can call it life. She showed me –" he swallowed again – "their blood is on my hands, too."

He stood, rigid. "You have your story."

Maena, unable to speak, nodded. The soft tread of shadows gathering filled the room – the shadows Nightingale hadn't been able to dispel.

"Now you see." Nightingale's voice was almost gentle. "I should have been with them – not whole and unharmed. The soldier is right – I sold myself away."

Maena finally found her voice – and what came out of her mouth was only anger. "I don't see a traitor. I see a fool wallowing in his self-pity."

Nightingale flinched away from her – his bird took flight, and came to perch high in the rafters, watching them both with listless eyes. "Maena –"

She came closer, stood towering over him. "You didn't sell yourself away, Nightingale. You were taken away. You were used. You were silenced."

His voice was a whisper, a thin, taut thread in the silence. "No –"

She reached towards him – and, as he had always done, he sought to withdraw from her. But this time she did not give up. She backed him against the wall, until he had no way out. "You were mutilated. Or did you think dead eyes weren't wounds? Did you think the silence in your heart, the shadows over your music, weren't wounds?"

He had both hands going to his ears now, his face twisted in the utter anguish of a man who has lost everything. "You're wrong. You're wrong –"

Maena's hands found his shoulders, grasped chilled flesh, soft and pliant under her fingers.

"You can grieve for the dead. You can pity the wounded," she said. "But you can't let them drag you down, Nightingale. You can't let guilt get the better of you."

"I should have refused," Nightingale whispered. "I should have –"

"You'd have died. And it would have changed nothing – just added one more corpse to her tally."

"Because you think *this* is any better?" he screamed. "This half-life without any meaning?"

"I don't know." Maena thought about what self-will it must have taken, to gather again his harp and trudge away from Linnabar – to attempt, however inadequately, to live on. "But I know you chose it. You could have died, back then. You could have given up. But you didn't."

He stared at her for a while, shocked. "No," he said, at last, "I didn't. I don't know why. I –" His hands clenched, unclenched. "I should have died," he whispered, and tears ran down his face, fell on the pallet with a sound like rain.

Maena said nothing. She drew him tightly to her, his cold skin resting against her chest. He was shaking, racked with crying spasms – and she held him as she'd never held the adult Thelos, flesh against flesh, claiming nothing, taking in his grief and rage and guilt – holding him, waiting for the spasms to subside and the grief to burn itself out.

As you weep, you feel the presence *coalescing under Maena's roof – something you have felt once before, but never so strongly.*
   You know, without looking up, what is happening.
   You know they have come.

Maena saw him: a tall, handsome man, flickering in and out of existence, his eyes two pits of darkness, his hands crooked out of shape – and even from this distance she could guess at the white scars on his knuckles. A dun-coloured bird was perched on his shoulder – and the bird's eyes, too, had been gouged out. That was perhaps even more horrible than what they had done to him.

"Sparrow," Nightingale whispered. He'd withdrawn from her, was staring at the ghost.

Sparrow did not move. He stood with his arms limp at his side. Behind him coalesced more ghosts, more College-trained with mutilated birds on their shoulders.

"Wren," Nightingale whispered. "Robin. Finch. Starling..."

On and on, until he had named them all. Maena laid a hand on his shoulder, and found him still shaking. It's going to be all right, she thought, torn between horror and pity. It's going to be all right.

They were singing – without tongue or hands to play an instrument, they filled the room with a slow dirge. They seemed to be...expecting something.

Maena thought of the reedy, monotonous voice of her brother Ys, entrusting Thelos's soul to the Wayfarers on the road, wishing him luck on his journey to the One City and the presence of the Divine.

You mourn the dead, she thought. You mourn the dead, and you move on. But you have to mourn first; to give them their due.

Her gaze, roaming the room, found the bulky shape of Nightingale's folk harp. Slowly, she went to fetch it.

"Sing," she whispered, placing it before him. "Sing for them."

His hands reached for it, stopped as if burnt. The ghosts watched him, emotionless.

Sing, Maena thought. Sing.

Nightingale was bent over his harp, wrapped around it as if to protect it. At last he raised his head, stared at the ghosts, at the hollow faces and the clawed hands.

"Sparrow," he whispered. "Wren. Robin. Finch..."

Lowering his hands on the harp, he began to play.

Minor chords filled the room: slow, crystalline sounds that echoed the song of the ghosts; plucked notes that ran up and down the gamut of the instrument: a slowly unfolding song that was the breath of the river, the eternal, unchanging rhythm of the seasons on the plains.

And the shadows came. They gathered in the corners of the room, grief and sorrow and anger waiting to consume everything.

Nightingale, Maena thought, desperately.

And then he opened his mouth, and sang.

"Weep for the voices cut short
Weep for the silenced songs –"

It was his voice at first, reedy and exhausted, quivering with tears. And then something else joined it: a warbling, whistling series of harmonics.

High in the rafters, Nightingale's bird had opened its beak, and was melding its voice with its master. It was the most beautiful sound Maena had ever heard: the voice of Nightingale, laid bare by fatigue and grief, as bare as bone glistening within a wound; and, in the background, gaining its strength from the silences, the high-pitched, sorrowful accents of the nightingale, mourning for night's end.

The shadows were receding – no, not receding, merely subsumed into the song until their pulsing hatred became the beat of the music, their darkness the shadows between the words.

"Weep for the mutilated
The victims who never knew
Weep for the silenced songs –"

The ghosts had fallen silent; the song wrapped itself around them until its rhythm became the heartbeat they no longer had, its accents the voices taken from them. They were wavering, growing fainter and fainter with every chord, with every verse, with every harmonic.

"In Linnabar of the Domes
Another song was born
A song for sorrow
A song for anger and grief
A song for all the silenced songs."

Nightingale's voice slowly faded away; the last chord echoed in the silence, and then, it too disappeared. The ghosts, by now almost invisible, wavered and vanished; but not before Maena saw them bow, slowly, the bow of College-trained at the end of a performance.

Nightingale was quiet, staring at the darkness with no expression on his face. Gently, Maena uncurled his fingers from his harp. "Come," she whispered. "Time to sleep."

After he fell asleep, she stood for a while, wondering how long it would take for the wounds to truly close.

She thought of Thelos and a body laid in the Temple of the Divine, and of mourning and moving on.

There are no dreams. Just black, featureless sleep that catches you within moments of laying on the pallet.
In the distance, someone is singing: a slow, mournful dirge – and the voice is your own, and it is the only one.

At dawn, Maena rose, and started chopping rosemary leaves to put into the morning's dough.

She had been at it for a while when a hand closed over hers.

"Here, let me," Nightingale said.

She moved away from the table, watching him wield the knife with slow, sure movements – as if all his life he'd trained for it.

He was dressed for going out: wrapped tightly in Thelos's woollen clothes, his bird on his shoulder, his harp hanging down his back. "You're leaving," Maena said.

He shrugged. "There's no other way. You know the soldier is bound to come back."

"I know." Maena watched the pile of chopped rosemary grow larger and larger – his long, white hands moving without a hint of a tremor. "You'll be missed," she said finally.

He'd finished with the herbs; now he turned and looked at her. His eyes were still the same dead, expressionless ones he'd had on first coming to the farm – there were, after all, no miracles, and not all wounds could ever be closed. "I'll miss here, too."

"Will you –" she stared at him, words failing her – "come back?"

He did not speak for a while. "He's bound to get discouraged. And with the war, the Emperor is going to be very busy – too busy, I think, to overly preoccupy himself with a lone poet."

"I see." Maena felt embarrassed, without knowing why. She felt as if she was losing Thelos all over again.

"You'll be fine?"

Maena saw herself, carding and spinning the wool, taking care of the sheep: pulling the farm through the winter – and, for the first time, not feeling the crippling emptiness left by Thelos's death. "I'll be fine," she said, and stopped before she mouthed, "I'll be waiting for you."

She walked with him to the road in silence, Blackhunt padding after them.

"Where will you be going?"

"There's a song that needs to be sung," Nightingale said. "Names that needs to be remembered, and I'm the only one with voice enough to speak for them."

"I know." Maena bit her lips. Her eyes stung, but she did not know why.

His hand reached up, stroked her face. "Thank you. For everything."

"It's nothing." Maena blinked furiously, struggling to remember the correct words for a parting. "May the Divine watch over you, and may our paths cross again."

He smiled, and there was nothing of bitterness in that expression. "They will, have no fear. They will."

She watched him walk away, a dark silhouette limned by the rising sun. There was a song in her mind, an endless song that would never be silenced – for all the dead that had moved on, for all the things that had to be remembered without crippling grief. She watched until he had disappeared from sight, and then stood for a while, not knowing what to do.

"Come," she said, stroking Blackhunt's head. "Let's see to that dough." And, the dog in tow, she walked back to her farm, to do what had to be done.

Figaro
Jackie Hawkins

The joke began at Med School. Well, not a joke exactly, that sounds too friendly. Like many spacer men, Harrison didn't have much time for women. But it was a point of contact between us, a spark. Sparks can burn, of course.

It began in a lecture on neural regeneration, a lecture given by the said Senior Medical Officer Trevor Harrison, MD, MNCP, (MCP). Specifically it was a lecture on regeneration after mindburn, so everyone attending was either already in, or hoping to join, the Navy. (Why do they call it the Navy. Space is black and twinkly. OK, I know, we have ships, but then why are they called ships?)

Back to the lecture. I *was* interested, or I wouldn't have gone. I was just a bit tired. And I shouldn't have sat at the front.

Next thing I knew, Harrison's hand slammed down on my notepad, jerking me awake.

"Wake *up*, Sarson," he roared in my ear, "No time for operas in space!"

At the time I was busy blushing, rubbing my eyes and trying to erase his handprint from the notes I'd made earlier. It was only later that I wondered how he knew what I'd been up to. Had he actually been to see the student production of Offenbach's Orpheus in the Underworld? *My* production, a sell-out? We'd even got a mention on some national music feeds.

The story soon spread, and within a week everyone was calling me Space Opera Sarson. But, as I reminded my tutor, theatricals are an Ancient Medical School Tradition. He was sympathetic, at least until he'd seen the sketch I wrote about him for the Grad Show.

Ten years on and I wasn't Space Opera Sarson any more. I was Captain Samantha Sarson, Captain of the good ship *Alphabet Boy*, and no-one aboard knew my old nickname, though there were some old friends who still teased me about it in private. We were a fast-response hospital ship, Grade C, with twenty-odd crew (and I mean odd) and space for two hundred seriously injured soldiers. Twice that if we freeze them.

Yes, the Navy calls us 'soldiers'. Even though most Navy personnel never fight, and we are nearly all sailors. What else would we do all day?

You see, like most human cultures we've found that mixed sex spaceships don't work very well - women make very good spacers, because we're better at dealing with the boredom. With some notable exceptions, men make the best combat troops (despite decades of sex-neutral education most women still have too much sense). So in the Navy there are some mixed ships but generally medical, support and survey ships are female, and combat ships are male. The result of which is that the local slang for homosexual is 'sailor'. Even though we're officially soldiers. Oh well, who expects things to make sense?

Male doctors like Harrison serve as front-line medics on Combat ships, and damned hard they work too, even in peacetime. All those bar-room brawls and lover's suicides to deal with.

I'd met Harrison a few times over the intervening few years: at the funeral of a mutual acquaintance, at a conference on high-g trauma complications, on a ship transferring a patient. Once I ran into him in a second-hand bookshop in Megaitaly. And on every occasion he never failed to recognise me and make some caustic remark about that long-ago lapse.

I'd been Captain of the *Boy* for two years when the war broke out. We'd done a lot of exercises and a few rescues and the crew was... *well rehearsed.* That's the real joke behind Harrison's comment. Don't forget that it takes months to actually get anywhere out in the black and twinkly. Ships often find themselves beyond all intelligible comms and have to make their own entertainment. The tradition is to sharecast with any nearby vessels. All you get from Combat ships are endless sports competitions, and a depressingly large number of female crews make nothing but tedious space soap-operas about thinly veiled versions of themselves. Others have more imagination. Debates, fashion shows, poetry readings, language classes, craft workshops, plays. So as Harrison knew perfectly well, there is actually lots of time for theatricals in space, and we'd kept up our medical traditions with a series of revues and musical comedies that we beamed out to the other ships on our missions.

We were orbiting Land's End, when the call came through, a boring little planet all on its ownsome at Chrysus A. To be more precise the *Alphabet Boy* was orbiting Land's End and I was orbiting Lisa. It was my turn. She's scrupulously unfaithful.

I pulled the duvet over her head and turned on the comm.

The Fiori had finally attacked. They had taken the McGowan system. We were to proceed immediately to a rendezvous with six other ships at Tegah and then go on with them to McGowan, joining up with the response fleet on the way.

The trip to McGowan would take four months. 'Proceed Immediately' could be taken with a pinch of salt. Red hair snaked invitingly out from under the duvet, and a long cool hand reached out to turn off the comm at the end of the message. No hurry at all.

It was not that I'd been thinking about my old foe, Harrison. I had been plotting something more ambitious for a while, waiting for the next long trip. Here was my chance; four months to prepare and rehearse followed by a premiere in front of most of the Navy. I've never thought small.

I wanted something to boost morale and distract from the coming battles. Something with style. We spent the week to Tegah in debate and Sal and I won.

For the delight of the Combined Human Naval Alliance of Falconer, Ydo and Gordon's Leap, the *Alphabet Boy* would present... *The Marriage of Figaro*, by Wolfgang Amadeus Mozart.

You may have noticed a problem here. Seven of the eleven characters in Figaro are male. Cherubino doesn't count, as since the disappearance of castrati the role has normally been sung by a woman. That leaves six. Some ships would use hologram recordings, but I felt that was cheating. We used a simple voice modulation programme, tweaked by Chris until it was fully capable of adjusting a soprano or alto voice into an authentic tenor or bass without losing any subtlety of phrasing or vibrato - or losing any of the adrenaline high of a live performance. Actually acting a male role was all part of the fun, and no more difficult than imagining ourselves into the right period.

Casting still wasn't easy of course. Of our crew, only a few have a good enough voice to take on a major operatic role. Of these, only

Carrie had the, er, *cocksure* quality to play Figaro himself. I was rather too curvy to play a man, so I got the part of Suzanna. Lisa asked to be the Count, and very predatory she can look, to be sure. Sal sighed and volunteered for Cherubino. We persuaded Bridie to sing the Countess, even though that would leave us short of a conductor - the computer plays all the instruments, of course, but you get a far more authentic sound and better integration with the singing if a human conducts the computer. The rest of the parts were filled with increasing desperation until we ended up with Furfoot as Antonio. It's not that Furfoot can't *sing*, it's that she can't really wear a sensible costume, not with the six legs.

So the weeks and days floated by. We singers learned our roles while Mel and Angela ran up the costumes (Holograms don't work for me – you don't move right if you're not in the right clothes, and anyway I for one can't put the same feeling into a role acting nude). Furfoot and I designed the sets - which *were* holograms, and Chris slumped in her usual chair, picked her teeth, and claimed that she was programming in her head. Our little group of ships joined another, and another, and then a large group of ships, until the whole of the black and twinkly around us was studded with the dull grey lozenges of the fleet, all going to war.

We planned our premiere carefully, a dress rehearsal five days from McGowan, then the first performance three days out. I hoped to put on a repeat performance in a few weeks time, for the liberated people of McGowan, but that was just my usual megalomania. The dress rehearsal went well, we announced our programme to the fleet and were gratified by the number of ships that called back to say they'd rearrange their own schedule to show *Figaro* live. Well, I was gratified. Sal had to go and throw up in the joan. An old student friend on another ship called over, and within an hour I was Space Opera Sarson to everyone on the *Boy*.

Orders came in four days from McGowan. The computer logged the courses. The only thing that snagged my interest was the news that the huge battleship *Nell Gwyn* had managed to catch up with the fleet after all. Nellie the Elephant. Apart from that I spent the day in my Suzanna costume, practising. You don't often have to wear a crinoline in the Navy.

Sal prescribed herself anti-nausea pills. Furfoot proudly produced a 'garden fork' she'd made as a prop for her character. I dare say if you were a three foot tall six-legged gardener you would use something like that to turn over the soil. I told Chris to subtitle her entrance, just in case the audience was confused.

We checked the orchestration and the scene changes, the hooks that linked the two programmes together, the coding on the voice recognition so there was no chance of Suzanna coming out baritone. Then I declared an official break. Carrie and I reviewed our orders. There had been a slight change since the arrival of the *Nellie*; she and two Viper class ships were to peel off in the afternoon and perform a diversionary manoeuvre. The *Alphabet Boy* and five other support vessels were assigned to wait for two hours and then follow 'cautiously'. Which sounded as though we were going to see action a little sooner than the rest of the fleet. You don't get adverbs in your orders until things hot up and you actually have to start telling the computers what to do.

At any rate, we didn't think it would affect *Figaro*. Our computers would handle the course changes and monitoring. We'd still be well within comcast range of the fleet.

Carrie's our pilot and she made sure the course was correctly set up. The two of us decided that we wouldn't tell the rest of the crew the details of our orders, just in case it distracted them from our *magnus opus*. I suppose that was a mistake.

The afternoon drew on. People began to get into costume. Lisa released her hair from the cap she'd had it in all day to reveal a glorious fall of auburn curls. I've never seen such a good-looking Count Almavira. Perhaps it explained his success as a womaniser. Furfoot broke a chair with her 'garden fork', probably because the cloth cap she was wearing kept slipping down over her eye. We didn't realise it was broken until Chris tried to sit on it. We do keep telling her to lose weight.

Thirty minutes. Most of us were in the big bathroom, checking our makeup.

"*Alphabet Boy, Alphabet Boy*, this is an emergency, emergency class two, do you hear me?"

I knew that voice from somewhere. I dropped my lipstick and grabbed the emergency comm. "This is the *Alphabet Boy*, Captain speaking, we copy, class two emergency, transmit details." I sounded calmer than I was. Out of the corner of my eye I could see Carrie running for the bridge.

"This is the *Easter Bunny*. This *was* the *Easter Bunny*." There was a pause. "Ship destroyed, repeat, destroyed by Fiori attack. Fiori now pursuing the *Nell Gwyn* and the *Pearly Queen*. Most crew are in boats or suits, relatively few casualties reported. Drive did not blow."

I felt the coarse thrust of our engines as Carrie switched the controls to manual. Getting the *Boy*'s arse into gear.

"But where are you, Captain?" I shouted. I was rattled by the people fussing around me. Okay, I knew I couldn't actually suit up in a crinoline, but did it take quite so many of them to unlace me?

"Captain and senior officers are all missing, presumed dead. Conference room took a direct hit. This is Commander Harrison, acting Captain until given further orders."

Harrison? That fun-hating, misogynist idiot of a doctor in command of a military emergency? Fuck, he wasn't joking when he said they'd lost all the senior officers.

Another voice broke in. "This is Sub-Lieutenant Cartwright, Sir, Ma'am. We are dispersed around the remains of the *Easter Bunny*, orbiting moon four, approximately 22-X-zero-theta-zero."

"Thank you, Sub-Lieutenant, we're on our way."

I broke the connection. My crinoline lay around me like an opened present. I stepped out of it and made my way towards the airlock, already planning how I'd tell Harrison he'd been rescued by Space Opera Sarson.

My EVes were all there before me, struggling into their suits, their stretchers and patch kits lined up. Lisa's red curls were filling her helmet, and Bridie's pretty stage makeup sat oddly as she checked everybody's failsafes. Behind us the inside crew were pulling up trolley after trolley, cross-checking triage criteria, calling us good luck. Sal was in charge here, briskly issuing orders despite being clad in Cherubino's brocaded jacket and absolutely nothing else. If her lovely butt and legs didn't cheer up those injured soldiers nothing would. We'd hardly need Furfoot's talents.

"Five minutes." said Carrie. We all paused, listening again to the power of the *Boy*'s engines as we arced towards the moon. We could see the wreck on the monitor now, an opened tin-can of a ship, surrounded by human flotsam sparkling like dust. There must have been some crossfire before the Fiori took the ship apart, for so many of them to have had time to suit up.

"Object avoidance programme initiated." That was Chris. Object avoidance indeed, those were people out there, even if they were men. But I bit my tongue. She did her job well. The *Boy* decelerated smoothly, on a long curve that found the widest of safety-margins between all those annoying 'objects'. As we neared stasis, I glimpsed the *Bunny*'s three lifeboats turning to rendezvous with us, their trails blue against the black.

Then the airlock began to cycle and I had to turn to the doors. I leapt out into this rather over-populated area of local space, leading my EVe team to further our noble mission of rescuing and healing humanity.

I must admit that I have spent some time practising my leap. It is difficult to look elegant in a space suit at any time, and jumping from an airlock tends to make you look like a 2D cartoon character, stranded by its own disbelief of falling. But I've always thought that élan was important for both actresses and leaders, so I got Lisa to teach me her technique. God knows how she acquired it but she can make even *removing* a space suit look sexy and uncontrived. So now I have this perfect... leap. It's all in the knee action, kicking harder than you appear to, while stretching your left arm out boldly as if you were being pulled along by a wire.

Never, in all my missions, have I executed a better leap. I never got Chris to admit whether she really forgot to cancel the programme, or whether she triggered it exactly then as a joke. But as I arrowed out into the black and twinkly, my team in formation behind me, the orchestra struck up. The scurry of violins, the perfection and anticipation tickling the hairs on my arms. The overture to the *Marriage of Figaro*.

And why not? As I finished my dive and turned on my jet pack I heard Lisa murmur just that and Carrie chuckle and agree very quietly. The music built up and up, and as I reached my first casualty the overture turned the corner and became the opening duet. And Carrie sang to me and I replied, the music carrying me on while the working part of my mind strapped the trooper's legs together and checked his vital signs. He gave me a thumbs-up, smiling. When you are stranded in space there are far worse things to find than a singing doctor.

We worked on through the first act. Many of the troopers closest to us were uninjured or only slightly injured - they had used their suit-packs to approach the *Boy*. As time went on the casualties got more thinly spread and more badly hurt. Once or twice our concentration slipped: "Non so pia cosa son, oh shit that's an artery," sang Sal as Cherubino, perfectly in tune, and Bridie stopped one of her recitavos completely to scold a soldier. His helmet was full of blood and he was in what you might call a *blind* panic. But it never slipped the other way, we never forgot our medicine in the music.

We worked our way towards the ruined twists of metal that had once been the *Easter Bunny*. Shards and splinters spun between us, catching the light like lethal tinsel. My EVes could easily avoid them, but the men immobilised by injury or suit failure were completely helpless. While the Countess, Suzanna and Cherubino hatched their plans to trick the Count, Carrie manouevred the *Boy* a little closer to the dangerous spiral of debris, saving us time on the to-ing and fro-ing, while others of the crew set up long lines to attach corpses to. We'd draw them into the ship once all who could be saved had been saved. *Amanti constanti* sang the chorus. The wedding began at the end of act three.

I'd hoped all along that it would be me. I kept itching to ask my Marcellina or my Basilio just whose body they had on their stretcher. But I'd not wanted to interrupt the music, the music that seemed to free my hands from shock and sorrow, enabling me to work better than I'd ever done to save life after life. Now I saw him close to me, the blazon on his suit clear as he drifted against a section of the *Bunny*. Commander Harrison, a Captain's sash drawn hastily across the large cross of an SMO. And my suit talked to his suit, and came up with the right answers. He was alive, only slightly injured in his paralysed suit and conscious.

The music's rapture caught me and I stopped in front of him, my voice sure and true as Suzanna, *Deh vieni non tardar, o gioja bella,* love sung slow and simple. Not just for Figaro but for all my crew and all my patients, even Harrison.

Behind the music I was preparing to jet over to him and strap him to my stretcher. I had my words ready for the end of the aria. "Space Opera Sarson at your service, sir." Blind and deaf to anything but the music, blind and deaf to any danger, I was singing my heart out, my soul alive to the climax of the opera, wishing that it could never be over, that I could sing for ever out here between the stars.

The ship blew. Not the main drive, or I'd not be here to tell you this, but something in the armoury. Harrison was directly between me and the blast, so that the great spear of metal took him through the chest, taking out his heart and lungs and spine and all his remaining suit support systems in one unstoppable moment. Took him spinning away, his blood already freezing. Took him, not me.

And what did I do? No-one could see the tears on my face and somehow I kept them out of my throat. So I sang on, to the bitter end, to the sweet end. I sang the music that had saved me and killed him and I could not stop crying.

If I'd not stopped to show off, if I'd moved straight over to strap him to the stretcher like a good doctor would have, that girder from the armoury would have taken my heart out instead. More Wagner than Mozart, wouldn't you say?

The last time somebody called me Space Opera Sarson, I punched him in the mouth.

Shostakovich Ensemble, The
Jim Steel

Greetings, Comrade!

Just kidding, Mark - nothing wrong with a burst of nostalgia now and again, eh? Anyway, my apologies for being so late with my entries for the album discography, but here's the last of them. Hope I haven't rushed it too much; these denationalised publishers seem to be driven more by deadlines than by quality (but please don't quote me on that). I know that you wanted me to try and cut out any references to myself, but I feel that the personal touch adds interest for the reader, and it would have made the entry on The Living Eyes impossible to write, for example, because I was in them. I know you didn't commission the Eyes piece but I take it you are going to use it? Our album may only have recorded on home-dubbed cassettes and sold at our gigs, but an album's an album. Think of it as being in the spirit of punk. Having said that, it might be best all round if I use a pseudonym for that one. If you've still got any doubts, we can discuss it in a couple of weeks when you see me to get your permit renewed. Unfortunately the recent departmental changes mean that this is no longer a mere formality, but I should be able to plausibly present your case. I can schedule an entire hour to talk with you if you think it necessary, providing you let me know now - I'd hate to see the entire project derailed at this late stage, especially after the work we've all put into it.

Besides, I feel, in this case, that sort of objectivity is entirely subjective, if that makes sense.

Regards,
Jim Steel

Shostakovich Ensemble, The

Formed Glasgow, 1978. Barry Good (guitar), Ross Macdonald (guitar, keyboards), John Powell (bass), Stuart Shaw (drums). The name was taken from an obscure Soviet composer who was 'disappeared' in the twenties. Originally a straight-ahead punk band, they rapidly became known for extended instrumentals. If they were starting out today they would probably have been classified as post-rock, but back then they were fairly unique with only the likes of Magazine, Eno and the early seventies German Movement sounding anything like them. Their gimmick consisted of pretending to be a classical quartet and they would take to the stage in full black tie regalia (Macdonald was a voracious Kraftwerk fan). This was pretty funny when sporting blue mohicans or dreadlocks, but as the years rolled by and the haircuts became more conventional, they came to look like the establishment figures that they were. Their habit of assigning opus numbers to all of their recorded songs also became pretty wearisome. Much of the music, however, stands up remarkably well and is long overdue a reassessment.

First Symphony (Stow 001) (1979)* * * *

Alleggretto/Allegro/Lento/Allegro Molto
This was the first release on the Stow College label, which was set up to enable students to learn all aspects of the music industry (three of the four were Stow students at the time). When revived after the clampdown of the eighties the label would be responsible for launching acts such as Belle & Sebastian, but in its first incarnation it only managed three annual releases, with Simple Minds and Orange Juice following the Ensemble. It is thought that the planned fourth release, by the wilfully obscure Joseph K, led to the label's shutdown and the arrest of the head of department. The Ensemble's first release proved to be an excellent collection of assured hard rock tracks that gave little hint of what was to come.

To October (GB 4455) (1979)* * *

To October / (other side by Dire Straits)
I hummed-and-hawed about including this (and the next) release in an album discography, but I have eventually decided to list both of them. Given the amount of non-album singles, compilation tracks

and soundtracks that The Shostakovich Ensemble released, it is difficult to do them full justice with their albums alone and, in the end, that is what decided me. They were signed to the state record company, GBM, within a week of the Stow release. It was customary for GBM to release two new signings on one album to gauge their popularity as, despite having a near monopoly, they still had no desire to lose money on an unknown commodity. However, it is fair to say that the two bands paired here were not carefully matched. It is said that all the copies of this record that turn up in second hand stores are worn on one side and mint on the other. One needn't add that it is normally the Dire Straits side that is worn flat. The Ensemble's nineteen-minute epic is not for the faint-hearted and is genuinely terrifying when the siren kicks in halfway through. That is followed by a massed chorus of whoever was in the studio at the time. It represented a break from their all-instrumental debut and hinted that this was never going to be a staple of their live act. The lyrics themselves are taken from a standard schoolwork assignment about Lenin and the Russian Revolution. Effective but hollow.

May Day (GB4489) (1979)* *

May Day / (other side by The Ruts)
In an almost unprecedented move, an obviously puzzled GMB released another split album, this time with the much more sympathetic coupling of The Ruts. If GMB had learned something from the last release, the Quartet hadn't; at twenty-six minutes, *May Day* was even longer. However, at least this time you could turn the record over without your fillings exploding in shock. It's a lighter piece, but again there's the massed choir and the textbook poem which has had more than one commentator wondering if it was recorded at the same session as *To October.* The title, though, has engendered much more in the way of discussion. A celebration of the workers' holiday, certainly, but was it also a cry for help? This was only a few months after the Tebbit takeover, and already artistic freedom of expression was feeling the pinch. Many bands, such as The Clash, fled to the USA to escape the clampdown, but most didn't have that option. Some simply gave up, but others buckled down and got on as best as they could. For many who were a-political and never got much beyond love songs, it didn't matter too much (the escapist New Romantic movement, for example, can be directly attributed to these events.) For others it was the dance of danger, wobbling

between accusations of collaboration and the threat of the labour camps. But the Ensemble felt that they were on the way up and were untouchable. One music critic (who will remain anonymous) has a story about walking below their changing-room window and being hit on the head by his own band's discarded demo-tape that he'd handed them only a couple of minutes previously. Times were changing, however, and the Ensemble would learn the inadvisability of making enemies.

Fourth Symphony (Alternative Tentacles 008) (1980)* * * *

Allegretto Poco Moderato/Moderato Con Moto/Largo-Allegro
The Ensemble had originally planned a rock opera as their first release of the eighties. They were big fans of The Who. However, their subject matter, Macbeth, ensured that the undertaking was under careful scrutiny from the start. The one performance that took place engendered accusations of nationalism, formalism and historical revisionism. The fact that it took place in a near-empty Hampden Park in the pouring rain probably didn't help either. The subject matter naturally drew comparisons with the overthrow of Heath by Tebbit only the previous year, although, of course, the group would have denied any allegorical similarity. How much of *MacBeth* was absorbed into the *Fourth Symphony* is a matter for debate. The band destroyed the score and the sole surviving audience recording of the Hampden gig only captures the first quarter of an hour. Ironically both support acts have been caught in their entirety but that does not concern us here. I was at Hampden and, in my opinion, the overlap between the two pieces was considerable. The band obviously thought so too, and they pulled the *Fourth Symphony* album. A dubbed cassette from the sessions somehow made its way to America and was released on a small independent label to little fanfare. Macdonald was the prime suspect but nothing has ever been proved. A couple of the band's singles were also banned around this time, with a curious result in the case of *The Nose*. It was withdrawn from sale and all shop-bound copies were destroyed before they reached the shelves. However, due to an administrative error, a broadcasting ban was not issued until a week later and promotional copies received ample airtime on late-night BBC radio shows. These were, of course, taped by avid listeners and black-market cassette copies were much sought after for many years.

5th Symphony (GB5001) (1981)* * * * *

Moderato/Allegretto/Largo/Allegro Non Troppo
It must be remembered that, around this time, several of their contemporaries were executed. We lost Howard Devoto, Mark E. Smith, Elvis Costello and Shaking Stevens. One can only dream of what these artists might have achieved had they lived. The Ensemble had an Arts Councillor appointed as their manager, and their interviews of the time are full of grovelling and apologies over their difficult experiments of the past. We had no right to expect anything much from their new material but they turned in a masterpiece that is arguably their finest work. Instantly accessible and yet capable of an infinite amount repeats without ever sounding dull, it is claimed that many of its sales resulted from people wearing out the notoriously poor GBM vinyl. The group also changed the titles of their symphonies from numerical names to Arabic symbols with this album and claimed that lazy music journalists had already made this decision for them. This was an exclusive that I obtained in an interview, incidentally.

6th Symphony (GB5112) (1981)* * * *

Largo/Allegro/Presto
The Ensemble, by now speaking only through their manager, announced in advance that this album was a conceptual tribute to Lenin. It may well have been, but who really knows? Was it an elaborate joke on their manager? On the censors? On their fans? Wonderful as it is, it defies interpretation. The official line was to take their statements at face value. Coincidently, at this time they were also sent on their first foreign tour at the request of the Italian Communist Party who apparently were under the impression from the track listings that at least some of the band could speak Italian. No interpreter was supplied when they reached Milan, and the tour proved to be at best a mixed success. They did, at least, manage to reach a couple of the venues on the correct nights.

Leningrad (GB5334) (1982)* * * * *

War/Memories/My Native Field/Victory
This was the first of a thematic trilogy on the Great Patriotic War. It almost feels like a film soundtrack, such is the strength of its imagery.

Shaw's incessant, military drumming is a key component in unifying the album, but in fairness all of them play their socks off. They were rewarded for producing such an ideologically correct work by having it premiered in its entirely on a special late-night BBC arts programme. Only after subsequent releases did people start to wonder at possible double meanings in its intent. Was the melancholic *My Native Field* in fact a requiem for the State's victims? At this time they were also encoring with an instrumental cover of *Dead Souls*. Curtis, of course, had been sectioned after Joy Division's first album and then executed for treason shortly after his release two years later.

8th Symphony (GB5150) (1982)* * *

Adagio/Allegretto/Allegro Non Troppo/Largo/Allegretto

What a bleak and uncompromising work this is. Recorded over the space of a single weekend at a studio in Ayrshire, it signals a return to their wilful obtuseness. Bad enough having the same name for tracks on different albums without repeating the names on the same record. I put forward the theory at the time that the band was in mourning after the death of their manager in a car crash during a recent short tour. The Ensemble had been following him in their van when his Rolls Royce skidded out of control and went over the edge of the Rest and be Thankful (a notoriously dangerous Scottish road). A police investigation cleared Macdonald, who had been driving the van at the time, of any involvement when he was eventually able to satisfactorily prove that damage to the front of the van had occurred in Oban during the previous night. Others, however, came up with different interpretations for the album. Paul Morley, for example, writing in Smash Hits just before he vanished, put forth the proposition that the group was lamenting America's neutrality in the War. Possibly, he wrote, the Ensemble were suggesting that much of the suffering back then could have been avoided if America had come to the aid of Britain and the Soviet Union. The war might even have ended as early as 1947. The unsaid heresy he hinted at was that the Iron Curtain might have fallen across the English Channel instead of down the middle of the Atlantic. My theory obviously seems to be the more plausible one from this distance in time.

9th Symphony (GB5199) (1982)* *

Allegro/Moderato/Presto/Largo/Allegretto

Another weekend recording, this time somewhere in Fife. The third in the War triptych, supposedly commemorating the sacrifices of the Great Patriotic War, this one puzzled everyone. Eventually the Party played safe and banned it a year after it was released. No charges were brought against the Ensemble, though, as no one could work out exactly what they were guilty off. It's cheery and light-hearted, which seems somehow sacrilegious given the stated theme. It barely dented the album charts as the public had been frightened off them by their previous album, and it is now almost impossible to get hold of second-hand copies.

10th Symphony (GB5600) (1984)* * * *

Moderato/Allegro/Allegretto/Andante

Ah, the difficult 10th! Classical composers have their cursed ninth symphonies, and rock groups have their cursed tenth albums. Many artists have fallen at this one: The Who, The Beatles and The Stranglers to name but a few. Despite preceding it with the second longest break in their recording career, the Ensemble sailed through it with barely as much as a blip. This dirge reflected much that was felt to be wrong in the country up until then. The recent assassination of Tebbit meant a lessening of censorship, and a changing of the guard of the Soviet Union brought a thaw in relations with America. This was the first of the Ensemble's records to gain an official release over there but it sank without trace. In this country also, they were playing to smaller venues despite a loyal core of fans. Some, although I shouldn't be numbered amongst them, decided that the album was a statement on Tebbit. Around this time the Ensemble also started referring to me as Stalin when they discovered that I shared the same birthday as the great Allied war leader (Steel = Stalin. Geddit?). I took it in the spirit that it was intended.

1905 (GB5668) (1985)* * *

Palace Square/January 9th/Eternal Memory/The Toscin

Brought out to commemorate the eightieth anniversary of the failed Russian uprising, it almost seems as if the Ensemble were trying to achieve a meltdown in filing systems with their titles. They also seemed to be writing by numbers in other ways as well. Make no mistake – this is a good album, but it doesn't show any progress from their material of a couple of years earlier. There has been talk that it was intended to provide a new score for Eisenstien's 'Battleship Potemkin', but as an Arts Council member at the time I can state, with my hand on my heart, that their name was never even considered and there was never any doubt that the Eurythmics were the best people for the job. Besides, just try playing *1905* alongside the film and you'll find that the two do not synch up to any noticeable extent. Rumours that the album was a commentary on the war in Afghanistan are also equally wide of the mark.

1917 (GB5710) (1986)*

Revolutionary Petrograd/ Razliv/ Aurora/ The Dawn Of Humanity

More of the same, and at the same time less. The Ensemble now seemed to be sleepwalking through their career. Shaw left twice, briefly, during 1986, and that probably didn't help matters. When I suggested to them, during an interview for the BBC Music Magazine, that they were merely slapping labels on instrumental songs in order to make the listener see something that wasn't necessarily there in the first place, they accused me of hypocrisy and referred me to my own essays on formalism. They apologised later, of course, in letters that we published in the magazine. One curious fact about *1917* is that the songs are intended to bleed into one another without a break. The band were apparently under the impression that they were about to have their first album release on compact disc, and they wished to utilise the new form to its fullest extent. Unfortunately the GMB CD pressing plant did not have the capacity for all of the planned releases and the Arts Council decreed that it had to concentrate solely on classical music. If this record ever receives a reissue, it is to be hoped that their wish is finally granted.

Babi Yar (GB5788) (1986)* * * *

Babi Yar/ Humour/ In The Store/ Fears/ A Career

Joy Division meets Black Sabbath. The title track, with its tolling bells and heavy guitar, sets the tone for this radical departure. Good performs the band's first vocal songs since the seventies. His hitherto unsuspected deep, powerful voice thrusts the lyrics into the face of the listener. And what lyrics they are! Working with a Russian poet (by mail), they seem, at first glance, to be about capitalist atrocities, but there is a heavy undercurrent of bitterness and irony that hints at a deep unhappiness with the People's Government. Later pressings were clumsily edited despite my pleas to the Ensemble to turn over the master tapes to the Arts Council. If they had done so, then we might have been able, by dropping just a couple of words or lines from the vocal tracks, to keep it reasonably intact. At the time I was thinking of several American releases of the sixties, such as the Doors' first album, where this had happened and the edited version is now the accepted one. Incidentally, there is no truth in the rumour that they wished to dedicate the album to myself, and I would modestly have forbade it if it were true (for it was certainly within my power to do so at the time).

14th Symphony (GB5804) (1987)* * *

De Profundis / Malagueña / Lorelei / The Suicide / On Watch / Madam, Look! / In Prison, At The Sante Jail / The Zaporozhian Cossack's Answer To The Sultan Of Constantinople / O Delvig, Delvig / The Death Of The Poet / Conclusion
Bleak beyond belief, this was the Ensemble's answer to the suggestion that they release an album of conventional pop songs suitable for daytime radio play. The situation in the country was uncomfortable at the time due to internal corruption and unavoidable global stresses, and the People's Government felt the need to cheer up the workers. What the Ensemble delivered was a collection of songs, based on the poems of Spanish revolutionary poet Lorca amongst others, which was obsessed with death. Powell, with a lighter, airier vocal style, split the singing duties with Good on this occasion. The group themselves stopped giving interviews (except to Arts Council officials seeking clarification, of course) and playing gigs. Individual members seemed depressed and informal contacts suggested that they expected to be arrested at any time for defeatism. They would only have had themselves to blame. Due to sales projections and other economic considerations, the album was only released on audiocassette. It failed to chart and no singles were issued from it.

15th Symphony (Creation 1004) (1992)* * * *

Allegretto/Adagio-Largo-Adagio-Allegretto/Allegretto/Adagio-Allegretto-Adagio-Allegretto

As the song titles suggest, this was an album infused with a sense of mischief. Their swansong was both funny and delightful, and a million miles away from the mood of the albums that they had been releasing prior to their own release. After surviving the seemingly never-ending drudgery of the Mull of Kintyre labour camp, the Ensemble was released along with most of the other political prisoners of the era when multiparty democracy was introduced. Claiming to feel free for the first time, it was ironic that, when they signed with Creation Records, the first (and only) album that they recorded for them was effectively a collection of cover versions. They stated that they wanted to liberate their back catalogue and set about re-recording an item from every single one of their previous fourteen albums. Injecting a riff from *Louie Louie* between the sections seemed to imply that they were, and had always been, a rock'n'roll band. Unfortunately the end, when it came, arrived from an unexpected angle. A Russian dissident called Maxim Shostakovich, using one of the new breed of nuisance lawyers, claimed that the group was profiting from the name of his father. The Ensemble, faced with crippling legal fees, had no option other than to split up. When I interviewed Maxim (I was, in fact, the journalist who tracked him down using the new open-access information laws), he seemed surprised and angry to find that a pop group had been profiting from his father's misery. His father, he insisted, would have been one of the leading classical composers of the twentieth century had he been allowed to carry on with his career. There is also an argument that the Ensemble had run out of steam. Delightful as the *15th Symphony* is, it is hardly a new work, and it must also be noted that all of the Ensemble's members have left the music industry after the split. Speaking as an executive member of the Musicians and Writers Union, I can also confirm that their memberships have lapsed and they cannot legally work in the industry unless they can renew them. Unfortunately the MWU has quite a backlog at this time, and many of our files remain displaced after the thaw. Do not, therefore, expect a reunion any time soon.

Arrhythmia
Neil Williamson

– and the music floods in, sluicing away the dreams of silence. It's the percussive chink of dishes, the rustle and snap of Dad's newspaper, the excited kettle, the burbling wireless ... and from the street outside the window, the muted, muttered march of the workforce heading out to the Factory.

Steve's eyes shutter open like aluminium blinds.

"Work, work, work," the workers drone. Their insistent rhythm heaves Steve out from the clingy embrace of the nylon sheets. "Work, work, work." He scratches the seam of his y-fronts, *scritch, scritch, scritch*, and hates that he did it in time with the song.

Fuck, fuck, fuck, he thinks.

"Fuck, fuck, fuck," he sings in the bathroom as he pisses, flushes, splashes his face with water.

"What's that, Son?" growls his dad from the kitchen. "Better get a shift on or you'll be late."

"Just humming a song," Steve mumbles as he dresses, wondering why his dad always says that. He's never late. He leaves half an hour earlier than his old dears for a start and, even if he didn't, no-one's ever late for the Factory.

Mum beams at him through a cloud of ironing-board steam. "Sit down, Son," she trills. "It's on the plate."

Two eggs, a pair of frazzled rashers and a chubby sausage arranged in a greasy face smile up at him, the latest in the daily parade of fixed breakfast grins. He slices through one yolky eye, but any satisfaction it might have given him is nullified by the scrape of the unyielding crockery behind the façade.

Steve chews his food, punctuating with grunts his dad's judgement on the contents of the paper, which amounts to little more than parroting the Governor's pronouncements on everything from efficiency and productivity to popular culture. He eats slowly, not because he's savouring the taste but because when he swallows, everything – the music, the chatter – sort of equals out. He's almost able to pretend it's real silence.

From within the music, there's a squeal of electric guitar feedback, and a cup clatters. A spill of milky tea spreads across the formica.

"Who does she think she is?" Dad baritones. His face is redder than the tabloid masthead scrunched in his fist. "Jumped up little strumpet." He brandishes the paper. A grainy photograph of the miniskirted singer from last night's Top Of The Pops is the evident object of this outburst. "Thinks she's better than the rest of us? Tarty little crumpet."

Steve looks at the picture and remembers the spiky flaming hair, the pvc boots, the screaming, the attitude, and the mercifully brief snippet of something that bore scant resemblance to music.

Arrhythmia. Jimmy Jensen had called her that when he'd introduced the band, before the TV was occluded by Dad's fat arse and that 'music' was abrupted by the click of the dial.

"*Sub-vers-ive*, that's what they're calling it." Dad throws the newspaper down on the table. "It's not *subversive*, it's obscene!"

"Subversive?" Mum looks perplexed. "I don't follow. What does that word mean?"

"It means..." Dad's face goes even redder because he doesn't know, not really. "It means..." The old boy's voice wavers as he casts angrily around the kitchen for something to vent his anger on.

Recognising trouble, Steve pushes his plate away, downs his tea and stands. "God save the Queen!"

Jerked out of his aimless rage, his father also stumbles to his feet, and his mother at her ironing board straightens herself smartly. "God save the Queen!" they intone together.

Mum's habitual, "And God bless us, every one," follows Steve through to the hall where he throws his donkey jacket over his overalls and grabs his satchel. "Have a lovely day at work, Son." The front door clatters shut behind him.

There are eight paving slabs between the door and the gate. The path exactly bisects the lawn and is bordered by roses. The plants are budding, but will not blossom until the first of May, signalling the start of summer. Their garden, and their neighbours', and all the gardens in the street, in the town. An orchestrated unfolding of colour. Steve hates summer because that's when the music quickens its pace, making the endless routine of *work, eat, play, sleep*, even harder to bear.

"Work, work, work." There are still workers filing past the gate, heading for the bus stop at the end of the street. As soon as Steve joins them, his feet fall into step. There is no escaping the compulsion to walk in time with the rest, to chant their morning mantra.

"Work, work, work," they all sing, but in Steve's mind the words are: *fuck, fuck, fuck*.

A gargantuan, multi-storied bus, red as a dragon in its Factory livery, lumbers away as he approaches the stop, but that doesn't matter because there will be another soon enough. There's always another bus for the Factory. A small crowd is already gathering and, while they wait, a portly man decides it's time for a song. He climbs up onto a low wall, sticks his thumbs under the bib of his overalls, and tenors: "Every morning at the count of eight, my friends and I all congregate, at our old street corner where we stand and wait for the daily ride to The Factory." It's an old music hall song, but it's eternally popular. People start to clap in time; a few hum along, encouraging the man to continue with the second verse.

"Well, we all pile in 'fore the toot at nine, and I takes my place on the production line, and consider it my fortune fine, to make my living at The Factory. But there's something on my mind all day. That I value more'n my penny's pay."

"I..." Some of the crowd join in, swelling the protracted note and beneath their voices the music too gathers for the chorus. "*Work, work, work* with all my might. So I can *munch, munch, munch* with my fork and knife. And then I'll *dance, dance, dance* to my heart's delight, before I *sleep, sleep, sleep* a peaceful night."

Since the bus has still not made an appearance, the man rolls on with the next verse and by the time the vehicle arrives most of the crowd appear to be in the singing mood.

"I'll *work, work, work* my natural life. So I can *munch, munch, munch* on gravy pie. And then I'll *dance, dance, dance* with my neighbour's wife, and only *sleep, sleep, sleep* when it gets light."

It's a song of optimistic fantasy whose many verses become progressively more ridiculous, developing from a hymn to duty and hard graft to claims of the kind of hedonism that none of these people have encountered outside of saucy postcards and the Lenny Harris show on TV. One reason that Steve leaves for work earlier than his parents is that he cringes at the gusto with which his father sings this song. And wants to die when his mum joins in with the actions.

"I *work, work, work* my blasted life. So I can *munch, munch, munch* til I split my sides. And then I'll *dance, dance, dance* throughout the night, before I *sleep, sleep, sleep* with my neighbour's wife."

The song continues as the bus jostles them through the city's ordered streets of identical red brick walls and postage stamp lawns, picking up more passengers, more singers of the song, until the enormous vehicle is full and it heads straight for the centre of town, for the towering stacks of The Factory.

"I'll *work, work, work* my neighbour's wife. And I'll *munch, munch, munch* on her gravy pie."

The last chorus resounds around Steve as the bus rumbles through the imposing gates.

"And then I'll *dance, dance, dance* til I'm beserk, and I'll *sleep, sleep, sleep* when it's time to...*work.*"

The workers spill out of the bus in good humour, traipsing up the steps and following the colour coded corridors towards their assigned hall of the day. The music blends seamlessly with the pounding of the engines of production. Inside the Factory, the two are inextricable.

Steve is a blue, and today his route is a long meandering one that leads him down to a sublevel of the west wing that he is unfamiliar with. He half hopes that today will bring an interesting, even comprehensible assignment, but he's been at the Factory long enough to know how likely that is, so he contents himself with the fervent hope of agreeable companions for the day's toil.

His thoughts circle around one particularly agreeable companion. Half a hope, half a fear. He knows exactly what his mother's response would be if he told her that he'd been stationed next to Sandra McReady three times this month. *Governor's got his matchmaking hat on, Son,* she'd say. *Is she pretty? I bet she's pretty.* In Steve's view, Sandra is in fact very pretty, but he doesn't see what business it is of anyone else's. Especially not the Governor's.

People like Steve's mum believe that everything that happens in life from birth to death – how well you do at school, what grade you'll rise to in the Factory, who you'll marry, and all points in between – are decided by the Governor. Steve can't think of anything more horrible and tells himself that such notions are for the weak-willed, the sheep who have never had an original thought in their lives.

Today's manufactory is a long room. There are narrow windows high on one wall, their light striping the face of the huge clock that hangs from the ceiling, and falling on the spaghetti nest of rubberised conveyor belts below. When Steve finds his assigned place in the assembly line he can't believe his luck, because there she is, already at her station. The trim, blonde figure of Sandra McReady.

She's reading the day's instructions, hazel eyes flicking over the numbered pictures as she memorises the steps. Steve watches her for a few extra seconds as he hangs his jacket on the peg behind his stool, before climbing up beside her. Sandra, he notices, is smiling. A small private smile. A deep, glossy, red smile. The kind of smile you'd expect to see dazzling the boys at a Friday social. Although, that lipstick– There's an off-pitch squeal that might be some misalignment in the factory's machinery, but which really sounds like someone badly abusing a guitar. The sound lingers, fades only reluctantly.

Sandra glances up and catches him staring. Her smile gets wider.

Then the hands of the clock tick on to the hour and the whistles pierce the air. The pulse of the Factory intensifies and the conveyors jerk into life. Steve has barely enough time to adjust the height of his stool and glance at his own instructions before Sandra is placing the first of her finished pieces back on the belt and it's Steve's turn. The module is a lump of grey plastic with moulded apertures, a few already plugged by components, looking like the surviving teeth in a centenarian's mouth. Sandra's contribution is a cream-coloured bakelite plug, Steve's is to twist into place two smoky glass bulbs that resemble the valves that glow orange in the back of the television set. His other neighbour will add a further contribution, and so on. What happens to the module once it is completed is none of their concern.

It isn't difficult work. It requires speed and dexterity, but it is easy enough once you get into the rhythm. And in the Factory, the music is at its most compelling. On the huge booming *one* of the great engines, the squeaking conveyor delivers a new module and Steve grabs a handful of components. On the *two* and *three* and *four*, he *inserts-twists, inserts-twists* his bulbs, and then the belt rolls forward again carrying the finished module on, and delivering a new one on the down beat of the next bar. Around the manufactory hall bodies move in time: reaching, tooling, assembling with the beat; breathing on the off-beat. At some point a bell will chime, the belts will still and the workers will be permitted to drink water or visit the toilet, but absorbed as they are by their tasks, compelled as they are by the music, no-one thinks about that until it happens. For now they work, and while they work, they sing.

"We don't know what we're making. We don't know what it's for. If it's destined for a hospital or'll end up in a war. We only know we're working. From dawn til end of day. An honest day's effort for an honest day's pay."

The song carries them through their shift. When their arms tire it lends them strength. When their muscles ache, it soothes them. It moves the hands of the clock around in stealthy intervals so that the morning passes almost without notice. The song thickens with harmonies, complicates with counterpoints. The hall resounds with impromptu calls and responses, but the basic song remains the same. The beat remains constant. The work gets done.

"Did you?" Sandra's eyes are fixed on her work, but this contrapuntal aside is pitched to carry to Steve and no further. "Did you see? Last night on the TV?" She risks a second of eye contact to make sure that Steve has heard her. When she sees that she has his attention, those red lips breathe: "Arrhythmia..."

Steve almost misses a bulb.

Sandra smiles.

The break bell sounds, the conveyors grind to a standstill and the worksong dwindles out, leaving only the boom of the deep engines resounding in the air, vibrating through their feet.

Sandra retrieves her handbag and her pretty beige macintosh. A nod of the head, a promise in her eyes. Steve stumbles after her. He follows her beyond the line for the water cooler, past the queue for the toilets. There is door, and a corridor, and then another door. And then stairs, stairs and more stairs. The astonishing silver-tipped heels of her ankle boots rimshot on the risers. Below the hem of her workdress, the pale flash of skin in the outrageously ripped stocking sizzles like a cymbal. The blue tail of a tattoo catches him off beat, makes him breathless by the time they reach the door at the top.

"We only have," Steve begins, but his voice comes out flat, atonal, in search of melody and scansion. "Fifteen minutes..." His words drift away over the flat roof, over the pipes and ducts and chimneys, up into the grey, silent air. Because here, by some quirk of architecture, some acoustic accident, there is silence. Or at least as close to it as Steve has ever experienced outside of his dreams. He can still *feel* the thud of the engines. It vibrates the tarmac beneath his feet, jumps through his fingers when he touches the brick chimney breast. But in his ears, there is nothing.

"Hey!"

"What?"

Sandra's red lips are a snarl. "You're the one," she accuses, her words spilling fast and angry. "You're the one! You're the one who's worried about time. Take this home." She's holding out a package. It's square, wrapped in a white polythene bag decorated with a poorly rendered skull and the words *Anarchy Records*. "Take it home. Take it home and listen to it tonight." Her eyes are blazing with something entirely alien to Steve. "And play it fucking loud, all right?"

Steve takes the bag. Then Sandra smiles, stretches up on the toes of her wicked little boots and kisses him. The kiss is short and brutal, and Sandra's lipstick is smeared when it is over. Without another word she re-enters the Factory and disappears down the stairs.

Part of Steve already knows what is in the bag, and part of him doesn't want to confirm his suspicion. He just wants to stand here in the silence a little longer, but there, faintly, is the warning bell that signals the imminent resumption of the shift.

Steve sighs. He flaps open the bag, acknowledges the mini-skirted harridan, the bilious spatter of her name. He closes the bag quickly, slips it inside his coat and reluctantly goes back to the beat.

"Are you sure, Son, that you don't want to come?" Mum fastens the top button of her coat, pats her hair into place. It's the second Tuesday of the month and that means drinks with the Hendersons. Steve stares at his pork chop and colourless, diced vegetables, shakes his head.

Dad enters from the hall. "Come on lad, it'll be fun." He winks and pats Mum's bottom, yolking the word *fun* with lurid potential.

"You can talk to..." Mum hefts a gift-wrapped box of Matchmakers.

"You can talk to..." Dad grabs the bottle of plonk.

"Jennifer."

"Veronica."

Steve's parents share a look of consternation. Of the Hendersons' two daughters, Jennifer is a year older than Steve and timid as a rabbit, while Veronica is a year younger and a precocious tease.

"No, thanks." Steve snaps his reply, forestalling his parents from saying any more.

When the front door snicks shut, Steve breathes out. One long, slow stream of air. He keeps on blowing out until he is empty, until his lungs ache, but he can still feel his heart. The music, reduced to its lowest volume. *Beat, beat, beat.*

Fuck, fuck, fuck.

Steve clears his dinner into the bin, rinses off the plate and cutlery, puts the things away. Then he goes into the living room and lifts the lid on the record player. To one side of the machine are Dad's records. Cheesy covers depicting men in dinner suits and bowties or women in lamé gowns and towering hair. Burt Goodman, Sylvia Hammond, and Dad's favourite, Charlie Montgomery. On the other side of the turntable, his mother's, much smaller collection of heartthrob charttoppers. All hair oil, leather jackets with the collars turned up and 'dangerous' winks. To watch his parents listen to them you'd think this music was capable of transporting you, but how can it? There are four measured beats to every one of those bars. No matter how chirpy and bright, how croony and swoony. Four beats. *Work, Eat, Play, Sleep.* Transportation? You'd be as well putting your ear to the factory wall.

Steve slips Sandra's record from the polythene. Holds the garish cardboard square by the corners, by his fingertips. He stares at the sleeve, drinks in the clashing colours, the jagged lettering, the snarling girl frozen in the act of smashing her fist through a pane of glass, teeth bared and red lips parted in a yell. He flips it over, devours the other side too. The track listings: A/ Smash Your Way Out, B/ Tear It Up. The writing credits, the copyright notice, the logo and business address of the record company. Behind the text, a close-up photograph of a bluebottle sandwiched between two plates of glass.

Steve's fingers are shaking as he slides the vinyl out of the sleeve. He tilts it, and the light swims around its glossy grooves. He rotates the knurled switch with a satisfying clunk. The turntable begins to move, and the speaker issues that expectant noise that is part hum and part hiss. Steve turns the volume knob from 2 to 3. The expectation rises. He feels sick, but he doesn't know why. It's just a record. It can't possibly give him what he dreams of. This will be anything but silence.

He drops the record onto the machine. It shrugs reluctantly, rebelliously down the spindle. He watches it for one, five, ten revolutions before plucking up the courage to place the stylus onto the leader.

He realises he is holding his breath.

There's a percussive chunk, followed by a wire-thin whistle of feedback that sounds taut, like a restraint. Then, off microphone: "*onetwothreefour*", and then a crazed, enraged musical beast is released. Growls of guitar, slashing steel claws of cymbals, raging, inchoate screams, barely comprehensible. "Kick 'em down. Beat 'em up. To a pulp. Scream and shout. Smash it. Smash it. Smash it. Smash your way out. Out. Out. Out!"

Steve recognises the hook. On Top Of The Pops that two seconds had been two seconds too long, but now he can't get enough of it. "Smash it. Smash it. Smash it." The song goes on forever. The song lasts two minutes and nine seconds precisely. It finishes with a final foundering thrash, and that is followed by silence.

Steve starts the record again. Nudges the volume up one more notch.

Some time later he is lying on the floor, and shouting: "Smash it. Smash it. Smash it. Out. Out. Out." He's lost track of the number of times he has played the song. The record player's volume is at ten now, and even though the ducks are jouncing against the wallpaper and the crystal ornaments jumping on the mantelpiece, it still isn't loud enough.

Then the music cuts in with a soap-opera melodrama that easily drowns the record out. The room fills with a sickening swell of impending familial discord and framed in the doorway are his parents faces: Dad's red, Mum's ashen.

"Your old man? He actually broke it, man? Snapped the plastic. Like elastic?"

On the Factory roof the next day, Sandra's face is impossible to read. She's done something with her hair, it looks weirdly asymmetrical at the front, ragged at the back.

"I'm so sorry." Steve sings low and earnest, and is perplexed by the huge grin he receives.

"That's so...so...fuckin' cool! Your 'rents are cardboard cut-out cruel. What a pair of waa-aaa-aaankers."

Steve thinks that's going a bit far, but he's not about to admit that right now, so he imitates her melody. "Waa-aaa-aaankers!"

"Too right." She looks up at him through her lopsided fringe. "You know, you're all right. What you doing Friday night?"

"Nothing." Which is true. If Steve had friends that he regularly went out with, or had ever shown any interest in attending the weekend socials at the Factory, no doubt his parents would have added restriction of his movements to the punishment that banned his use of the television and the record player for the rest of the month. But since all Steve ever did was go to work then come home, it had clearly never occurred to them.

For the rest of the week Steve does what is expected of him. He goes to work at eight, he eats at six, he puts his light out and sleeps at eleven. His mother tries to interest him in conciliatory after-dinner board games, but the living room is radiant with Dad's constant glare, so he opts to retire early with a book whose pages he turns but doesn't remember. He doesn't see Sandra again that week, but that doesn't matter. She's written the details down for him on a scrap of paper that is pressed between the pages of his book. On Friday it is a simple matter to repeat the pattern of the previous evenings, then lie awake until the rest of the house has retired before stealing downstairs and slipping out.

The Makers Mark is located at the lower rent end of the Parade. It's a cold night, needles of rain prickling Steve's face and a ragged wind plucking at the tails of his workshirt. He's familiar with the Parade from helping Mum with the Saturday shopping, but that's during the day. These night time shuttered frontages are alien to him, like turned cheeks. The warmly lit windows above, blind eyes.

The segs of his workboots beat their ingrained, infuriating four on the pavement. Steve forces himself to break the rhythm, interspersing lopes and shuffles into his gait. Nothing calamitous happens. but the novelty quickly wears off. It's simply easier to go with the music.

Fuck, fuck, fuck. Steve's breath mists the air, becomes a song he hadn't known was there. "I feel." His melody is low, threaded with minor intervals. "Outside of everything. Outside of living and dying, and laughing and crying. And anything that matters." Near the grocer's there are some broken food crates. Steve scoops up a piece of wood, drags it along the wall as he continues to sing. "I feel ... unreal. Brittle and paper thin. Fragile as butterfly wings, the most delicate things. Touch me..." As Steve rounds a corner he belts the stave satisfyingly against a lamppost. "...and I'll shatter." The upper third of the wood snaps and dangles by jagged splinters. He swings it around in circles as he advances down a side street. "I feel my own rhythm but I'm ruled by the beat. I'm light as a feather, yet chained by my feet."

Ahead he sees a pub. It must be the one he's looking for because there's nothing else out here.

"I know where I'm going from the first step to the last," he murmurs, "but the bus that I'm riding is going too fast." He comes to a halt, throws the broken stick away. He wishes he hadn't come, wants to go home. He wants to be anywhere but home. "I just want to make it stop. I just want to breathe. Jam the hands upon the clock. Hide between the beats." He hasn't a clue where he wants to be.

"I just want to be me," Steve whispers, and finds that he is moving again, closing step by step on the beery lights, the well of muted noise. "I just want to be me. Me. Me ..."

Steve breaks off when he realises that there is someone leaning against the wall beneath the swinging pub sign. The corpulent man is wrapped in a woollen coat. He takes a puff of a chubby cigar and blows out exotic smoke. If he heard Steve's song, he gives no indication, but when Steve falters at the door, he glances at last his way. "And if you can't stop moving?" The melody apes Steve's down to the last note, but the clear tenor voice, unmistakeable from the television, is what is amazing. "If there's no such thing as silence? Why not indulge in a little noise and violence?"

"You're the – " Steve begins, but the Governor raises a fat finger to his lips. Then with a tap of glowing ash, he straightens up and saunters off down the Parade, apparently oblivious to the muffled blare that has been issuing from the building all this time.

There is perhaps a measure less of anticipation in Steve's heart as he eases open the pub door and walks into the buffeting cacophony, but it is quickly forgotten when he finds Sandra's hand and manages to lose himself completely in the all consuming noise that, in the end, is almost as good as silence.

It is only many years later, when he and Sandra are married, that he will look back and feel cheated. Sandra and the others will remember a genuine moment of rebellion. Even if the only thing that gets *torn up* and *smashed out* are the walls of the old Factory, making way for a shinier, sleeker, more productive replacement. Even if people still spend their lives doing the same meaningless, incomprehensible jobs. Even if the changes to come that will feel so fundamental at the time are acknowledged in the end as merely superficial. They will remember Arrhythmia and claim a small part in what they'll call a revolution.

A revolution that began: *onetwothreefour.*

But Steve won't have that. Instead he'll remember the Governor's words. The way they lingered in the air like the cigar smoke, staining everything to come. The way they fell in perfect time with both the music and the pub's muffled chaos, equally bound by those four simple, inescapable, beats.

One, two, three, four.

Work, eat, play, sleep.

Live, marry, fuck, die.

It is only all those years later that he will acknowledge the truth that it seems he has always known. Sometimes, the music might change its tune, but it will never end.

Act III

Dybbuk Blues
Richard Jay Goldstein

What it was

He played like a fucking angel, but then he was dead, and nobody could hear him play after that.

Some mighty fine shit

One night Roosevelt showed up at a gig where Len was playing, in a little downstairs club on the East side, on St. Mark's Place. Roosevelt planted himself at the bar and during a break Len moseyed over.

"Howdy, Roosevelt, how y'all doing?" said Len in his sweet Georgia drawl.

"My man," said Roosevelt. "Say, listen, I got some mighty fine toot, if you might want to step around back and try a snort."

"Well, sure," said Len. "Sounds like it might be interesting." That's what Len thought of most things, except he'd say it *innerestin.*

So the two of them, bulky Roosevelt and lanky Len, walked up the steps and onto St. Mark's, out into the gritty evening. Saturday night traffic jerked and muttered along the jammed street. It was late summer, hot and sticky. Up above the jagged skyline the sky was orange and ragged with gray veins.

Roosevelt and Len walked up St. Mark's and onto Second, then turned into a narrow alley. Their feet crunched through broken glass. They stopped behind a pile of trash that smelled like cedar packing crates and leaned against the greasy wall. Light from Second Street dripped and drizzled around them.

Roosevelt got out his dope kit and they snarfed up some coke with his little silver straw.

"Land o' Goshen," muttered Len pretty soon, commencing to giggle. "Pretty mighty fine shit y'all got there, sir."

"Yes indeed, yes indeed, yes indeed," said Roosevelt.

"Well, sir," said Len, "I gotta get back in for the next set, but I might be interested in some of this interesting shit."

"Oh, man," said Roosevelt, "what you need to go with *this* shit is some even *finer* smack that I got back at my place. Tell you what, why don't you drop by after the gig and I'll turn you on to a little?"

"Right on," said Len. "Might do that. After all, *The hope of the righteous is gladness, but the expectation of the wicked shall perish.*"

"What the fuck's that supposed to mean?" asked Roosevelt, frowning.

"*That which has been is that which shall be, and there is nothing new under the sun.* Ecclesiastes."

"Bullshit," said Roosevelt.

They started back for the club. At the entrance to the alley they walked into a sea of sound. Len stopped and looked up at a street lamp above him. It flickered green gray against the orange sky. He could hear it buzz, a counterpoint to the pulse of traffic. He stood staring at it a while, tapping his foot.

Len

Len was a tall skinny white guy who came up from around Atlanta to the Big Apple to play jazz. He was a horn man, played cornet. Not trumpet. Cornet.

He blew into town one day like a sugar wind from the South. One minute he wasn't there, the next minute he was all *over* the place. New York eats people, swallows whole crowds of sweet babies just for a snack, but Len was a brandy cherry, a hot pepper in the jello.

Everybody on the scene knew it right away. This cat could play like a fucking angel.

Len was also Jewish. He had a fine and mellow southern drawl, said *y'all*, always called men *sir* and women *ma'am*, but he was still a Jew, just like the regular Jews from New York. He'd been a *bar mitzvah* and could read Hebrew, and thought of himself as a kind of hipster Jewish mystic scholar.

He was always doodling Hebrew characters and numbers and circles and musical notes all over napkins and phone books. If anybody asked him what he was doing, he'd say, "Well, sir, magic and music are both mathematical, ain't they? So I'm translating kabbalah into numbers, and numbers into music, that's all."

But then he'd go on about cat-fishing, or chiggers, or eating grits, or whatever. People could never tell if they were talking to a rabbi or a redneck.

Len actually never thought of himself as being white, because he grew up thinking white meant the local white trash, the ignorant folks who patronized his family's store, and he always knew that had nothing to do with him.

One time Len was in a cafe in Harlem, at about half-past zero in the morning. He had just gotten done with a gig, and he was filling up his tank with coffee to get him back downtown. He was eased back in a booth, with his long legs stuck out into the aisle, when two black guys wandered in. These were pretty tough customers, who figured this cafe was their turf.

They walked up to Len's legs, and one said, "What we gonna do about all these white guys coming in here?"

And the other one said, "They like roaches, man. You got to keep getting rid of them."

So Len looked up, and got up, and stood teetering at the top of his pipe-cleaner six-foot-five, and said in his molasses southern drawl, "Are y'all calling me *white?*"

One of the guys pretended to look around the room, then said, "You the only white boy here, looks like."

Len put his hand over his heart and said, "Why, no sir, I ain't white. I'm *Jewish.* Y'all talk to some *real* white folks down south, they'll tell y'all Jews ain't white. Never have been, never will be."

Whereupon the two guys went off and got their pie and coffee, because it was clear that this was one crazy mother.

Len did use a lot of drugs. Most days, he'd snort, smoke, shoot, or eat just about anything if he thought it would be an interesting trip. *Innerestin.* But it would've been hard to say Len was an addict, exactly, because he'd take all sorts of different stuff, whereas most addicts tend to specialize.

"Oh, wow, man," some bass player might say, his eyes the color of a hooker's lips. "Me and Len sure got wasted last night, man. We snorted a couple of lines, then did up a doobie with some cats we ran into. Then we went to a party to jam and ended up drinking a fifth of Cuervo. So we were in the bathroom, you know, to do another doobie, and we found these pills and popped 'em. Wow, man, I don't even know what those pills were *for,* man."

"Yeah," Len would say. "It was really *innerestin.*"

Len was one of those people who never had to learn music, never needed any formal training. He had perfect ears and a righteous head, so he always knew what was going down just by listening. He could have played any kind of music, but jazz was where he found the fewest walls between himself and the music that always surged inside him. For him music was something that went on all the time, everywhere. It never stopped. People talking in a room with different cadences, that was music. Guys slamming trashcans around at five in the morning, that was some *serious* music.

When Len came north from Atlanta, he brought with him an incredible horn, an old E-flat cornet. It was a family heirloom from Bavaria, probably 150 years old or so, which had been brought to this country, through Ellis Island, around the turn of the century by Len's grandfather. It had a fine delicate curve which fit nicely in your hand, like a cat laying in your lap, and a rich brassy glow that took the light and played it back in a minor key. It had a husky, musty sound, that made you think of old things, or maybe about quiet little alleyways hidden in the heart of town.

When Len played it your senses would be filled, meaning not just your ears, but your eyes and everything else. You'd feel a forgotten touch on your fingertips, or taste some flavor you almost remembered.

Len and his horn moved through a tune like a river through a canyon, like sap through a tree. He'd bend tones around until you thought your heart might break. He could make people see things with his music. Sometimes you'd think he could see your dreams and play them back to you.

It was magic the way Len played. He played like a fucking angel.

Syble

Len had a girlfriend, a black woman named Syble.

Syble was a tough hustler from Philly, relocated to New York. She had about a million skills, could cook, manage an office, write grant proposals. At the time Len was hanging out with her she ran a little Cajun restaurant called *The Perloo Palace*.

The Perloo Palace was about the size of a big closet. It was all one room, including the kitchen, so you could watch Syble slinging pots around at the big Wolf stove while you ate. There was no menu, either. You ate what Syble cooked, and you ate it when she cooked it. There was one sitting for lunch, and two for dinner, first come first served. The place was always packed.

Len liked to sit behind the stove with a cup of coffee or a beer, his head whirling with music and dope, watching Syble working. In his quirky way Len loved Syble. She grounded him, kept him from floating off altogether.

She turned him on too, second only to music. Her body was a kind of touchstone for him, where he could test his grip on reality. He loved to disappear between her round breasts, loved to bury his face between her legs. There was something oceanic to him about Syble's salty juices, her seaweed pubic hair. When he'd been with her a lot, his music took on a liquid quality, crashing like surf rolling in from Antarctica.

For her part, Syble wasn't sure exactly why she was hanging with this skinny white Jew from Georgia. She wasn't a groupie type at all, had always gone out with educated black men. But the first time she heard Len play, something came out of Len's old cornet as if it would pierce her very breast, and brought her a puzzling vision of dry mountains and distant shadows and silent stone temples. She couldn't bear the thought of losing him until she had seen what lay within the temples, knew whose shadows moved in the shimmering distance.

She was also fascinated by the constant groove in which Len moved.

There was one sweltering summer day, when New York felt like a giant pizza under a heat lamp. The air was molten, and the layers of racket filling the streets weighed a ton. Len and Syble were waiting for a bus. They were slumped on a bench in the thin shade of a kiosk, nearly cooked.

The bus arrived, stood at the curb, idling. After a moment, Syble said, "Let's go, Lennie, we gotta get on the bus."

But Len sat up straight with his hand on her arm and said, "No, wait. Listen to that far-out rhythm." And he sat there with his eyes closed, nodding his head, and the bus was going *pop-pop-poppity-pop-pop-poppity*, in 7/8 time, and Len was right with it. The bus pulled away, and Len and Syble were still sitting there, snapping their fingers with big grins on their faces.

They didn't exactly live together, Syble and Len. Len's place was just a single room in the Battery, with a mattress on the floor and stacks of books in Hebrew everywhere, and nothing else. So when they were together they were either at Syble's apartment on the West Side or at a gig or at the restaurant with Len stashed behind the stove, grooving on the symphony of sounds that Syble dished up.

Len was easy for Syble. He wasn't mean or demanding. And he played like a fucking angel.

Roosevelt

Everything would've probably gone on like that, the way things do, if Roosevelt hadn't gotten so weird about Syble and Len.

Roosevelt was another guy in the music scene. He was black and made a big deal about it. For instance, he'd hassle white musicians about being racist, guys who could hardly remember what color they were themselves without looking. Or, conversely, he'd hassle black musicians about not being involved in the revolution, guys who had maybe studied at Julliard and knew a thousand tunes by heart.

Roosevelt played a little horn too, but he wasn't good enough to make a living at it. For money, he dealt dope of various kinds to the music scene. His dope business was always in good shape because he always had the best shit, and gave a good deal. He never ripped anyone off, and was silent as the pyramids when he needed to be.

Naturally, he'd tried to pick up on Syble the first time he saw her. This was in the little downstairs bar on St. Mark's, where Len used to gig.

Syble was sitting at the bar, her hands curled around a glass of house red, when Roosevelt came in to deliver some dope. Roosevelt took one look at her, took a deep breath of the dark, smoky air, and forgot about his business. He sat down next to her.

"Say, baby, what's shaking?" he said.

"Get lost, nigger," answered Syble.

There wasn't much even Roosevelt could say to that, so he did get lost, at least temporarily.

The first time Roosevelt saw Syble and Len together, he said to Len, "Say, man, what's this fine black princess doing with a skinny honky like you?"

Len knew Roosevelt pretty well, so he didn't pay much attention. "Well, sir," he said, "it's all in the Bible. Right in Kings One. The Queen of Sheba was black, and I'm descended from King Solomon. *And the Queen spoke to Solomon of all that was in her heart, and King Solomon gave to the Queen of Sheba all her desire, whatsoever she asked ...*"

"Bullshit," said Roosevelt.

"Right on," said Syble.

Len was just as mellow with Roosevelt as he was with everybody else. Besides buying weed and dope from him, Len was encouraging of Roosevelt's music. One time Len was at a jam somewhere, and

Roosevelt wanted to sit in, so Len said to him, "Let's do *Straight No Chaser.* Y'all know it, the Monk tune?"

Roosevelt said, "Well, I think I know it, but, you know, not note for note."

And Len said, "That's okay, Roosevelt, just play the notes y'all know."

The icing on the hate cake for Roosevelt was that Len played like such a fucking angel, played just the way that Roosevelt *would've* played.

And the cherry on the icing was the horn, Len's Bavarian cornet. Roosevelt knew, just *knew*, that if he had that horn he could play like Len. Maybe better than Len. The horn began to gleam in Roosevelt's dreams, like the Statue of Liberty torch, like the red light above the door of Satan's whorehouse. When the horn was his, in his dreams, he could play like a fucking angel too.

And when he played like an angel, Syble would be his. And all the music, and everything that Len was, that Roosevelt could be and do so much better.

Roosevelt deals some shit

After the gig, Len folded away his money into his horn case and took a cab over to Roosevelt's place near 4th and Avenue B. Roosevelt lived in a crumbling brick building filled mostly with elderly people living on welfare. He was on the ground floor, as befits a dope dealer. Len had been there before to score so he knew to ring twice, then pause, then ring once. After a minute, Roosevelt buzzed him right on in.

Roosevelt's apartment was clean as a whistle and sparsely furnished. In the front room was a sofa covered with a Madras bedspread. A boom box sat on the floor in one corner playing old Coltrane. A thin green carpet covered the floor in every room, even the kitchen and bathroom. Len came in, put his horn case by the door.

"Hey, man, all right," said Roosevelt. "Let's not dick around." He guided Len to the sofa, then produced a shoebox from which he pulled a rubber strap, some syringes, an envelope, a spoon, and a candle.

Roosevelt cooked up the smack and loaded a syringe. He helped Len get the strap around his arm, then Len slid the needle in and pushed in the juice, popped the strap and waited for the sweet rush, the Toonerville Trolley through the Black Forest, the cicada solo between his ears.

Roosevelt watched Len slide back on the chair, watched him loll his head back, watched his breathing grow shallow, watched him not breathe at all, watched him roll off the chair onto the green carpet like a sack of catfish, watched him turn blue.

Roosevelt got up, put away the dope box, including the envelope of uncut heroin, then stuck Len's horn case away in the closet in the back room. Finally, Roosevelt picked up Len's long lanky and dead body and dumped it out the back window. He climbed out after it, picked it up again, carried it through the alley behind his building, then stuck it into the back seat of his car, which he'd parked by the alley entrance earlier.

Roosevelt drove uptown, stopped by a dumpster somewhere near the Port Authority, dumped in the body, and drove home.

The body was discovered a few days later by sanitation workers. Len never carried any kind of ID so they had a hard time figuring out who he was. Finally, Syble reported Len missing and somebody put two and two together. Syble identified the body. Len's parents in Atlanta were notified. They had the body sent back south, so it could be buried in the Jewish cemetery near where Len grew up. Syble went to the funeral but was snubbed by the family and came back to New York pissed off.

And that was that.

What happens to Len

After shooting up he drifts off, like always, a laughing fish in cool blue water. But the water becomes cooler and cooler, and bluer and bluer. Something clamps down over his face, buzzes. Something big swells up in his chest, then explodes. He feels pain, then sweetness seeps over him. It's dark. There comes a taste of oil. Then suddenly he's filled with a searing golden light and golden music lances through him and is him.

Roosevelt plays the Dybbuk Blues

A week after Len was sent to Georgia to be buried, Roosevelt took the Bavarian cornet out of the closet and over to a pawn shop in the Village and pawned it. He left it there a month, past the due date. Then he went in and bought it.

Leaving the pawn shop, Roosevelt could sense a current running up his arm from the horn case. His fingers began to itch to get around a golden flow of notes. His chest ached to breathe life into the brass body of the horn, his horn now.

He found himself walking the streets for hours. It grew dark. He was outside the club on St. Mark's Place. He could feel music surging in his heart. He went in.

A quartet of guys he knew were playing. Syble was sitting at the bar, her hands curled around a glass of house red. Seeing her, Roosevelt felt like he could make anything happen, anything at all.

The band was just taking a break. Roosevelt approached the piano player, a guy named Phil.

"What's doing, Phil?" said Roosevelt.

"How's it going, Roosevelt?" said Phil.

"Hey, you mind if I sit in a little?" asked Roosevelt, holding up the horn case.

Phil scratched his head, said, "Well, I guess it's OK, Roosevelt, if it's OK with the other guys. Sure, I guess so."

Waiting for the set to start, Roosevelt went over to the bar and sat down next to Syble.

"Say, Syble," he said. "How you been?"

"How you expect me to be?" she said, not looking up.

"You need to forget Len, Syble," said Roosevelt. "He's gone and buried. You need to get on with your life. Have some fun."

Syble took a drink of her wine. "Fuck off," she said. "I suppose you got just the thing for me, right?"

Roosevelt spread his hands out effusively. "I'm your friend. No need to be uptight with me. Listen," he said, "I'm sitting in next set. Check it out."

Syble took another drink, sat silently.

Right then the band started getting back on stage, so Roosevelt got up, got out the horn. When he stood up under the lights, Syble sat bolt upright. She leaned forward, squinted at the horn. Roosevelt smiled at her.

The first tune was *Nights in Tunisia,* which Roosevelt knew pretty well. Everything was going his way. He was as right on as right on could be.

He played it like an angel. It was like his fingers had eyes, like his lips had fingers, like the horn was wired to his brain.

At the bar, Syble leaned back with the first note, her eyes closed. She could taste sand on her lips, hear a dry wind scraping rock. A tear squeezed out from under her eyelid, ran down her cheek.

The set passed like a blur for Roosevelt. They did a couple of standards, *Satin Doll, Night and Day*. They did some Monk, some Mingus, some Sonny Rollins. Some original tunes of Phil's. Roosevelt played everything like he'd written it. When the set was over the guys all slapped Roosevelt on the back, shook his hand. "Too cool," they said. "Right on. Far out. Mighty fine." Phil even gave him a few bucks.

Roosevelt went back over to the bar. Syble hadn't moved.

"That's Len's horn," she said as he sat down. "You got Len's horn."

"That's right," he said. "Found it in a pawn shop over in the Village. Knew you'd recognize it."

"How'd you get it?" she asked, eyes still closed. "You kill Len for it?"

"Wow, baby," he said, "how can you say something like that? I just told you. I found it in a pawn shop. What I figure happened was Len was walking late at night, like he did, and some creeps mugged him for the horn. Look here, here's the receipt." Roosevelt dug in his pocket, pulled out the receipt from the pawn shop, dropped it on the bar.

Syble opened her eyes, glanced at the paper. "I didn't know you could play like that," she said.

"When I got the right person to play for," he said, "I can play like a fucking angel."

"I never thought I'd hear music like that again," said Syble.

"Say, Syble," he said, "you want to go somewhere?"

"I would," she said, looking him in the eye. "I would, but I can't tonight. Come up to my place tomorrow night. Bring the horn and play for me. Will you do that? Play just for me?"

Roosevelt nodded, Syble staring at him. "Tomorrow night," she said again. "My place. Play for me." She turned back to her drink.

In a daze, Roosevelt went behind the bandstand, stuck his money into the case, packed up the horn and wandered out onto the street. Behind him Syble sat at the bar, her hand over her eyes. Tears ran down her cheeks. "He killed him," she whispered, "the fucker killed him."

Outside, Roosevelt was barely touching the pavement. How could it be any better than this? Now he had it all, just like he'd dreamed. He could still feel the power from the horn, like a warm glow around his lips and hands. He could still hear himself play, still feel the way the music poured up from his chest and through that far-out horn and out into the light. And the music was still there, still inside him. As he walked, the music became louder, pressed against the inside of his chest, his forehead. He wanted to let it out, flowing like a river. The music was *everything*. Why hadn't he seen that before?

It became clearer and clearer to him. The world was filled with music, everywhere, every second.

He saw he was walking toward the East River. He quickened his pace. Syble didn't matter anymore. She never had mattered, if he could've seen it. Nothing mattered but the music.

He crossed over FDR Drive, crossed the bike path, squeezed through a sagging chain-link fence, and walked out onto a deserted wharf. The river and upper bay spread out before him. The lights of Jersey City were like jewels across the water. He'd never noticed how incredibly beautiful New York was.

Roosevelt put the horn case down, unsnapped it, and took out the cornet. It seemed to glow in the dim light.

He walked up to the edge of the cement and faced out toward the shimmering oily river. Behind him a swirling finger of breeze spun his money unnoticed out of the horn case.

He placed the horn to his lips, took a deep breath. Almost without effort the sound came soaring out, smooth and clear. He played an ascending run that seemed like it would never stop.

He took another breath.

He played another run, starting a third up. He felt like his soul was coming out through the horn.

He started a third run, another third up, without taking a breath. But he *needed* a breath.

He couldn't stop. The sound welled up crystalline and flowing. The ascending runs gave way to a series of staccato descents. Roosevelt's eyes bugged out. The horn pressed against his lips like a french kiss. Its warm brass curves gripped his hand. The valves moved up and down with his fingers riding them, glued helplessly.

The sound flowed like a river, echoing out across the water. He was playing notes he didn't know, notes *no one* knew, loops and curves of exquisite minor changes. His lungs were empty, burning, but the sound, the clear brass tone, never diminished.

The big veins stood out on Roosevelt's neck, great gaps appeared in his vision, like giant whole-notes of fog. His body sagged, as if it was suspended from the glittering, wailing horn. The burning in his chest was an unendurable agony, like all the music there was trying to get out all at once. The burning swelled up and burst inside him, a volcano of molten brass.

Another ascending run began, climbing up forever in thirds and fourths. At the top it went higher, and higher. The sound soared out in a thin diamond tone almost too high to hear, then held, and held, then faded away into the sigh of the wind.

Roosevelt collapsed into a heap on the wharf. His eyes stared sightlessly up as if trying to follow the path of the last note. The Bavarian cornet lay like gold across his still chest.

Len plays like a fucking angel

Len feels the dazzling light fade and give way to a sweet quiet darkness. He runs back out of Roosevelt's fingers and lips, back out of the horn, like warm water, like smoke. The wind picks him up and blows him after the music. Turning and turning he sees the humming, syncopated city below. There's Roosevelt, lying dead on the docks.

It's funny how music'll do that to a guy.

The Accompanist
Susan Lanigan

I live on the second floor of the Academy of Music and Performance, founded in 1842. I am the only person left here. The whole building was condemned not long ago.

The room in this Haussmann-era city terrace is bare. Its long, panelled front windows face north and are covered in dust; any light that manages to get in past the street buildings is always blue-dim in colour, as drab as the blue wallpaper that slowly turns grey all around me. It is bitterly cold inside, with no furniture to break the draught but a grand piano and stool in the room's very centre.

At that piano I sit and begin my routine, running stiffly through a few chromatic scales, my fingers aching with cold and arthritis. The sound jars at first, breaking through the silence, but then the notes become more muffled, the damp in the woodwork absorbing the sound. As I play my fingers warm up, the knuckles cracking less often, the cold and pain vanishing as always. I like the symmetry of the scale in contrary motion, starting on D, left hand and right hand radiating out of the centre like ripples on a lake, until they reach the edges. When I pause, there is only the sound of the wind creaking in the joists; I listen, by instinct, for its vocal, try to guess what chords it needs, settling on some heavy triads in C sharp minor, like Rachmaninov's Prelude. And so I play with the wind while it blows.

If Herr Robert were here, he would be pleased at my progress. I have lost all the usual compulsions: sleep comes only fitfully and I am rarely hungry. The evening shadow falls on the page of notes in front of me, yet I feel no need to turn on any light. Just as well, since the electricity has long since been cut off.

Herr Robert's soft, commanding voice comes to me once more through the fog of time. "Stop what you are doing. Play *Träumerei*," it says. So I start the first few bars, slow enough that the piano strings echo and settle before moving on to the next chord. There is no shortage of time, after all.

I play it for my boys, in memory.

When I first came to the Academy, decades earlier, the building was noisy and full. Its rooms echoed with the clashing scales and bars of musicians' practice, a wave of sound that swept over me the moment I first entered the building and lingered by the stairwell. A flight of granite steps led up to the large, panelled door – all the paint has peeled off now, but then it was bright red – and I stood at the bottom, on the footpath, with nothing but a manuscript case in my hand and the memory of my father's last words to me: "Do you think we ran away from Idi Amin and made a life here just so you could waste it all with this piano nonsense? Do you want to make your mother cry? Go on, then, go. I can't stand the sight of you."

And so I ran away – from that grim, litter-strewn street in the industrial city in England where we lived; from the stale smell of chips, samosas and cigarette butts in my father's taxi office; from my thin, nervous mother's constant bewailing of our lost life in Africa. But most of all, I ran from my father's strangling love.

I cannot blame him for being possessive; my mother and I were all he had after his import-export business was burnt to the ground and we were forced to leave Africa for good. Although he was born in Uganda, in the eyes of his country's rulers he was an Asian, a foreigner, not to be trusted. So then we settled in England, a grey place, the masses cold and white in the everlasting rain – "petals on a wet, black bough" as Ezra Pound says – and were once again strangers in a strange land. The three of us clung to each other. He married young, to a woman who did not understand him, so all his energies went into controlling me. His intentions were my life: I would get a good degree and marry well. Music was not something that he could grasp. Music alarmed him. It was unpredictable, dissolute, no job for respectable people.

But for me, music was the home I never had. So, against his wishes, I kept practising in that mildewed little room with the out-of-tune upright – the only musical instrument available in the comprehensive school I attended. (My classmates were wary of my odd and slightly precocious nature, which came from being in the company of adults. They largely shunned me, to our mutual relief.) Every afternoon I went there, even though my audience was limited to the building's resident collection of rats. When I refused to back down and my father ordered me out of the house, I gathered what little money I had and took the ferry and train across to the Continent, to the great city where the Academy was located.

When I reached it, I was almost too nervous to go in. Times were different then; I feared the people at the reception desk would look oddly at a young Asian woman turning up alone with only her music, some schoolgirl French and a crumpled letter of recommendation from her old music teacher, addressed to Professor Heuffer, a retired concert pianist and one of the Academy's senior staff, to recommend her.

But the Professor was in the reception hall himself and hearing me ask for him, welcomed me without hesitation – I was accepted. For the first time in my life, anywhere. I was granted a stipend and moved into some modest rooms over a baker's shop nearby. To my dying day, I will remember waking each morning to the sound of the church bells ringing across the city and the warm, sweet smell of croissants.

That did not mean my hopes of being a concert pianist were to be fulfilled. One rainy afternoon, after twenty minutes of lacklustre Czerny exercises, Professor Heuffer sat me down and gave it to me straight: as a pianist I would do, but never more than that. I remember getting up and walking out to the front steps, then standing outside in a drizzle, listening to someone playing an easy Chopin Prelude and feeling more lost than I had ever felt before. Light spilled out onto the wet footpath and I leaned against the railings. It was probably the hardest moment of my life. I had not travelled so far and gone so definitively against my parents' wishes, for it all to come to this.

So began the introduction to my lifelong career – no, *vocation* – as an accompanist – with that moment of crushing disappointment all accompanists experience. But with hindsight I know it was for the best. Another path opened out to me. The art of good accompaniment is delicate and – pardon the pun – unsung. One must be the subtlest of coaches, guiding the singer, the dancer or the instrumentalist towards the most ideal expression of his lines, while being able to blur or finesse over his mistakes. One must not only accept the reality of being unpraised and unnoticed, but strive for it. When I play with a soloist, I stay in the background, controlled and understated. And throughout my life, I have done well at my job. My renderings have been complimented many times for their exemplary invisibility; I even once got a mention in the Friday review column of the *Allgemeine Musik-Zeitung* for an accompaniment to a cello sonata. One can find it about three quarters of the way down the page, next to the church service calendar.

And of course, there were my boys.

First Redmond Kane, the Irish violinist. He had a weak chin and long, dexterous smoker's fingers. His long face and its floppy fringe looked just right bent over the violin. It always took ten minutes of conversation before a note was played by either of us, but such entertaining conversation! I could easily forgive him. And then there was Fruebeck, the strutting little baritone. He always walked into a room as if affronted, ready to take offence at the quality of music, or food or even the goddamn room temperature. I had little enough opinion of his voice, which was boorish and forced, sounding as if it came from his tightly-collared yet near non-existent neck. But there was a time, after one difficult rehearsal, when he cleared his throat and, rummaging in his waistcoat, presented me with a bottle of the finest whiskey, "to be mixed with two-thirds water and a slice of lemon, please." When I looked up, I saw the timid eagerness in his eyes and was touched.

Then there was Paul Estepha. He was a tenor. He meant something to me.

He had soft eyes, fine hands, and a warm lyric timbre that filled the confines of our practice room. In his presence I allowed myself a licence I never did with the other students; my own playing became softer, more *rubato*, as I let my fingers circle around the key before touching down, my wrists arching and coming to rest, both the gesture and result as suggestive to the eye and ear, to one observant of these things, as a low-cut top and a flash of suspender.

When he and I worked through the *Lieder* of Schubert and Brahms, his timbre was a perfect balance between passion and control. A tenor in full voice commands a power that most men keep chained and leashed, and Paul Estepha's unleashing of that power created such an intense passion in me that it was all I could do to obey the little black stems that wavered in front of my eyes as my fingers ranged the keys with varying degrees of dexterity.

Of course there was a girl, an Italian flautist with high cheekbones and hair that shone as brightly as her tote bag. She always picked the male accompanists, never me, so we did not meet in any arena where I might have had even the faintest advantage. Away from the piano, standing beside her, I felt as if she looked into me and dismissed me. The word she had in mind, a cruel, hateful one reserved for use against people of my background, might never have been uttered aloud but was implicit in every sentence she directed at her boyfriend when I was present.

It was only when my fingers were on the keys, rounding on them, cherishing them, lingering on them – then I had confidence. A confidence that came from practice and accomplishment – something I never could have learned above a taxi driver's office in Sheffield, or confined at home to wait for a suitable husband. A confidence that disappeared the moment I went out on the street, and into my shell.

But what matter. I might not have had requited love, but I had my boys, whom I worked with through happy and hard times.

Redmond, Fruebeck, Estepha, and many others – they were my boys. And I killed them all.

It started after one practice with Estepha, as I packed my score into my music bag, preparing to leave for the day. I noticed that Estepha lingered. He was looking at me in a concentrated way.

"Shobnam," he said at last, "do you know the Dichterliebe?"

"The Schumann? Oh yes."

"Herr Robert wants us to run through it with him. He thinks we might be ready."

I looked at him in surprise. Herr Robert was the most revered teacher in the Academy, spoken of with hushed tone and a reverent expression, but he rarely *taught* anyone. One could not demand classes with him; he would drift into a music room to listen as the mood took him and more than likely drift out again after about two minutes. Or so I heard from others who were lucky enough to know him; he had never made any of these visitations to me. Or so I thought.

He was sometimes called the Old Man, but always *sotto voce*. Nobody really knew what age he was – some said he had been a refugee from the war. When I asked "Which war?", the response was always "oh, you know, the last war" and a dismissive wave of the hand. I sometimes passed him in the corridor, wandering along, shirt loose from his trousers, collar undone, his hair a shock of grey-silver, his face sallow and handsome with a sweet smile that implied some wondrous secret he did not wish to share with anyone. He always wore pale green shirts and smelled of cigars, though I never saw him smoke any.

"When does he want us?" I asked.

"At nine tomorrow."

I sighed. Mornings were not my best time, and I never wanted to be at less than my best in Paul Estepha's company. But back then I was in love and any excuse to be with him was enough. I took out my small, cheap moleskine diary and scribbled in the appointment.

"You are late," were the maestro's first words to us when we entered the room at five past nine the following day. I glanced around at Estepha but he did not look in my direction. My heart sank: this was not a good start.

Waving away our hurried apologies, Herr Robert directed us to begin. Without waiting to see if Estepha was ready, I played the opening arpeggios of the first song, *Im wunderschönen Monat Mai*. At his cue, he was able to join in with a rather ragged vocal, no doubt caused by irritation at me for not giving him the nod as I usually did.

This piece is simple to play, but I have always found it strange – unlike most of the songs of the time, it does not resolve into the original key but ends in an unrelated one altogether. The melody made the longed-for May month sound like nothing more than a lost dream. Out of the corner of my eye, I saw Herr Robert lean his head back against the wall, with a faraway look on his face, as if he were dreaming too. But when we continued to *Ich will meine Seele tauchen*, he called out at us to stop.

"You know," he asked, "the *Dichterliebe*, where it comes from?"

As we were both silent, he supplied the answer himself. "From Heine, when he was young and romantic, before he rejected all that. He wrote these poems, *Dichterliebe* – it means 'the poet's love'. Love is always a serious thing; it is never trivial. To love and to be loved – that is the supreme goal. All music is only a reflection of that truth. But you! – you play and sing as if love were a trivial matter."

I glanced over at Estepha; the effect of Herr Robert's words on him appeared to be profound.

"To know of that love," Herr Robert continued, "must be your sole and highest aim when you play this music. Nothing more and nothing else will suffice. Now – begin again."

So I started those strange arpeggios once more and this time Estepha was with me straightaway. He sang each phrase without effort, unwinding the notes as if they were long ribbons blown about in a breeze and occasionally floating higher in the air, yet at all times supported, anchored down in a vocal that showed true mastery. I had never heard him sing like that before: in the past, he had been prone to wandering off in an unsupported croon, trying to show off his higher register and forgetting the deeper tones that must compliment every male singing voice like the kick of a mouthful of coffee.

Uninterrupted thereafter by Herr Robert, we went all the way to *Die alten, bösen Lieder*, the dark, final song. There is a long interlude at the end where the singer is silent and only I play – usually at this point we would stop and take a break, but this time Estepha stayed standing, mute and swaying, while I continued the long, final stretch. When we ended, Herr Robert raised his head: he had tears in his eyes.

Clara, he whispered.

Then he turned his gaze beyond us, up at the high window, withdrawing into a reverie so deep that after a while I realised the class was over and beckoned to Estepha to come on out.

But when Estepha turned to me, I recoiled in shock. His loved, dreamed-of face was now a lifeless mask, cheeks and jowls hanging flabbily off the bone. His eyes, glazed and lost, wandered about like a blind man's. Eventually, after I called him a few times, he followed me out, walking like someone in a deep slumber.

He had never sung so well in his life, I will wager. But now, looking back, I can see all too clearly what it cost him.

Suddenly, Herr Robert was everywhere. On one of our meetings, I was out walking in my favourite city park.

"Shobnam! I am glad to see you."

"And I you, Herr Robert," I replied, in happy surprise that he knew me by name. It is not unusual for accompanists to have their names permanently unknown.

"Walk with me a moment," he said, offering his elbow.

As we promenaded along the path, I couldn't help but feel like a lady of another century, in a different continent from that of my ancestors, escorted by a benevolent father down the long central lane with its lime trees on either side. Indeed it seemed that the more I looked at the other ladies, the more their clothes seemed to blur and then resolve into tightly cinched waists and wide hips, gaiters and waistcoats…Or was it a trick of the setting sun? I blinked, and the people looked ordinary again.

"You are enjoying our classes together, the Schumann?" Herr Robert enquired, breaking into my reverie.

"Yes, I am," I replied, "but I'm worried about Estepha –"

"*Ach*, don't worry about him. He will be all right. He is so young, such passion. Young men, they are trouble." Then he added, as if he were commenting on the weather, "I could kill them without remorse."

"What?" I began, but ignoring my shock, he expertly guided me towards a small glade of trees, in the middle of which stood a painted summerhouse which smelled of creosote and apple blossom. "I like to walk here. It is *so schön*...so peaceful. Don't you think?"

"Yes, it is nice."

"Places like this are good. So often I have run – and here I can stand still." Seeing me look at him questioningly, he added, "Of course, you understand that. Your family ran from war, did they not?"

"War?" I said perplexed. Then, "Well, I suppose so. They had to flee Uganda in the sixties. Amin's thugs chased them out. But how did you know that?"

Herr Robert smiled. "You think I do not follow the lives of all my pupils? Yes, I do know, and I concern myself deeply. Because you have known persecution –"

"Well, I haven't personally –"

But Herr Robert wasn't listening. He put his hand on my arm. "I would do anything to protect you, my Klärchen. You who have been persecuted for my sake. I would have dealt with your father's anger. Promise you will not let it happen. Promise you will not let them take you away from me again."

His grip on my arm was tight. I wanted to say, "No, my name is Shobnam – and you're hurting me!", but my mouth and tongue felt dry and stiff, my throat closing over. He was looking at me like a man in love, his eyes shining, his smile gentle but determined. I felt numbed in a fog of happiness that did not come from me, but which was all-enveloping, even stronger than my fear which grew in almost parallel leaps and bounds.

"Promise," he said. "*Versprich mir.*" He was nearly cutting off my blood circulation at this stage.

"All right!" I said. "I promise."

He let my arm go and put his hands on my shoulders. His gaze was intense.

"Poor girl," he said at last, "You have never known what it is to come home. You will know soon." His accent made the "u" in "soon" a deep one, like my father's. He inclined his head; that too reminded me of Papi.

But Papi was by this stage an elderly man; when I looked at Herr Robert's face, I could not tell what age he was.

The classes got harder. Herr Robert got angrier. Estepha and I were kept back time after time, practising the same pieces.

"More!" he shouted at Estepha. "More! Where is your fire?" He banged his hand down on the top of the piano, making the strings vibrate discordantly and putting me off.

"I did not ask you to stop," Herr Robert said acidly.

"Then stop banging my instrument, please." I was satisfied to see him step back in surprise at my tone. Few people dared speak to him like that, least of all Estepha, who worshipped the ground he walked on.

He turned back to Estepha. "To feel this music, you must give everything." In his anger, the "v"s became "f"s. *Gif Efferthing.* Oddly enough my father spoke those consonants similarly, even though his background and language were different. "You must not hold back anything of yourself. We have discussed this before. You are too polite, too cautious."

Estepha hung his head, gripping onto the stand. For a moment, I thought he would collapse, and was about to rise from my stool to catch his fall. But he steadied himself, passing his hand across his forehead. He looked in great pain.

"Now, we go again from the *da capo*." Herr Robert instructed, pointing at Estepha's score. I led in by half a bar, then Estepha joined me, his diaphragm jumping, his face alternatively red and pale. When we reached the *forte* he overdid it and nearly broke the windows.

Herr Robert folded his hands against his chest in a Namaste gesture. He looked down and allowed himself a little smile.

"*Ausgezeichnet*," he murmured, "excellent."

I dropped my hands in relief and weak as he was, even Estepha smiled.

"Yes," Herr Robert whispered almost to himself, "you have it exactly how I always wanted it."

When the weather was fine, I often wandered the narrow streets of the city alone. I would spend my spare time in the theatre, watching cheap matinees, or in one of the many cafés dotted around the small town squares near the Academy building. One afternoon, sitting in a café around the corner from the Academy. I was surprised to see

Estepha's girlfriend shove the door open, cross the floor and pull out the chair opposite mine: surprised, because we were not friends.

"Just what do you think you're doing?" she said, without greeting or apology, the door behind her still swinging on its hinges where she had banged it.

"I beg your pardon?"

She put her elbows on the table. "I'm only going to say this once. Leave him alone."

"What do you mean?" I said coldly.

"As if you don't know. He is really sick now. He won't eat the good food I cook for him. He sits and stares out the window or puts on music for hours and hours. Always and only Schumann. He looks out the window and shivers as if the life has been taken out of him." Her voice cracked a little.

I said nothing. What could I do? I had seen Paul Estepha's sad deterioration for myself. The stronger, sweeter and higher his tenor voice became, so the more frail the body that held it, with its sweet, cloying smell of sickness. Gone were the halcyon days when we romped through the *Erl King*, he goading me to come into the forest, I hastily tripping after him with those lethal semiquaver triplets in the right hand. I never heard a spoken word out of him these days. Technically we were far beyond any previous standards; personally, I could not help but be saddened at watching him fade away before my eyes.

"Well," his girlfriend spat, "I know you are putting some spell on him. You and that crazy Kraut. I want you to stop, both of you."

"Stop what?"

Her face darkened. "The hell with you!" she cried, shoving my cup off the table. I cried out as the still-warm coffee spilled on my belly and my lap. "*Sporcha… sporcha…*" she hissed. Although I know little Italian, experience taught me that she was on the verge of uttering some ethnic slur, but she held back, as if afraid to unleash all that power in one instant. "You are evil to the core. I hope you die a painful death."

And with that last malediction, she turned on her heel and left the café, leaving the male staff staring after her in admiration, wiping down their cups and saucers and gaping in her wake.

Smoothing out my wet skirt, whose worsted material absorbed the liquid badly and chafed my thighs, I felt nothing more than a faint regret about what might happen; I could only hear those rising arpeggios, their progressions as natural and expected as the falling rain. Already since I had seen Herr Robert that morning, I was withdrawing from the world.

I could not help her or my beloved Estepha, no matter how much I might want to: I had made a promise.

By the next class, Estepha could hardly stand. When he did sing, a note would come out so pure that it would nearly make me weep. For all that, Herr Robert ignored him, directing all his comments at me. At the end of class, he waved at Estepha to leave, and watched, impassive, as the tenor staggered out of the room, leaning against the doorjamb to catch his breath. I could just about hear his faltering shuffle down the corridor – one step, two step – before returning my attention to Herr Robert, who was giving me instructions for the next class.

"I have a baritone for you to accompany. Paul Fruebeck." Although I was surprised at Herr Robert selecting that particular singer, I merely nodded assent.

"*Gut*," Herr Robert smiled. "We shall play the *Three Sonnets of Petrarch*. You know it, I am sure."

"No. Not Liszt." I said sharply. "I can't bear him; you know that." The spasm of revulsion I felt startled me. I had always loved Liszt - where had this outburst come from? It felt like the last one, mine but not mine. Herr Robert seemed to be expecting it. He put his brow in his hands.

"Always the same argument," he sighed, "always the irrational prejudice."

I was about to apologise, tell him I hadn't known what came over me. but he said, without looking at me, "All right. We play Schubert now. I prepared for this eventuality and brought another score."

And so when the baritone arrived, instead of the *Three Sonnets* I played the tender introduction to *Du bist die Ruh*, waiting for him to chime in and ruin it as he usually did everything he touched – but to my astonishment he sang with a full, proud voice, hitting the difficult F at the climax without effort, using the kind of fully supported vocal that singers took years to master. And as the piece concluded, his voice reminded me of my father's – I felt all the years that separated me from my parents and my home. When I was small and we still lived just outside Kampala, I remember my father tracing letters in the dust outside his shop and I would copy him. Now he was nowhere.

To know of that love... Nothing more and nothing else will suffice.

And out of some other nowhere, I began to cry. I could not control myself. I could not even stop playing. I knew that if I did, some deep, unnameable grief would take over. So I played on, returning to the beginning even as I reach the end, to keep what was left of my composure.

But Herr Robert stopped me.

"Shobnam," he said, placing his hand on my shoulder, very gently, as if the skin and bone were tissue paper that would crumple at a firmer touch. I stopped mid-bar.

"*Sei ruhig, sei ruhig, mein Kind.* Don't cry, Clara," he whispered, "I never want to see you cry. I'm sorry for everything I did. I was cruel."

Through my tears I saw Fruebeck walk to the window and fume self-importantly. I could sense his impatience and embarrassment with every tiny motion of his body as he held himself almost rigid. The back of his head was tonsured like a monk's. I felt no reciprocating shame to his embarrassment. I was too distressed to care – and Herr Robert's arm was about my shoulders, my head pressed to his chest. Beneath the green cotton shirt front, smelling faintly of cigar, his heart beat, warm and living.

I did not even look up when the angry baritone left the room, somewhat more halting in his footsteps than when he came in.

That evening, I entered the little-used room that served as the Academy's library. It was near the back of the building and always dark – its one window was a small four-pane set high in the wall. Low-watt bulbs were constantly on, covered by tasselled lampshades on desks which looked as if they were hurriedly shoved in between the bookshelves that lined the walls. Students tended to come here only to grab scores, rarely leaving them back when finished, as the gaps in the bookshelves testified. Me, I was there for a purpose. I walked past all the scores lined up in alphabetical order and pulled out the Q – V edition of the huge encyclopaedia down near the bottom to look up Clara Schumann.

Of course she wasn't listed, not by herself, only referred to in passing under her husband's entry. I knew the bones of the story: Robert Schumann came to study under the direction of Clara's father, Friedrich Wieck, wooed and won Clara, took her father to court so that he could marry her, infuriating Herr Wieck. And why should he not have been angry? I thought. Schumann, while not yet mentally unstable to the extent he would become in his later years, had little money and was a poor prospect for Clara. Other than that, the article told me nothing new about Clara Schumann.

I turned to the biographies, up a few shelves. There I found a children's book entitled *Clara Schumann – a Life* that sat uncomfortably beside the scholarly analyses on her male counterparts. Among the many pictures dotted here and there to whet the child reader's curiosity, I read the truth: Clara Wieck's life had been hell. Her mother had had the unheard-of courage to leave her father, who had a monstrous temper, but Clara was barred from seeing her. The bounds of Friedrich's anger seemed limitless as he roared and threatened and wrote angry letters to his estranged wife. Clara was so traumatised by the continual shouting, the book said, she did not even speak until she was four.

That particular detail startled me: I too, was a late speaker. My father had even been worried that I was becoming, in his words, an imbecile and had taken me to the doctor while we still lived in Africa. But they could find nothing wrong with me, other than the tendency to withdraw into my own world. My heart went out to little Clara: I knew how it felt to have a heart too full for words to express.

I continued reading. Like my own father, Friedrich completely mapped out his daughter's destiny, first putting her on the stage at the age of eight. By her teens, Clara was playing up a storm all through Europe, receiving accolades from Chopin and Liszt, bestowed with the honour of the Austrian "Royal and Imperial Chamber Virtuoso". Friedrich had done well.

Then a pupil and composer called Robert Schumann, who had lived in the house since Clara was eight, undid all her father's hard work. Surely Friedrich could have seen that coming a mile off? The inevitable marriage took place and eight children followed. A sentence jumped out at me – "Schumann wanted a traditional wife, not a musician." But Clara continued to play at concerts. She had no choice: Schumann's already precarious grip on reality was further weakening. (I remembered the look in Herr Robert's eyes: *Versprich mir*. It was of a man half-mad.) And there, bald in black and white, was Clara's hatred for Liszt. Her removal of Schumann's dedication to him on one of his pieces after his death. Her refusal to play his pieces in public. Irrational, beyond explanation. Yet I had felt a profound irritation when Herr Robert had mentioned Liszt. It was almost as if he were goading me.

His love for her was all-consuming. He wrote his *Lieder* for her, as well as his sprawling, lovely *Fantasie* for piano. She was his Muse.

Yet two years before he died she put him into the madhouse.

Fruebeck did all our lessons now. Herr Robert never discussed it with me, but we both knew Estepha was too far gone. His successor was also succumbing: I could see the signs even with a constitution as robust as the baritone's: a pronounced pallor (even more noticeable in Fruebeck than Estepha, since he had a broad, pale Northern look, unlike the tenor) and hands that shook constantly, as if he had been pilfering ever more of that whiskey in the morning, though I knew for a fact that he never drank the stuff himself, preferring to share it among others.

During our next lesson, a very distressing event took place. All was brought to a halt by a loud cry of anguish: Estepha's girlfriend rushed into the room. As soon as I saw her, I knew – and the knowledge was like something cold in my gut. Kicking me.

She opened her mouth to say *He's gone*, but nothing resembling words came out. Just sounds, the most awful, groaning sounds.

I knew what would happen next.

She made for me, dragging me out into the corridor. I did not resist her. As I felt those delicate, perfectly hard knuckles rain blows on my face along with her inarticulate howling – the cries of grief which I had held back – I found myself swaying, felt the cold, tiled ground against my cheek, then knew no more.

Things became tangled. Somebody brought me to a sickbed, where I drifted in and out of consciousness. I remember Herr Robert pressing a cool, damp cloth to my forehead. His voice was soft, Germanic and concerned. "I am sorry, my dear."

My head hurt and little bullets of black light were shooting across my eyes. "What for?"

"The young man. He did his duty admirably. Like all young men do, in war and in peace."

To my woozy eyes, the indentations around Herr Robert's mouth and neck had smoothed out, the peppery grey hair was now light brown. His eyes seemed larger, fresher.

"There was one young man whom I loved like a son. He was only twenty when I let him into my house and taught him everything I know. Then I became ill. They say I went mad. I don't know, all I know was that something broke inside. In the meantime he fell in love with my wife, my Clara. He made love to her with his music, chastely. They visited me together at the hospital and thought I was too far gone to know what was going on. But I knew. I knew how that young man betrayed me. I could see it in both their eyes."

"And he..." Confused as I was, I wanted to know if it was Estepha, but Herr Robert shook his head.

"Brahms," he said. "His name was Johannes Brahms."

The baritone fell soon enough; after him, a few string musicians playing Schumann's only piano quintet, poor innocent Redmond among them. This piece put Herr Robert in a particularly bad mood; he railed at me, claiming I was trying to outdo him. I did not understand what he meant until he once again addressed me as *Clara*; a quick trip to the library made everything clear. His all-consuming jealousy meant that he could never forgive his wife for playing so well in that last quintet of his. He hated when she tried to compose, or give concerts to bring home the money he couldn't.

Just as he had hated Brahms for his youth, genius and beauty. Brahms could give Clara so many things that Schumann could not. He hated Clara's father too – but behind her father's rage lay concern for her life and career. The madness in Schumann's eyes was apparent to him, a man of experience, in a way it could never be to a nineteen-year-old girl in the first flush of love.

But then again – Clara herself wrote: "I once believed that I possessed creative talent, but I have given up this idea; a woman must not desire to compose – there has never yet been one able to do it." And she had a stubbornness of her own. *I won't play Liszt. I can't bear him.* To the day she died, she would not be in the same room as him.

The young men all went the way of Paul Estepha. But here I must point out: they went *willingly*. Herr Robert had not been lying when he said nothing less would suffice. Had they not given their paltry lives to his service, they never would have created such wondrous music.

And I?

I was born to accompany. An accompanist is a lot like a traditional wife. But without an accompanist, there can be no song. Like Clara, I know my place. I have learned it now, I think.

Herr Robert was uncomfortable that I was not as beholden to him as those singers, who would have gone through fire for him. His wife caused the same discomfort. He cannot separate me from Clara – race, time, language are as nothing in the face of such emotions. Nor can I separate him from – I hardly know what, except a deep sense of *home* that no earthly tie can overcome. Now I understand what love is, why it strangles so. Why it lasts so obstinately after everything that inspired it is gone.

The air grew colder in the Academy. Year after year, fewer people walked its corridors, until only Herr Robert and I were left. All the music that filled the building got fainter, until each room went silent, querulous teachers and protesting pupils all fading. Herr Robert and I continued, even after the last person had gone, even when there was nobody to sing the *Dichterliebe* any more. I lost track of time.

Then one day, even Herr Robert could not go on. The longest-living and most strong-willed person needs food and sleep some of the time, yet he'd had neither for many years – the music had enthralled us both too deeply. I came across him that morning, frozen and inert on the floorboards, his eyes wide open and sightless. In an attempt to warm him up and revive him, I spat on my hands and rubbed them together, laying them on his cold forehead, whispering his name: *Robert, meine Seele*. But when he failed to answer I knew there was nothing I could do.

I wanted to weep for him, but had fallen out of the habit. What use crying, anyway, against the howling of that everlasting, cold wind? I got up, pulled my shawl around me, and returned to the piano. The keys were rigid with a thin layer of ice. I hit them repeatedly to loosen it, the loud discords making the walls shake. Then I played those same opening arpeggios, even trying to sing *Im wunderschönen Monat Mai* in my cracked, untrained voice, as if I could somehow conjure up such a season when the joists hummed in the north wind and the windowpanes were covered in frosty lace. It sounded more like the call of a banshee, even though there was nobody left to die.

I let his body stay there until it began to putrefy and the crows got in to eat away what was left of it. The room stank, but I hardly cared. When there was nothing left but a skeleton, I put a clean bone next to my cold cheek and for once let my tears flow freely.

Then I got on with it. After all, Clara outlived Robert. She did what was necessary, even after Brahms abandoned her. Did Schumann ever know that? Would he have been proud of her?

It has been years now, decades, since anyone besides me has been in this room. Without doubt, I am the Academy's longest resident. Surely it cannot continue like this forever? But I don't know how to let go of this life. Death implies time and progress, but this dry cold that has the shawl around my shoulders, this bare room, the piano upon which I play – nothing alters. I cannot make a new life. I can only play out the old one. Father gone, teacher gone, all of them gone.

Oh my boys. My poor boys.

The Legend of Left-Hand Lewis

Maxwell Peterson

In the top room of an eccentric old house on Rowan Street, Lewis Light was standing on a chair with a rope around his neck. The rope ran from his throat up to the ceiling fan, and from there down to one of the legs of the neatly made bed.

At the moment, Lewis was not killing himself. He was taking notes.

He stood still for several minutes, observing how the room looked and smelled, and how the rope felt around his neck.

The rope did not feel particularly dismal or desperate. Rather, it was loose and comfortable, and did not restrict his breathing at all. The room was bright, and a gentle breeze carried the smell of early summer in through wide, high windows. Lewis was disappointed.

He had rented the room to record his first and final album. Just him and his acoustic guitar and raw emotion, to be wondered at and written about and hailed as genius after he was dead. His final poignant letter to the world. It would be found and wept over. It would inspire academics to write papers about the tragedy of his life. It would make him a legend. It would be haunting, and bleak, and utterly, unabashedly honest.

The only problem was that Lewis couldn't think of anything to write.

He slipped the rope from around his neck and stepped down from the chair, crossing the room to the bed. He had purchased a small, black, unlined notebook and a fountain pen at an arts and crafts store on the way out to the house. Lewis had still not quite mastered writing with the fountain pen, and the pages he had written on so far were spattered with ink. Still, he kept at it. Lewis Light was perseverant.

The wind, he began, in the notebook. He stared at the words for a few moments, then crossed out what he had written and began again.

The breeze comforts me (line break) *in the end.* He picked up his guitar and ran the pick through a few chords, but none of them seemed to be particularly haunting or poignant. He tried humming a few lines to a chord that sounded as if it might have eventually been sad, with a little dressing up, but it always ended up sounding like an advertising jingle. He set the guitar down again.

The man who had taught Lewis how to play guitar was a member of a polka band, and had refused to teach Lewis any minor chords, insisting that, on the whole, things were pretty good. What need would Lewis have for sadness?

Sadness, the old man used to say, was counterproductive to happiness.

Lewis agreed with him, but happiness was not Rock and Roll.

A banging sound came from somewhere far below him, shaking the walls of the room slightly, and setting the strings of his guitar vibrating. Lewis listened to the sound of his guitar strings resonating with themselves. He liked it – the way each smaller note harmonized to create a larger unified sound.

Then the banging stopped, and the sound stopped with it.

Harlan (the owner of the house) had told Lewis that the loud, heavy banging sound was the hot water heater turning on, that it happened often, and that he should not worry about it. He had advised Lewis to avoid going down to the basement at all, as one of the other tenants in the house was a photographer, and used it as a darkroom.

There was a shave-and-a-haircut knock at the door.

"Coming," called Lewis. He untied the rope from the leg of the neatly made bed, stepped up onto the chair, un-looped the rope from the ceiling fan, and tossed it into his open luggage bag. He moved the chair back into the corner, where it had been when he had arrived the day before. Then he closed the luggage bag and opened the door.

The old man who owned the house was lying face down in the hallway in front of Lewis's door. His white hair was messy. He was not moving.

"Mr. Anderson?" said Lewis, quietly. There was no reply.

He knelt and placed a hand on the old man's back. It was cold. How fast did dead bodies cool? Lewis didn't know. He looked up and down the hallway, but saw nothing out of the ordinary.

Lewis gently shook the old man. "Mr. Anderson?" he said again. He wondered if he should call the police.

The old man rolled onto his side, then creaked his way to his feet. "Sorry. I got old and died while I was waiting for you to answer your door. Had to change out of your women's clothing, eh?" He winked at Lewis. "And if I have to tell you not to call me 'Mr. Anderson' one more time, I'll fuck your eyes out and use the juice for jelly on my toast. 'Harlan' is fine." The old man gave him a friendly punch on the arm.

"You haven't told me not to call you 'Mr. Anderson' yet," said Lewis.

"Well, consider yourself warned, then. 'Mr.' is for old people."

Lewis nodded. "Okay." Harlan was at least sixty.

"Good. C'mon. You can be a fairy later. Right now, you're going to learn the ancient, manly art of cooking."

Lewis stepped into the hallway and closed his door behind him. He had only been living in the house for a day, but he found already that he liked it enormously. "What are we making?"

"Minced lamb brioche."

"Really?"

"No. Are you out of your fucking mind? We're making hamburgers. I said 'manly art,' not 'I cry myself to sleep at night.' Jesus Christ." The old man grinned, and punched Lewis on the other arm. "Come on."

Lewis followed the old man down the hallway, toward the spiraling staircase that led to the lower floors. There were Polaroid pictures in frames on the walls, at different heights, and with no discernible pattern. Lewis looked at the photograph in one of the incongruous frames.

It was a picture of a man sitting in an office cubicle, stacks of paper like a miniature cityscape sprawled across the desk. The man had a confused look on his face, but he was smiling. There was a signature in the lower right-hand corner. Lewis couldn't make out the name.

"The pictures'll be there later, Light. There's meat to pound and play with downstairs. I'm sure you're good at *that*, right?" The old man laughed. He was standing at the staircase, one hand on the worn wooden handrail.

Lewis walked down the remainder of the hallway, glancing at the other pictures as he went. There was a fast food employee, smiling awkwardly; a homeless man; an old woman standing behind what looked to Lewis like the front desk of a library. There were signatures on all of the photographs.

"Who are these people?" Lewis had reached the staircase. The old man moved slowly on the steps. Carefully.

"Hell if I know."

"Well, who takes the pictures, then?"

They had reached the second floor. Harlan pointed down the hallway. "Edgar does."

Lewis looked down the hallway. The walls were adorned with half a dozen framed Polaroids like the ones outside of his room.

"Why?" Lewis asked, as they reached the ground floor and the kitchen.

"Because I know everything there is to know in this world, I'm going to be an asshole, and not tell you." Harlan leaned against the countertop and pointed to the refrigerator. "The meat is in there. Have at it."

Lewis opened the refrigerator and took out an oval serving platter. Three packages of ground beef were thawing on the platter. The meat sat in a small pool of dark brown blood. The liquid had soaked into the bottoms of the packets, dissolving the butcher paper.

"So," said Harlan, "why here?"

"What?" Lewis was looking though the cupboards for another plate to place the meat on, out of the brown puddle.

"Why'd you come here? I charge too much for rent, there's no view, the other boarders are as crazy as cock-hungry nuns.... Why are you here?" He ran a hand through his hair. It was sticking out at odd, unlikely angles, and as his fingers passed over it, his hair sprang back to its original position. "The plates are in the cupboard by your knees."

"Aren't you going to help?"

"Don't worry. You're doing fine."

"Well," said Lewis, transferring the meat to the new plate, "I wanted a place to record some songs."

"An artist," said a woman's voice.

"We're living with an artist," agreed a second voice. A man's.

Lewis turned around. He had started a pan heating on the stove, and had just begun rummaging through the drawers, looking for a knife to cut up the tomatoes and onions he had seen in the refrigerator. There was a short man standing in the doorway to the kitchen. A woman stood behind him. She was at least a head taller than the man.

"Hello," said Lewis.

"He's not an artist," said the woman. "He is a musician."

"Yes. Not an artist at all," agreed the man.

They were both unbelievably thin. The short man was dressed in a checked waistcoat and brightly polished black shoes. His clothes hung on him like skin on a skeleton. The woman had on a black silk dress and long, black, silk gloves. There were pearls around her neck, and she wore a violently red cloche hat.

"But is not music the noblest form of art? Of course he is an artist, Dino. Pay attention."

"I'm going to kill you two," said Harlan.

Lewis began forming the meat into flat, round patties. The tomatoes could wait.

Later that night, in his room, Lewis shook a handful of breath mints into his palm.

The click of death, he wrote into his plain black notebook. He picked up a bottle from the floor next to the bed. He had considered, briefly, buying actual alcohol, but had decided to buy sparkling grape juice instead. He had never been a drinker.

Lewis dumped the mints into his mouth. The taste of peppermint was overpoweringly strong, but he gritted his teeth and raised the bottle to his lips. He was committed. He had come this far. He couldn't turn back now.

Lewis swallowed. It wasn't difficult. He was a little disappointed: he had expected to have to choke the "pills" down. He had even pulled the chair from the corner and situated it next to the bed, in case he had begun to choke and had to perform the Heimlich maneuver on himself.

He set the bottle back on the floor, lay back on the bed, and imagined he was dying.

He imagined his heartbeat slowing, his breath becoming shallower as his eyes lost their hold on the walls and ceiling, the world becoming blurry and dim. He thought about the numbness in his fingers; the clumsy way they slipped off the strings of his guitar as the synapses in his brain faded to black, like a power outage in slow motion.

In death, he wrote, *I wish for wintry breath.*

Lewis picked up the acoustic guitar and tried a few chords, quietly singing the lyrics he had written down.

He had forgotten to set up the camera.

Lewis set down his guitar and opened his luggage bag. He pulled out a tripod, a camera bag, and a thick spring with a threaded bolt attached to one end.

Lining up the edge of the bed in the viewfinder, Lewis set the timer on the digital camera for fifteen seconds and hit the button on the top. He tapped the camera, lightly, setting it bobbing. He walked back to the bed and picked up his acoustic guitar. He made the most pensive face he could manage, and looked at an electrical outlet, away from the lens.

Lewis had designed and constructed the tripod himself. The spring meant that when the camera took a picture, it would be blurry – something that wouldn't normally happen with a tripod. It would become part of his legend, he was sure: Who was with Lewis Light in the days before he died?

The camera beeped. Lewis stood to reset the timer for another shot. As he reached the camera, he heard a whisper in the hall.

Lewis picked up the tripod and set it in the closet. He opened his bedroom door.

The short man and the tall woman were standing in the hall.

"Hello," said Lewis.

"What is your name?" asked the short man.

"Dino," said the tall woman to the short man, quietly, "that was unforgivably forward." She turned to Lewis. "Please excuse my husband. He forgets himself, on occasion."

"It's fine," said Lewis. "My name is Lewis, but people call me Left-Hand Lewis." This was not strictly true. Nobody referred to Lewis as "Left-Hand Lewis" except Lewis himself.

"It is a pleasure to meet you. *My* name" – the tall woman had placed a hand delicately on her collarbone – "is Lynnette Gravely London."

"I'm Dino," said the short man.

"Nice meeting you," said Lewis.

"My husband and I were conversing, earlier in the evening – well, speculating, really – on your vocation and the curious and contradictory silence which seems incessantly to emanate from behind your door, although to say it aloud now, it seems problematic to suggest that silence might emanate from *anything*, silence being by nature and definition the lack of emanation, I suppose." She stared very hard at Lewis, her brow furrowed as though he himself had invented this troubling paradox. "At any rate, my husband and I decided that you might offer some satisfaction and elucidation upon the subject."

"Um. What was the question?" asked Lewis.

"If you're a musician," said Dino, "why don't we ever hear music from your room?"

"Oh. Well, I'm still writing the lyrics."

"I see," said the woman. "How are they coming?"

"Wonderfully. These are songs that have been living in me for a long time. They're going onto the page like Legion into the pigs."

Lewis had rehearsed what he would say if anybody asked him about his songs. He had discovered Jesus' expulsion of multiple demons into a herd of pigs while researching famous exorcisms on the internet. When the last people who had seen Lewis alive were asked what he had been like in his final days, Lewis wanted to be sure that they would have interesting quotes to give the biographers and documentary filmmakers.

"That's from the bible," said Dino.

The tall woman nodded approvingly. "A musician *and* a Biblicist. Your songs are of a religious nature, then?"

"Well, no. They're about my life, and. Um. Other things. Haunting stuff." Lewis was taken aback. He had not considered that people might think he was religious. This was enormously upsetting to him. Christian music was seldom successful, Christian rock especially. "It's going to be just me and my acoustic guitar," he said, hoping to change the subject.

"Oh? I do *so* love Easy Listening. What are you going to call it?" asked the tall woman.

Lewis was becoming increasingly distressed. His final, lingering masterpiece had been called "easy listening" before it had even been recorded. "It's not Easy Listening," he said. "More like letters to the world. The songs aren't religious. I mean. Not at all. Religious."

"I see," said Lynnette Gravely London. "What will you call it, then – the album?"

"I'm calling it 'Devil at a Dead End: The Ditchwater Tapes.'" Lewis was especially proud of the album title. He had been born on the third of May, which, according to an evangelical website he had discovered, was the day that the devil and his angels were cast out of heaven. Lewis didn't believe in the devil, but he thought the title was edgy, and mysterious. It had that "Bad Boy" thing.

"Ah, yes. Very clever." The tall woman was beaming at Lewis. She nudged her husband with an elbow. "Did you hear, Dino? Mr. Light is working on a record hailing the end of the devil and the inevitable and glorious second coming of our Lord Jesus Christ."

"Hallelujah," said Dino. "All hail Jesus, Destroyer of Worlds."

Lynnette Gravely London stifled a yawn. "Well, Mr. Light, Dino and I really must be getting to bed. We wish you well in your work. You'll join us for breakfast tomorrow morning, of course?"

"Of course," said Lewis. He did not know what else to say.

"Goodnight, then," said the tall woman and the short man, in unison.

Lewis watched as they disappeared down the staircase to the second floor.

Back in his room, Lewis scanned through the pictures on the digital camera. He had taken a few dozen the first morning he had been there, from different angles around the room while he pretended to write, or to play his guitar. None of them were particularly good. At any rate, they didn't look haunting, mysterious, or bleak. Mostly, Lewis thought, they looked blurry.

He set down the camera and picked up the small, black notebook. He stared for a long time at the handful of words he'd written there.

At six o'clock the next morning, Lewis woke up and took a shower. After he got out, he shaved. He left a patch of scruff around his mouth, black and bristly. Lewis did not like the facial hair, finding it itchy and not particularly attractive, but it added to his "tortured artist" edge, and besides, all the virtuosos – Cobain, Morrison, Hendrix – had all had facial hair in their final days.

Lewis pulled on a clean, black tee shirt and a pair of black jeans with the knees cut out. There was a knock at the door.

"Don't pretend you're not awake in there," said Harlan, through the door. "I can hear you masturbating."

Lewis opened the door. "Good morning, Harlan," he said.

"Come on. We're going grocery shopping. I'm out of gin."

"It's six-thirty in the morning."

The old man's mouth dropped open, and his eyes opened wide. He clutched at his chest.

"What? What's wrong?" Lewis was worried that the old man might be having a heart attack.

"You can tell time." Harlan was still holding his chest, but he was smiling now. "There's a place in town. Come on. You're carrying the groceries back."

"Okay," said Lewis.

"Meet me downstairs in ten, or I'll come back up with a gun," Harlan said as he made his way down the stairs.

Lewis lifted his leather jacket off the back of the chair in the corner. He had purchased the jacket at a consignment shop in northern Kentucky. It had several buckles, and was so worn that it was really more gray than black. He did not particularly like leather, and he'd cleaned the jacket thoroughly before he had worn it. Lewis did not hold well with dirty or unsanitary things.

Downstairs, Harlan was waiting by the door. He was wearing a red and black flannel shirt.

"I like your shirt," said Lewis. "Very nineties. Seattle."

"I like your jacket," said Harlan. "Very homeless drug addict."

It was a fifteen-minute walk to town. The early June morning was clear and cold and bright. The dew made the grass on the edges of the road shimmer like the sea.

"Beautiful morning," said Lewis.

"Gorgeous as God's balls," said Harlan.

They walked in silence for a while.

"So," said Harlan, "how's the album going?"

"You're interested?"

"Not really. The sexually charged silence was giving me a hard-on," Harlan said. "And that would just be awkward."

Lewis laughed, and the old man smiled.

"Well, honestly," said Lewis, "I'm having some problems with it."

"How'd you mean?"

"I can't really think of anything good to write. I mean, I'll start a song, or some lyrics, or. Anyway. They just all seem to be..." Lewis shrugged.

Harlan thought for a moment. Then he said, "What kind of music do you play?"

"Punk Rock and Alternative," Lewis said, proudly.

Harlan looked blank.

"Rock and Roll," Lewis tried.

The old man shook his head. "No you don't. You're too polite to be a rock star."

Lewis laughed. "Go to hell."

"Watch your mouth."

"Sorry."

"See? My point exactly. *I'm* more of a rock star than you are," Harlan said. "Just ask your mother."

They had reached the town. It was small and cheerful.

The girl behind the counter at the grocery store was pretty and blonde. Harlan bought two bottles of Gordon's gin, two dozen eggs, and three packages of bacon. She put the groceries in a paper bag and handed the bag to Harlan, who handed it to Lewis.

There was a television behind the counter. A man with very black hair was reading the news.

"Authorities say no progress has been made in the search for local librarian Nancy Wyndham, who was first reported missing nearly three months ago," the man said.

"Come on," said Harlan. "You can help me make breakfast."

That night, Lewis took more pictures. He didn't think any of them looked particularly legendary.

He had considered, briefly, writing lyrics in black permanent marker on the walls, but had decided against it. Someone would have to clean it up afterwards, and Lewis hadn't wanted to cause trouble for anyone.

There was one that he liked. It was a picture of the room. Lewis wasn't in the frame – it had been taken when he had accidentally pushed the shutter button before he had set the timer.

The picture showed one corner of the bed, and the sunflower-print wallpaper. Lewis had been holding the camera, so the frame wasn't blurry. He especially liked how the sunflowers on the wall looked, in the dim light of the single bedside lamp. The center of each flower was pale brown, each petal pale yellow. They looked overexposed, as though before they had been sure of what they were, the sun had come along and dazzled them, and they had been washed away in the flood of what they aspired to be.

Lewis turned the camera off and set it on the bedside table.

A muffled sound came from somewhere lower in the house. It was a steady creaking, too quiet to be the sounds from the basement.

Lewis got out of the bed and turned off the lamp on the bedside table. Out in the hall, the sounds were louder. He locked his door and started down the staircase. The sounds grew louder as he went down the stairs.

They stopped as he reached the kitchen. He looked around, but couldn't see anything in the darkness. He thought the sounds might have been coming from Harlan's room, down the hall. Lewis groped along the wall for the light switch. His fingers brushed against it, and he flipped it on. A single bulb flickered to life, dimly illuminating the kitchen and casting long shadows on the walls.

There was a man sitting at the kitchen table.

"Having trouble sleeping?" said the man. His voice was very quiet.

Lewis nodded. "What was that noise?"

The man smiled. He had gray hair with streaks of black in it, and he wore a gray knit sweater. His eyes were very dark, and Lewis could not guess his age. "You're the new boarder, yes?"

"Yes."

The man chuckled. "It really isn't my place to say, but you would have learned for yourself eventually, and I think my telling you will save both Mr. Anderson and yourself considerable embarrassment."

"Harlan?" Lewis sat down at the kitchen table, across from the dark-eyed man.

"Yes. He and his lover, Charles, are —" The man paused. "How best to put this? Doing the dog's rig."

Lewis thought he knew what this meant. "What's your name?"

"Edgar St. Clair." There was a glass of water on the table in front of the man. He picked it up.

"You're the photographer," said Lewis.

"Yes. And you're the musician."

"Oh, sorry. My name's Lewis Light," said Lewis, and he extended a hand across the table. "But everybody calls me Left-Hand Lewis."

The man took Lewis's hand in his and shook it. "Do they?" he said. He was smiling.

Lewis looked at the man a moment.

"No," he said after a while. "But they will when I'm gone."

"I see," said the man. He raised the glass to his lips, but did not drink. "And when will that be?"

"I don't know," said Lewis.

"*But of that day and hour no one knows, neither the angels in heaven nor the son, but the Father alone.*" Edgar had closed his eyes, and set the water glass back down on the table. He opened his eyes and looked at Lewis. "May I ask you a question?"

"Sure."

"What's the worst thing you have ever done?"

Lewis was quiet for a moment. "I don't remember," he said after a while. "I was three years old. I remember police, and my Mom and Dad crying, and I know that they were crying because of something that I did, and that it was really bad, but I can't remember what."

"Are your parents still alive?"

Lewis sat back in his chair. "Yes. I mean, I think so. I don't really know where my Dad is, but my Mom lives up in Maine."

Edgar took a drink from the water glass. "Would you like something to drink? I believe there's gin in one of the cupboards, and soda in the refrigerator."

"Just water, thanks," said Lewis. Edgar stood and filled a glass with water from a carafe. He set the glass in front of Lewis.

"Thanks."

"You're welcome," Edgar said. "You know, I can hear you playing your guitar sometimes, during the day."

"I came out here to record some songs."

"How's that going?"

Lewis took a drink of his water. The creaking bang had begun again, down the hall. "It's going good."

"Going *well*," Edgar corrected. "How nice. Are you nearly finished?"

Lewis paused. Then he said, "No. The songs aren't coming along at all. I can't think of anything to write."

"But your playing is quite good. Very engaging."

"But it isn't haunting."

"Why must it be haunting, Mr. Light?"

"You can call me Lewis."

"Lewis."

Lewis spun his water glass against the table. "Because these songs will make me a legend, when I'm gone."

"I see. Your final aria, to cement your place in the musical pantheon."

"Yeah. I mean. Look at the legends. Kurt Cobain. Jim Morrison. Jimi Hendrix. These guys died young, and they left behind these songs that –" Lewis paused. "I don't know. Had so much more meaning after they were dead."

Edgar nodded. "Sylvia Plath. Virginia Woolf. I see your point." Edgar folded his hands on the table in front of him. "Why do you want to be a legend, Lewis?"

Lewis thought for a moment. "I've never told this to anyone," he said, "but when I was little, I wanted to be a dinosaur." He laughed. "Not because they were big, or ferocious, or – well, maybe for those reasons too. But really, I wanted to be a dinosaur because there weren't any left." He paused. Edgar said nothing.

"We don't know anything about them. Nothing real, or substantial," said Lewis. "All we have are the bones. They might've been boring, but that doesn't matter, because they died before anybody *knew* that they were boring. People are dying to know about them, because now they can't find out anymore." He scratched at a stain on the dark wood of the table. "People are fascinated by them. Love them."

"All of the legends are dead," said Edgar, and something in his voice made Lewis look up. "The love and adoration and interest don't do them any good. Tell me, Lewis, those people you mentioned before – were they happy, when they died?"

"No," said Lewis. "That was sort of the point. They were tortured visionaries. The tragedy was what made them so famous."

"I think, sometimes," said Edgar, "that our fascination with pain is the greatest tragedy of all."

Neither of them said anything for a long time.

"What's the worst thing *you've* ever done?" Lewis said, eventually.

Edgar St. Clair smiled, politely, and said nothing.

There was a muffled sound at the end of the hall, then silence.

Edgar stood up, slowly. "It's getting late. I think I will retire for the evening. Good night, Mr. Light."

Something had been bothering Lewis.

"Mr. St. Clair?"

Edgar was at the base of the staircase at the far end of the kitchen. "Yes?"

"Why do you take those pictures? Who are those people?"

Edgar smiled. He looked at Lewis with his dark eyes. "I'm making the ordinary legendary," he said. "Those people. They were all happy." He started up the stairs. "That's something worth remembering."

Later that night, Lewis sat hunched on the bed in his room. He was writing in his black notebook with a blue ballpoint pen he found in one of the drawers in the kitchen. Occasionally, Lewis would pick up his acoustic guitar from the stand next to the bed and strum C major, or E, or D, humming along. Then he would set the guitar down and resume writing.

The camera and the tripod sat on top of the tee shirts and underwear in his luggage bag.

The morning was cold. Harlan looked out the window between the second and third floors as he climbed the staircase. The sky was clear and bright.

Harlan walked down the hallway, quietly. He paused outside Lewis's door, checking that the fake blood was convincingly applied to his body. He was wearing an old white tee shirt, and had cut holes in the stomach earlier in the morning. With any luck, Lewis would still be asleep.

He pounded on the door, then lay down on the cold wooden boards in front of Lewis's room.

Harlan waited for a few seconds. Silence. He pounded again, moaning loudly for good measure.

Silence.

He got up and rapped on the door with his knuckles. "Light? You in there?" He tried the handle. It turned, and Harlan opened the door.

One of the windows was open, and the apple-scented early-morning air filled the room. The wooden chair was in the corner. The bed was neatly made.

The room was empty.

"Light?" said Harlan, but even as he said it he knew Lewis Light was gone. He stepped into the room. There was a white cassette tape on the bed, in a clear plastic case. Harlan picked it up.

"Sunflowers and Dinosaurs" was scrawled in black marker across the face of the tape.

There was an envelope on the bedside table. The word "Rent" had been written on it with a fountain pen, in a neat, spidery hand. The amount due was written beneath it, and the envelope bulged, slightly.

Harlan wondered where Lewis had gone. Back to the city? Back to his job, and his life?

A banging sound came from the basement far below him, shaking the walls of the room, slightly.

He stood for a moment, next to the bed. The fake blood was drying on his shirt and across his brow.

Then Harlan placed the cassette tape in his pocket and left the room, closing the door behind him as he went.

Lacuna Blues
Stephen Gaskell

For so long all Oba had wanted was to hear the song.

It teased his days, haunted his nights. He was convinced he heard it in his dreams, but when he awoke, limbs heavy from the colony world's tough gravity that never got any easier to bear, he could never bring it forth. It was like the faintest of mists burnt up in the harsh light of dawn.

Now that he had a chance to find it, he hoped he'd still recognize it.

Jump-time.

Reality fractured, shattering into a thousand million pieces. Oba always imagined himself as an observer, cowering in the middle of an enormous, mirrored dome as a hundred thousand micro-incendiaries detonated. The noise was colossal. A roar to rival an ocean swell breaking against marble cliffs. The glittering shards would be on the verge of striking him, when everything – really, truly, *everything* – unmade itself.

No light. No sound. Not even a vacuum.

It was known by many names. The Dirac Sea. The Void. The Garden of Good and Evil. He simply thought of it as the un-space.

Then everything came rushing back in a cacophony of white noise. The mirror reassembled itself. The last sliver of glass tumbled upwards into the mosaic and silence reigned again.

He realized he'd been holding his breath.

He exhaled. Inhaled. Exhaled again.

Commander Ikari unhooked himself from his surge blister while analyzing the feedback that skated across his floating vSplay. He was a flat-faced man, heavy-set, and he needed a couple of good tugs to free his arms from their straps. "Well, we're not dead – or worse."

He'd made the words his own. It was a mantra that the jump-crews out to Mimosa's helium-rich gas giants had slowly learned to love.

This wasn't any in-system jump though, Oba thought. This special two-man expedition had covered *light-years* not light-minutes. No-one had jumped that far since . . . he shook away the thought not wanting to dwell on that day, sixteen years past.

While his superior concentrated on jump-ship integrity, Oba brought up the astronomical metrics. They may have jumped safely, but had they jumped accurately? Un-space connected everywhere with everywhere. That was its power – and its terror. They might've been half-way to Andromeda for all he knew.

The core processors worked overtime, grinding through the wealth of spectral data from a hundred million motes of light. Through the ceramo-chitin composite hull he heard the whirr of motors as dozens of space-scopes roved their eyes over the heavens.

"Where are we then, Oba?" Commander Ikari asked, irritably. "Can we cast the *radio-nets?*" The tone of his voice was dismissive, condescending.

It was a tone Oba had gotten used to over the years.

Radio-net was a crude name for the technology that he had dreamed up and then, with the help of other engineers, made real over the last sixteen years.

From the scantest traces of electromagnetic radiation in the 3kHz to 300GHz range – radio waves as they were once quaintly known – Oba's nets could amplify the waves to receivable quality. In essence, they could collect history. Not the filtered, censored history in the odd data-conch that the colonists had brought with them, but real first-hand history.

Radio archeology.

Many dismissed the worth in trawling the dead shells of radiation that had been emanating from Earth for over a century past. Why take a risk, however small, over one of the colony's only three jump-ships?

But those dead shells could help them answer many questions: What forces brought us to this state of affairs? How can we avoid the mistakes of the past? Who, ultimately, are we? More than that, those shells contained a large slice of the cultural heritage of the species. A heritage that might be lost forever if they didn't act.

Those reasons were important, and Oba, as well as enough others, believed in them, but they weren't what drove him.

All he really wanted was the song.

The processors completed their calculations. It was good news.

"We're exactly one hundred and thirty light years from Earth," Oba said. "Outside the sounds of 1921 are rolling past. Somewhere out there Rudy Vallée is crooning."

He'd found the name on an encyclopedia-conch.

"Rudy *who* is doing *what*?"

"Never mind. I'll get the nets deployed."

Eighteen years earlier, Oba had stood in the atrium of the United Nations Secretariat Building that overlooked New York's East River. The pride he'd felt for being chosen for the colonization mission still burned bright back then, and he'd stood tall amongst the groups of smartly dressed attendees. The buzz of chatter filled the air, while hover-bots carried salvers of champagne flutes between the guests.

A Texan Congressman, girth straining his belt, talked at Oba. "And now I'm standing next to a man who is going to jump *Lord* knows how many light-years across the galaxy in six months time." He lowered his voice. "You know, off the record, I can't tell you how happy we are that we've beaten the Near East Bloc on this one. Without something like this the whole world would've soon been getting their prayer mats out and getting down on their knees a dozen times a day. Hoo-ee!"

The man kept talking while Oba looked for an escape route. Like himself, the other dozen or so representative members of the UNSA were all pinned down, blue striped uniforms occluded by scrums of suits. I could say I need a comfort break, Oba thought, as his eye drifted towards the exit.

At the glass doors an uncommonly beautiful, animated Asian woman in a smart two-piece suit was arguing with a mountain of a security man. Evidently she'd forgotten her ID. The man shrugged his shoulders and pointed at his own pass. She delved into her handbag and pulled out a sheaf of papers, only to spill them a moment later.

Ah, what the hell, Oba thought.

"Excuse me," he said, and left the Congressman before the man had a chance to reply.

"About time," Oba said when he reached the woman who was now on her knees retrieving her paperwork. "We need you in the conference room right now. Commissioner Albright won't sign the Land Division Treaty without consulting the final draft of the Marshall Report. Commander Wilson is fuming."

The security guy loomed over them, a pillar of muscle. "Sir, this woman doesn't have the correct identification. I can't let her in, sir."

"Did you hear what I just said?" Oba asked. "Look, just note her down as my guest. I'll take the heat if there's any trouble."

The security guy looked back and forth for help. He gave a little shake of the head when he couldn't find any and waved the woman in.

"Marshall Report? Land Division Treaty?" she repeated incredulously when they'd gotten to the other side of the atrium.

"Sound plausible, huh?"

The woman laughed, lively and genuine. "Why'd you do that?"

"I always have my eye open for easy acts of chivalry towards beautiful women." Oba grinned. "And Congressman Field was wearing me out. His politics are always a little too nuanced for my liking."

"Let me guess, you're the colony comedian." The woman began checking nearby faces. A hover-bot breezed past, and Oba swiped a flute. He handed it to the woman. She downed the champagne in one, then looked around some more.

"Actually, I'm a Communications Specialist. Nothing turns me on more than a hi-gain RF signal."

The woman laughed, showing a perfect set of enamels. Oba felt his heart hammering against his chest.

"So, *do* you know who I am?" she asked.

"You're . . . it's on the tip of my tongue . . . you're-"

"You don't have a clue, do you?" She grinned. "Lakshmi Rawaldini. BBC America." She offered her hand, and they shook. The hairs on the back of Oba's neck bristled in delight at her touch.

Lakshmi went on. "I've got to file a report-" she checked her watch "-within the next thirty-six minutes or my editor's going to kill me."

"Talk to me then."

"It's a political piece."

"Political is my middle name." He watched her calculating. "Seriously, as an UNSA representative I'm privy to a lot of interesting things."

She locked eyes with him, then fiddled with a blood-red data brooch pinned to her jacket lapel. "Okay, give me a brief bio first."

It may have been for the report, but Oba talked as if it were just for her. For some reason she made him honest. He told her about his father's death in a meaningless accident on an auto-dirigible production line when he was fourteen years old. How he'd hated everything for a long while after, and how finally he'd drifted into the air force as a maintenance grunt. There somebody had seen his potential as a Comms Specialist and pulled him out. When the opportunity of moving over to space exploration came he'd jumped at the chance.

"I've got a lot to thank the air force for, but in the end their whole philosophy was too much. I was just a small cog in this great war machine and I wasn't buying all this talk of doing it for world security."

"And you think this new phase of expansion into space is different?"

"I don't know. I hope so."

He could see she thought him naive, or hopelessly romantic, but she didn't say anything.

"So, tell me," she said, "how does it make you feel thinking of how far you'll be from Earth?"

"It'll be tough, I know that. The psychologists have done a lot of work with us. We'll be lonely, homesick, frightened . . . I'm one of the lucky ones though."

She met his eyes.

"How's that?"

He knew he was tempting fate, inviting complications, but he couldn't resist. "There's nobody special in my life right now."

Not yet, at least.

"Still waiting to meet your soulmate?"

He couldn't tell whether she was humoring him or not.

"Something like that."

They dropped the topic after that. Lakshmi probed him for juicy details that could flavor her report. The best he could do was drop hints that the lack of Saudi pilots on the mission was due to more than just operational concerns. Afterwards, she disappeared to file the story.

He was on his way out of the building believing he'd seen the last of Lakshmi Rawaldini, when he bumped into her in the lobby.

She looked flushed with excitement.

"Oba, you're not going already, are you?"

"Well, you weren't around any longer asking about the politics of the UNSA High Command. I got bored."

She slapped him on the arm. "My editor loved the piece, and it's lined up to be a lead story. I need to celebrate. How about some R & R? You can tell me all about signal compression technology."

"A fascinating subject," he said. "How long have you got?" He lead her out into the balmy afternoon, his grin so wide his jaw hurt.

For three days the fine filament nets had been cast like spider's webs across the vacuum. In that time the photopolymer data conches had snared a good cross-section of the crackly broadcasts of 1921. Now it was time to haul the nets in and weigh anchor.

Now it was jump-time.

They leapt a light-year closer to Earth – a light-year further from their new home on Mimosa IV – and into the radioscape of 1922.

In this manner they would leap-frog towards Earth one light-year at a time, building a library of sounds – and eventually moving pictures – of years past. They could even shoot for important dates.

Oba imagined the jump-ship as a vast vessel pitching up and down on an ocean of history. The radio waves passing by were real waves, and they rocked the vessel according to their cargo. Most were gentle waves: inconsequential news broadcasts; variety shows; melodramas.

At other times the vessel was tossed by great foam-spitting waves that marked momentous events in humankind's past: the harried voice of an announcer telling the world of the great stock market collapse beginning on Black Thursday, October 24, 1929; news of the Manchurian Incident – an explosion of a Japanese-run railway in Manchuria in 1931 – which was a catalyst for World War II; the birth of the Golden Age of Jazz, when Pee Wee Russell and Benny Goodmen aired their 'Chicago style' jazz right across the United States, and marked an era of hope for society's dispossessed.

As the Earth had spun, so the radioscape changed. Four hours after listening to Pittsburgh's KDMA station, the 'scape would fall silent as the vast emptiness of the Pacific Ocean came to bear on their line-of-sight. Six hours later they would hear radio out of Tokyo, then Beijing, Mumbai, Cairo, Rome, Lagos, and a hundred other cities as the rest of the world came and went. The Earth was a spinning wheel of aural fireworks, majestic in its diversity of sounds.

Commander Ikari unearthed an early Louis Armstrong recording, and the great jazz musician's gravel-laden voice filled the jump-ship. It was one of those pieces sung with odd syllables instead of words.

The Commander lightened up, snared in the sheer joy of the music. He joined in with gusto. "Da doo wop dee bee da boo . . . wait till we get this back on Mimosa IV, Oba."

Most of the five hundred and sixty eight colonists had thought they were going back to Earth in two years, five tops. They hadn't brought nearly enough music to sustain a world.

Oba enjoyed the lively, light-hearted sounds, but the song he wanted to hear more than anything came from a later, more somber period, he was sure. As he once again tried – and failed – to dredge up its aching refrains from the silt bed of his mind, melancholy settled over him.

She might be listening to it at this very moment. *Right now.* If he could hear it too, then, even light-years apart, they'd be together in a sense . . . if she was still alive. Not knowing was the hardest part.

A pair of headphones floated nearby. He slipped them on, killing the music. The 1931 archive was almost full and he wanted to hurry-up and finish the year so they could jump another light-year.

Nearer to a time where he might find the song.

Three weeks after Oba had met Lakshmi, he'd taken her up to Martha's Vineyard. It was off-season and they walked along a windswept beach under grey clouds pregnant with rain. A catamaran toiled in the choppy water a few hundred yards out to sea.

"You'll be like the men on that boat," she said. "Too caught up in the moment to notice you've left the rest of Earth behind."

She wore a gray cashmere sweater and an ankle length skirt of the same color. She seemed equally at ease here as in downtown New York.

"Not true. There'll be work to do, but every day on Mimosa IV will remind me that I'm not here."

Sea spray whipped across the beach, and a couple of gulls banked higher, crying as they rose. Oba led Lakshmi away from the water.

"What is it like? The planet, I mean," she asked.

"One and a half times the size of Earth. Hot and humid. Surface is one third water. Vegetation covers most of the bodies of land. Atmosphere is breathable. Much more than that we don't know."

"I'd be terrified." She squeezed her arms around her chest. The first drops of rain started to fall.

"I don't think so. Exploring a new planet pales next to interviewing our Secretary of Defense."

She'd laughed at that. Flung her head back and laughed a natural, healthy laugh. "Humans I can deal with."

"You call that creep human? All those overtures to Taiwan — talking about freedom and democracy and rights just to unsettle China. The guy's a tinderbox. You should see some of the EYES ONLY stuff."

Lakshmi held Oba's eye, thinking. "Interesting."

Oba felt a paralyzing chill. *Was she using him? Feigning romantic interest to get a story?* Before he could say something she was off running along the shore.

He chased her as the heavens opened and unleashed a downpour. By the time they found shelter under the awnings of a dilapidated beach house they were both soaked through.

Lakshmi squeezed out water from her sweater while Oba marched back and forth on the peeling deck work.

"I always wanted to explore an abandoned house," Lakshmi said, shivering. "Let's go-"

"What do you want from me?" Oba said softly. He picked up a pebble and hurled it out to sea, his back to Lakshmi.

"You think I'm using you for a *story?*"

"Are you?" Oba felt his drenched jeans gripping his legs like irons.

She moved in front of him. "You wanna frisk me?" she said, raising her hands above her head. The fabric of her sweater clung tight, revealing the shape of her breasts, her hard nipples. "Well, too bad, spaceman." She stormed off the decking into the squall.

"Wait, Lakshmi, please." The rain drops felt like lances of ice. She kept walking, so he got in front of her and blocked her way. "Wait, please."

She stopped. Strands of her silky black hair stuck to her flushed face and ran into her eyes, but she didn't brush them aside.

"I'm sorry," he said. "I screwed up."

She looked hard into his face. "There's something happening between us, Oba. I felt it the first time I laid eyes upon you."

Oba felt his heart hammering.

She went on. "Your job? Mine? Our histories? None of that matters. But if we don't have trust? Then we're finished before we've even started. Do you understand?"

Oba took Lakshmi's hands in his own. "I understand very well." *He did. All too well.* He gripped her hands tighter. "I just want you to know that I don't do anything half-heartedly, Lakshmi. If I commit to something, I commit to it fully, wholly, passionately. I can't be any other way. And I need you to know-"

"I'm exactly the same." She pulled him close, sheltered against his chest. They kissed a little after, but what Oba remembered the most was her trembling body next to his.

"Listen to this," Commander Ikari said.

He killed the Pinetop Smith number, a boogie-woogie classic with an energetic piano theme, and replaced it with crackling static. Oba bit his tongue. A man had no soul if he could stop a tune like that mid-song.

A thunderous voice with a hint of a lisp boomed around the jump-ship: "— we shall fight on the beaches, we shall fight on the landing grounds, we shall fight in the fields and in the streets, we shall fight in the hills —"

The voice was charismatic, but Oba still felt a deep revulsion towards the rhetoric of politicians. Especially war rhetoric. All he wanted to hear was music. Music was pure and clean; trawling it offered the possibility of finding *the* song. It was nearby. He could feel it.

"You know who this is?" Commander Ikari asked.

"Another fool."

Commander Ikari turned off the recording. "Winston Churchill. He was a great war leader."

"Isn't that a contradiction in terms?"

Commander Ikari turned his back, summoned a vKeyboard and vSplay, and began flicking his fingers as if he were playing an invisible piano.

Maybe I'm being too hard on him. There he is, trapped in this empty, cavernous cathedral of a vessel with the most significant events of the twentieth century rushing past outside, and all his crewmate wants to do is wallow in the music of Fats Waller and Duke Ellington.

Oba tried to make amends. "Do you think what happened was inevitable?"

Commander Ikari spun about. His face was flat and expressionless. "You mean, do I think humans will always succumb to war?"

Oba nodded.

"I don't know, Oba. I don't know – but I have to believe otherwise."

*

Lakshmi's skin was the color of pale caramel. When Oba licked it he tasted the faintest trace of chili. They lay in the bath together, Lakshmi leaning back against Oba's chest, her hair tied up with a pencil.

They'd found a common ground in almost everything: maple pecan pie being better without the cream; the Administration's slashing of the developmental aid budget as dangerously reckless; knowledge of the obscure two-letter words that made playing Scrabble a deliciously Machiavellian game.

The few things they didn't share – favorite cities, musical tastes, appreciation of contemporary art – were undiscovered lands waiting for exploration by the other.

Over her shoulder, Oba was halfway through reading an article about China's naval blockade of Taiwan, when she tossed the paper to the floor.

"When you're there I'd like you to write my name in the sand," she said, splashing lukewarm water up her arms, nearly extinguishing one of the small candles arranged around the bath. "The planet does have sand, doesn't it?"

"It does. I'll write Oba loves Lakshmi."

"And Lakshmi loves Oba."

"I'll be the first interplanetary graffiti artist," he said, biting her neck.

She tried to pull herself up, painfully knocking his knees against the porcelain sides, but she was trapped. "Oh God, you can't go. I won't be able to stand it." She tried to twist about but her hips were locked between his legs. "What if there's an accident? What if the jump-drives fail? What if you fall in love with another woman while you're gone?"

"I don't think Mimosa females are up to much."

"I'm serious." She elbowed him in the stomach, causing him to gasp. "You don't know what might happen. You don't know what effect this planet might have on you."

"It's just work. Off-planet, that's all. After a year – when the colony is well-established – I'll be back."

"It's too long."

"I told you. I don't do things by halves. I've committed to the mission. And I've committed to you."

Lakshmi stretched her arm back, brushed her fingers through his hair. "You bring me such peace, Oba. Peace and joy. I've never felt so . . . happy. You better come back."

"I will," he said.

And he would.

Neither of them could know that she would be the one in danger.

The jump-ship ploughed on through the invisible seas, buffeted by an ever-increasing wash of music, news, interviews, dramas, debates, and commercials. By the time the 1950s were streaming past, television broadcasts were a rich part of the swell.

Commander Ikari slaved one of the vSplays to NBC's transmissions, and, while Oba didn't listen, everything from early westerns to the McCarthy hearings silently flickered in his peripheral vision.

He ignored the visuals, focused on the radio broadcasts.

He heard musical styles flirt with one another like young lovers, consummating their passions in fiery unions. Jazz hit it off with the blues and the fast-paced, driving beat of rhythm and blues was born. Country and western gate-crashed the party and soon rock and roll was the hottest thing in town.

As the world spun he might hear a dozen schools of music – from the fluted-pipes of Muslim qawwalis to the mournful laments of costumed *mariachi* bands.

Oba was swept up in the energy of the time, bopping his head, clapping his hands, and yelling any lyrics he could follow like the Elvis fans he saw on Commander Ikari's vSplay. The constant questing for that one song never went away though, and whether it was Jerry Lee Lewis, or Fats Domino, there was always a bleak, empty place inside.

This was the era he'd find it though.

It was as if he was a musician and it would be himself who finally pulled that song out of the recesses of his mind rather than the whispers of the vacuum. The song was melancholic but hopeful, grand but heartfelt, from an age when people still lived the terrible war in their heads, but smiled at the future. Rockets and whimsy, innocence and love.

He could taste it!

He scoured the airwaves. Every time a disc jockey introduced a track on a likely station, Oba waited with baited breath. The stations multiplied. When he listened to one frequency he found himself terrified he was missing the melody on another. He skipped between the waves like a dog searching for a stick on a wild, wave-racked shoreline.

The song never came.

The last time he'd seen her had been the night of the Leaver's Ball at the Sagan Institute in Washington DC. It was the first – and last – time he'd heard the song. They'd danced alone in the deserted hall, Lakshmi convincing the string quartet to one last request before they packed up.

Afterwards, under the moonlight, they'd walked along the bank of the Potomac. The aroma of cherry blossoms laced the air.

"What happens if you meet someone?" he asked over the gentle whisper of the river. He thought he was asking in jest until the words left his mouth.

"Then I won't have to worry about sneaking around, what with you God knows how many light years away."

Her flippancy stung him. "It might happen."

"I'm not going to meet anyone."

"How do you know?"

"I know."

"How?" he said, too loud. "*How* do you know?"

She stopped, faced him. "You still don't trust me, do you?"

He'd seen hurt in her eyes. He'd apologized, of course, but the damage had been done.

The timing was terrible. Their schedules meant they only exchanged a few cursory voicemails over the following days. A few hours before he left she left a message telling him she'd be waiting for him when he came back.

He left for Mimosa IV before he had a chance to tell her he couldn't wait for that day.

The radioscape intensified into a hyperactive cacophony where once it had been a single, clarion call. With each jump closer to Earth the data conches filled faster and faster, and their time spent in the electromagnetic wash of each year grew shorter and shorter.

Oba didn't sleep.

Commander Ikari told him he looked like shit and should get some rest. He didn't. He spent the endless night squinting at his analytics, listening to the opening bars of the wrong songs before switching frequencies and hunting elsewhere.

Of course, he'd have time to peruse the conches at his leisure when they returned to Mimosa IV, but once there he'd be powerless to change their contents. The thought made him crazy wild.

He tracked the threads of musical history. Rock 'n' roll quarreled and split. Roll slinked away never to be seen again, but rock reinvented itself in a dozen incarnations: folk, psychedelic, progressive, punk, alternative, teen. The cold war came and went. Musical genres fizzed past, their existences shorter than jump-times. Dance, techno, house, garage, drum and bass, trip hop, trance, electrowire, culthead, mirage, ghost, sprint. Music accelerated, bifurcated, ceaselessly recreating itself.

The mission was coming to an end. The love song remained elusive, still lost at sea, smothered by a raging ocean of radio flotsam from wireless podcasts to the most inane implant conversations. It was like searching for a single, unique star in a galaxy of billions.

"That wraps it up," Commander Ikari said not long after they'd jumped into 2029's wash. "We're done. We can go home."

"Not yet. I need more time."

"We're done, Oba. The conches are full."

"I need more time!" He tried to slam his fist against his vSplay, but only succeeded in passing his entire arm straight through the holographic. The light text wobbled then stilled.

"It's over. We're going back." Commander Ikari wheeled about and pushed towards the helm. "Surge blister. Now." After settling into his own cradle, he called forth a vSplay and began inputting the jump-vectors.

Oba looked around frantically. Across the command chamber the bubbled ridges of some Med-X vesicles caught his eye. He floated over to the consumables rack, slyly grabbing one of the vesicles on the way. Back to his Commander, he took a couple of airfoil-shaped pouches and filled them with generous measures of the eye-watering distillate that went for alcohol on Mimosa IV.

"What are you doing, Oba?"

"We have to celebrate, Commander," he said over his shoulder, easing a good dose of the liquid into one of the pouches.

He floated over to Commander Ikari, handed him a drink. The Commander stared at the copper liquid that slid around the sides of the pouch, then brought it up to his nose.

"Not exactly a well-blended malt whiskey," he said, with a look of distaste.

"We make do," Oba said.

Commander Ikari raised his pouch. "To the past – and the future."

Oba echoed the words, then slurped the alcohol down in one long, messy motion, the crude liquid burning his throat. Commander Ikari did likewise.

"I'm sorry," Oba said.

"Sorry for what?"

"The sedative."

The Commander stared at his empty pouch, disbelieving. "You better be . . . be . . ." His voice trailed off into a meaningless slur. A slick of drool trickled from the side of his mouth. His head lolled.

Oba took the pouch from the Commander's hand, made sure the man was comfortable. He drew the vSplay closer, began editing the jump-vectors. 1960. Surely there, if he searched long enough he'd find–

He stopped, finger frozen in the pale white light. *Who am I fooling?* He could go back. Now. She might still be alive . . .

He remembered when they'd jumped back into Earth orbit, sixteen years earlier. First a shared cry of joy at once again laying eyes on that brilliant azure, cloud-flecked marble. Then the cheers dying down, replaced by a growing uneasy chatter as the whole panoply of comm devices, from tightbeam lasers to quantum congloms to microwave radios, failed to detect a single transmission from the usually seething datasphere.

Nothing.

"Talk to me," Flight Administrator Zakaris had growled over Oba's shoulder.

"There's nothing out there, sir."

"How can there be nothing out there? Check your–"

"Wait. I've found a signal." Oba let out a long breath. "It's for us. From UNSA High Command. Decrypting."

A one-time transmitter aboard a ring-fenced commsat squirted a terse message through the jump-ship's comms relay and onto Oba's vSplay. The last few lines drew his eye, brought ice to his heart.

You must return to Mimosa IV immediately. You must never come back. No exceptions. No delays. These are your orders. The fate of our race lies in your hands. God speed.

Oba twisted, watched his superior's face pale, then harden. "Prep for jump," Zakaris said resolutely, although he couldn't hide the tremor in his voice, "we're going back."

Earth had fallen. They called it a soft plague. Who attacked who was unclear, but the results were not.

A self-replicating coded cancer that destroyed every networked computer from sub-cortical implants to supercooled military networks. Auto-dirigibles would've fallen from the sky. Doc-bots would've frozen in the middle of complex surgical procedures. Energy grids would've shutdown. Banking systems would've collapsed.

Civilization reset.

Twelve billion people thrown into a new dark age.

Oba shook away the thoughts, focusing on his hand, motionless in the pale white light. He could go back. She wouldn't be easy to find, if she could be found at all –

Commander Ikari murmured in his unbidden sleep. Oba wasn't only playing with his own life. What would the Commander do back on a transformed Earth? How would life on Mimosa IV change if they lost one of their only three jump-ships? The colony was stable – flourishing even – but even simple tech like ceramo-chitin manufacturing, not to mention sub-baryonic stitching, was decades away.

They might never recovery from such a blow to their collective psyche.

Oba grunted. He'd made his choice.

He sequenced a new jump-vector.

Jump-time.

"Where are we?"

Oba didn't glance away from the raft of vSplays that hovered around him like the individual lenses of a gigantic, shimmering compound eye. He knew Commander Ikari would come to eventually.

"Or maybe I should ask *when* are we?"

Oba didn't answer, his gaze sliding between the vSplays according to some unfathomable, stochastic routine. An over tanned man on the Crazy Consumers channel demonstrated how to use an automated-wardrobe. An Asian woman in a bright yellow jacket talked animatedly in front of a Buddhist shrine. A dour-faced politician with a Houses of Parliament backdrop droned monotonously on BBC America.

Beyond the low blabber of the channels, he heard Commander Ikari working himself out of his surge blister. He sensed him drift closer, hang in mid-air over Oba's right shoulder. He carried a faint whiff of sweat and alcohol.

There was note of dread in the Commander's next words. "We've jumped to the day it happened, haven't we?"

"A few days before." An adequate safety margin. The soft plague was still more than seventy-two hours away for the tanned man and the Asian woman and the surly politician. Nothing in their demeanor gave any clue as to what they would soon experience.

"Why?"

Oba began killing the vSplays, one lens of the compound eye at a time. He spoke slowly. "In New York there lived a woman named Lakshmi Rawaldini. She worked as a journalist for BBC America. She was very good at her job. She earned high praise from her superiors and great respect from her colleagues."

Only a lone vSplay floated ahead of Oba now. A female presenter stood in a bright studio unveiling demographic graphics with a light wand. BBC America.

"Her dream was to one day present the news. That day never came for her." Oba extinguished the final vSplay. "Lakshmi Rawaldini was my lover."

Oba felt Commander Ikari's heavy hand clutch his shoulder. "We all lost someone that day."

Oba stared at the empty space in front of him.

Months later, Oba sat alone on one of the bloated roots of one of Mimosa IV's most iconic pieces of flora: the crystal tree. He liked to sit under the sway of the tree's white shard-like leaves, feel its rubbery bark beneath. A breeze rippled through the foliage that he still found so alien, and the air carried a sweetly laced scent reminiscent of juniper.

When he wasn't working he'd come here for an hour or two, listen to the songs they'd captured. He had tens of thousands from the 1950s alone.

At this moment, cradled in the gentle melody and rich baritone of a Nat King Cole number, he felt sleepy. He closed his eyes, drifted into daydreams . . . and suddenly the voice he'd been seeking for years was in the air, filling every word with yearning.

See the pyramids along the Nile . . .

His heart soared.

In his daydream Lakshmi was back his arms. They rocked together to the song.

"I should've stayed," Oba whispered, inhaling her scent, her rawness. "Why didn't I stay?"

She put a finger to his lips, then pressed herself against his chest. He held her tighter, losing himself in her.

Just remember till you're home again
You belong to me.

As the song ended, the gentle rustle of leaves brought him back to the present. He was back on Mimosa IV once again.

A truth came to him with the force of a knife to the lungs. The search for the song had been his shield all these years. A shield to protect him from the utter bleakness he now felt having finally found it, heard it, lived it.

Under the bloated alien sun, he whimpered, heartbroken.

Deep Field
Sean Martin

I: *A Discourse on the Eighth and Ninth*

I was in the front room of Prolands in Hampstead. St Andrew's abided under an imminent dusk; dark birds circled its spire. Beyond the church, I could see a stand of beech trees gently shed their golden leaves onto the banks of the bathing pond. Governesses hurried children homeward for tea and cake. And then came that unmistakable hum. I searched the massing clouds and then saw them: a wave of zeppelins coming in from the south. I reached for the opium.

Captain Dudley came into the room. "James, we're under attack. We must start the Ritual now," he said, and then nodded toward the opium pipe. "Do you mind?"

"Not at all," I said. I handed him the opium pipe and he inhaled. He handed it back to me. I got a good lung full. The room was becoming vague, although the prospect of imminent bombardment kept me lucid. Dudley went to the gramophone and put a recording of Hans Richter conducting Bruckner's Eighth Symphony. I squinted through the brass telescope that sat on a tripod near the window. The zeppelins loomed nearer as the first scratchy bars of the Bruckner made themselves present in the room. I could make out markings on their sides, numbers and black crosses.

"The *Apocalyptic* symphony," Dudley said. "I think it's appropriate, given our situation." I looked at him and nodded. "Are you ready?"

"I think so," I replied, feeling uncomfortably amorphous from the drug. The opium helped in the Rituals, especially at times of emergency, like this, when we had had no time to get into the right mindset through meditation and breathing exercises. Drugs were the necessary short cut. Dudley handed me a jewelled circlet of battered, dull gold. We nicknamed it the Crown of Lights, a slightly sinister thing of unknown provenance. Stories varied as to who had originally acquired it: looted from a monastery in Tibet by Younghusband, or found in a fleamarket in Cairo by Aleister Crowley and then accorded high ritual status. It didn't matter; it's what we've always used, and it had acquired its own mystique over the years. I placed it on my head and got down on my knees before Dudley. "My Father, yesterday you promised that you would bring my mind into the Eighth and afterwards into the Ninth. You said that this is the way of tradition."

"My Son, this is indeed true," Dudley intoned. "For when I conceived from the fountain that flowed to me, I gave birth."

"Then, my Father, I have many brothers and sisters, if I am to be numbered among the offspring. Your word is true, Father; it has no refutation. My Father, begin the discourse on the Eighth and the Ninth, and include me also with my brothers and sisters."

The Bruckner was slowly building. In all my years of training, this was the most difficult movement to get over, especially in Richter's version. I had heard legends of him conducting at the Royal Albert Hall where people were so overcome by the music they were weeping and staggered out into Kensington's night air, their very selves annihilated. I wanted that. I wanted annihilation, anything to get me out of this world. Out of existence.

Dudley put his hand on my head. "Let us pray, my Son, to the Father of the universe, with your brothers and sisters who are my offspring, that he may give the spirit of – "

Dudley was cut short by an explosion. It shook the room, and we were flung across the floor like dolls. The cabin pressure alarm started to wail. Another bell rang from somewhere in the corridor outside. Looking up, I could see the windows flickering like a silent movie screen. Hampstead's green and pleasant land and the zeppelins were replaced by an intense whiteout, from which emerged the image of a silver and black ship, a lean intergalactic sprinter.

"Fuck!" I whispered. It was the *Dominica*: our doppelgänger, our dark, obsessive twin. She had caught up with us at last, and was greeting us with cannon fire. There was a pressure blast. The noise went to the inside of my brain. I covered my ears. Blood flowed from my eyes and my head felt like it was compressing under Jupiter's gravity.

In that split second afterwards, all I could hear was breathing, but I was not sure whose it was.

I heard Dudley whisper, "Eloquence". It was the word he was trying to say when we were attacked. It was the last word he ever spoke.

II: *Strange Days*

The Hampstead I noted in my diary, this diary of our last days I've left for posterity, was an illusion. A Lord Kitchener-wants-you, cricket-on-the-green, *Dad's Army* England; a HoloDeck game. We liked games. Helped pass the time when you're in deep space, especially the distances we've come. No one had ever travelled further, using wormholes for our crazy, epic zigzagging away from the *Dominica* and her taskmasters. Sometimes I preferred the HoloDeck games to reality; sometimes I had trouble telling them apart. Sometimes I just forgot about it all, and just enjoyed the ride. As a song in one of my playlists had it, *This is the strangest life I've ever known.*

We were the last of a kind, and we'd been running for hundreds of years. Or what seemed like hundreds of years: using wormholes the way we did threw your sense of time completely. Roma had put a bounty on our heads, and we had the high and mighty of every galaxy after us. Or, more often than not, bounty hunters who were just as desperate and mad as we were. But we had the last Krasnikov hybrid sprinter of her class, the *Theia*, whom we liberated from the test fields on Voss Eigen back when I was still just a rookie, learning about why we were all, as a community, heading towards the Eighth and the Ninth. She was hybrid as in part machine, part sentient. As with much else, I never did figure it out. I've felt like I've always been on *Theia*. I received a new education aboard her, a new life. I love her, and I love how she reacts, to me, to each of us, like a lover. We named her after the Titan Theia, from the Greek myths. She was the lover and sister of Hyperion, God of Light. Her name meant *the far-shining one*, and she was said to have given birth to the Sun. We thought the name apt, given our beliefs, and she seemed to like it.

III: *Damage Report*

McNamara paced on the bridge. She was a big woman, and her flight suit made her seem all the more solid and powerful. She reminded me of prize fighters I'd seen on the moons of Antares, in those hellish shanty towns set up for the miners, where all you did was dig and drink, and then try and fight your way out. McNamara gave us all sombre looks. Me, our pilots Krishna and Mouse, systems admin Nix and the Count, our chief engineer. "I have to inform you that we've lost Captain Dudley. I shall now be assuming command on this trip. Or what's left of it."

We nodded.

"Dudley's body is in cryo, but I doubt if there's anything that can be done to bring him back. Unless where we're going has some surprises in store for us."

"Was it the *Dominica?*" I asked.

"Yes, it was the *Dominica*," McNamara said. "She must have calculated our position from entropic algorithms. Or just gotten very lucky."

"I thought it was her," I said. The *Dominica* was the very last ship still on our tail, Roma's very own hit squad.

"I thought we'd shaken them off in the D80s," Nix said.

"Scariest ride in the funfair," Krish said, trying to lighten the mood. He'd taken us through the D80s, quasars dotted with nova clusters – remnants of four galaxies that were being torn apart by gravity storms – and it had been hell to get out in one piece.

"You didn't do all the driving," Mouse said. "I was there for some of it." She poked her tongue out at Krish. Typical Mouse: petite (hence the name), crazy; every day was April Fool's for her. She had *Reality Sucks* written on her helmet.

"Their pilots must be as good as you two," McNamara said. "And got them through those clusters. They're still on our tail and, as we now know, still want our blood. How are the systems?"

Nix checked her screens. "We've lost some of the external cloaking. So we're visible. And vulnerable."

"The Dorms?"

Nix pulled up more data. "They're OK. Everyone's sleeping like babes."

McNamara turned to the Count and arched a questioning brow.

"It's going to take a few days," the Count said, chewing gum thoughtfully. "Unless we can give the old girl some TLC."

McNamara looked at me. I was still in my HoloDeck gear – plus-fours and tweed, although my decorum was sadly depleted by blood, dust and scorch marks. I looked like I'd wandered into the wrong party. "Can you render your services, James?"

I nodded. "I'll go see the Elect."

"Good. Get to work everyone. We're going to be passing the last known solar system out here, G32W, in 16 hours, and after that, we'll be near our Novikov co-ordinates. We need to be ready by then."

"Yellow Brick Road, here we come," said Krish and Mouse gave him a high five. It was time to go to work.

IV: *The Elect*

We like to work to music. Our people have always valued creativity in all its forms. We believe, unlike the *Dominica* and Roma, that it is the way to the divine. Or, I could also say that the divine is more fully present in us when we are creative. And all art, as they say, aspires to the condition of music, which is nothing other than the condition of the divine, our God of Light. So we are all writers, singers, musicians, actors, jugglers, clowns, jongleurs, minstrels, bards and troubadours. Some nights, when we know we're safely on our own in the void of deep space, we let our hair down. Song, dance, colour: our very own renaissance fair. Roma stood opposed to all this; it was the black iron prison of the closed, fearful mind. And there were few things they hated more than people who did not obey them.

Work music tended to be loud: guitar-driven or industrial, something to get the blood up. The Count had a fondness for The Who; for Mouse, Nurse With Wound did the trick. Nix and McNamara claimed to like everything, as long as the job in hand got done. Music for the Rituals, on the contrary, was quiet: plainchant, polyphony, whatever the inductee liked best. With Dudley it was Beethoven; for me, Bruckner. The Elect, who nourished the ship with intimate care, preferred drones or sitars. Something Indian, repetitive.

The Elect were just that: above us in terms of our religion. Our priests and leaders. We were the Listeners. We listen to the teaching of the Elect. We were soldiers of the soul, soldiers of *gnosis*; in our dreams, we sailed on Lightships of the Pure. I'm a Sethian, who trace their lineage back to the children of Adam and Eve; Seth was the brother Cain didn't kill. We were the visionaries, the mystics, halfway to being Elect. I was the only Sethian on *Theia*, which means I had certain duties that the others didn't.

The Elect stayed mainly in their small suite of rooms a few floors down and back from the bridge. For a long time they had been in the ship's Attic, their chambers glass-roofed so they could meditate on what we were fleeing fast away from: galaxies, nebulae, clusters, countless worlds. But a few close run-ins with the *Dominica* had made the Attic an untenable place for such valuable people, so we suggested that they moved to reinforced rooms near the heart of the ship. Without them, we'd be like children without parents.

Anna answered the door. She was in her usual lilac toga, head shaved, eyes piercing. I've never been able to figure out how old she is – sometimes she's like a teenager, other times a crone. I don't know how much regen she or Anders have done. I'm only on my second, but some of the others are older. Dudley was nearly 500 (and used to joke he didn't look a day over 350), so he must've been through 7 or 8 regens by the time the *Dominica*'s cannons did for him.

"James James," she said. "Come in."

Their rooms were lilac, too, and low-lit. You couldn't read in that light, but it was good for meditation. Or sleep. Anna turned to me. "And what can we do for you, my dear Listener?"

"TLC," I said. "To help speed the repairs."

Anna nodded. She knew I was – unlike the others – of the Race of Seth. Pure blood. Pure everything. (Except my personal history, which was a little chequered. I'll come to that in a moment.) "She needs love. Anders is with her now." Anna nodded toward a door, the inner sanctum of the Seeding Room.

I frowned. Surely the Elect, unlike the Listeners and Sethians, were not allowed physical relationships?

Anna read my thoughts. "He talks to her. He's a good comforter."

The Seeding Room door opened, and Anders walked out. He was almost identical to Anna, the shaved head, the piercing eyes, but taller. Anna explained my presence. Anders looked at me and nodded.

"She needs you, James. She has been asking for you. She even sang a song for you."

V: *Seeding*

The Seeding Room was a small steel chamber with a small fountain trickling water down out of one wall. There was also a chaise longue and a fruit bowl. I'd often thought it was an attempt at an ancient Roman townhouse, some sort of Villa of the Mysteries for the intergalactic refugee. Rubbery tendrils with gaping mouths snaked out of the fountain. They reminded me of seaweed. I put on the preprogrammed blastgoggles and earbuds. Bruckner's Eighth greeted me again. But apart from that, I had no opium, or any other enhancer.

So. In this most desperate of escapes, I now had to show my love in the most obvious way. Such is the nature of *Theia* that she could transform human body fluids into the fuel she needed to keep speeding us on our way, further towards the deep field. She knew about Mouse and I, so the goggles and headset showed me virtual Mouses. Sometimes, when I've had to do this before, I've had images come up from the past. E in particular. We met in 1967, when I was working at the British Library. I was 24, she was 16. Well, nearly 16. She had run away from the family home in Cambridge and was in the big city big time, discovering all life had to offer. She discovered me and soon we were offering each other all we had. Her laugh was infectious. Her tits were amazing. And she introduced me to Pink Floyd. We went to the 14 Hour Technicolour Dream at Ally Pally. Things were never quite the same again; reality had shifted. In retrospect, this was good grounding for my later training with Sethian mystics and teachers. After all, E had given me plenty of experience when it came to altered states of consciousness. You might say it's become my one true calling.

But now, in my goggles, it was Mouse. There she was, in all her shaven, pierced and tattooed glory. The blastgoggles beamed into me the feelings I needed to give *Theia* what she wanted. I eased myself into one of her tendrilly mouths, and she had all of me. I'm sure at that moment, I could hear a woman singing somewhere, softly.

VI: *A Holiday Camp with a Difference*

I came out of the Seeding Room and the Elect's quarters to the unmistakable strains of The Who's *Tommy*. Work mode was still in full force. The Count nearly ran into me.

"Good morning, Campers!", he said, mimicking the Who song. "*Hard* work, was it?"

"Very funny," I said. He disappeared down the corridor smirking. He liked wordplay. His ship title, Chief Engineer, didn't last long before he changed it to Chief Buccaneer, which he felt to be more fitting a man of his piratical proclivities. His real name was Eric Geiger, hence Geiger Counter, and finally Count, or the Count, as if he were an aristo. But he's not. Like the rest of us, he's a fugitive. An outcast with an attitude.

Nix came up from the Dorms. "How are they?" I asked. We had fifty fellow travellers with us in suspended animation, fellow dissenters who were dreaming the trip away.

"Good. All soundly asleep. You look like you could do with a kip yourself," she smiled. "We all know what you've been up to."

She was right. I was tired after my encounter with *Theia*, and made my way back to my room. I recalled my former life, centuries ago, before we slipped down the rabbit holes of time, and what it was like to be with someone. E. And then these bastards on *Theia* introduced themselves to me, telling me I was a chosen one, of the Great Race of Seth. I had been helping organise a conference on the Dead Sea Scrolls and heretical religions at the British Library in 1968 when the very people we were talking about showed up in a spaceship. I seriously thought Syd Barrett was probably saner than I was at that point. Was there something in the water? Or something in me? And that was the last I saw of London. To be honest, I was glad to be out of the place, although I did miss E. Christ almighty. I told them I needed her, ranted and raved about love and sex and drugs. They told me I had religious potential, and put me in one of their sleep pods. I spent months (or was it only days?) in a weird country house in Sussex. Runhill Court. They trained me there. I met Dudley and forgot, for the time being, about E.

I slept and dreamed of the crazy times. There were times we weren't travelling, making necessary pit stops to overhaul *Theia*, or raising funds to carry on. This was where the Count came into his own as a buccaneer, swindling and defrauding as he went, cutting a lucrative swathe across fifty galaxies. In my dream, he had a peg leg and eye-patch, just like a real pirate on the Spanish Main. Mouse, our other loosest cannon, had spent time running an Ice Bar on Andromeda for Offworld entrepreneurs; in reality it was a high-class clip joint, making a million clicks a month from her girls. The dream showed her working shows on feelgood ships running high-pressure booze cruises through Jupiter's atmos, 1000 miles down. I saw her ship heading through the Great Red Spot; Mouse was wearing a party hat, loving the maelstrom outside as if it were nothing more than a high tide in autumn. And then she turned into E, peachy, free in a Cambridge April, smiling with those big dark eyes. And all around us the doll's house darkness of Syd Barrett, and he's whispering to us, *Set the controls for the heart of the sun.*

I was woken by a thudding on my door. "Come in," I said, not knowing where I was.

It was Nix. The work rota had made her ebony skin glisten. "Red giant outside! And it's fucking huge!"

I was on my feet and following her down the corridor before I knew anything else. My god, the things we've seen.

The bridge was bathed in the red glow of an evening unlike others. The Count had Ray-Bans and a cowboy hat on. Mouse sported pink tail-fin sunglasses, a leftover from her Jupiter days. They went well with her Mohican haircut. Everyone looked at the main screen, marvelling at a star that would make Antares look small. The opening bars of Bruckner's Ninth kicked in. I smiled. Someone had left my playlist running. It went well with the view: nuclear reactions, hundreds of millions of miles of them. Ironic, really, given that we got into the deep field via the constellation of Fornax, which means 'furnace'. (Or, I should say, the ultra deep field, where we now were, amongst the oldest, remotest stars from earth. Stars that were formed when the universe was very young, the first travellers away from the centre of all things out toward the great unknown.) The star was a beauty. Even the Count seemed impressed, chewing his gum more thoughtfully than usual. In a million years or less, this big old girl would be a white dwarf twenty thousand times smaller than she was now, her fires dulled forever. But by then, we'll all be long gone.

Mouse stepped up and put her arm around me. "She's dying," she said quietly, looking at the star as if it were a family pet.

McNamara turned to me and smiled. She had a good smile, which belied her size. "James, you need to do the Ritual."

"What do you mean?" I asked.

"If you can reach the Eighth, we can relay it via the Crown of Lights to the HoloDeck and the screen in here. Should help everyone prepare themselves for when we reach the beginnings of the Ninth. You are Sethian, after all. The seers."

"Any news on the *Dominica*?" I asked, glancing nervously at *Theia's* screens.

"She's offline," Nix said. "Probably behind a nova cloud. MKV 347's close. Pretty much the only place to hide out here. But they won't hide for long."

I nodded. "So its back to Hampstead?"

McNamara nodded. "Fraid so. You'll have to have a woman as your Father. We're a bit short of available men."

Krish and the Count gave me looks. I shrugged.

"No problem," I said. "As long as they can put up with Bruckner."

VII: *A Brief History of the Manichaean Heresy*

I must leave a record of this before I do the Ritual for what will probably be the last time. I want you to know what the Eighth and the Ninth are, and what we have been running from for these last hundreds of centuries. We had been in existence long before they came for me in 1968, when E and I were entwined to the sounds of *The Piper at the Gates of Dawn*. We were in existence before the

Victorians said that there would be no more inventions after 1900 because, by then, they would have everything they would ever need. Bless their little cotton child-and-country-abusing socks. They had not intuited that they, as human beings, were on the edge of eternity. Instead they ignored the best that was in them, the shard of divine light, and fed their young men to the mud of the Somme and Passchendaele.

Yes, the edge of eternity, which is the same as saying the edge of death. What we've been running from. And it's not the Kaiser this time. Come on, what century are you reading this in? Surely you must know, now, who we are? No? I will tell you, one last note before we are lost forever. Or, if we are not lost, we will begin again, new Columbuses in a new universe.

We came into the world in the third century CE. Our leader, Mani, the Blessed One, had a great vision of us all moving closer together, all humans as one family on our little blue planet. He came from a sect called the Cathars, the Pure Ones. He knew the words of Jesus, and how the Church Fathers had corrupted them. He knew the words of the Buddha, and how all life is suffering, but we all possess the means of escape. A means within us. He knew the words of Zarathustra, of how the Light and the Dark are in continual conflict. He knew how we leave this world – whatever world we are on at the time – he knew of the Soulships and their flight to the moon, that Ship of Death, and how they head then towards the Light along rivers dug in the cosmos. That was how he described them in the year 260, before the rich and powerful silenced him. Christ was only on the cross for 6 hours, tops; Mani had 26 days of it in that prison cell in Babylon. That's how powerful his message was. They feared him much more than Jesus. And when the blessed Mani was in the Light, our People had a thousand years on Earth of persecution. We fled east, to China, and then north, into the Mongol steppe. Our greatest teacher in the west, St Augustine, betrayed us after going mad in a garden in Milan. Evil children whispered to him from beyond the wall, tempting him over to Roma's way of thinking. We made sure our children kept their silence when playing outdoors, and taught them to stop their ears lest whispering voices summon them to the other side of that wall, and we lost them.

Rivers in the Cosmos, Mani called them. We know them as wormholes, Einstein-Rosen bridges, white holes. That's how we've escaped, hop-scotching across time and space into the ultra deep field, thirteen billion light years from Earth. Thirteen billion light years away from Roma and all she represents. Now we are finally at the Edge, the Fulcrum, and the bastards are still with us. But the *Theia* is faster than the *Dominica*; as soon as we hit our Novikov coordinates, we'll be gone. They will never follow; they're scared of what's out there. We know: it's the Ninth sphere, spoken of so long ago by our forebears. And the Ninth is the edge of Heaven.

VIII: *Late Heavy Bombardment*

I was in my room, changing from my flight suit into a new set of tweeds. You couldn't do the Ritual without dressing up, it was all part of the game. And then the lights went out. Or at least, that was my memory of it. First the dark, then the explosions. The *Dominica* was back. I held onto a hand rail on the wall, bracing myself for more. Nothing. Not even music. Just the hum of the *Theia*, her heartbeat. I scrabbled around in the dark for a helmet. Putting it on, I activated its light. I'd have to take it off for the Ritual, but it might help keep me alive until then. *Theia* occasionally needed my seed, but the Ritual needed my head.

The Crown of Lights, as we dubbed our antique tiara, had had its jewels replaced with small diamond transmitters. Sensors on the inside of the crown touched my head, and what was in my head would end up on the screen, via the diamonds: the state of my soul, the soul of the universe, or a glimpse of the World of Light. It all depended on the Ritual. We had many rituals, most written down centuries ago. I was both the conduit for higher worlds, higher spheres, and a lucky mascot. And the Elect's pupil. I wondered whether Anna and Anders were OK when further cannon fire rocked the room, propelling me towards the wall at speed.

I don't know how long I was out for, but the helmet had saved my life. The next thing I knew, I could hear machine gun fire coming from the corridor. I had the sudden feeling that we had ghosts aboard. I grabbed the nearest weapon, which turned out to be a rusty Mauser from the HoloDeck, and ran out.

The Count was out there, decked in body armour, with one of the big assault weapons mounted on a tripod. Nix had a gun in each hand.

"They're trying to gatecrash via teleport," the Count said. "Last ditch attempt. They must be getting desperate. Unless they want to read us the Last Rites. When they come through, we blast them to fuck."

I nodded. We always liked a good shootout. It was another game to us by now. We'd almost forgotten we could get killed at any moment. We watched the corridor as its empty space grew fuzzy. Two armed men appeared. They flickered on and off, coming into reality and then out of it again like the image on a badly tuned monitor. The Count and Nix donned infrared goggles. The commandos came in again, and the Count either screamed or said something. I couldn't hear over the volley of gunfire that had turned the corridor into a meltchamber of white light and white noise. My Mauser was useless, no better than a cap gun. Smoke was everywhere, the heat from the guns tangible.

They stopped firing. The Count scanned the smoke.

The atmosphere in the corridor began to clear, and I could see two bodies lying at odd angles. Odd because pieces of them had been blown off by the cannon.

The Count stepped forward, inspecting the *Dominica*'s hitmen. "They're cat food," he said.

IX: *Tales from Turfan*

As you might have guessed, we're the crazies. The lunatic fringe of the Manichaean faith. The rest of them are back there, somewhere, making their homes on obscure, peaceful worlds untouched by the taint of intergalactic, inter-species politics. Stay out of trouble could be their motto. But it was never Mani's. You couldn't keep the man down.

He told a story once, found by some German archaeologists when they were digging at a ruined monastery in a Chinese backwater called Turfan around 1900. These were the Manichaean Dead Sea Scrolls, the Master's works, all of them mildewed and moth-eaten. But they could reconstruct this:

In the beginning, there was Light and Dark. The Dark attacked the Light because it was jealous. Ambitious, greedy, insecure, *agitated*: the way politicos and businessmen are. The God of Light emanated the Primal Man, the ultimate superhero, to defend the Light; but instead, he committed the world's first act of military incompetence, being defeated by the Arch-Devil with fog and scorching heat (think surface of Venus, or any given Gulf War). The Primal Man prayed for release, and the Friends of Light and the Messenger, created to rescue the Primal Man's soul, swung into action. The Messenger distracted the Dark Lord's minions, the Archons, by splitting himself into many different men and women, who proceeded to seduce the Archons.

(Kinky stuff for a creation myth, huh? That's probably why I'm a born Manichaean, given my relationship with E and *Theia*.) The Archons got so aroused they accidentally let some of the Primal Man's soul go, enabling the Messenger to take it back to the world of Light. Some of the women Archons, however, got so hot and bothered they gave give birth to abortions, which become the material world. Our Earth. A mish-mash of Light and Dark, hopelessly intermingled. It is the lowest sphere of creation, while the Eighth and Ninth are the highest.

The Arch-Devil feared losing the remaining soul-portions, and embedded them in two mockeries of the God of Light, Adam and Eve. When they had children, Cain, Abel, Seth and the rest of the human race, those Light particles got further dissipated, making the Messenger's job of retrieval all the harder. All of nature, although the work of the Dark Lord, has the Light, or soul, within it. Mani predicted an apocalypse: the Hunter of Light, the final emanation, would appear at the end of time to rescue the final pieces of Light, and imprison forever the last shards of Dark. Eternity will begin then, but we hoped to get there sooner.

Our logic was simple: the material universe is inescapably evil. Therefore, as good Manichaeans, we had to get out of it. Hence our lengthy hop-scotch into the ultra-deep field. We know more about wormholes than anyone else, and put that to good use, *Theia* becoming the needle in the quantum haystack (her class of ship's nicknamed a corkscrew, and for good reason). Once we're beyond the earliest known galaxy, G32W, we are out of the known universe. Or well on the way to the big bang, depending on how you look at it. Either way, we're out of the clutches of the *Dominica*, and Roma. As another song from my druggy London days put it, *Time we left this world today.*

X: *Grantchester Meadows*

Nix and I were back at Prolands. Hampstead lay under a blanket of snow.

"Someone's feeling chilly," I said, putting on the Crown.

"Maybe *Theia* is," Nix replied. "It's almost absolute zero outside, after all."

She was right. The only sources of heat out here were from the occasional red giant, whose heat was beginning to fail them, despite their size. I brought up the actual view from the HoloDeck. The screen showed us the saddest of sights: a binary star, white dwarfs both. They were the first stars ever to have flared in this part of space, amongst the earliest nuclear reactions in the universe, when created matter first began to play. I shook the sentiment out of my head and brought the view of Hampstead back.

Nix consulted her notes. She did not know the Ritual by heart, but it wouldn't matter. The words, the play, were what mattered. She would assume the role of the Father, and we could summon up the Messenger and the Friends of Light to help us onto the Yellow Brick Road and into the Ninth sphere.

"The Bruckner record's broken, sir." She said, holding up one half of the record. "Looks like your opium pipe fell on it during the last attack."

"Is the Beethoven there? The *Ode to Joy?*"

She flicked through the record rack and nodded.

"You know it's actually not about joy, but about freedom? Might be better than Bruckner's *Apocalyptic.* It'll do us. Let's get started," I said, and lit the opium pipe.

On the bridge, everyone was strapped in, helmeted up. Strains of Beethoven filtered through from the HoloDeck. Everyone was at their stations, expectant.

"G32W passing," Mouse said. "Last house on the left. Looks like the lights are out, and no-one's home. Goodbye cruel universe."

"Anyone picking up the *Dominica?*", McNamara asked, scanning her own screen for our nemesis.

"I think *Dominica's* fallen back," said Nix.

"We're clear here," Mouse said.

The Count squinted at his screen. McNamara held her breath. And then he said, "Empty sky."

"Finally,"McNamara said. "Finally gone."

"Yellow Brick Road's coming up, boss," said Krish.

"Move up to three-quarters light speed," McNamara said.

Krish and Mouse saluted, increasing the ship's speed. Krish turned to Mouse and said, "We ain't going to be in Kansas anymore."

She smiled.

I was on my knees in front of Nix with my eyes closed, the Crown of Lights on my turned head, my cheek pressed against her belly. The pungent smell of opium lay heavy in the room. On the record, the singers of the Berlin Philharmonic belted out Schiller's lines:

Brothers, above the starry firmament

A loving Father must surely dwell.
Do you fall down, O millions?
Are you aware of your Creator, world?
Seek Him above the starry firmament!
For above the stars He must dwell.

Nix and I chanted, our voices an odd unison:

"Lord, grant us wisdom from your power that reaches us, so that we may describe to ourselves the vision of the Eighth and the Ninth. We have already advanced to the Seventh, since we are pious and walk in your law. And your will we fulfil always. For we have walked in your way, and we have renounced evil, so that your vision may come. Lord, grant us the truth in the image. Allow us through the spirit to see the form of the image that has no Deficiency, and receive the reflection of the Pleroma from us through our praise. Acknowledge the spirit that is in us. For from you the universe received soul –"

Nix stopped. I wasn't aware something was wrong at first. "James," she said. I opened my eyes and noticed that the view of Hampstead was fading out. I could feel the crown humming on my head, its dusty jewels sparking into strange life.

"Is it the *Dominica* coming back? I thought we'd lost them."

We watched as the familiar faded from view.

And then E appeared on the screen. Or it appeared to be E. It was Cambridge, 1969. She was in Grantchester Meadows, wearing a white dress with red flowers on it. She knew she was being filmed, and smiled coyly for the camera; it looked like one of our old Super-8 home movies. For one terrible moment, I thought she might slip out of her dress, and the whole crew would see her naked.

"Who is she?"

"A Friend of the Light," I said, banishing thoughts of a naked E from my mind. And then E changed, or Cambridge changed, fading like Edwardian Hampstead. I knew what this was. All was now white, E changing into a serene, noble being. Someone who looked like Anna, or Anders, I couldn't quite tell. They seemed to be both male and female, alive and dead at the same time. Was it a Friend of the Light, or even the Messenger himself? We all watched, Nix and I on the HoloDeck, the others on the bridge, as we passed the Fulcrum that marked the edge of the universe. Before us, all was white. Was it the light of the Big Bang? Or Mani's world, the Light world of the Ninth and higher spheres, that had been waiting patiently for us since the beginning of time? Whose game was this? Whose dream? I could no longer tell as we headed into it at near light speed, and the face on the screen once more became E, and she waved goodbye.

Singing Breath into the Dead
L.L. Hannett

It is twilight in the upworld: the time of seduction, of passing thresholds, of becomings. The sun, though setting and veiled with battle smoke, is much yellower than Swan expected. The rubble-strewn path is a stream of chalk mortar, russet bricks, rich charcoal beneath her bare feet. Scattered shards of glass are redder than the painted spots on her skin, bluer than the shadows beneath her eyes. Grass, which is always pale turquoise or sepia in the faded pictures she lovingly studies, now shines the same green as her irises. Every colour is saturated, outlandish; even commonplace grey zings beyond her optical range. Up here, grey is so vivid it hums.

Swan shivers as she moves away from the vaulted tunnels of her childhood, takes her first steps above ground. She and the rest of Thevessels, with their faux-freckled complexions and fairy-floss waists, are laced into white corsets, robed in sheer fabric and begartered with lingerie ribbons. Soft veils fall before their kohl-rimmed eyes, which are kept modestly lowered, as Themothers lead them up into an unfamiliar shade of evening.

The sky seems limitless despite its bracketing clouds. Leafless bushes click-clack in the wind, their branches twitching like mandibles as the women brush past. This year's Ladyday girls swarm out and around the downworld's largest trapdoor, a din of nervous giggles and snippets of well-rehearsed tunes. They won't venture any further without Themothers' permission. Staccato echoes of artillery in the distance ricochet around the group, bouncing along the pockmarked asphalt that had, until that moment, been the only sky Swan had ever known.

"Will you pass through the gate?" Hermother asks, offering Swan the first of two tickets. It is small and faded, paper worn thin from generations of use. Working her tongue around her mouth, Swan tries to dredge up the moisture speech requires. It is useless. Swallowing hard, she quietly takes the lucky scrap from Hermother's outstretched hand. Her stomach roils; her throat convulses and throbs. The taste of pent-up worry is thick on her tongue.

"Will you lay yourself bare, fresh skin to fresh earth? Will you dig for your unborn soul?" *Nod*, Swan mutely replies, heart palpitating. *Nod, nod.*

Themothers tut-tut her lack of response. Swan had hoped they'd mistake silence for excitement, for speechless anticipation, for awe at finally being chosen. Instead, Hermother's tone is clipped, irritated. *You know what's at stake*, her expression screams. Of course Swan knows. Of course.

"Will you pay the toll and absorb new life?"

Nod, nod.

With well-practiced movements, Themothers circle around the duo to conclude the ritual. All the women take it in turns to add ochre dots to the girl's fair cheeks, to share choruses of birthing songs, to infuse her skin with the expectation of pregnancy. Their gestures and incantations temporarily transform her: no longer Swan, today she has become Avessel.

Hermother presents the second ticket. Smiling, the matriarchs turn, and wait to hear Swan sing the accepted refrain.

They give her more than enough time, but their patience is rewarded with silence. Swan's lips quiver while she tries to convey, with devout gaze and solemnly clasped hands, that she won't disappoint them. That she will contribute, just as they have, just as all the downworlders have. That she will transcend her skills as a painter and today praise Themarys by becoming Amother. She wants to say she *will*.

She can't.

Thevessels, ushered away from the trapdoor, look eagerly ahead. But Swan lingers at Hermother's side, hoping to catch a glimpse of encouragement, a sign that she'll be welcomed home soon. Any sign. Hermother's features, once so nurturing, might be made of stone for all the hope they impart. The girl watches, unblinking, until the door clangs shuts behind Hermother's perfectly straight back.

A sulphurous breeze roughens Swan's skin into goose bumps; unbidden tears well in her eyes. *May it be to me as you have said*, she thinks. Still unable to give her answer voice.

The sunset is too bright. Whoever is responsible for painting this sky should've invested in a stick of amber Conté. Swan shields her eyes. This palette is too gold, the application too heavy. Its weight presses on her like a stranger's unwanted embrace. She looks at her hands, inspects the rims of her nails that still bear the stains of her trade. Patches of brown, deep green, and burgundy: far more fitting colours with which to honour Themarys. She has used them all, mixed their tints out of mushroom ridges, kaolin, mould and iron oxide; sanguine dyes for the septet of Marys adorning her chamber walls, drawn on old sheets of newspaper.

Swan yearns to imitate the illustrations she creates. To be like Themarys, plump and freckled, blue-robed on red cushions, with saturnine faces surrounded by bees, caterpillars, peonies, strawberries — evidence of fruitfulness she has only seen in two dimensions. All her knowledge of fecundity has come from Themothers' books: from abstract words, wan photographs, bleached memories. Freckled babies have been born and raised in the downworld — this all girls have seen. But how they get there remains a secret until Themothers bestow the rights of Avessel. Until then, the girls wait, and prepare.

For sixteen years Swan has pored over pages graced with Themarys' likenesses: at first admiring without understanding; then appreciating the gift of creation; then inventing artworks of her own. At night these images fill her dreams; three times a day she sings them into being while rehearsing her summoning-song. Dreams echo through her vocal chords, promising to quicken life within her.

Now she hunches, watches Elizabet's approach through the sheen of her veil. Swan hasn't slept for days — she practiced so hard, sang so true, and for what? Today her voice is thinner than paper, breathier than a puff of steam on the upworld's horizon. She scowls and digs her fingernails into the soft flesh at the base of her thumbs.

Her cousin has never looked more joyful. "Don't be afraid, dear Swannie." Elizabet air-kisses each of Swan's cheeks to avoid smudging makeup, squeezes her hand, and softly chirps out a blessing: "Themarys favour you." The title breezes through her cousin's lips in a rush, too sacred to linger in profane mouths. Swan averts her gaze, unconvinced.

"Your song is amazing," Elizabet continues. "Relax, you'll be fine. Soon those freckles will be real." Then, *sotto voce*, "There's no way you won't have a girl."

Shhhhhhhhhh! Themothers' hiss shreds the still air; brows furrow, eyes blaze. The procession falters at Elizabet's jinx. Her face turns lucent with shame; her betraying mouth is pressed shut by Swan's trembling fingers.

Take it back, Swan silently implores, searching her cousin's face for hints of malice, finding none. Hurriedly, Thevessels make the sign of Themarys. Swan closes her eyes, imagines all the colours she'd use to paint over Elizabet's mistake. A prayer of hues: indigo, cerise, even brash gold. But not beige, no. And white is out of the question.

The procession passes quiet steel shells on the way to the cemetery, structures that go *up* instead of down.

It's all so ancient, Thevessels whisper. So impractical.

"Why build with such fragile material?" In her work as a scribe, Agnes makes exceptional connections, joining thin stroke to fine curves as easily as breathing. In the upworld, it seems, her mind isn't as dexterous as her hands. "Such crumbly rock," she continues, gesturing at the decrepit buildings. "Look — it's too heavy for its ribs and has fallen all to the ground!"

Concrete, Swan thinks, looking at row upon row of rectangular hulks lining the boulevard's left bank. *Not rock*. It must have been sturdier once.

Thevessels titter and shake their heads at Agnes. Such stupidity is bound to turn her skin tan, to see her burdened with a Lacuna child. Wouldn't that teach her? Give her a boy and confine her up here forever; then she'll learn how the upworld works.

"How many upbuildings have been felled by men's battles?" Thevessels demand. Humiliated, the scribe remains silent. "Hazarding a guess would be futile," they agree on her behalf. "Like trying to pinpoint the end of infinity."

A flash of green arcs high above their heads. In its unholy light all footsteps slow; some splash to a stop in late-spring puddles.

"A falling star!"

The child can't be blamed for her ignorance. Ruby is only twelve — too young to be here in Swan's opinion — and though she still has a hard time differentiating between psalms and hymns, the girl's descant won't be denied. Summoning-songs don't discriminate by age; they ring true but once, when Avessel's time is nigh. No matter if she is young or youngest.

Not a star, Swan thinks, as two sparks break away from the blaze overhead. *It's a —*

"Boomer!" Agnes cries, trying to redeem herself in her sisters' eyes by stating the obvious. Upbuildings loose showers of stones;

Ruby squeals and breaks into a run. Themothers herd their charges: arms outstretched, they shoo the girls quickly toward the cemetery gates, casting worried glances skyward. They've travelled far from the downworld door; even if they could safely return before nightfall, none of them would. Ladyday magics are most potent at dusk and Thevessels can't afford to let the opportunity pass.

They press on.

Swan trails behind, but not far enough to go astray. Elizabet drops back to join her. Their pace is brisk and ungainly.

"I heard Lacunae hang their enemies from the street signs up here," she whispers. "You know, as a sign of conquest." Strobing boomer flares illuminate the sharp planes of Elizabet's face. For a moment she is plunged in a wash of emerald, as though submerged in Swan's paintbrush waters. A blink later, the glare dies, and the upworld is once more burnished orange in the sun's dying glow.

Acrid smoke billows across the broad street and breaks against the buildings' vertical husks. Swan turns away from her cousin and tries to find a pocket of fresh air. She takes shallow, wheezing breaths that taste like ash and lung. Lifting a hand to her mouth, she stifles the hacking cough that claws at the base of her throat.

Where do Lacunae find shelter in this forsaken country? Nothing is whole for miles, apart from the statues flanking the cemetery's entrance; dozens of tall men, all bronzed sternness and corroded gestures. She knows they're men, or meant to be, even though they remain utterly still, not fighting. Perhaps that's how Lacunae sleep? Standing, dressed in foreign garb? Surely they must sleep between sieges. Even tanned ones must crave respite sometimes.

Even those whose songs have failed need rest.

Thinking of the Lacunae seems to conjure them into being. As Thevessels and their entourage file past the avenue of statues, they grow wary of men skulking in the shadows. Stone scrapes across stone, a stream of sun-darkened forms emerges — but from where? Swan can't tell. Increasingly, she can smell their sour breath, the sweat seeping through their dappled shirts, the scent of scalp and decay. Lacunae appear in broken troops, uniformed in brown and grey splotches; like magic, the fabric makes them disappear when not directly in Swan's line of sight. Looking away is a relief.

The men prowl the cemetery's perimeter, emboldened by their proximity to Thevessels. By the chance some of that fair skin will be filled with murky children, growing tan before the sun sets completely. They scratch their browned faces, clutch dangles of metal tags, and wait for their numbers to increase. Boy children are theirs by treaty, as are their mothers. Though their contempt for the downworlders is plain, these men willingly exchange protection for the promise of replenished legions — and for women to raise them.

Holymarys, Swan prays. *Save me from that.*

Unwilling to process the desperation, the hunger, she sees in the Lacunae's appraising glances, she focuses instead on the statues' scarred faces above. The head and shoulders of the tallest are coated with splotches of — what? Paint? Trickles and splatters of white that coat heroic features to the point of erasure.

She tries not to interpret this as an ill omen.

The cemetery's gate is always open. Its hinges support nothing but air — there's no need for a door. Lacunae enter its forbidden grounds but once in their lives and none, to Swan's knowledge, have ever returned from that journey.

Several girls run through their scales as Thevessels pass under the gate's rusted archway, *so-la-ti-dos* keeping vocal chords warm for the ceremony. Elizabet wraps her arm around Swan's waist, squeezes tightly, smiles a rainbow of happiness. Swan trembles with fever, her skin sweaty despite the evening's chill. Red jealousy gnaws at her innards as she listens to notes projected with perfect pitch, from voices that aren't her own.

It isn't supposed to be like this.

Each time Themothers heard her summoning-song they'd exchanged significant glances. They'd asked her to demonstrate it again and again until everything in the women's bearing — from their sinfully tapping feet keeping time with her rhythm to their poorly suppressed grins, hovering between pride and relief — *everything* told Swan she would be chosen first. That she would sing to bear them a girl, and earn her promotion to prime illustrator. For that, more than anything, she promised to be a most devout Mother.

But as she steps through the gate and is confronted by its keeper, fear leaches her envy and leaves her shaken, hollow. Her throat too dry for singing.

"Absterget marianae omnen lacriman," Themother says as Swan exchanges her first ticket for entrance to the inner sanctum. *Themarys shall wipe away every tear from their eyes.* Swan doesn't want to cry, but can't seem to stop. Her tongue edges out of her mouth, catches a few moistening drops on its tip. The gatekeeper reaches beneath Swan's

veil and dabs her cheeks with a woollen sleeve, then hands her a faceted lachrymal vase.

"Drink from this," the woman says, the timbre of her voice lower than Swan's spirits. "If it hurts. You know, when the time comes."

Gum trees, naked as ghosts, criss-cross the cemetery's lawns. Their slender trunks guide Thevessels through the labyrinth of plots, but otherwise there seems no method to their planting. Saplings spring up of their own volition, heedless of barrier or design. Roots infiltrate decorative plinths and hasten their decomposition; garlands of ivy choke marble cherubs; branches reach skyward from mausoleum roofs like grizzled undead hands. A symphony of crickets greets the girls as they creep through graveyard districts. Swan listens for nightingales or owls or bats, but hears nothing but the pattering of bare feet and wind sighing at their passing.

Ants crawl across paths in orderly lines, tiny foot soldiers more disciplined than the ragtag procession of girls. Swan avoids stepping on them though walking is treacherous; in places the gravel is fused together in solid, uneven slabs. There is much hobbling from stubbed toes.

Long shadows intersect with walkways, directing Thevessels to their graves, which need to be fresh to serve their purpose. A week or two old, three at most. Unbleached titanium, a colour paler than oatmeal though not yet ivory, stripes the soft grass at the path's edge. Swan inhales sharply as she scrapes the ball of her foot on a ribcage, scatters the exposed skeleton.

With a tail of that length, the bones must be animal. The thought gives her pause. What do Lacunae carcasses look like? Surely they're bigger than this one. And dug deeper. But for all Swan knows they could very well have tails.

Themothers draw to a halt. With low voices they sing a few notes, the tune an aural blueprint of the cemetery. Taking well-rehearsed cues, Thevessels join the motet until its polyphony reveals to whom each allotment belongs. Swan's temperature rises, sweat beads her forehead. When her turn comes, she mimes a verse (a mezzo-soprano's G, below middle C), and prays for her song to return. She nearly chokes on its lack.

Grave after grave is assigned to full-throated girls. But not yet for Swan. A horrifying thought nearly brings her to her knees.

What if there aren't enough?

One row over, a marble headstone, carved with bas-relief crosses. Two plots beyond that one, a limestone pillar, broken in half. A few granite tombs guard an equal number of newly-dead. Three sandstone markers, etched with intersecting swords, retreat over a low hill — none of the girls will approach those tanned monuments. Beneath the western wall, a copse of pine trees shelter seven or eight wrought-iron urns, which are perched atop decorative steles, nestled in the dank scent of turned soil.

Will there be enough?

Swan spins around. Thevessels' voices slide up a key change her ravaged larynx can't hope to accommodate.

Will there be a grave for her?

She turns again, her breath coming hard and fast in the upworld's asthmatic air. One, two ... five, eight ... Summoning-songs take flight all around her; Swan raises a hand to her parched mouth. She feels disoriented.

How many are there?

And Elizabet? Where's Elizabet?

Will there be a grave for her?

A figure clad in hoarfrost and winding sheets peels away from a mausoleum nearby. Swan stumbles to the ground; her lachrymal vase skitters out of reach. The figure's strong hand, pale as Swan's own, scoops up the small vial and holds it out. Swan takes it, and the extended hand. She nods her thanks as she stands and checks that the vial remains securely stoppered.

"Have you got your ticket?" the figure asks. Her voice is soft but strong, its cadences familiar. Swan bends to retrieve the crumpled slip, taking the opportunity to peer up into Theexhumer's shady cowl.

"This way," the woman says, lowering her hood to afford Swan a better view of her face. Swan's mouth opens in a silent gasp. Theexhumer strides toward a marble plinth that beckons from the cemetery's north-east corner. She doesn't turn back to see if Swan follows.

Ohmarys.

Under the dirt, under the winding sheets, under the layers of unkempt hair, she looks exactly as she had two years ago. Her name had been Judith before her mark was erased from the hymnal. Elizabet had partnered her in more duets than Swan could count — until Ladyday broke their harmony, leaving Elizabet to sing solo.

Swan hurries to catch up. Her guide's skin shines like white silk, utterly clear. Never Amother then, but Anexhumer.

A lost one.

Holymarys, Swan prays. Looking around, she sees Thevessels being similarly led by unhooded figures shrouded in smoky garments. Ruby has taken her guide by the hand. Some have reached their destinations; Elizabet and Agnes are now presented with boxes. All of them, singing. Calling out for new life and a skin full of freckles.

Theexhumer stops at the foot of the grave. Up close, the plinth proves to be decorated with a flock of swallows. *A good sign*, Swan thinks. *A symbol of motherhood.* Her throat constricts.

Will it be enough?

The soil is loose; a regal brown, thank Themarys. This one hasn't been buried long. Swan fidgets with her veil. She sticks a corner of it in her mouth hoping to generate some moisture. All around the cemetery, Thevessels raise their voices, pitching them to fill the up and down worlds; projecting their summoning-songs from this realm into the next.

"Now is the time for singing," Theexhumer says, passing Swan a wooden box.

She grasps it in both hands and wiggles her numb feet, burrowing them into the life-giving earth. Tears fill her eyes as she releases the brass latch. Her song had been so beautiful. She'd practised so hard. Without it, what good are such tools?

The hinges creak as Swan lifts the lid; the box exhales lily-scented perfume. It is upholstered with plush crimson, possibly velvet. She has never seen anything so luxurious.

"Now is the time for singing," Theexhumer repeats, then collects a spade from behind the marble plinth.

Tears plink with metallic splashes as they land inside the box. One drops on the knife's silver blade, the other on the fork's steel tines.

Such precious bone handles will be destroyed in the dirt. She takes both utensils in one hand; working from tip to end, she individually polishes them with her flimsy skirts. *Not clean enough — any paint left in the bristles will ruin a brush's point.* Starting again, she methodically cleans knife and fork until the hem of her garment is snagged into webs. And again, until cutting edges gleam.

And again, until Theexhumer tires of Swan's stalling and starts digging.

I can't do it.

The knife rasps along the plinth's edge, growing sharper with each stroke. Swan's arm jerks back and forth, a canvas-stretching rhythm.

She closes her eyes briefly, ignores the ache in her throat, and pretends that's all she's doing. Beginning her next tribute to Themarys, preparing the surface upon which she will paint.

Magenta will do nicely as undertone, she thinks, but her imaginings vanish when she feels the knife warming in her grip. A foothill of dirt has accumulated beside her; Theexhumer's task is nearly complete.

Swan sneezes out a kerchief's worth of grave dust. Her eyes redden beautifully as they water. The air smells of silverware and worms; all around her, it rings with Thevessels' arias, their cantatas, their recitatives, their fugues. Summoning-songs tear through the cemetery's atmosphere, accompanied by the shrill of knives on tombstones.

This must be a nightmare. Thevessels conclude the first round of their songs and Swan has yet to sing a single note. Air wheezes in and out of her lungs. In and out, in and out — quickly, try again. No sound follows no matter how she forces her breath. She grows light-headed.

Below, Theexhumer straightens and seeks a way out of the grave.

Ohmarys, Ohmarys, Ohmarys, Swan prays. *How will the soul know where to settle, if I don't sing it home?*

Theexhumer hoists herself out of the dark trough carved in the earth. Swan worries at her lips, bites at them, swallows.

Please let this be a nightmare. Oh, please.

Theexhumer brushes chunks of soil off her shroud, then gestures at the open grave. Swan leans over the verge, paralysed at the sight of her life bundle. So shrivelled. So exposed. So silent.

Sing, she tells herself. *Sing now.*

The cemetery is quiet. Thevessels' songs soared while knives pierced decaying flesh; they crescendoed while forks crushed their ancestors' rotting bones; but now they have hushed to sonorous humming. It is impolite to chew with mouths open, but humming is more than acceptable — songs mustn't be broken until final mouthfuls are swallowed.

"Eat that which is good, and let your soul delight itself in fatness," Theexhumer says, gently nudging Swan closer to her meal.

What am I supposed to do? she wants to ask. But words don't follow her mind's directions. Her mouth freezes in a pinched "o" shape, tries to make a "w" sound.

Air escapes out the aperture of her pursed lips — and is followed by a tiny, musical breath.

Swan's heart flutters in her chest, beating her into swift action. *Thank Themarys!* She takes a quick swig from her vial of tears, grabs her knife and fork, and lowers herself into the open grave.

Her whistle is sombre and wavering, its tempo leaden. It falls from her lips like a reluctant secret, a heavy oesophageal echo. Through pinched lips the cadences of her summoning song are unrecognisable; the tune sounds like a dirge as she slices into Lacunaic flesh. Between bites, her whistle wavers with thoughts of baby girls. Swan gulps down a crumbling tendon.

Are lyrics needed to lure spirits into our bellies?

So hard to whistle with a mouth full of corpse. Swan thanks Themarys for the gatekeeper's gift and takes another sip from her lachrymal vase. Salty tears sting the insides of her cheeks; her whistling melody falters more than it soars. So hard.

Three times she cycles through her summoning-piece (she had *sung* it so beautifully), repeating it until all the tender bits are settled in her stomach. Silence greets her when at last she stops whistling. Silence and empty skin.

Clutching the utensils (their handles unrecognisable with mud) Swan grips the grave's ragged lip, braces her feet against its crumbling walls, and hoists herself slowly up. The effort leaves her breathless, lying on the patchy grass, half in and half out of the earth. Across the cemetery, she sees Elizabet, covered in dirt and freckles, returning her dinnerware and its gorgeous box to Theexhumer at her side. Her cousin looks stunning, bespeckled with child. She seems lighter, more confident; her spotted feet glide over the uneven ground as though she's walked it a thousand times.

Swan resumes her whistling. Of all the girls, if Elizabet is freckled then surely it isn't too late for her. *Happy Elizabet*, she thinks, watching the Newmother drift away. *I wish she had said goodbye.*

Her whistling grows more fervent. All around, Thevessels pepper with spots, replace their cutlery, and float along the path home. Even Ruby, the youngest proving Themothers' faith warranted.

No tans so far, just freckles, thank Themarys. A mottled harvest of baby girls. Swan imagines Themothers' joyful faces as their pregnant daughters descend, leaving no fodder for the Lacunae. She stares at her skin. Is that a dot on her knee? A smattering of deep brown on her wrist, a spattering on her thigh? Swan *wills* freckles to appear.

She whistles and whistles. The only spots she sees are blue, swimming in front of her eyes from lack of oxygen. Too soon, the cemetery is vacant.

Theexhumer sidles over, places a calm hand on her shoulder. Reluctantly, Swan lets the sound die. The utensils slide from her fingers, rejoining the body that had made their fine handles.

Night has fallen. The time for quickening has passed.

Swan shrugs Theexhumer's hand off, turns her back on the woman's sorrowful expression. Three plots away from her own, a similar play is being enacted. A waifish girl — Swan can't remember her name — sobs the final notes of a lullaby while her guide prises the knife and fork from her slender fingers.

That waif is too thin to bear girls! Swan thinks. *Her song always falters in the downworld; it's rumoured she hasn't a taste for it.*

Up here, the girl's allotted carcass is picked clean.

And still she sings. And still she remains as pale as Swan.

Why was she chosen this year? The question is plain in the lines creasing Swan's brow as she watches the girl refuse to accept defeat.

"It is not for us to decide how, or for whom, salvation will come to pass," Theexhumer says, replying as though Swan has spoken aloud. "Our task is to ensure an opportunity is unearthed, nothing more."

"This?" Swan's voice rasps, resists each syllable. "Salvation?" She shakes her head. Emptiness consumes her disappointment and leaves her feeling almost nothing. Loss is more palpable than hope, and more confusing. If she's not to be Amother, if she's not to paint, then what point is there in being "saved"?

Theexhumer reads the girl's despair; recognises it as a mantle she herself has worn many times.

"Such thoughts are best left in the downworld, Swan." No longer Avessel; this failure has stolen her past accomplishments and has left only her name. "In time, you'll see things differently. Now come."

Stepping around piles of dirt and bones, Swan lets her new sister slowly draw her toward the nearest cluster of mausoleums. The path is black, difficult to distinguish in the moments between boomer flashes, but Theexhumer's footsteps are assured. She moves swiftly, confident that the childless girl will stay close if only to avoid being alone. Eyes cast down, Swan negotiates the route, from rough patches of midnight blue grass across colourless flagstones, into the depthless ink clinging to the crypt's facade.

She slips into the shadows as if into a new robe. Darkness is a comfort; it conceals her unfortunate skin more effectively than any winding sheet, any uniform. Tears warm her cheeks, erasing ceremonial spots. The tomb's chill is pervasive; Swan is soon shivering uncontrollably.

"Here," says Judith, offering a swathe of dusty grey fabric. The pads of her fingers, rough with calluses, scratch as she unlaces Swan's white corset and replaces it with Anexhumer's garb. The veil is unpinned, a hood lifted in its stead. A shovel is placed in Swan's shaking hands.

"Come. We must gather bones and fill the graves before dawn. There's bodies aplenty next field over that need preserving. It won't take long, but watch your step — you don't want to get caught by an earthsplosion."

Swan nods. Swallows and swallows but the lump lodged in her throat shows no sign of moving. She clutches the spade, knuckles white, feet rooted to the floor. Looks at the flecks of paint around her nails and wonders how long they will take to fade.

"What colour is morning here?"

Judith pauses. She looks outside, away. "Vibrant enough to shatter dreams."

Swan sniffles. *Ohmarys* — She stops. No more prayers, not to them. Seven coddled Marys: never alone, always singing. What can they do for her now? They've given nothing but the residue of hope, drier than the paintbrushes she'll never again touch, emptier than her womb.

Shuffling toward the tomb door, Swan turns away from blessed, familiar dark, and steels herself for the bleakness of a bright future.

Coda

Fugue
Gavin Inglis

As the crash began, what he felt was relief.

There were no lights on this remote road; only a wary half-moon through the black branches of overhanging trees. His fingers were on the car radio, flicking channels, his attention on its green display as it hissed static and snatches of tedious DJ talk. He didn't notice that the curve had tightened until his front wheel scraped the edge of the road.

Instinct made him yank the steering right, away from the looming trunks in the headlights. The car lurched across the central line. Only then did he see the lamps of an oncoming vehicle, its twin beams growing in his windscreen –

He wrenched the wheel back to the left. The car squealed, hit the kerb at a hard angle and began to roll. As his stomach rose into his throat, he thought: *well, that's it then.*

Blood pounded in his head as the car tumbled towards the trees. Windows shattered and the headlights died. In the last moment before impact he fancied he heard something strange: voices through the trees, a distant assembly of singers drawing together in a rich, dark anthem.

Then he hit.

The ceiling was painted cream. It came into focus slowly. His chest felt as if it had been in a clamp and his neck was rigid. He wasn't dead. Reardon closed his eyes again and sighed.

"You've been here for three days." The nurse had a soft Highland accent. "I'm afraid your car was completely wrecked. You're a very lucky man."

He looked at her until her smile faltered.

"It's a terrible stretch of road," she said. "Should we contact anybody? Maybe your wife?"

"You might find her. But she wouldn't come."

The nurse frowned.

"I heard singing," he said. "At the crash. I heard singing."

She patted his shoulder. "The doctor will be along shortly."

The hotel was ten minutes from the hospital. He could have taken a bus, a train; but he had nowhere in particular to go. Reardon checked in and went to the tiny bar without bothering to take his suitcase upstairs.

Ten minutes later he was nursing a bad whisky, studiously keeping his eyes off the framed Burns songs that adorned three of the four walls. He had driven to Scotland to escape the pad of blank manuscript on his piano back in London, the torn scraps on the carpet. As recently as six weeks ago he could write phrases: opening lines he recognised immediately as derivative. Then he was reduced to clichéd progressions, dull chords. Latterly he just tore up the empty sheets.

Reardon ordered a gin and felt drowned in the old irritability, the old restlessness. The barman came over, drying a pint glass. "On holiday then? You're off the tourist trail here."

Reardon looked up. "Not exactly a holiday."

"Oh aye. What's your business then? Developer, is it?"

"No. I'm a composer."

"Really?" The barman sounded genuinely pleased. "I've got a few classical CDs myself. Brahms and so on. Much money in that, is there?" He slotted the dry glass above the bar and picked up another.

"Not much."

"I suppose these old masters have cornered the market, eh? And they're not even here to enjoy it. Would I have heard your stuff?"

"Ever go to a chamber recital in London, say eight years ago?"

"Afraid not."

"Ever seen a film called *Helen's Angels*? Or *The Elevation*?"

"No..."

"Well, you haven't then."

"Would I find some in the shops?"

"I doubt it."

"So how long does it take you to write a, what, a symphony then? A couple of weeks? A month?"

Reardon smiled and ordered another detergent whisky.

The barman moved off with the empty tray and picked up a different cloth. He began to polish the bar. After a minute he paused. "Here," he said to Reardon, "a composer you say? Have you heard about the accident?"

Reardon looked over and opened his mouth to explain that he *was* the accident.

"The choir? Couple of years ago?"

Reardon closed his mouth.

"I'm surprised you didn't read about it. Terrible business. Going to Glasgow for some festival. Eighteen of them in a minibus. There's a road out west of here, weaves through a wood. The corner's tricky. They say the driver lost control and hit a lorry on the other side of the road. All killed." He shook his head. "Terrible business. The council said they'd make changes to the road. In the end they just put up a sign. That lasted two months then some drunk kid drove into it. They never replaced it." He shook his head again.

Reardon felt a strange excitement. "A choir? Singers?"

"That's what they said. Going to Glasgow."

"Whereabouts is that place?"

"Not far. Down to the main road, turn left, follow it for two miles or so. But there's nothing to see. For a while people left flowers. But now you never see them."

"Thanks." Reardon drained his whisky.

"Here. Don't go down there now. There's no pavement. You have to walk on the road. People drive too fast round the corner. It'll be dark soon. Wait and go tomorrow."

"Sure." Reardon spotted a cheap rum behind the bar and reached for his wallet.

He waited until he was sozzled before he left the hotel. At the end of the lane he had trouble remembering whether the barman had said left or right. He went towards the trees.

The breeze was cool on his face. Dim fields receded on either side. He walked on the road, facing the traffic as his mother had taught him. His clothes were dark; it would be hard for drivers to see him. "Fuck 'em," he muttered. "Fuck all of 'em."

The first couple of times he saw headlights, he stepped off the road into the muddy grass. It squelched beneath his shoes. The cars blew past him in a roar of engine and wind. In time he stopped bothering to step off the road.

He came to a bridge over a motorway. Here there was a token pavement and a moonlit view. The guardrail was dry beneath his fingers. He hoisted one leg over it, then the other.

Reardon sat on the rail and watched the cars below. They peeled from slip roads onto the motorway, piercing the dark with their twin shafts of light, humming through the gap beneath him and on into their evening. Perhaps their drivers were going to the cinema, a restaurant, home to a lover.

It didn't seem so long ago he'd taken a drunken walk like this with Penny, singing Schumann to her at the top of his voice. Had she looked at him with contempt even then? When he was still working, rehearsing, moving in the right company and pressing the flesh? He thought perhaps not.

Reardon smelled exhaust. He could try to time his drop so he hit a car. Even if he missed, he'd end up unconscious on a motorway. It would be pretty reliable.

But the singing. He needed to know about the singing in the trees.

He pressed on. Past the bridge, the first car gave him plenty of room, as did the second. But when he reached the trees the curves became tighter, the lines of sight shorter. A taxi flashed past in the middle of the road. Drunkenly, he listened to its tone plunge: the Doppler effect. F to D. A minor third.

He had heard some stuffed shirt from the Guildhall on Radio 4 talking about the miracle of music, the endless variations possible with just twelve notes. He had broken a bourbon bottle over the radio. An empty one, of course.

Around the next corner the road began to seem familiar. He watched two beams ease around the trees ahead and turn to bathe him, dazzling. They lurched abruptly away as the driver saw him, and the car whistled past Reardon's legs, horn blaring. He didn't even look up.

Finally he glimpsed it: a shape to the trees, a bend he remembered. He saw the exposed stumps of freshly chopped trunks and two long, black skidmarks on the moon-polished road. Caterpillar tracks marked a clearing by the side of the tarmac, a clearing he now guessed had been created two years ago by another intrusion of tumbling metal.

A car flashed through the bend like a blazing knife. Reardon was already off the road, among the torn ground. He smelt bark and engine oil.

So this was the spot. Had they been singing as they went into the corner, with the simple joy that tired people get from song on buses late at night? Reardon closed his eyes and stood silent. He took a deep breath and listened.

Leaves rustled above. The wind cooled his face and he felt the beginnings of a light rain. Somewhere far off, a dog was barking.

He heard a car pass, then a second, going in the opposite direction. Reardon opened his eyes again. Red taillights slipped up the hill ahead.

No singing. No unearthly choirs. He sighed and wished he had thought to bring a bottle of something from the hotel.

He trudged towards the trees, feeling his feet sink into the mud. Might be elms. It was too murky to tell. Penny had given him impromptu botany lessons, little tests, when they walked in the countryside. The memory was so dim. He groped into the wood, feeling his way from trunk to trunk.

Within thirty seconds he was through to the other side, staring at an empty field. Stalks waved gently in the wind. This wasn't even a wood; just a strip of trees. The rain was heavier now, and he was two miles from the hotel. What was the point in even starting back? His little mystery, the choir in the trees ... he had imagined it as he tumbled towards death. Reardon turned away.

On a stump he sat and let the rain hit him. It was soft and cold. Vehicles burned past in both directions; cars, vans, lorries. He might have wept a little. Nobody stopped.

He got the urge to sing, and used the first song that came to mind, his voice weak and drunk and muffled in the damp air.

Swing low, sweet chariot,

Comin' for to carry me home.

And he felt it. He was ready now. He was ready to give it all up. He would just walk onto the road and lie down. He was wearing a dark jacket. There wouldn't be long to wait for a car.

A gust rattled the leaves behind Reardon.

He felt a faint vibration in the ground, the air, as if somebody had started farm machinery nearby. He frowned. Nobody harvested in the middle of the night.

The vibration built, and the back of his neck tingled as he recognised it as a hummed note, a hum in unison. A hum from an assembly of singers, laying the bass for ... for ...

He closed his eyes and sang the next lines out into the night air.

I looked over Jordan and what did I see,

261

Comin' for to carry me home?

The voices behind him shifted softly, spreading out across the clearing, men and women feeling their way into the melody.

A band of angels comin' after me,
Comin' for to carry me home.

The altos picked up the words, their voices reaching towards the glowering sky. The sopranos followed, then soared to a higher note still, sustaining a harmony as the altos descended and the male voices rose to meet them.

Reardon turned to look, rising from his tree stump with damp hair in his eyes, turning to see...

To see an empty clearing, suddenly silent.

He froze. All he could hear was the wind through the leaves, and distant traffic.

Reardon turned back to the hellish road, covering his face.

He had ended this music too.

A chorus exploded behind him, a hallelujah which shivered his wet shirt, a triumphant cascade which plunged like a waterfall only to rise back in resonant steps. He had no idea what they were singing now; it wasn't English, it wasn't Latin, it was no language he recognised. Yet the unfamiliar syllables gave a new timbre to the notes, a taste of possibilities unexplored. The passage twisted and forked, the voices teasing each other in discord before drawing back into unison. He could hear more than four parts now; surely eight, or more. Each voice explored its own route, sliding through the spaces between notes, riding the arpeggios while the whole remained unaccountably in harmony. The choir poured its anthem into the night.

Reardon found he could join in.

His baritone was sluggish, out of practice, but he snaked it through the weaves of the melody, now countering a bass line, now sitting on a sixth while octaves enclosed him. He threw open his arms and sang to the empty road, shedding inhibition like an old suit, delighting in the movement of the music, the simple notes. These twelve notes.

He found he was dancing – and laughing! – swaying around the clearing in graceful, muddy steps, carried by the curves of the music, the sweep of the voices. He threw off the booze and coasted along like some Renaissance noble at a ball. He lost himself in the movement, alive in the moment, treading paths and steps he had been missing for years. And still he was singing, part of this company whose glorious phrases resounded from the trees –

A horn blared and Reardon gazed directly into headlights, his arms raised like a failing ballet dancer –

As the brakes squealed, he threw himself aside. His ankle bent beneath him. He smashed into the verge, breath departing with the impact. But he was off the road.

He heard the wrench of a handbrake, a car door opening, and approaching footsteps.

"Hey Mister! Mister! Are you okay?"

Sprawled in the mud, Reardon didn't want to answer. He was composing.

Contributors

Chris Amies lives in London. His first published stories appeared in small press magazines and the *Midnight Rose* series of anthologies. More recently he has been published in *The Mammoth Book of Future Cops* and *Strange Pleasures*. A novel, *Dead Ground* was published by Big Engine. "Cow Lane" was written in Hammersmith while he was living near the places it describes although when he moved into the area those pubs had already closed down. He has been taking photographs of derelict public houses for several years and "Cow Lane" incorporates his favoured themes of pubs and music. He is sure that nothing like that happened to the real "Red Cow", but it did stand empty for several years and the establishment now on the site has a different name. Chris also writes songs and plays guitar just sufficiently to accompany himself. He does publicity work for a small government organisation.

Tom Brennan lives on the coast in Liverpool, UK, with wife Sylvia and many cats. His regular job is an Emergency Medical Dispatcher taking 911 calls, but he enjoys writing a wide variety of fiction, particularly SF, Fantasy and Mystery. His short stories have appeared in *Paradox, Writers of the Future, Story House, Neo-opsis, Indy, Baen's Universe* and *Year's Best Fantasy and Horror: Nineteen*. His favourite question is "What if..."

Aliette de Bodard lives and works in Paris, where she has a dayjob as a Computer Engineer. In between programming sessions, she writes long and short fiction: her Aztec fantasy *Servant of the Underworld* is now out from Angry Robot, and her stories have appeared in venues such as *Interzone, Asimov's* and the *Year's Best Science Fiction*. She was a Campbell Award finalist and a Writers of the Future winner. Visit www.aliettedebodard.com for more information and fiction samples.

Stephen Gaskell lives in London, where he private tutors, plays football, and, on his daily cycle to the British Library to write, colourfully curses bad drivers. He studied rocket science at University College, Oxford and artificial intelligence at the University of Sussex, but thinks his most beneficial graduation came from Clarion East at

Michigan State Uni. His work's been published in *Nature*, *Interzone*, and *Cosmos Magazine*, amongst other places. He's neither visited other planets nor travelled into interstellar space, but he has been to New York. He occasionally blogs at www.stephengaskell.com

Richard Jay Goldstein has been writing fiction and non-fiction for about twenty years. He lives in the mountains east of Santa Fe, New Mexico, where it's nice and quiet, thanks, but at one time he lived in New York City, where he knew many musicians who played like fucking angels. He's a retired ER doc. His wife, Polly Tapia Ferber, is a professional percussionist. They have two grown boys, now twenty-five and thirty-five, and two really cute granddaughters. He's published forty-something stories, essays, and poems in the literary and fantasy/sci-fi press, including a couple of anthologies. He's had two Pushcart nominations, but neither got in.

Lisa Hannett was born and raised in Canada, She now lives in Adelaide, South Australia — city of churches, bizarre murders, and pie floaters. She has sold stories to venues including *Clarkesworld Magazine*, *Fantasy Magazine*, *Weird Tales*, *Electric Velocipede*, *ChiZine*, and the *Steampunk Reloaded* anthology. Her story "On the Lot and In the Air" appeared on *Locus*'s Recommended Reading List for 2009. Lisa is a graduate of the Clarion South Writers Workshop. She aims to complete her PhD in medieval Icelandic literature before she grows older than her subject matter.

Jackie Hawkins was born in Surrey but has lived in Cambridge since her student days. Her first career was in human genetics and she spent several years researching mutations in leukaemia. After a career break she had the opportunity to take a change in direction and she is combining her lifelong interest in both storytelling and the visual arts through studying for a BA in Illustration at the Cambridge School of Art. She has been writing fiction on and off since she was five years old and she is currently working on a young adult novel. Her other interests include ferrying children around, gardening, keeping chickens, and rehabilitating her neurotic rescue dog.

David H. Hendrickson has published over nine hundred works of nonfiction ranging from humour and essays to scientific research and sports journalism. He has been honoured with the Scarlet Quill and Joe Concannon awards. His short stories have appeared in anthologies, literary journals, and magazines, including the DAW anthologies *Swordplay* and *The Trouble With Heroes*. His story "In Another Life" placed second in the *Flash Me Magazine* Readers' Choice Award. His two latest novels are currently under consideration by New York publishers and he is at work on a third. A lifelong resident of New England, he resides north of Boston. His website is www.hendricksonwriter.com

Andrew Hook was born in Norwich in 1967, and apart from bouts of extended travelling has lived in that fine city for most of his life. He began writing in 1987, although his stories didn't start appearing in print until 1994, the first being "Pussycat" in the Barrington Books anthology, *The Science of Sadness*. That publication was pivotal as the anthology heralded the new wave of 'slipstream' – a genre which Andrew realised he had been writing all along. Since that date, he's had over 70 stories published in a wide range of magazines and anthologies, but has always remained faithful to his slipstream roots, crafting fiction which touches on the edges of other worlds and possibilities, whilst remaining anchored in the present day. In addition to magazine acceptances, Andrew's short fiction has been collected in three books: *The Virtual Menagerie* (Elastic Press, 2002), *Beyond Each Blue Horizon* (Crowswing Books, 2005), and *Residue* (Half-Cut Publications, 2006). Whilst primarily a short story writer, Andrew has also written novels, with the comic satire *Moon Beaver* appearing from ENC Press in 2004, and a shorter work, *And God Created Zombies*, published through NewCon Press in 2009. Andrew's website can be found at www.andrew-hook.com

Gavin Inglis lives in Edinburgh. For a thankfully brief period he earned a living busking as half of a saxophone duo. He served as Jimmy Destri in tribute band Gentlemen Prefer Blondie despite looking nothing like the slim dark New York keyboardist. Gavin's fiction has appeared in many anthologies and magazines, from *Nova Scotia* to *Grunt and Groan: The Anthology of Sex And Work*. His eerie little novel for grumpy teenagers, *Mirror Widow*, won a competition at the Edinburgh International Book Festival. A collection of flash fiction about ineffective apparitions, *Crap Ghosts*, is currently available. Gavin brought together his musical and literary interests to collaborate with the Glasgow electronic bands Spylab and Cinephile. He is also no stranger to the stage, having run a five-star spoken word show, *Underword*, at the 2009 Edinburgh Fringe. Gavin teaches a night class in flash fiction at Edinburgh University, and prefers short biographies.

Susan Lanigan is a programmer and writer. Twice shortlisted for the Hennessy New Irish Writing Award (2005 and 2009) and winner of the 2009 Dublin One City One Book Award, she has had short fiction and poetry published in a variety of magazines. She runs writers' workshops in short fiction at www.joyofwriting.net. Susan currently lives by the sea in Bray, County Wicklow.

Vincent Lauzon was born in Montréal, Canada, in 1969. He published his first book, *Le pays à l'envers*, when he was eighteen years old. It was nominated for the Governor General's Award, Canada's most coveted literary prize, in 1987. It didn't win. He went on to publish ten books for children and teens, all of them in French. Then real life intervened and he stopped writing for a decade or so. A few years ago, he decided to give it another go, this time in English. "Festspeel" is his first story published in his new language of predilection. Next up, German. Vincent Lauzon lives in the suburbs of Montréal with his wife and five children.

Sean Martin is the author of several non-fiction books, including *The Knights Templar: The History & Myths of the Legendary Military Order, Alchemy and Alchemists, The Cathars: The Most Successful Heresy of the Middle Ages* and *The Gnostics: The First Christian Heretics*. Researching the latter provided the inspiration for the story "Deep Field." He is also the author of *Andrei Tarkovsky*, a study of the Russian filmmaker, and co-directed the documentary *Lanterna Magicka: Bill Douglas & the Secret History of Cinema*, an exploration of the late Scottish director's fascination with pre-cinema optical devices and the making of his final film, *Comrades*. Sean Martin was born in Somerset, but now lives in Edinburgh.

Maxwell Peterson is currently living in Michigan, in the United States, with a cat that isn't his. He has been writing feature stories for *The Drummond Island Digest* since 2004, and his short story "Daughter of God" is in Gill Ainsworth's anthology *The Blackness Within* (Apex Book Company). He is a hat person (or he thinks he is) and writes all of his first drafts in fountain pen. There always seems to be ink on his fingers, but he secretly suspects that inky fingers are a good thing.

Cyril Simsa was born and brought up in London, has a degree in zoology, and has worked as a librarian, museum curator and university administrator. Since the 1990s he has been living in Prague, where he tries to avoid the fate of his near-namesake in the Kafka story. He has been writing on and off since his mid teens, and has contributed reviews and articles to a wide variety of genre publications *(Foundation, Locus, The Encyclopedia of Fantasy, Wormwood)*. His stories have appeared in *Electric Velocipede, StarShipSofa, Darkness Rising, Here & Now, Central Europe Review, New Horizons* and *New Writings in the Fantastic*. He has also published translations of Czech writers.

By day, **Vaughan Stanger** works as a research manager at a British engineering company. This is less interesting than it sounds, which may explain why, thirteen years ago, he began setting himself homework. The resulting short stories have been published in *Nature, Interzone, Postscripts, Hub* and *Neo-opsis*, amongst others, with translations appearing in Polish and Hebrew. He is working on a novel, but then isn't everybody? "Star in a Glass" arose from Vaughan's oft-used tactic of mining ideas from *New Scientist* and then letting his imagination go completely off the rails while listening to loud rock music. Having tortured twelve attendees at a Milford Conference plus his friends in the OSB writers' group with various versions, all radically different, he finally relented and sent the story out on tour. He is thrilled to see it find the right venue.

Jim Steel is editing a collection of his music journalism that will initially be published in hardback with a limited-edition slipcase containing a CD of *The Living Eyes* album. Jim is also an executive member of the MWU and an A.O. in UKAC. He lives in Glasgow. You can contact him through official channels but please don't waste his time. However, you can be assured that he will most certainly contact you when it becomes necessary. If this happens, remember that he is your friend and offer him your full cooperation.

Neil Williamson's fiction has been published in a variety of magazines and anthologies. Some of his stories appeared in *The Ephemera* (Elastic Press, 2006), and he also co-edited *Nova Scotia: New Scottish Speculative Fiction* with Andrew J. Wilson. Neil lives in Glasgow where he can be found crossing opinions with other members of the fierce literary duelling school known as the Glasgow SF Writers Circle.

Jill Zeller is the author of numerous short stories and novels, living near Seattle, Washington with her patient and adoring husband, one self-centered tuxedo cat and one pit bull mix named Jack. Her works explore the boundaries of reality. Some may call it fantasy, but there are rarely swords and never elves. More to the point, she prefers to write as if myth, imagination and hallucination were as real as the chair she is sitting on as she writes this. Maybe it is because she was raised as a Christian Scientist. Jill, a registered nurse, wanted to write a story about a woman suffering from multiple sclerosis who once was a talented concert pianist. Rather than exploit the maudlin possibilities of this, she preferred to examine how Schubert, and a little cannabis, cures not only her body, but also her heart.